Till We Meet Again

Roy W. Penny

D1520146

Published by Shawnee Publishing, LLC
Copyright 2013 Shawnee Publishing, LLC

ISBN-13: 978-1482676181
ISBN-10: 1482676184

Map of Indian Territory and Oklahoma 1890 reproduced courtsey of
David Rumsey Map Collection, www.davidrumsey.com.

Chapter 1

One hot summer noon in the 1890's, a skinny young girl in a long, dingy dress came limping barefooted up a mountain road that straggled westward out of the Ozark Mountains of Arkansas. In her right hand she dragged a long willow switch, and her left hand carried a sunflower blossom on a short stem.

Stopping on her good foot, she wiped the sweat out of her eyes with quick swipes of her sunflower hand, which sent her dark pigtail flying back and forth across her shoulders. She squinted up ahead to a pair of brown horse colts nipping grass in the road, and farther on to a black cow tied to the rear of the nearest covered wagon. Then she turned back to the mountainside spread below her.

For years she had dreamed of becoming a schoolteacher like her Aunt Sis down there and never getting married. Yet here she was leaving Arkansas for Oklahoma Territory—swollen foot and all—and her only thirteen years old.

Earlier in the week she had stepped on a rusty nail sticking out of an old board down at the hog pen. She limped to the house, where

Mama put coal oil on the bloody spot to keep it from festering and had her put on one of Bob's socks to keep out the dirt. Last night the heel started throbbing anyway, and this morning she couldn't bear to touch it to the floor.

At breakfast, Mama took one look at the heel swollen up the ankle like a fence post and said, "Child, you cain't walk on that. Tell your papa you'll jist have to ride in the wagon."

Greatly relieved, she sat down at the table between Emma and Tommy. Mama, with Ben on her hip, went back to helping Alice put breakfast on the table.

In a few minutes Papa and Bob came in from the barn, washed their hands at the washstand just inside the kitchen door, and everybody sat down to eat. They all bowed their heads while Papa "returned thanks"—all except Ben, who had already started his breakfast at Mama's breast.

As soon as Papa said, "Amen," she told him what Mama had said to her. Without even looking in her direction, Papa raked three fried eggs and a slice of ham off the platter onto his plate. "Mattie, I done told you," he said, and stopped to clear his throat, "you got to foller them colts for two or three days till they learn to keep up with their mammies."

Her eyes flushed hot with tears and she shot a look at Mama to save her, but Mama seemed to be giving all of her attention to Ben, who was now pushing her breast away with both hands while fretting through milky lips trying to find the nipple again.

More for sympathy than help, she looked around at Bob, but his hint of a shrug only told her what she already knew—nobody argued with Papa—not even Mama unless she was boiling mad about something.

Papa's hard voice seemed to have scared the talk out of the whole family. Not another word was said until he finished bolting his ham and eggs and pushed himself back from the table. "Hurry up, Bob," he said, getting to his feet. "We're aw'ready late as 'tis."

She knew better than try to get Papa to change his mind, but hoping he might, she kept her eyes on him as he walked to the kitchen door. When he took his hat off its nail, he did turn around, brushing a crumb out of his mustache as he looked down at her, his blue eyes steady.

She held her breath and took heart.

"You heered me now, Mattie. Sore heel or no sore heel, you got to foller them colts."

That was such a mean thing for Papa to say that later in the morning she didn't see how his conscience would let him kneel down in the yard with their friends and neighbors—after they had all joined hands and walked around the house singing "God be with you till we meet again!"—and on his knees ask God for His blessing on this journey to a new land.

She had limped along all morning, trying not to let her sore heel touch the ground, for when it did, the pain shooting up her leg was almost more than she could bear.

At the first creek they crossed, she broke off a long willow switch to help her scare the colts along. Later when she passed a strip of sunflowers alongside the road, she broke off the biggest flower she saw saving it till they stopped the wagons again to let the teams rest.

Only then would she have enough time to sit down, pull the sunflower petals out of their circular bed, one by one, and find out if she and Bob were really and truly going to get their secret wish.

Bob didn't want to go to Oklahoma Territory either, and the two of them had made a secret vow that as soon as they could make enough money they were going to run off and come back to Bear Valley and live with Grandma Hale and Aunt Sis. She knew Bob wanted to come back because he was sweet on Lena Mae Baker, but she never let on to him that she knew.

Now as she limped up the road again, she caught up with Pat and Browny, their front legs spread wide and their little tails flicking back and forth as they nipped at the grass. She swung her switch and shouted at them, but they were used to her threats by now. They kept on grazing until the switch touched, or almost touched, their fat little rumps before they ran a few steps up the road and dropped their heads to start grazing again.

Once Pat kicked up his heels at her as he ran away, and in

spite of the misery she felt, she had to stop and laugh at his didoes. It was then she noticed that the wagons had stopped and people were climbing down—just what she wanted to happen.

Turning to the lower side of the road, she limped over to the edge to see if she could see Grandma's house from here. She pushed back the limb of a sassafras bush and slid under it on her knees. As she came to rest on an outcropping of rock, she scared a pair of grasshoppers out of their shady spot and sent them sailing out in the sunshine, chattering as they went.

She cupped her hands to her eyes and worked her gaze down the mountainside. Her eyes stopped at the river, which wound along the bottom of the valley like a cow path.

It was at that yellow-brown oat stubble field, where Bear Creek ran into the river, that they had been late this morning in meeting the Bartons and the McDermits. But it couldn't be helped. Not only were there lots of good-byes to be said, some people who had bought things at the sale had not picked them up yet—things like the cookstove, the kitchen table and chairs, and Mama and Papa's bed.

It would have been safe enough to leave all of these things at the farm until the buyers got around to picking them up, except that everything had not been paid for yet. And from the arguments between Mama and Papa that she had listened to for months, she knew they would need every penny they could lay their hands on to get them to Oklahoma Territory and settled on a homestead.

Many times she had heard Mama ask Papa, "And what we goin' to eat if we run out of money before we git this homestead?"

To which Papa always gave Mama the same aggravated answer, "Pshaw, Mandy, let me worry 'bout that."

Starting at the stubble field, she followed the river upstream with her eyes until they came to the familiar bend at Mama's home place. Last night after a big, family supper there, she and Aunt Sis cried in each other's arms saying good-bye around a corner of that old log house.

"Mattiee!"

She jumped as if she had stepped on a snake, and her pigtail caught on a limb of the sassafras bush. At the same instant she realized it was Emma's voice and was mad at herself for being scared. She jerked her pigtail loose and started to answer, but then she thought she would make her sister pay for scaring her.

She pulled herself out of sight under the sassafras bush, and turned so that she could see up the road. The first part of Emma she saw was the hair, always bleached so light by the sun this late in the summer that no one would ever take her for being part Indian.

It was always a mystery to her how Emma could have light colored hair and dark eyes, and her have dark hair and blue eyes, when they both had the same amount of Cherokee blood in them.

She saw Emma carrying a drumstick of chicken in one hand and a biscuit in the other, holding them way out in front of her as if she was anxious to get rid of them. Every few steps she stopped and shouted, "Mattiee!"

Half-hidden behind Emma she saw little Tommy, moving and stopping whenever his sister moved and stopped, but never ceasing to give most of his attention to the piece of chicken he was gnawing on.

She waited until Emma was about past the sassafras bush, and then she gave it a hard shake. Emma screamed and leaped away, drumstick and biscuit flying in the air. Tommy stopped dead still for a long second and then rushed silently to Emma and threw his arms around her waist.

Laughing at her sister, she stuck her head out from under the bush. "What's the matter, Em? Think a bear had you?"

Emma's face went from white to red. "Jist look what you made me do! Made me drop your old dinner!"

Still laughing, she watched Emma find the drumstick in the grass, give it a swipe against her own dress and shove it towards her, saying "There! You're so smart you can go find your old biscuit yourself."

"Well don't get mad, Em," she said, taking the leg of chicken. "I was just having a little fun."

"It ain't funny."

"Aunt Sis says you're not supposed to say 'ain't.'"

"I will if I want to. Ain't! Ain't! Ain't!"

While she waited for Emma to cool off, she watched Tommy pick up her biscuit, wipe it off on his overalls and bring it silently to her.

"Thanks, Tommy," she said, and kneeling down in front of him, she pushed the dark hair out of his eyes, "Did you think a bear had *you*?"

Nodding solemnly, Tommy looked at her and his eyes suddenly brimmed with tears. She grabbed him in her arms and gave him a big hug. Ever since he nearly died last year from having measles and scarlet fever at the same time, he had been hard of hearing and almost stopped talking. Much of the time when he did say something, his words were so slurred it was hard to understand him.

"Now, Tommy," she said, "For being such a good boy and bringing me my biscuit, you can have half." She broke the biscuit carefully in half and gave the grinning boy his choice.

In a voice suddenly friendly, Emma said, "Matt, can I hep you drive the colts this evenin'?"

"No."

"I can chase'm and you won't have to run so much on your sore foot."

"You have to look after Tommy."

"Alice can do it."

"She has to help Mama with Ben."

Emma wrinkled up her freckled nose, "But it's so hot in the wagon! And they's flies ever'wheres. And Ben is jist squallin' and squallin'.

"Em," she said, changing her tone, "look up there at old Blackie. Looks like she's got her foot caught in her rope again. Better hurry up there and tell Bob before that crazy old cow gets all tangled up and hurts herself."

With a little more urging, she soon had Emma on her way back up to the wagon, Tommy silently following.

Once more she slid under the sassafras bush. She still had a lot of chicken leg left to finish eating, but first things first. She laid the chicken leg on the edge of the rock, licked the taste of chicken off her fingers, and slid the sunflower stem down her left hand until she

8

had the head of the blossom facing her.

She closed her eyes, and felt for the first petal. When she had the petal tight between her thumb and first finger, she said out loud for nobody but herself to hear, "I, Martha Louella Lane, and you, Robert Hale Lane, *will* come back to Bear Valley to live with Grandma Hale and Aunt Sis."

Opening her eyes, she pulled the yellow petal out of its black, green-edged bed and, saying out loud, "We will come back to Bear Valley," she put it carefully on the rock near her drumstick of chicken and reached for the next petal, saying as she pulled it out, "We won't come back." This petal she threw out in the sunshine and watched it flutter out of sight below the rock.

Still speaking out loud, she pulled another petal out and laid it across the first one. The next petal she threw out in the sunshine. Slowly the little stack of petals on the rock grew into a second stack. When she had just a few petals left to pull out, she could see what the answer was going to be, and she hurried her fingers and her words.

Finally she took hold of the last petal and paused for a deep breath. Then, forcing herself to speak calmly in spite of nearly bursting from wanting to shout, she said, "We WILL come back to Bear Valley and live with Grandma and Aunt Sis."

She jerked the petal out, hugged it to her chest and chanted, "We WILL. We WILL. We WILL!"

She was so excited she wanted to run up the road and tell the good news to Bob, but when she gathered up the piles of petals and squirmed out from under the sassafras bush and saw no colts, she suddenly felt sick.

If she had let the colts slip past her, Papa was sure to give her a good whipping. Scrambling to her feet, she looked up and down the road. All she could see was the empty mountainside. The two colts, the four covered wagons with Old Blackie tied behind the last one, and Papa and Mr. McDermit on horseback had all disappeared. She was all by herself on the mountain.

She sucked in a sudden breath and started limping up the road as fast as she could go. At the top of the rise she could tell from all the fresh horse manure where the wagons had stopped. Here the road sloped down into another valley and disappeared around a spur of the mountain.

She was about to leave Bear Valley for the first time in her life. In spite of what the sunflower petals had just told her, she felt a sudden pang of fear—afraid she and Bob might never find their way back.

Quickly she turned for another look. The river, the oat stubble field, and Hales Bend had now grown too misty for her to see even a corner of Grandma's house.

Holding back her tears, she turned away, and with a wad of sunflower petals in her left hand and the willow switch in her right, she started limping as fast as she could go towards the spur of the mountain.

Chapter 2

In less than a mile the rough road joined a well-used road, and she started limping even faster. Sweat poured down her face and body until she was drenched all over, but she never once thought about stopping to rest.

Eventually she came to a long stretch of straight road and saw, way up a head, four covered wagons with a pair of horsemen in it out in front—Papa and Mr. McDermit. But what relieved her most was seein' the colts in single file behind Old Blackie.

For the first time since leaving the sassafras bush, she was no longer scared. That was a narrow escape from a whipping, and she had better never sit around daydreaming again and let the wagons get out of her sight.

She lifted her gaze to the front wagon—Old Lady McDermit's light farm wagon bought brand new just for this trip, with Clyde Spencer hired to drive it and look after her. She knew that old Lady McDermit, like Momma, had tried her best to stay on the farm, but since she was too old to live there by herself, and since her son was as bound and determined as Papa to move to Oklahoma Territory, she had to give in and go along with him and his family.

That family, his wife and four children, was in the heavy wagon just behind Old Lady McDermit's. Junior McDermit was only eight-years-old, and then three little girls, all kind of puny looking. Only Junior took after his parents in size, and he was so big and strong for his age that he was allowed to drive the horses, although his Mama was right there in the wagon if anything went wrong.

About the people in the third wagon, she didn't know very much except that they were a young couple named Barton, and that Mrs. Barton was nursing a baby. They joined Mr. McDermit at the oat stubble field that morning.

Papa had put his wagon at the tail end because he didn't want the colts running in and out among the wagons to find their Mamas. When she caught up with the colts, she could see they were also tired. Instead of trying to grab a mouthful or two of grass and then scamper catch-up with the wagons, they were drooping along right behind Old Blackie, their heads down, passing up good grass on either side of the road.

She slowed down and kept her distance. Hour after hour she limped along behind the colts on a road that kept winding around the side of the mountain. Now and then it cut across a little valley past fields of corn and sorghum, with a row or two of tobacco here and there. But no matter how much the road wound on this way and that, it always headed back toward the slanting sun, so that most of the time she had the heat of the full sun on her face.

When the sun was still about an hour high, she watched the wagons pull off the road and stop at the edge of a stand of trees. By the time she reached the trees, Emma and Tommy and all the other children were already wading in the shallow bed of the creek.

Too tired to wade out into the water, she flopped down on the bank and let the cool water play over her feet. It felt so good on her throbbing heel she thought she could stay like that forever.

Yet when she heard Bob calling for her from down at the wagons, she got up and went limping through the trees to find him. Bob said he was going to take Old Blackie back on the road and stake her out on a good grazing spot, and they started back along the road together.

Right away Bob began talking about how great it was to be seeing all this new country, and how he could hardly wait to see what was ahead of them in the days to come.

She could hardly believe that Bob had suddenly forgotten the months of sadness they shared over having to leave Bear Valley, or how happy they were when he came up with the idea of saving their money until they had enough to run away back to Bear Valley.

To remind him of what he should be thinking about, she said, "Guess what, Bob." When he couldn't guess, she told him what the sunflower petals had told her.

"Oh, Matt," Bob said, stopping so suddenly that Old Blackie almost ran into him. "You don't still believe that silly flower stuff, do you?"

This didn't sound like Bob, and she was hurt. "And what if I do?"

"You're still a baby, that's what."

"Well you're not so grown up yourself."

One word led to another until they were soon having the worst quarrel she could remember. Finally she put her hands back over her ears, left Bob standing in the road holding Old Blackie, and returned to the creek.

It was not until after supper that she was able to get Mama to look at her heel. Mama had her get a bucket of water from the creek and heat it over the coals until it was so hot she could just barely keep her hand in it. Then Mama stirred a fistful of salt and told her to give her foot a long soak.

In a few minutes the foot began to feel so much better, even though it kept on throbbing, that she almost fell asleep sitting on the rock. Later when they were getting ready to go to bed, she saw Old Lady McDermit climbing down the special ladder at the back of her wagon. The bent old lady made her think of a witch out of a fairy tale as she came hobbling by in her white night dress and ruffled nightcap, leaning on her cane.

"Why, land sakes, Mandy," the old lady said when she saw

Mama handing down quilts and pillows for pallets. "It ain't right for them girls to be sleepin' out in the open like that with all them men around. Girls," she went on, peering around at Alice and Emma and her, "you jist fetch them pallets right over to my tent. They's plenty room."

Momma "thanked" her and tried to say "no," but the old lady's mind was made up, and she hobbled away calling for Clyde. He had set up her tent on a flat piece of ground near the creek, and she had him go in now and move her feather bed to one corner of it—the chair and chamber pot, too.

Sometime during the night her sore heel, throbbing fit to kill, woke her up. She was about to call Alice to get up and bring Mama to do something about the pain, when Old Lady McDermit's heavy breathing reminded her of where she was.

Afraid to say or do anything that might wake the old lady up and maybe make her mad, she bit down on the corner of her quilt and waited for morning to come. Hour after hour she lay wide awake in the darkness, listening to the sleepers breathing all around her and feeling the steady throbs of pain coming up her leg from her heel.

This went on until the first light of day began to turn the tent gray and she heard birds chirping outside. She must have fallen asleep then, for the next thing she knew, daylight had come and Alice and Old Lady McDermit were gone from the tent. But the pain was still shooting up her leg.

Rousing Emma, she sent her grumbling off, still half asleep, to bring Mama. In a few minutes Emma was back with a plate of breakfast for her and saying Mama was too busy to come just then.

It was not until after sunup, when breakfast was over, the wagons loaded and the teams hitched up and ready to pull out that she saw Mama, her milk leg making her limp, coming towards her, followed by Emma.

Clyde had long since taken down the tent and carried it away to the wagon leaving her sitting on her pallet beside her uneaten breakfast, plaiting her hair and trying not to think about her throbbing heel.

Mama spoke to her, felt her hot forehead and told her to lie down while she had a look at the foot. One glance and Mama was shaking her head and making little sucking noises through her teeth.

"Em," Mama said. "Run quick and get your papa."

In no time Papa came riding up on Nellie and got down in a rush, frowning and complaining about the delay just when they were ready to pull out. He took hold of the injured foot and twisted it around to get light on it.

When she cried out, Papa said, "Hush," and went on twisting the foot for a better view. "Well, Mandy, they's no doubt another salt soak would prob'ly hep. But we ain't got no time fer that now."

While she was looking up at Papa frowning and shaking his head, Mr. McDermit rode up on Prince. He swung out of the saddle and strode over to where she lay. She watched while he stuck his face within inches of the throbbing heel for a moment and turned to Mam, saying quietly, "Got to cut it open."

She began to tremble even before Mama nodded and Mr. McDermit asked if someone would run and tell his wife to send him his razor. It seemed to her that Emma had hardly disappeared before she came racing back, gripping a yellow leather razor case.

Mr. McDermit pulled the case apart, slid the folded razor out between his thumb and fingers and flicked the blade open. She winced as he started stropping the scary blade back and forth on the heel of his hand. Yet scared as she was, she couldn't take her eyes off that flashing blade.

Mr. McDermit stopped stropping, turned his hand over and shaved off a few hairs. "Aw'right, Jim," he said, "you hold that leg steady. And Miz Lane, I guess you better put a little weight on her shoulders, jist in case."

She wanted to ask, "jist in case of what," but she was too scared. By the time Mama had pushed her shoulders hard against the ground and Papa had her leg gripped tight in both hands, she was too terrified to breathe, but she had made up her mind not to make a noise no matter how much it hurt.

She could not see her foot now, but she saw the hand holding the razor. It moved, and something stung her like a red-hot needle. She screamed and saw bloody pus spurting up on Mr. McDermit's hand.

She came to jolting along in the wagon on Mama's feather bed, the throbbing all gone and Mama humming as she cooled her face with a damp cloth. She felt so good she began to drowse and was pleased to let herself go.

A few days later the heel was almost like new, but she was still riding in the wagon because the colts had learned by themselves to keep up with their Mamas.

One morning Papa stopped the wagons before a stack of rocks covered with splotches of weathered red paint. He said this was the start of the Cherokee Indian Nation. "We'll be crossin' it fer a few days, but we ain't got nothing to worry about if we mind our own bisness."

"Well, I do declare," interrupted Old Lady McDermit. "I hope them heartless creatures let a body alone." And she gave the stack of rocks a jab with her cane to show she meant what she said.

"Oh," Papa said, "there ain't no more of that."

As people were walking back to their wagons, Tommy grabbed her hand and asked if they were going to meet some wild Indians. Before she could answer, Bob said, "Nah, Tommy. They'll look jist like Grandma. If they had feathers in their hair I'd be scared myself."

"I scared now," muttered Tommy and held on to her hand.

Even before Papa had stopped at the Indian boundary mark, she had noticed, from her seat beside Bob, who was doing the driving, that the wagons were rolling down the last of the foothills. The road began to twist across ridgetops, and she caught glimpses of a great open space off to the west that stretched as far as she could see.

By early that evening the road came to more or less level ground, but instead of the open prairie she expected, the road entered thick woods. After more than an hour of this, she started hoping they would get through the woods before camping time. For in spite of what Papa said about these Indians being friendly, if any wild ones just happened to be around, she thought these woods would be the perfect place for them to hide and wait to scalp white people passing by.

When the wagons turned off the road while the sun was much

higher than their usual camping time, she was still thinking about wild Indians, but she soon saw it was a camping place no one could pass up.

A creek made a big half circle around a meadow of grass so green for this late in the summer it was hard to believe. Here was enough good grazing to last the horses for several days if the men wanted to use it.

She forgot about wild Indians, and when Bob stopped the wagons she hurried back to untie Old Blackie and lead her to water. Then she staked the old cow at the lower end of the meadow where the grass was the best, near where the creek ran through a plum thicket.

Now free to play, she hurried across the meadow to the row of wagons back up a few yards from the creek, and led the children back to the plum thicket. After they had eaten their fill of plums, they played "blackman" until supper. Then Bob took them back along the road leading down from the main road to a big tree stump that had washed in from somewhere.

No sooner had Bob said this would make a good home base for a game of hide-and-seek than everyone shouted that he had to be "it." As the oldest and biggest, he could have said "no," but he didn't. Instead, he leaned his forehead against the stump, shut his eyes, and started his count to one hundred. Everybody else scattered, looking for places to hide.

She found a redbud tree that was easy to climb in spite of her sore heel, and soon she was twenty or so feet up among its branches, looking down on the horses and colts grazing in a bunch near Old Blackie.

By the creek, at the near edge of the meadow, the women were gathering in the washing they had put out before supper, while the men were sitting around drinking coffee.

So busy was she watching everything going on in the meadow that she forgot to keep an eye on Bob. He spotted her in the tree, easily ran back to home base ahead of her and patted the tree stump three times.

They played several games of hide-and-seek before the sun went down and their mamas started calling them to come in for bed.

They agreed among themselves to play one more game, and since she was "it," she decided to count fast. She whispered in a rush through the first fifty numbers; and then she began to count out loud, slower and slower as she got closer to the magic number: one hundred.

"Ninety-eight, ninety-nine..." she stopped counting and called the usual warning to the hidden players, "ready or not. Here I come with my eyes wide open."

And then, thinking she heard a noise behind her, she braced herself to be ready if Bob pulled his favorite trick of hiding a little way behind her, and rushing in to pat home base after she had counted to one hundred, but before she had her wits enough about her to simply pat him out on the home base she was leaning against.

Ready for Bob now, she shouted, "One hundred!" and spun around to face two Indian men, black hair reaching their shoulders, looking down at her from a pair of dark horses.

Chapter 3

In a deep voice the older of the two Indians on horseback said, "Howdy do."

Hearing herself spoken to in her own language was like a breath of fresh air, but she was still too scared to answer.

A young man's voice said, "Papa was afraid we would scare you. That's why we waited for you to finish your counting."

She answered with a nervous laugh and said, "You scared me anyway."

He smiled and said, "We played "hide-and-seek" at the Academy in Talequah." When she merely nodded at this, he said, "My papa wants to talk to your papa."

"Oh," she said, stepping away, happy to oblige, but other frightened children had already spread the word and the men were coming out to see who it was.

Papa and the others spoke friendly enough to the Indians, but she noticed they didn't ask them to "git down and come in," something they always said to white visitors.

Except for his deep-throated "howdy do" the Indian man let his son do the talking. The son explained that they lived nearby and had seen the smoke of the campfire. He said rain was coming tonight and this was a dangerous place to camp. A heavy rain always flooded this meadow, often deep enough to swim a horse. That was why they never planted a crop here. The young man finished by saying there was a good place to camp about a mile ahead on another creek.

As the Indians rode off in the twilight, the men walked back to the wagons looking up at the cloudless sky and doubting to each other that it was going to rain anytime soon. Yet once the women heard about the Indians' visit and what they had to say, they were for moving out immediately.

Mama said they ought move to a safer place because of the children, but Papa said, "Pshaw, women. They'll be plenty time to thank about packin' up and movin' out if'n when it starts rainin'."

Mama just shook her head at Papa and started shooing the children off to bed, but Old Lady McDermit had more to say. "Why, son," she said, shaking her cane at Mr. McDermit, "We'ud be fools to stay here after what them Indians said."

When Mr. McDermit laughed in his mama's face and told her that she had nothing to worry about, she started yelling at him. He yelled back at her, and in a quiet voice she said, "Aw'right, son, I cain't make you mind me no more, or we'ud still be back there safe and sound on the farm.

Turning to Clyde, the old lady told him to go put her bed back in the wagon, and he hurried off without a word to do it.

Next morning, as usual, Alice was already gone from the tent when she woke up. She was still trying to get Emma awake when Clyde called through the tent flap, saying he had to get the tent down in a hurry. Leaving Clyde to deal with Emma, she went out in the early daylight and walked away from camp to relieve herself, plaiting her hair as she went.

In spite of hearing faint rumbles of thunder during the night, she noticed it had not rained a drop around here. Yet even as she was looking at the sky, she saw lightning splinter a dark bank of clouds way off to the northwest. Soon a rumble of thunder came from that direction and she reckoned it might be raining over there.

On her way back to the wagons, she stopped by the creek to wash her hands and face. Last night the water in the creek was running in a clear single channel, but now the whole creek bed was filled with dirty water swirling by carrying sticks and leaves.

She turned and ran to the wagons to tell the grown-ups, but they already knew about the creek rising. That was why they were hurrying around, loading the wagons and harnessing the teams, even though the children had not finished eating yet.

"Mattie, you been off playin'?" Mama asked.

"No, ma'am."

"Well, here. Hurry up and eat this. We're leaving soon's we can git loaded up."

Left holding a plate of biscuits, gravy and fried potatoes, she took it around to the front of the wagon where she could eat by herself and look out at the meadow.

She set her plate on top of the front wheel and began to chew slowly on her first bite of biscuit. In spite of what Mama had said, and all the rushing around she could see for herself, she guessed she had plenty of time to eat because they never left as soon as they said they were going to.

She watched Bob hurrying across the meadow towards her, carrying the milk bucket. Trotting along beside him to keep up was Tommy leading Old Blackie. Behind them the first of the sun was bursting through streaks of fiery clouds behind the plum thicket.

From far up the creek in the direction of the thunder and lightning she heard a cracking sound like a rifle shot or somebody snapping a dead limb off a tree. From the same direction a doe, followed by a fawn, bounded down into the meadow and past the tree stump until it saw the people and wagons. Suddenly it veered off and ran across the meadow and up in the woods past Old Blackie, white tail waving, the fawn racing to keep up.

She saw the old cow stop in her tracks and throw up her head so suddenly she jerked Tommy off his feet. Bob set the milk bucket down and grabbed the rope out of Tommy's hands. Just in time, too, for in the next instant Old Blackie turned as wild as a deer herself.

Her tail flicked up in the air like a buggy whip. She spun around and ran after the deer, snorting like a horse and jerking Bob along behind her.

Laughing so hard at Bob that she let her breakfast spill to the ground, she watched him run after the crazy old cow, calling "Sook, Blackie. Sook, Blackie," until they both disappeared in the woods.

She was about to call to Tommy so they could have a good laugh together when a rumbling started somewhere up the creek. She looked around at the bank of black clouds off in that direction, but they seemed farther away than before. Yet there was no doubt about the rumbling, and it was getting louder. So were the popping and crackling sounds.

She thought of an earthquake and could imagine the earth opening to swallow them up, teams, wagons, and all. Then she heard Mr. McDermit shout, "Git'n the wagons! Git'n the wagons!"

Children started screaming and men shouting. She jumped up on the hub of the wheel, scared by all the noise but seeing no reason to climb in the wagon. Yet she could see children and grown-ups rushing to the front of the other wagons and scrambling up to get inside. One of Mr. McDermit's horses, wearing only a bridle and a collar, plunged past her and went loping across the meadow, tail up and head swinging right and left. In seconds other horses, already harnessed up, ran after it.

All of this commotion puzzled her more than it scared her. If this was an earthquake, she couldn't see how hiding in the wagon would save her. An earthquake could swallow up a wagon as easy as anything else.

Turning to look towards the loud rumble, she couldn't believe what she saw happening up the hollow beyond the road. Bushes were swaying and bobbing. Even small trees were waving like some giant was shaking them. The rumble was now a roar and getting so loud she could barely hear the noises around her.

Not until she saw the bushes beyond the road fall towards her and a wall of foaming water burst through did she realize a flood was on them. Scared stock still, she watched the flood gush across the road and sweep down into the meadow. It splashed high against their home-base tree stump, knocking it over like a straw. The wall of yellowish foam came rushing towards the wagons, seething and frothing like soapsuds boiling in a wash kettle.

"Tommy!"

At Mama's scream she turned and saw Tommy crouched out in the meadow, facing the coming flood. She leaped from the hub of the wagon wheel, throwing her empty plate to the ground, and went racing towards him, hiking her skirt up with one hand so she could run faster.

Seeing that the wall of water was going to reach Tommy before she could, she yelled, "Run for the woods!"

She kept yelling and running, and Tommy kept staring at the flood rushing towards him. When she was a few steps from Tommy, he heard her and looked around, but instead of running for the woods he threw up his arms and ran screaming towards her.

As she leaned forward to scoop him up, the wall of water hit them. Down they went together, the flood swept over them, picked them up and sent them rolling across the meadow like a log.

She thrashed out with her arms until she got her head up for a breath of air. A weight dragged her under and she realized Tommy's arms were around her waist. She found his arms and tried to pull him up, but his weight was too much for her. Once more she churned the water with her arms and legs and forced herself up for another gulp of air.

Time after time as they were swept along, she fought her way up through the foamy water for a quick breath only to be dragged under again. Once she sucked a mouthful of water and went under choking and coughing.

Scared now that Tommy was going to drown her, she clawed at his arms. Her ears began to pound and her head roar, but she kept on clawing and pulling to get free of the weight holding her down. Her clawing fingers caught Tommy's hair and in frenzy she jerked his head away from her body, jerked and jerked and was still jerking it when the current rolled them over a bed of hot needles, slammed them against something hard and left her jammed against it.

She lay vomiting and sputtering in a bed of foam, afraid to

move. Minutes passed. Then slowly she raised a hand to her face and scraped the foam away. She was lying on the plum bushes, caught and held against the trunk of a dead tree. Foamy water was still swishing and gurgling through the bushes all around her, but the roar of the flood was dying away downstream.

She thought of Tommy and grabbed at her waist. Gone! With a cry she grabbed with her other hand to make sure. The current swung her around and she grabbed for the tree again and held on, crying out for Tommy, sure now that he was somewhere under all that foamy water.

Suddenly overcome by guilt, she began to cry, shivering all the while in spite of the warm sun on her face. Tommy had run to her to save him and she had pulled and kicked and clawed him until she got rid of him. She could not believe what she had done. It was like a dream, yet the water running through the plum thicket all around her was no dream.

Still shivering, she pulled herself up the slippery tree trunk to where she could stand out of the water on a stump of a limb. How long she stood leaning against the tree and looking into the foamy water and wishing she could die, she had no idea, but she was still standing there when she heard a shout.

She looked around, but she didn't see anybody until she heard the shout again. Then she saw Papa riding Nellie towards her, splashing through the shallow water just below the woods. When Papa got closer, she saw he had been in the water himself. His clothes were soaked, and the brown hair slicked down on his head looked as black as hers.

She waited, scared all over again, as he forced Nellie into the thorny plum thicket, which was now hardly belly deep in water to her, and when the mare was close enough, she put her hands on Papa's shoulders and threw herself on behind the saddle.

No sooner was she safe on Nellie than she dropped her head against Papa's wet back and began to cry again. Between sobs she tried to tell him what happened to Tommy, but he stopped her.

"Hush now, Mattie. Maybe Tommy ain't no more drowned than you are." And then Papa started telling her what had happened to him. He had been riding Nellie up to the front of the wagon to unsaddle her when he saw the flood hit her and Tommy. He rode out on Nellie to try to help. The water knocked Nellie over, too, and he had been lucky to grab hold of a stirrup when she got back up and started lunging for shallow water.

While Papa talked, she had time to think about what she had almost confessed, and she was relieved she hadn't been able to tell Papa what she had done to Tommy. He might have given her a whipping first and asked questions later.

She was reminded of the time Jimmy ran Nellie all the way home from Shades Crossing in the heat of the day. Papa didn't take a second look at the mare's heaving sides before he had a butt line in one hand and Jimmy in the other, and he didn't stop whipping Jimmy till his back was all bloody welts. That night Jimmy ran away from home and hadn't been seen or heard from since.

She could see that most of the meadow was still covered with water, but it was no longer flowing like a fast river, and Nellie had no trouble wading through it. When they got close to the wagons, the first thing she noticed was that the flood had turned Old Lady McDermit's wagon on its side and ripped the wagon sheet off. In the next wagon all the McDermits were standing in a huddle near the spring seat.

Nellie splashed past them and then she saw Mama and the others standing in the wagon, Mama holding Ben and everybody staring big-eyed at her. She knew they were wondering where Tommy was, and she lowered her eyes, ashamed to look at them. She didn't know how she was ever going to face all those eyes.

Papa stopped Nellie right next to the front wheel, but even then she didn't look up. Climbing over the sideboard, she jumped down in the wagon bed. She had made up her mind she wasn't going to cry any more, but when Mama handed Ben to Alice and reached out for her, she was crying as soon as she felt Mama's arms around her.

"Old Lady McDermit's wagon got turned over and she got washed away like Tommy did."

"Hush, Emma," Mama said, "and git in the back of the wagon."

"Is that so, Mandy?"

She looked up to see Mama nodding to Papa. Without another word Papa reined Nellie around and splashed back towards the McDermit's wagon.

She stopped crying and looked around bleary-eyed at Alice and Bob. They were staring at her like she was some kind of strange animal. She felt better when Mama shooed Bob away, got a dry dress out of the chest under the spring seat, and helped her get her wet one off and the dry one on.

"You get some sleep now," Mama said, spreading a quilt on the chest.

She didn't feel in the least like sleeping, but she lay down and shut her eyes. Almost as soon as Mama finished wrapping her up in the other half of the quilt, she stopped shivering and was asleep.

Chapter 4

The sun in her eyes woke her. She turned her face away from it and saw she was lying on the chest under the spring seat. Closing her eyes again she tried to remember why she was sleeping there in the wagon in broad daylight, and then her mind leaped to Tommy.

Throwing herself upright, she bumped her head against the spring seat and stood up to look out of the wagon. The horses and colts and Old Blackie were grazing at the far end of the meadow. She was about to breathe easier, when she noticed a mud-covered log on the ground where Old Lady McDermit's overturned wagon had been.

"Nooo," she wailed, dropping back to the chest and covering her face with her hands.

"You awake, Matt?" Alice called from the back of the wagon. "They found Old Lady McDermit. She's dead. Stuck between two trees. Way up in the air. They had to chop one tree down to get her loose. So far they ain't found a trace of Old Caesar."

Her heart started to pound even harder when Alice went on to say the men and two Indians were still looking for Tommy, all except Clyde. The men had put his wagon back on its wheels, and he was taking Old Lady McDermit's body to a settlement up ahead where there was a graveyard and maybe, the Indians said, a preacher.

"We're all goin' straight there," Alice said. "Soon's they find Tommy."

It was nearly sundown before the men straggled in, soaking wet and dirty as hogs from searching the muddy undergrowth along the creek. As soon as they washed up, everybody gathered for supper.

Her mind was so full of shame for what she had done to Tommy that she didn't want a thing to eat, but Mama insisted she try a few bites. Once she started eating, she found she was starved and had to ask Mama for more. Even so, she was surprised that everybody but Mama was eating and talking as though Tommy and Old Lady McDermit had never existed.

There sat Mr. McDermit, finishing off his second plate of butter beans and cornbread as fast as the first one, and talking along as easy as you please. If he was sorry he had lost his mama and his old hound dog Caesar, he never acted like it.

After supper, she and the other children hung around the fire. The women went to work washing up and putting away, while the men stayed squatting or sprawling where they were, and little by little went to talking about the coming search for Tommy.

Finally the men agreed they would spend the next day looking for Tommy, if it took that long to find him. If they didn't find him, they would hitch up and drive through the night to the settlement where Clyde had gone. Mr. McDermit said he would ride on ahead of the wagons and have the funeral arrangements made for his mama by the time they all got there. That way they would not lose another day on the road.

Next morning the creek was back in its channel again, and she was put to work with the rest of the children to hunt along it for pots and pans and other things the flood had carried away. About mid-morning, while she and Emma were dragging in Prince's muddy saddle blanket, the sound of a gunshot came from downstream. That was the signal to draw the men to where something had been found, and she shuddered at the thought of looking at Tommy's dead face.

In a few minutes Bob came panting up to the wagons, all in a rush for a shovel. He said the Indian boy's papa had found Tommy's overalls sticking out of a mudbank, and they were going to dig there for the body. She let go of the saddle blanket and thought she was going to faint. Later when she saw Mama go up in the wagon to nurse Ben, she climbed up after her and slumped down beside her on the feather bed.

"Mama," she began, "I wish I was dead, too." Between spells of crying she told Mama about Tommy's drowning, just the way it happened. After she had told it all, she felt better, but she was so scared of what Mama was going to say that she kept her wet face pressed hard against Mama's shoulder.

For a long time she waited for Mama to say something, but Mama only kept softly stroking her head. Finally she felt the hand stop and heard Mama say in a tired voice, "I reckin we'd all done about like you done, Mattie. So they ain't no need for you bein' too hard on yourself."

"Oh, Mama!" she burst out, and broke into more tears, crying harder than ever.

"Jist the same," Mama went on after awhile, "they ain't no need sayin' nothin' about this to the rest. You hear, Matt?"

She nodded and moved away, but she was too upset to get out of the wagon and face the others. She was still there on the feather bed when Bob came back again by himself, carrying the shovel and the muddy wad of Tommy's overalls. Bob said they had dug the mudbank down to bedrock without finding another trace of him.

Through her own tears, she looked at Mama when Bob held out the overalls to her. But Mama never shed a tear, just called Alice to come and take care of Ben, and Emma to get a bucket of water to put on the fire.

Climbing down from the wagon, Mama got out the washboard and soap. When the water was hot, she scrubbed the overalls almost to pieces to get all the mud out of them. Then she rinsed them in a bucket of clean water and hung them on the front wagon bow to dry.

Later, while the overalls were still damp, Mama had Emma bring her the flatiron she had put on the coals. Wiping the ashes off on her apron, Mama ironed the overalls dry on the spring seat, folded them carefully, and laid them in the chest.

The sun was touching the treetops by the time they had eaten supper, loaded the wagons and hitched up. She was sitting next to Emma in the back of the wagon, looking out at the colts tied next to Old Blackie. The old cow didn't seem to mind, but the colts were not used to being tied up and were fidgeting around and jerking back on their ropes.

The Indians had said there were panthers around here, and Papa was afraid the colts might wander off down a side road during the night, and one of them wind up as a meal for the panthers. Thinking of that, she soon had a picture in her mind of panthers digging Tommy out of a mudbank and eating him.

They pulled out of the meadow onto the road and the mares clip-clopped down to the creek and splashed it. When Old Blackie and the colts reached the edge of the water, the colts pulled back on their ropes before plunging in, but Old Blackie merely raised her tail up like a pump handle and waded calmly across.

When it got dark, she hunted her pillow and quilt out of the pile and began to make herself comfortable for the night. She slept off and on, crammed tight in her corner by the others sleeping next to her. Every time she woke up, the wagon was still moving, yet when she woke up for good, the sun was shining and the wagon was standing in a clump of oak trees. The other wagons were close by and the women were cooking breakfast.

While they were eating, Mr. McDermit rode up, freshly shaved—his mustache trimmed shorter than Papa's—and wearing a clean shirt. Between sips of coffee he told them the funeral had to be put off until after dinner. A boy from a bunch of wagons passing through on the Texas Road had been kicked by a horse last night after supper, and during the night, he died. The preacher was burying him this morning. So they would put the teams out to graze and wait for their turn with the preacher.

After breakfast she saw a family of Indians drive by in a wagon and got the idea to visit the little Indian settlement a short way up the road beyond the clump of oaks. Emma was willing, and the two of them struck out up the sandy road.

It turned out to be not much of a place, just a few log houses and a store and that was about all. When they got close to a gathering of people standing in the road, it turned out not to be Indians, as she had expected, but white people—maybe two dozen men, women, and children. They were milling around in front of a blacksmith shop and sort of drifting under a brush arbor next to it.

At the far end of the arbor a few people were already sitting on the front bench, and an Indian man in preacher's clothes was standing behind the pulpit, waiting for the rest of the people to come underneath and sit down.

As the others moved under the arbor, she was busy counting up the days on her fingers since they had left Bear Creek. She decided this was not Sunday, and she wondered what kind of a church service this was. But when the preacher opened his Bible and began to read "the Lord giveth and the Lord taketh away"—and the people down on the front row started sniffling—she knew this was no revival meeting.

And then she noticed the coffin in front of the pulpit and realized this was the funeral for the boy kicked by the horse. From the size of the coffin, she reckoned he was about Tommy's age, and that started her trembling. "Let's go back," she whispered to Emma.

They found Papa and Mama in the wagon having a big row over the funeral for Tommy. Papa wanted the preacher to just say a few words about Tommy at the same time as he was talking about Old Lady McDermit, but Mama wanted him to have his own coffin, with his overalls in it, and the old double-bladed barlow he had found and she was keeping for him until he got a little bigger.

Papa kept muttering this was heathenish, and finally Mama got so mad everybody could hear her shouting, "Heathenish or no heathenish, Jim Lane, I ain't goin' one step from this place till that boy's coffin is in the ground. Now you jist make up your mind to that."

The row ended with Papa storming down out of the wagon and

off on Nellie to get the man to make another coffin. So it was that there were two coffins in front of the altar that evening, although she had eyes only for Tommy's.

The preacher sounded a lot like Reverend Farthing at Shades Crossing, yet when she looked up at him she was surprised at holy words coming out of an Indian face, a face that had a streak of soot on the chin to boot. She had heard that the blacksmith shop next to the arbor belonged to this Indian preacher, and he was a blacksmith in his spare time, or maybe it was the other way around. He also made coffins, and Tommy's was so light she and Bob picked it up after the service and carried it like nothing to the graveyard back of the brush arbor.

After both graves were filled in and rounded up, they all walked back through the hot sand to the wagons. On the way, the men decided it was so late they would be better off to stay camped where they were for the night.

Lying on her pallet in Old Lady McDermit's tent after supper, she thought how glad she was that Mama had made Papa get the coffin for Tommy. Even if he was not in it, the idea was a comfort to her. His name burned into the headboard was so clear anyone could read it a long way off: Thomas Hart Lane...6 yrs... drowned.

"Drowned by his own sister," she whispered to herself and put her hands to her mouth so her crying would not wake Alice and Emma. In spite of being glad about the coffin she shivered at the thought of Tommy lying naked back there somewhere along that creek, and hungry panthers finding him and eating him.

At breakfast next morning, she could hardly believe her ears when Clyde told them he had been awakened during the night by Old Caesar licking his face. He said he guessed the old hound had found his way back up the creek to the campsite and then followed the scent of the wagons.

When the wagons pulled out and reached the far edge of the Indian settlement, instead of going on west towards the open prairie she had seen from the mountains, they turned south. Bob told her that Papa had told him that they had to follow this big Texas Road south until it crossed the Arkansas River. Then they would turn west again and be on their way to Oklahoma Territory.

Wheels and hoofs had powdered this busy road finer than if it had been plowed and harrowed, and a puff of dust flew up from anything that touched it. Even the birds stayed away from the dust-clouded road. She missed seeing the birds, but as for people, she saw more that day than she had seen on the whole trip, so far. Most of the wagons, hacks, buggies and men on horseback were headed south, but some were going north, probably to St. Louis, Papa said.

After their hottest day yet, they stopped on the far side of a broad creek that already had a string of travelers camped along it. During the night she and her sisters were awakened by what sounded like some gigantic, angry animal rampaging through the countryside towards them, getting closer and closer with each bellow, howl or whatever it was.

By now they were all three holding on to the tent pole, whispering nervously to each other every time the noise came screaming through the night—"It's closer!" "It's closer!" "Someone'll shoot it!"

No one did, but the sound stopped. No sounds came from any of the campers up or down the creek. Alice was just saying it must have turned away, when a piercing wail slashed through the tent, faded away, and then came back louder then ever. Again and again it shrilled like a riled up monster. Emma started screaming and ran for the flap and kept screaming as she ran out into the night.

Up and down the creek people started hollering, but from inside the tent neither she nor Alice could understand what they were saying. The next time they heard the scary sound, it came from farther off, and Alice said she guessed it had turned away.

The tent flap jerked open and a whimpering Emma was pushed inside, followed by Papa's angry voice. "Now all of you git to sleep. The idea makin' all this fuss over a railroad train."

The next day she listened in dread and wonder to the wails of another railroad train passing nearby, this one coming from the north. For many miles the railroad tracks passed within sight of the road, and she got to see more than one railroad train. Yet she never got over thinking of them as fearful, smoking monsters streaking through the countryside, screaming now and then for no reason she could see.

The weather was hotter every day now, so hot that nobody complained when a rain cloud black as night blew up out of nowhere late one evening and started settling the dust with a cooling rain. The trouble was that it turned the road into one mudhole after another. In the worst places the teams went up to their knees in the mud, and in one long stretch the mud clogged the spokes so much the wheels could not turn. The men put two teams to one wagon at a time and dragged them out of the long mudhole like sleds. After this they gave up trying to go on, and camped at a spring for two days while the road hardened up.

They were in good farming country now, and once they got underway again they were able to buy fresh eggs and a bucket of honey for themselves, and corn for the horses. Every time they stopped to buy something, she and Emma nosed around the place to see what they could see. She was surprised that most of the women who came to the door of the farmhouses they stopped at were white. Yet maybe it was like her own family, Cherokees and whites marrying each other for so long it was hard sometimes to tell a Cherokee from a white.

When they came to the Arkansas River, it was flooding out of its banks, and the ferries could not run until the water went down. Fording such a big river even at its normal level was out of the question, so they found a place to camp in a pecan grove well away from the river in back of other wagons waiting to cross.

Chapter 5

For several days they camped in a grove of pecan trees among more and more arriving families waiting their turn to cross the flooded Arkansas River on the ferryboats. She spent her mornings playing with Emma or wandering through the camp, talking to girls and boys from faraway places. One family had come all the way from Ohio, yet from what she could tell, they looked and talked about the same as everybody else.

She noticed that she was not the only one pleased to stay in one place for a few days. The wait gave the women time to get a little rest and catch up on their washing and mending, and the men to patch up the harnesses and wagons.

Sunday came and Papa led them, scrubbed, and dressed in clean clothes, to the far end of the pecan grove—where all the graves were—to listen to a Methodist preacher, a little man with a big voice. He stood in the back of a wagon, and after lining out a hymn with them, he preached for a good hour about not looking back once you put your hand to the plow. From the way he was sweating like a field hand, she figured he earned all the money he got when Papa and a couple of other men passed their hats for him.

One morning a few days later, the sun was halfway towards noon when Papa and Mr. McDermit came up from the landing, announcing, "Well, today's the day." This was the news everybody had been waiting for, and the bustle commenced at once. The men and Bob hurried off to catch up the stock and bring them in, and the women started gathering up all their cooking things. Within an hour the wagons were loaded, the teams hitched up, the colts tied next to Old Blackie, and everybody ready to pull out.

Everybody except the Bartons. He was always talking, but this was the first time she had ever heard Mrs. Barton raise her voice.

Yet there was Mrs. Barton beside him on the spring seat—a crying, squirming baby in her arms—shouting to her husband again and again that he was breaking his promise. Yet the tears didn't seem to bother Mr. Barton.

He jumped down from his wagon, which he had already pulled half way out of the group, and began calling to Papa that he had suddenly decided to go on to Texas. "If Texas don't work out," he lowered his voice to add, "you may see me one day in the Territory. Or I may try Colorado, or even Oregon. There's a lot of West out there to see, and I aim to see it before I settle down on my own piece of it."

As she watched Mama and Mrs. McDermit climb down to say good-bye to a tearful Mrs. Barton, it crossed her mind that the three women had much in common. Mrs. Barton was the only one crying out loud, but she knew the two others hadn't wanted to leave their home. Yet here they were, a scary river to cross and more and more miles to travel, with no home for sure at the end. Maybe it was husbands who liked to travel, and the wives just went along, even if they really didn't want go. Without a husband, she would never have to worry about that, and the thought made her feel better.

But on reaching the landing, she was nervous once more at the thought of having to cross all that shiny water, and the sight of a man having trouble getting a scared span of mules to pull the wagon up the planks and onto the ferryboat set her to trembling. In spite of his whipping and cursing the mules, and the shouts of the other men trying to help him, the mules refused to step up on the ramp.

Finally the mules were unhitched, and a swarm of men, including Bob, pitched in and helped the Indian crew roll the wagon on. The mules were then blindfolded and backed up the planks, with more shouting and cursing and whipping by the driver. Before the ferryboat was fifty yards out in the river, the cursing and shouting started all over again, and she held her breath as she saw a rearing mule spin around and leap over the side of the ferry into the river. It came up almost before it went under, but no sooner did its head and neck show than the current rolled the body over belly up, legs kicking in a tangle of harness, and pulled it under.

She kept looking and hoping the poor animal would come up again, but it never did. As Bob came back to their wagon, she couldn't help saying, "See that?"

But Bob just laughed and said, "You ain't got nothin' to be skeered of, Mattie. Less you're plannin' on jumpin' in."

In no mood to joke about the drowned mule, she didn't say anything else, although it did seem to her that Bob was losing the kind nature he used to have. That poor man with only one mule left and no telling how far he and his family still had to go.

Noon came and went, and everybody was hungry and hot and cranky, what with the sun and the flies and the stink of fresh manure everywhere. Only Mama and Mrs. McDermit were too busy to complain. They comforted the children, gave them cold biscuits to eat and put the smallest ones, including Emma, down in the wagon bed for a nap. And they still found time to make a little fire and boil a pot of coffee for the men, as if the day was not hot enough already.

When the time came at last for them to drive their wagon onto the shaky ferryboat, she did not need Papa's order for all of them to sit down and keep quiet. She was too scared to do anything else, and she kept on being scared even after the wagon wheels were scotched, and Papa and Bob had unhitched Babe and Doll and tied them to the front of the wagon. But for some reason it made her feel a little better to notice that the colts, now tied between Nellie and Old Blackie, were trembling, too.

The ferryboat was big enough for two wagons, one behind the other, so when Mr. McDermit decided to keep his wagons together and take the other boat, the Indian crew rolled a grasshopper buggy with yellow wheels up behind Old Blackie, Nellie and the colts, and tipped the shaves up in the air. Following the buggy came a lean, red-faced man leading a long-legged chestnut buggy horse that shied and danced until he tied it close to the back of the buggy, and even then it snuffled and rolled its eyes at every movement of the ferryboat.

She felt Emma poke her in the ribs, and knew her sister was trying to get her to look and laugh at the sharp nose and turkey-red face of the man with the buggy, but she was still too scared by the shaky boat and the great stretch of red water ahead of them to laugh at anything.

When she felt the ferryboat start to move, she caught her breath and held it while the gap of water between her and the river bank got wider and wider. She clutched the top of the sideboard of the swaying wagon with both hands. Then she closed her eyes and held on, waiting for the wagon to tip over and throw them all in the water.

After awhile she slowly opened her eyes. Looking cautiously up the river, she watched a green branch come sliding along and crash against the side of the ferryboat. Soon another branch passed behind it. To take her mind off her fright, she started playing a game with herself, picking out something floating towards them and guessing whether it was going to pass in front, behind, or hit them. Happily for her peace of mind, most of the floating limbs and sticks and chunks of wood missed the ferryboat.

Near midstream she noticed the old Indian in charge of the crew playing the same game. She heard him give a sharp grunt and the chanting stopped, and so did the forward movement of the ferryboat, which now began to rock. This time she kept her eyes open even though she was sure something bad was about to happen. She looked up at Papa, who was standing on the wagon tongue between Babe and Doll and pointing out something upstream to Bob.

Now she saw it, too, and at first she thought it was what a big alligator might look like, slipping along fast in the current with just the top of its back shining out of the water. On and on it came, getting bigger all the time, and then it wallowed by, barely in front of the ferryboat, a log about fifty feet long and from the little of the top she could see, half as big around as a wagon wheel.

The Indians took up their chant, the pulleys squeaked and the ferryboat moved forward again, even as the red-faced man was shaking his head and whistling his relief at the near miss—the same relief she felt as she watched the big log disappear downstream. In another few minutes she saw the blobs on the riverbank ahead turn into bunches of men and wagons much like the ones they had left back on the other bank.

She watched them grow bigger, and in what seemed no time at all she felt the ferryboat jar softly and stop. She was so pleased to be on solid ground again she did not mind at all when Papa made everybody but Mama and Ben get out of the wagon to lighten the load. The mares were hitched up again. Papa stood on one side of them and Bob on the other. Just before the front wheels of the wagon rolled off the planks onto the sand, they both shouted and whacked the mares on their rumps.

As one animal Babe and Doll lunged into their collars, their hoofs dug into the sand, and they went plunging up the slope more at a run than a walk. Old Blackie and Nellie and the colts had to hurry to keep up or they might have been dragged off their feet.

When she caught up with the wagon, where Papa had pulled it off the road to wait for Mr. McDermit, she climbed in and turned to look back at the water. Her eyes followed the red curve of the river to the far shore, and on past it to the dark smudge of the pecan trees and cane brakes. Beyond were the low hills they had passed through, and somewhere way, way, way beyond that was Bear Valley.

Never mind that Bob was no longer as anxious to get back to Bear Valley as she was. There was no such thing as going back on your word, and when the right time came she would remind him of their vow. Clyde and Mr. McDermit passing by took her mind off Bear Valley, and when Bob pulled Babe and Doll into the road after them, she began to take notice again of the country around her. They were still in farming country, bottomland now with flat fields running back as far as she could see.

Passing a big field of rows of skimpy bushes about three feet high, with what looked little stringy snowballs mixed in among the green leaves, she realized she was seeing her first field of cotton. Papa's family had grown cotton in eastern Tennessee, and she had heard him say many times what a lot of work growing cotton was, but she had never actually seen a boll or a stalk of cotton.

She and Emma jumped out of the back of the wagon and ran to see who could be the first one to pick a boll of cotton. She snatched at the first fluffy, white boll she came to and was closing her hand on it when something like a needle pricked her finger and made her cry out and drop the cotton. She heard Emma make the same kind of noise and looked around and saw that her sister had dropped her cotton and put her fingers in her mouth.

Taking care not to prick her own fingers again, she reached out and cautiously pulled a boll apart, piece by piece. She saw that each boll had four parts inside a half-opened husk, which had four needles hiding at the outer edge of the full boll of cotton, just waiting to stick into anything trying to pull the cotton ball out of its husk. She stripped two bolls, stem and all, off the stalk to show the others, and ran to catch up with Emma and the wagons, thankful that she would never have to pick cotton. At one cotton field they passed, the pickers were near the road, and she was surprised to find that the men, women and children she had thought to be Indians were Negroes. So were all the other pickers she saw close up.

She had not expected to see Negroes living among Indians, and at the first stop she asked Papa about it. He said they were in the Creek Indian Nation now, and the Creeks brought their slaves with them when the government moved the tribes West before the Civil War. "Nowadays," he said, "you cain't tell 'em apart cause they've bred like cattle in a pasture." She didn't know what Papa meant and was afraid to ask. She did know she was scared of both races.

The next morning they turned off the big road running south to Texas, and headed west on what was little more than a trail. According to Papa, this was a shortcut that would bring them to

Oklahoma Territory in about four or so days if nothing went wrong. Within a few miles they left the rich bottomland behind, and also the Indians and Negroes. It was wild, open country now, no farms, no fences, and so far, no other travelers.

All she could see in any direction were strips and patches of scrub oak and blackjack on upper slopes of the rolling hills. Strung out along the creeks they crossed were willows and cottonwoods, and trees she didn't know the names of. On the long slopes in between yellow brown grass flashed in the sun, rippling under a wind blowing hot from the south. In most places the grass was waist high, but along the bottomland of the creeks it was as tall as the top of the wagon bed.

A while before sundown they met a string of four wagons, each pulled by two spans of mules hitched one behind the other, but only the first and last wagon had a driver. Bringing up the rear was a little old man wearing a dirty beard and riding a sorrel mule. He neck reined the mule around and shortly led them off the road past the red mounds of two fresh graves and on down to a spring beside the dry creek bed.

Once she had watered Old Blackie and staked her out to graze, she and Emma walked over for a closer look at the little old man, now squatting in the creek bed talking to Papa and Mr. McDermit. White hair hung out from under his hat and a dirty white beard all the way to his chest. When Papa asked him the shortest road to the Territory, he answered, "Oh, the place to go out there is Kickapoo."

The name started her and Emma giggling, but the little old man took no notice of them. On and on he went, telling what a great town Kickapoo was. At last, with the butt of his blacksnake he started to trace in the sand where to turn off for the best road to Kickapoo. Every now and then the little old man paused and sent another blob of tobacco juice looping over his shoulder, wiped his mouth on the back of his hand and went on talking. The sun was ready to set by the time he stood up to go.

At supper, although the hot wind from the south had not dropped with the sun, no one said anything more about the heat. The stories of the little old man had made Oklahoma Territory seem so close and so exciting it was all the talk.

Yet as she listened to this one and that one of the grown-ups saying what it was going to be like when they got there, she kept thinking of the two new graves back up the slope towards the road, two people who never would get to see Oklahoma Territory. After she had finished eating, even though it was already getting dark, she gave in to the urge to walk up and see the graves again. During daylight they had been two long mounds of fresh red dirt, but now they were twin dark shadows in the moonlight inside a circle of trampled down prairie grass.

A prickle of fear touched the nape of her neck. Under those two shadows lay two human beings who maybe day before yesterday were as alive as those she could hear talking down at the fire. But these two would never talk again, or feel the fire on their faces again.

For a long time she stood looking down at the two shadows in the moonlight, shivering as she tried to imagine what it would be like to die, to be dead and put under the ground and have the dirt piled up over you, and you stay in there forever and ever. She could understand other people being dead—Tommy and Old Lady McDermit, for instance—but not herself. No matter how hard she tried, she could not see herself down there under one of those shadowy mounds of dirt, and the family and Old Blackie and the colts going off up the road without her.

Chapter 6

At sunrise the next morning, she stood at the spring, letting Old Blackie get a last drink of water before she tied her to the back of the wagon. Breakfast was over, the wagons were loaded, and everybody was about ready to leave. Slowly the bony old cow sipped and sipped, taking forever to get her fill.

Seeing Old Blackie suddenly stop sipping and throw her head around toward the wagons, she looked around, too. Four horsemen were riding down from the road to where Mr. McDermit and Clyde were doing something to the wagon sheet on Clyde's wagon. The leading horseman pulled up there, but the other three kept on past the wagons and came towards the spring, as if they knew all the time it was here.

They swung down from their lathered horses within feet of where she was now trying to pull Old Blackie away from the water. She stopped pulling to stare at their big hats and pistols and spurred boots.

"You all cowboys?" she asked, something she had heard about

but never seen.

The first two men brushed past her without answering, squatted at the edge of the spring within a few feet of Old Blackie, and began scooping up water in their cupped hands and slurping it down. But the third man, who looked almost as young as Bob, grinned at her and said, "Sure, ma'am. Want me to twist that old cow's tail fer ye?"

This was not what she meant, and she was ashamed to seem to be asking a stranger for help—and a man at that. Yet he had called her "ma'am," and that must mean he thought her older than she was. Quickly she looked down at her dirty old dress and felt her face getting hot. She jerked Old Blackie around, led her up from the creek bed and tied her to the back of the wagon. But instead of getting in the wagon herself, she ran up the slope to see what the other stranger looked like.

Papa and Clyde and the lean faced stranger, dressed in cowboy clothes like the men at the spring, were standing near a tall black horse all crusty white in the flank with old sweat. Mr. McDermit straddled the horse's near front leg, and had the hoof curled up between his knees. With a pair of tongs he was prying a piece of broken horseshoe off the hoof, while the lanky stranger leaned forward, watching.

Mr. McDermit handed him the piece of broken shoe, and touched the tongs to the frog of the hoof, saying, "Looks like it dug in here perty bad."

The stranger said something, but his voice was so low she couldn't hear what it was. Mr. McDermit shook his head and said, "Well, if he was mine, I shore wouldn't ride him for a few days."

The stranger nodded, straightened up and looked around at the three other horsemen, who had returned from the spring and were now sitting on their horses a little way away. He looked back at Mr. McDermit, and said, "In that case I'm sorry, Mister, but I'll have to borry your roan for a spell."

Mr. McDermit dropped the curled up hoof and pushed away from the horse. "Now jist a minute," he began, the tongs half raised in his hand.

She shrank away towards Papa, scared from the look on Mr. McDermit's face that something awful was about to happen.

The stranger lifted his own hand and quietly said, "Just hold it now." He looked at Papa and Clyde. "You all take it easy and nobody'll get hurt." Back to Mr. McDermit, he said, "Now, Mister, I'm gonna leave Beauty with you for the time bein'. And no offense, but he's worth two of your roan any day."

She could see Mr. McDermit was mad as hops. But he never made a move as the stranger stripped the saddle and blanket off Prince and put Beauty's blanket and saddle on in their place. It was then she noticed the rifle in a scabbard hanging from the stranger's saddle. She looked around at the other horsemen. And sure enough, every saddle carried a rifle. The stranger swung up in the saddle and calmed the snuffling Prince with a few soft words and a few soft pats on the neck. Then to Mr. McDermit he said, "If you tell me your name and where you're headed, I'll try to swap back with you soon's I can." He repeated Ed McDermit's name back to him, and touched spurs to Prince.

The horse went plunging down the slope, and the rider never looked back as he crossed the creek and headed the roan cross country at an easy lope. One by one the other horsemen followed a few lengths apart, the young man who had grinned at her, and called her "ma'am" spurring away last. He had just reached the creek when she heard Bob shout, "Can I shoot now, Papa?"

"No!" roared Papa and Mr. McDermit at the same time.

Thankful that the polite young man had not been shot, she saw Bob jump down from the wagon and come fuming up to them, the shotgun still in his hands.

"Papa, I could've got him easy. Whyn't you let me shoot one of them horse thieves?"

Before Papa could answer, Mr. McDermit said, "You want them outlaws to come back and shoot us all?"

"Outlaws?" Bob looked as if he'd seen a ghost. After a few seconds he said in almost a whisper, "Maybe it was the Dalton gang."

"Naw," Clyde said. "They done been killed off. But I tell you one thang. I bet them saddlebags were fulla money. Bet they jist held up

45

a bank somers."

While the others stood around talking outlaws and looking across the creek, Mr. McDermit put a handful of axle grease on Beauty's cut foot and wrapped the hoof in a piece of tow sack. After he led the limping horse down to the spring for a drink, he tied it behind Clyde's wagon so he could keep an eye on its limp while he drove his own wagon.

Once they were on the road, she had to explain to the family what had happened, since no one in the wagon had any idea what was going on until Bob saw the man taking Prince and grabbed the shotgun.

By mid-morning the sky began to cloud up from the south, and by noon a solid layer of clouds hid the sun. This should have cooled things off, but the road was going through an endless blackjack thicket that cut off the south wind and left them sweltering in the worst heat they had been in yet.

Nothing stirred in the thicket. Even the birds in the trees stayed where they were while the wagons passed, their wings drooping and their bills hanging open. They reminded her of the chickens at home, squatting around in the shade on the hottest days, bills hanging open like dogs panting for air.

By late evening the clouds were gone and they were out of the thicket into farming country once more, but the farms were small here.

At supper, Papa made everybody laugh when he looked up at the newly cleared sky and said his bad leg told him it was going to rain.

Yet sure enough, she had hardly fallen asleep before she was awakened by thunder. Flashes of lightning lit up the tent, and Clyde came around to drive the tent pegs deeper into the ground. The thunder and lightning came closer, and Emma began to complain that she was scared and wanted to go to the wagon. But Alice calmed her down by telling her that lightning would strike the wagons before it would the tent because of the iron rims on the wagon wheels.

All at once the south wind stopped and the tent went slack. This south wind had been blowing without stopping ever since they crossed the Arkansas River, and it scared her to feel it stop all at once. With lightning blinking and thunder grumbling, she sat up on her pallet in the still tent, waiting to see what was going to happen next.

Suddenly the tent thrashed around like something alive, and wind shrieked in from the north. Flash after flash of lightning blinded them. Thunder ripped the sky open and crashed over their heads. Something splattered against the tent like a handful of gravel. The splattering kept up, and she crept to the tent flap and put her hand out in the storm.

It was hail all right, big as her thumb and so cold she put a handful in her mouth without thinking about it. After all the weeks of heat, this was too good to be true. She bent down and scooped up a double handful, passed it around to Alice and Emma, and went back and got some more for herself. After several minutes the steady splatter of hail on the tent eased off to a passing dribble. Then it stopped.

The wind kept on blowing, carrying the thunder and lightning off to the south. Long after she stopped hearing the thunder she could still see a little flicker of lightning against the tent.

Once she looked out through the tent flap and could hardly believe what she saw. Instead of the hot, brown prairie at sundown, everything was white and cold, and the moon was racing across gaps in the dark clouds.

The next morning when she came out of the tent, all the hailstones had melted, leaving the ground damp and cool, and the air as chilly as a fall morning. During breakfast Bob told her they would be getting to Oklahoma Territory in a few hours, and that Papa had told him he could ride Nellie this morning and be the first one to cross the border. Right away she asked Papa if she could ride with Bob, but he said, "Better hep Alice. Your mama's feelin' poorly this morning."

Before they finished eating breakfast, the sun came up in a sky as clear as if there had never been a storm, although the cool breeze coming from the north was a reminder of it.

No sooner were they on the road than they could see other

reminders of the storm. Every field of corn they passed was laid flat, the leaves cut to ribbons and beaten into the ground. Cotton was torn out of the bolls and hung in ragged locks on the stalks, or was beaten into the ground like the corn. The trees in every orchard were stripped clean, and the ground littered with leaves and ruined fruit.

At one orchard a skinny Negro farmer, out looking at the damage, came over to the fence and called to them to come in and help themselves. "Dat hail done finish 'um," he said to Papa. "No two ways bout dat. Dis lak las' year."

She was the first one out of the wagon and into the orchard. At the first tree she picked up a yellow apple to be eating on while she went from tree to tree looking for her favorite fruit, Elberta peaches. When she came to several trees of them, she picked up and ate all she wanted, and then picked up a skirtful of the best ones and carried them back to Mama.

Later, after riding along beside Papa in the cool, morning air for a while, she decided she was no longer jealous of Bob, and didn't mind seeing him riding around on Nellie and trotting off down every side road he came to. From one of these trips, he rode back alongside the wagon to tell everyone there was a river in the green strip across the prairie ahead of them, and that Oklahoma Territory was on the other side of it.

As they neared the green strip of trees, the road dipped down from the prairie and cut a sandy swath through grassy patches and vine-covered thickets of wild plum, sumac and other bushes. Open stretches of sand showed that water had been in this low land recently. It was a scary looking place, and she was glad she was sitting next to Papa instead of off riding with Bob. She did not mind a bit when he trotted by and disappeared ahead to be the first one to get to Oklahoma Territory.

In a few minutes Bob came back at a fast lope. He shouted something to Clyde and Mr. McDermit that made them stop their teams, but he kept on to Papa's wagon before he pulled Nellie up short.

"They's a nigger hangin' down there," he shouted, his voice cracking, his eyes as big as Nellie's.

Papa stopped the mares and said, "How's that? Hangin'?"

"Hangin'! I mean he's hangin' from the limb of a tree!"

Clyde and Mr. McDermit came back to find out what the matter was, and it was agreed that even though there had probably been a lynching up ahead, all they could do was go on.

Mama made Bob get in the wagon, and Papa got on Nellie and rode off without seeming to pay any attention to Mama's saying, "You be careful now, Jim."

With Papa riding just in front of Clyde's wagon, and Mr. McDermit walking beside him, they started off again. In a quieter voice Bob told the family how he had been riding along in the shade of some big trees when the road curved and there ahead of him was the river shining in the sun.

"Before I got to it," Bob said, "I seen what looked like a broken limb hangin' over the road. When I got closer, Nellie she started to snortin' and shyin' around. Then I seen it was a man hangin' from a limb. A black leg was hangin' out where his pants was all tore. And then I seen a bunch of men off to one side. White men. Some was sprawled on the ground. Some was standin' around holdin' their horses. By now Nellie she was jerkin' at the bit. So I turned her around and let her go."

When Babe and Doll came to the curve in the road, the other wagons had stopped, and Papa and Mr. McDermit were talking to a bunch of men. Bob drove the mares right up against the back of the McDermit wagon, jumped down and hurried up to where the men were. A few minutes later, he came back all excited again.

He said it was true one Negro had been lynched, and the men had a second one surrounded in a nearby thicket. They said the two had robbed and murdered a white man near a settlement just across the river.

According to Bob, the men just laughed when Papa tried to get them to let the law handle the hunted man, but they made no objection when Papa kneeled down in the road beneath the dead one and said a prayer for his soul.

Bob said one man took it for some kind of a joke. "Hey, Mister," he said to Papa, "you better say a few words for that other black bastard at the same time, cause he's goin' to be hangin' up there next to his friend soon's the hounds get here."

When the wagons started moving again, Mama told her and Emma to get down off the spring seat and get in the back of the wagon and stay there. Once at the back, she told herself she was not going to look at the hanging man, but she did want to see what kind of men would do such an awful thing.

She was looking out the back when the wagon passed about a dozen rough looking, red-faced men carrying six-shooters and rifles. Others had already sprawled on the ground in the shade, talking and laughing and passing a bottle.

She was about to look away, when almost at the level of her head a pair of feet slipped into view, and then a whole body was hanging right there in front of her eyes.

Caught by surprise, she looked without meaning to look. At first she could not take her eyes off the bloody feet—actually only one foot because the other had a bloody, worn-out boot on it. And then her eyes moved up the torn, bloody trousers and bloody shirt to the dark face. It hung twisted to one side like a man trying to look over his shoulder and up at the sky at the same time. When she saw where the rope had cut into the neck and all the blood, she closed her eyes hard, ashamed that she had looked this long.

She felt Emma nudge her to show she had seen it, too, but instead of answering, she left Emma and scrambled forward to the spring seat and climbed up beside Bob. She had to look at something else, and put that twisted, black face out of her mind, and those awful men drinking and haw-hawing right there in plain sight of it.

She looked at the river without really seeing it until the colts splashed into the water ahead of the mares, and then she watched them lunge through the knee-deep current like big dogs. Bob began tightening up the lines and started talking to the mares, getting them ready for the hard pull up the far bank where Papa was sitting on Nellie, watching to see if everything was going to be all right.

As the front wheels rolled out of the water and up the rutted slope of red clay, it came to her that she and Bob were getting to Oklahoma Territory at the same time after all. She took this to be a good sign, and for the moment she forgot the twisted black face of the hanging man.

Chapter 7

Although the twisted face of the hanging Negro man was soon again on her mind, she could not help noticing as they drove away from the river that the land here in Oklahoma Territory was the same as it was on the other side of the river. Yet when the road came out of the trees into a little settlement, she saw one difference right away—saloons.

The sign on the first one read Black Dog Saloon, and right across the street from it the longest set of horns she had ever seen on a cow was hanging above a sign that said Longhorn Saloon.

Knowing how dead-set Papa was against whiskey, she couldn't imagine what he had in mind when she saw him stop Nellie at the Black Dog Saloon and get down to talk to two men standing under the sign. She was not able to hear what Papa said, but she saw that the men listened without moving until he hooked his thumb back towards the river. Then one of the men started wagging his finger in Papa's face. It ended with the two men shaking their heads and going into the saloon.

Papa led Nellie back to the wagon and handed the reins up to Bob. Mr. McDermit came back and Papa told him the two men had said the niggers were getting what they deserved. The men said it was probably true that Sandy Nelson was drunk—he usually was— and that he might have fallen off his horse and hit his head on a rock the way the niggers claimed, but that did not account for them suddenly having a lot of money to buy whiskey. Besides, the men said they were no-good niggers anyhow, always coming over here from Indian Territory to get drunk and cause trouble.

She could tell that Mr. McDermit was for moving on, but Papa was not going to let this first setback stop him. He said if he had to ask everybody in this place for help he would do it, and he and Mr. McDermit spent the next hour going from place to place—the Longhorn Saloon, two stores, the blacksmith shop, and even private houses—trying to get someone to go across the river with them to keep the second Negro from being lynched.

While they were doing this, she and Emma got out of the wagon and walked the length of the settlement, up one side of the road and down the other, looking at all the buildings. Outside a store they came across Papa and Mr. McDermit talking to a fat woman with a snuff stick in her mouth.

She was trying to convince Papa that he was wasting his time. She said the county seat was about twenty miles away, and even if a sheriff or a deputy could get here in time, neither one of them would ride one inch inside Indian Territory to stop a lynching or anything else.

"Nosiree," she repeated, taking the snuff stick out of her mouth to spit. She put the stick back in and gave it a couple of twirls while frowning up at Papa's worried face. "Why, Mister," she said, "them saloons is the trouble. They ain't legal in the Territory and the law knows it. They wouldn't be no trouble here if the saloons was gone. Talk to the people in Kickapoo about that."

But Papa kept turning towards one end of the settlement and then the other, as if he expected the people to suddenly change their minds and come rushing out to help him. When nothing happened, he proposed to Mr. McDermit that the two of them ride back across the river by themselves and see what they could do.

Mr. McDermit balked at this idea. "A waste of time, Jim."

After a lot more head shaking and soul searching, Papa agreed, but not before he said again and again, "Ed, you know it ain't the Christian thang to do."

And every time Papa said it, Mr. McDermit came back with, "I know, Jim. I know. But circumstances alters cases."

Finally Papa had to leave it at that. He asked the woman the shortest way to Kickapoo, and they drove on through the little settlement and out into farming country again.

Apparently the hailstorm had not reached here for none of the crops showed any sign of damage. And the road itself was as dry and dusty as the one they had been on yesterday, though the air was cooler.

Right away she noticed something else different about Oklahoma Territory that was even more unusual than the saloons. The whole countryside was marked off like a big checkerboard, with roads or traces of roads cutting straight across each other every so often.

Since leaving Bear Valley they had been traveling on roads that wandered across the country like a cowpath, but here someone had gone to the trouble—for what reason she could not guess—to make the roads run north and south and east and west, straight as a string, no matter what the lay of the land.

When they stopped for rest around noon, Papa explained that the roads cutting across each other were a mile apart, and that each square mile of land was called a section. Every homesteader was allowed a quarter section, if he could find one without a farmer already on it. And all for nothing! Oh, he would have to give the government a little something a few years down the road, but it was actually so little it was just like getting it for nothing.

"Jist thank," Papa said, "A hundred and sixty acres. Why that's around you, Mandy. Nary a rock. And all free."

"We ain't got it yet," Mama said.

Kickapoo turned out to be farther away than they expected. But Papa said his heart was set on getting there today, and they pushed the tired teams on past sundown. When they got to the edge of town they couldn't find a place to camp, and had to put up at a wagon yard. It had pens and stalls and sheds and watering troughs for the animals, and empty rooms off to the other side where people could bed down under a roof.

The wagon yard man sat around with them and drank their coffee during supper, and from him they learned that all the land in the county had already been homesteaded. There was talk that the government was going to open up some more Indian land farther on out west in Oklahoma Territory. Of course, it might be a year or two before that happened, but it was bound to one day.

"Them Indians out there ain't got no use for all that land," the man said, wagging his head over his coffee cup. "No earthly use a'tall."

Watching the other men wagging their heads in tune with the wagon yard man, she was pleased by the first part of his news. If all the land was already homesteaded, Papa and Mr. McDermit might have to turn around and go back to Bear Valley.

Papa never seemed the least bit upset about the homesteads being all gone, and her hope for the family going back died when Papa said he reckoned he might be willing to move on west by and by, if and when they did open up more Indian land out there for homesteading. But for now he aimed to get his hands on a piece of land right around here, somehow.

The wagon yard man shrugged at this, but said if they wanted some work in the meantime, there was always plenty of cotton picking starting this time of year across the river west of Kickapoo.

At this news she could feel the burr of that first boll of cotton sticking in her finger like a needle, and her heart sank. But as she heard Papa asking for particulars, she made up her mind that if picking cotton was what she and Bob had to do to get their hands on enough money to take them back to Bear Valley, she would never complain.

The next morning a hot wind was blowing from the south

again. She was already sweating by the time it came her turn at the washstand, but the looking glass on the wall took her mind from the heat for the time being.

From habit she had already combed and plaited her hair without a looking glass, and now she saw the part was all crooked. But she had no time to do it over, so she shrugged and hurried off to breakfast. There she learned that the McDermits had decided to split off here and go to the south end of the county, where Mrs. McDermit had relatives.

After a long breakfast, and many good-byes and promises among the big people to keep in touch, the families drove off in different directions, hands waving.

Papa remembered it was Saturday and rode back to trade places with Bob, saying that with the town full of people, Bob had better ride Nellie and let him drive the team. They were going straight through Kickapoo, and he was afraid Bob might not be able to handle the mares if something scared them.

"They may be one of them horseless carriages around," Papa said, shaking his head as if he hoped not. "Ain't no tellin' what Babe and Doll might do if one of them thangs come snortin' along."

She had given her place on the spring seat to Alice and was now standing behind it. Hearing about a horseless carriage, she turned to look at Emma standing behind the other end of the spring seat and found Emma turning to look wide-eyed at her.

A horseless carriage? She knew what they were, but she had never seen one in Bear Valley, and she had never expected to find one way off out here in Oklahoma territory either. First a railroad train, and now a horseless carriage! What next? This country sure was different from Bear Valley after all.

As soon as the wagon pulled out between the tall poles holding up the wagon yard sign, Papa turned west up a wide road the wagon yard man had said was the main street and ran right through the town.

In no time at all she could see that Kickapoo was a hundred times bigger than Shades Crossing. It spread across the prairie for what looked like a mile or more, and before long the road was a street lined on either side with buildings jammed so close to each other there was no space in between.

And people! She had never seen so many people and horses in one place; so many noises and smells, and more dust than on the Texas Road. But it was the hundreds upon hundreds of people, and the way they were scurrying along, that made her shake her head in disbelief. She had never ever thought she would see so many people in one place. Most of them looked as if they were already late for wherever they were going, and were trying to make up for it. They reminded her of chickens rushing to be fed, necks stretched out and wings half spread.

Hardware stores, hotels, livery stables, lumber yards, and more livery stables. Lines of horses stood tied along in front of other buildings, while out in the middle of the street, horses of every size and color were coming and going, pulling wagons, hacks and buggies, or carrying men on their backs.

Among teams of big plow horses like Babe and Doll, and matched pairs of brown, blacks, bays and whatever, spans of flop-eared mules dozed along in spite of all the bustle around them. By the time they came to what she guessed was about the middle of Kickapoo, the dust was so thick she had to squint to see anything at a distance. And the moving hoofs and wheels kept stirring up more dust all the time.

All at once there were "whoas" all around, and the two lines of teams stopped. She looked out and saw that a wagon in front of Nellie had tried to turn left in front of another wagon. The two teams had run together, tangling up their neck yokes.

While watching the men untangling the neck yokes, she noticed up ahead, leaning forward in a buggy and trying to hold still a fidgety bay horse, the most beautiful lady she had ever seen.

The beautiful lady was wearing a wide-brimmed yellow hat wrapped in a veil tied under her chin. Her long gloves gripping the lines of her horse were also yellow. But the sight of the white face and red red lips were what took her breath away. Not even in Aunt Sue's book of paintings had she ever seen such a beautiful face.

When the teams started again, she leaned as far out over the sideboard of the wagon as she could, anxious for Papa to hurry up and get closer to the buggy. She paid no attention when she heard Papa say, "Whoa, now," and the wagon stopped, but she could not believe what she saw happening next.

The beautiful lady turned her horse across in front of Babe and Doll and gave it a little slap on the back with the lines. The bay sprang forward. A nod of the yellow hat and a smile of thanks to Papa from the red red lips were the last she saw of the beautiful lady before the back of Alice's old brown dress blotted her out.

With a little cry, she rushed across to Emma's side of the wagon, on the way hearing Alice say, "Oh, look at her, Papa. Must've stuck her head in a flour barrel."

Looking over the top of Emma's head, she groaned as she saw the tail end of the buggy bouncing down a side street almost out of sight in its own dust. She watched as long as she could see anything. Then she slumped to the floor of the wagon bed, mad at Papa for letting the buggy cross in front of him and madder still at Alice for making fun of such a beautiful lady.

"You feelin' aw'right, Child?" Mama called from back in the shade of the wagon sheet.

Sitting up and nodding, she blinked away her tears. Mama was sitting on the doubled-up feather bed this morning, her bad leg propped up on a pillow as usual. Her face was yellowish-brown and shiny with sweat. Her lips had no color at all. Remembering the lips of the beautiful lady, she ran a finger over her own lips, trying to imagine them red and curved. She looked at her brown hands and wrists. They were never white, even in wintertime, and she thought how brown her face had been in the looking glass that morning.

Once more she slumped down on the floor of the wagon bed. When Emma called to look at this or that, she just grunted. She had lost all her interest in Kickapoo. She heard Emma ask Papa about the horseless carriages, but she didn't care about them anymore either. She would have traded all the horseless carriages in the world for one more look at the beautiful lady in the buggy.

It was not until she heard Papa say, "Well, I reckin there's the last river we'll have to cross for a while," that she roused herself from the floor of the wagon bed and stood up to look around. Watching the road bend a little to hit the river head-on, she saw the end of a wooden bridge come in sight, the first bridge they had seen on the whole trip.

The mares clattered onto the noisy planks, shying and snuffling more than they ever had at any of the streams they forded. Since the bridge swayed and creaked as if it might fall in the water any second, she could understand why the mares were scared. But the bridge held up, and when they reached the far side, Papa stopped the wagon and told Bob to drive while he rode Nellie.

The road sloped up to bottomland flat as a stove lid, and ran straight west across it to a line of hills a couple of miles away. Fields of cotton, corn, and alfalfa lay on either side of the road.

At every farmhouse they came to, Papa rode up the driveway to ask if they needed any cotton pickers, even though no one was picking in the cotton fields. Sometimes no one was at home, but when he did find someone, he reported back to the wagon that the cotton crop was a little late this year. Yet he kept on stopping, and one time he came back saying the woman told him she had heard that Fred Carpenter was starting to pick, and she told him where the farm was.

It turned out to be the last farm on the bottomland, and the buildings were in the edge of the hills behind a clump of cottonwoods. Mr. Carpenter had gone to Kickpoo, but his skinny wife came out in the yard and told them to drive back to the shade of the cottonwoods and wait for him. "Y'all come fer?" the woman asked, walking up to the wagon.

When Alice told her, the woman nodded and said, "They's a right smart Arkansas folks hereabouts. Lots come futher'n that and didn't git nothin'. Most of them done gone on. Or gone back where they come from. Goners, we call 'em."

She and Emma moved to the side of the wagon to get a better look at the bony face burned almost black by the sun. At once she thought of the white skin of the beautiful lady in the buggy, and later when the others were resting in the shade of the cottonwoods she climbed back up in the wagon where Mama and Ben were.

She borrowed Mama's looking glass and sat turning her face this way and that, inspecting her skin. Everything she saw, including the crooked part in her hair, made her frown. No matter what she looked at, from her widow's peak to her chin, it was all dark as leather. She had never thought much about the color of her skin, but now that she had seen that beautiful lady in the buggy, she wished her own skin could be just as white.

"Mama, reckon I'm ever going to have red lips and white skin?"

Mama was sewing a knee patch on a pair of Bob's overalls. Without looking up from her needle, she said, "What do you mean?"

After hesitating a moment, she told her about the beautiful lady in the buggy. "I was just wondering if I could ever look like that when I get big, is all."

"Oh, I spect you'll look purty enough... if you wash your face good ever day with soap and water."

"She was the prettiest lady I ever saw."

"Well, purty is as purty does. Painted lips and a powdered face sounds like a bad woman to me."

"Bad how?" When Mama didn't answer right away, she looked around at her, but for a long time Mama just went on sewing and never said anything. At last she made a knot in her thread and bit off the rest. "Ever hear the preacher talk about harlots?"

"I guess so."

"Know what a harlot is?"

In spite of the calm way Mama asked, she felt a little uneasy, and her voice trembled as she said, "I don't reckon I do."

"Well," Mama said, putting aside the overalls and fastening the needle to the collar of her dress, "you're gitten old enough to know about them thangs. Hand me a diaper out of that box next to the chest."

She leaned over and picked up a folded flour sack soft as cotton from countless washings, and gave it to Mama.

"A harlot," Mama said, "is a woman that takes money from a man to let him have his way with her body. I'm not surprised they'd be some in a place like Kickapoo. Whores, some people call them.

No decent man would have anything to do with such a woman."

As Mama went on talking, she was glad she was sitting half turned away from her because for some reason she felt ashamed and didn't want Mama to look her in the face. One thing she didn't understand was what kept harlots from having babies. She knew that every time Papa took the mares or the cows away to be bred, they always had babies the next spring. She wished she knew what kept the beautiful lady—if she was a harlot—from having a baby, but she was ashamed to ask Mama.

As soon as she could leave the wagon without seeming to be hurrying, she climbed down and wandered away to the last cottonwood and leaned against it. Her mind was so full of what Mama had just told her she didn't want to see or talk to anyone, not even Emma.

Chapter 8

It was late in the evening before Mr. Carpenter and two boys came rattling up to the cottonwoods in a light wagon pulled by a span of fast-stepping mules. Mr. Carpenter jumped down to talk to Papa and told the boys to go on to the house and unload the wagon. When the older boy kept looking at her even as he was driving away, she put her hand to her head, guessing he was noticing the crooked part in her hair.

After Papa and Mr. Carpenter talked weather a while, Papa asked about cotton picking and heard the good news that they could start picking Monday. "No pickin' on Sunday," Mr. Carpenter said with a little laugh. "Don't believe in workin' on the Lord's day, 'ceptin' for chores."

As for a place to live, he led everyone but Mama and Ben along the driveway past the lawn and up alongside the hill behind the house to a dugout in the south slope of the hill. At first all they could see was a log wall against the side of the hill with openings where a door and window had been. The twelve-foot wide dugout was bigger inside than out, running some twenty feet or more back into the hill to a cookstove set on a rock base.

"She's a good enough stove yet," explained Mr. Carpenter, "but nothing would do Effie but a new stove to go with the new house. One thang leads to another with womenfolks, you know. You're welcome to use it."

They camped out at the dugout Saturday night, and moved in Sunday after Papa cut poles from the Indian land nearby and made a tent frame out front of the dugout. With the wagon sheet stretched over the frame, they had a tent roof they could eat under, protected from sun and rain.

Yet as things turned out, they were not able to start picking cotton Monday morning, even though they were up and ready by sunup, because they had no cotton sacks to pick in. Papa thought Mr. Carpenter would furnish them, and apparently it never crossed Mr. Carpenter's mind that they wouldn't know they had to furnish their own cotton sacks.

Mad at himself and everybody else because he had neglected to find this out ahead of time and was losing half a day of cotton picking as a result, he threw the saddle on Nellie and loped off to Kickapoo to buy material for the sacks.

By mid-morning he came loping back with a roll of white canvas tied on behind the saddle, and with Nellie drenched in sweat. Mama looked at the heavy canvas and wished out loud that she had had room to bring her sewing machine instead of letting it go at the sale for almost nothing.

But Papa said Mr. Carpenter had already told him she could use Effie's machine. He pulled out his watch, checking with the sun at the same time, and said he hoped the sacks would be ready by dinnertime.

While Alice stayed behind to make dinner, she and Mama followed Papa to the Carpenters with Nellie's roll of canvas. She helped Mama measure and cut it, and watched her run-up a cotton sack for each one of the family but Ben. Mama said she expected her leg to get better as soon as cool weather came, and when she started feeling like it she would pick in the evenings.

When the job was done, Alice had a dinner of cornbread and beans waiting. Then with their new cotton sacks slung over their shoulders, and with Bob carrying the same tow-sack covered water jug they used on the farm back home, they followed Papa around the hill past the Carpenter's house, and down past the barn and the cottonwoods, to the bottom land where the fields were.

She and Emma trailed a few steps behind the others, shuffling their toes through the hot sand and trying to step on every grasshopper they came across, and not to step on any horned toads, while at the same time joking with Alice about how funny she looked in a worn-out poke bonnet of Mama's.

They passed a field of corn and came to a cotton field that looked half as big as the whole farm at home. A wagon with double sideboards stood at the near end of the field. The wagon tongue was slanted about halfway up in the air, propped there by the neck yoke standing on end under it just in front of the doubletree. Emma wanted to know why the wagon tongue was slanted up in the air that way, and Papa pointed to the set of iron scales hanging from the end.

"It holds them scales they weigh up the cotton with," he said.

The Carpenters were already in the field, even Mrs. Carpenter, who had her baby riding on the end of her cotton sack. Mr. Carpenter came back to the wagon to show them where to start picking, and how to go about it, in case they didn't know. He talked about picking all the open bolls on a stalk and about keeping the cotton clean, and things like that.

"Got to have clean cotton," he said for the third time, laughing his little laugh each time. "If it ain't clean they dock me at the gin. So don't put no leaves, ner sticks, ner green bolls, and that kine of stuff in your sacks. You'll git the hang of pickin' soon enough. Mostly it jis takes a stout back."

She reached out and pulled a lock of cotton out of the nearest boll. The cotton was just as soft as she remembered it, although when she pressed it hard she could feel the seeds hidden in it, like buckshots in the rabbit's skin. Carefully she reached for another boll, and another.

Seconds passed before she realized she was actually picking cotton, and when she did, her first thought was that she was earning money that would take her back to Bear Valley. Each time she slid a handful of cotton into her sack, she saw herself putting money in the pocket of her dress.

She stopped picking to watch Bob's hands grab at a stalk of cotton, his fingers snatching the white locks from the bolls faster than her eyes could follow. Already he seemed to have the knack of it. In a couple of seconds his full hands disappeared inside his sack and flashed out to grab more bolls. He was picking so much faster than she could that she was ashamed of herself.

She tried to copy him, grabbing at the bolls as fast as she could. When her fingers stabbed against the end of a burr, she didn't cry out like Emma, or say a word. She just kept on picking, and when an extra sharp burr made one of her fingers bleed, she pressed a piece of cotton against the spot for a couple of seconds and then went on picking.

This was worse than picking blackberries, because the cotton burrs were mostly hidden. Besides, with blackberries, when you stuck a thorn in your finger you could stop picking and eat a few berries until the pain went away. Now within a few minutes she had pricked her fingers several times, but she knew better than complain to Papa. She had listened to Emma try that and heard Papa tell her to be quiet and keep up with her picking or he would take a switch to her.

The cotton stalks in this rich bottomland were almost as tall as she was, and when she bent over to pick the bolls near the ground, the limbs of the stalk caught in her pigtail and she would have to stop picking and pull them loose. She realized now how smart Alice was to be wearing a poke bonnet, and she made up her mind she would get Mama to make her one as soon as possible.

Besides pricking her fingers and getting her hair caught every few minutes, she found that pieces of leaves and sticks from cotton stalks were falling down the back of her dress, which was sopping wet with sweat from the waist up. Each time she pulled her cotton sack forward, the strap of sack pressed the leaves and sticks into her neck and shoulder.

But worst of all was the close, sticky heat down here in the bottom. With tall stalks of cotton all around her, she felt like she was wrapped in a hot, white blanket. There was no wind, just the sun boiling down on her head and the glare of white cotton all around.

Every few minutes she wiped the sweat out of her eyes with a handful of cotton and kept on picking, trying as hard as she could to stay up with Bob, who was picking two rows to her one. She was almost at the far end of the field when she started feeling lightheaded each time she bent over, and before long she felt a wrenching and knotting in her stomach that told her she was going to throw up.

Dropping to her knees, she wiped the sweat, now cold, from her forehead and face with a double handful of cotton and waited for the vomiting to start, dreading it, yet knowing it had to happen.

When it was over, when all the bitter, stinking cornbread and beans had come spewing out of her mouth, clogging her nose and bringing tears to her eyes—and after her stomach kept on heaving even when there was nothing else left to come up, and she was too weak to move—Papa called back, saying, "Better go to the wagon and drink a little water. But not too much now, Matt."

Once back in the shade of the wagon, she took a sip of warm water from the jug and felt the churning in her stomach about to start all over again. She wanted to lie down until she felt better, but she knew Papa would never allow that. Waiting only long enough for her stomach to calm down a little, she took another sip of water and hurried back to her sack before Papa could have any excuse to call her.

At the first weighing up, although she still felt so weak she wanted to lie down as she watched closely as Vernon, the oldest Carpenter boy, picked out her sack first and hung it on the scales. Grabbing the iron weight—the pee, she heard Papa call it—hanging from the end of the wagon tongue, Vernon hooked it on the long arm of the scales, apparently at what he guessed the weight of the sack of cotton. He came so close to guessing it right that he had to move the pee only a couple of notches to make the arm balance a little better than level with the ground.

She looked at her cotton sack, doubled up and swinging from the scales, and even though her fingers were scratched and bleeding and she still felt weak all over from vomiting, she was proud of this first sack of cotton she had ever picked.

"Twenty-six pounds, sack and all, Mattie," Vernon called, looking at her and smiling. "Make it twenty-four cotton."

Twenty-four pounds seemed like a lot to her, but when in a couple of minutes she saw that Emma had picked almost as much, she was not so pleased with herself. As Vernon weighed up the cotton of the others, she was even less pleased, for each one of them had picked more than twice as much as she had. Bob was the winner with sixty-five pounds, beating Papa by two pounds.

When everybody's cotton had been weighed up, Papa and Vernon each brought out a little notebook and wrote down the pounds picked. After the cotton had been emptied in the wagon and the water jug passed around, Papa pulled out his watch, looked at it and then squinted at the sun.

"I reckon we got time fer another good weighin' between now and sundown," he said. "If we hurry."

Papa did keep them picking after the sun slid behind the hills and threw one big shadow over the whole cotton patch. The shade cooled the air a little, but it brought out so many gnats and mosquitoes she wished she had the sun back, hot as it was.

The next time they weighed up she was too tired to feel ashamed that in spite of trying harder she had picked only twenty-one pounds to Bob's fifty-nine. She had never worked so hard in her life, and now all she wanted to do was go to the dugout and fall down on her pallet and go to sleep. She didn't even want to wait for supper or help bring the stock in for the night from where they had been put out to graze.

Papa thought it was safe enough for the horses to graze there in the daytime, since they would not wander away from Babe staked out on a long rope. But at night he wanted them in Carpenter's old lot, which he and Bob patched up with some new poles from the Indian land.

At supper, as Papa was returning thanks, the smell of hot

cornbread floating her way changed her mind about not wanting anything to eat. She opened her eyes just enough to see the yellow-brown pieces of cornbread stacked on the platter, then let her glance slide to the bowl of brown beans steaming beside it, and on to the big white pitcher, which she knew was filled with sweet milk fresh from Old Blackie. When grace was over, she could hardly wait to help herself to everything, and later she had a second helping. Before she finished eating, she was ready to fall asleep, but first she had to help Alice gather and wash and dry the dishes.

By then Mama had a complaining Emma scrubbed clean. Now was her turn to wash up, but she was considered old enough to do it herself. Tonight she didn't feel like doing a good job, but she did, knowing that, like as not, Mama would inspect her by the lamplight, especially her neck and ears.

When Mama saw all the red scratches on her hands, she clucked her concern and had her get some coal oil out of the can and rub it on them. Only then was she allowed to get her quilt and take it outside to her place under the wagon sheet and curl up for the night. Not even the stink of the coal oil on her hands kept her awake very long.

She woke to find Alice shaking her and thought she had just fallen asleep. Before she could ask what the matter was, Alice told her to hurry up and get ready for breakfast. By sunup they were back in the cotton patch, along with the Carpenters. All day they picked without stopping, except to weigh up, and to hurry to the dugout at noon to gobble their food and hurry back to picking.

As she walked home in the near dark for the second day, she was too worn out to talk, and she guessed Alice and Emma were, too, for no one said a word from the cotton patch to the dugout. Again she was sure she was too tired to eat anything, but she ate a big supper and as soon as possible was on her pallet, anxious to get every second of sleep she could before Alice woke her for another day of picking cotton.

Day after day it was the same, picking from "can see to cain't see," as Mr. Carpenter put it, returning to the dugout to eat supper by lamplight, and then to bed. She never vomited in the sticky hot

68

cotton patch again, but she was tired all the time now.

Sunday came, but instead of a day of rest, Papa had other ideas. Although they had never done the washing on Sunday before, they had to do it today while Papa and Bob drove to Kickapoo for groceries and things. This way everybody would be free to go back to the cotton patch on Monday.

The washing was finished—hung out, dried, gathered in, folded and put away—by the middle of the evening when Papa and Bob pulled up in front of the dugout with the wagon loaded. Besides flour, cornmeal, beans, potatoes, sugar, coffee and the other things Mama had Alice write down for them to get, they brought home a bedstead with springs for Mama and Papa, a window for the front of the dugout, and a stack of lumber.

After sending Bob to the shed with the team, and telling him to hurry back with the hammer and saw, Papa said, "Now, Mandy. You have Alice and Mattie git that kitchen stuff cleaned out of back of the stove. Me and Bob'll have you some shelves up in there by sundown. Soon's I can, I'll make us a front door. Till we git our own place, looks like we'll have to make do with a homemade table and set on homemade stools."

"Never mind what we have to set on," Mama said, looking up from mending one of Papa's newly washed shirts. "Or eat on either. I'm jist right glad to see them shelves goin' up, Jim."

After weeks of picking, fingers became so tough the burrs no longer brought blood. Mama had made her a poke bonnet out of the tail of a worn out shirt and a few strips of cardboard, and it kept her hair from catching in the cotton stalks. She had learned to pick as fast as any of them for short periods, but she was never able to keep her mind on her picking hour after hour the way the rest of them seemed to.

In spite of trying and trying to do it, before long she would forget and fall behind while she stopped to look at a late flower or listen to a meadowlark. She would not even realize she had stopped picking until Papa's shouts for her to get to work woke her out of her daydream.

One morning after Papa had shouted to her twice within an hour, she made up her mind once and for all to forget about birds and flowers and the like, and to pick without stopping, no matter what. She had been picking hard as she could for what seemed like hours when a pair of butterflies came chasing each other right under her nose, twisting and turning in the sunshine like falling leaves. One butterfly landed on the handful of cotton she was holding, and there, not a foot in front of her nose, it started slowly opening and closing its wings.

She gazed at the orange wings with their black velvety edges sprinkled with pale blue dots, watching them lie flat against the white cotton for an instant and then flash up and come together, flash down wide open on the cotton only to rise again. Down and up, open and close the wings went while she held her breath at such a beautiful sight, afraid to move a muscle for fear she would scare the butterfly away.

Something jerked her arm and the butterfly fluttered away. Gasping, she threw her head around into Papa's angry face just in time to feel a stinging whack against her legs. Crying out, she tried to pull away, but Papa's grip was too strong. Down came the whiplike limb of the cotton stalk again and again.

As each stinging lick cut into her legs she flinched and screamed. But this seemed to have no effect on Papa. He kept hitting her until her legs were numb with pain. When he did stop he shoved her arm away and said in a hoarse voice, "Now git to work and ketch up. You hear me?"

Afraid to look at him, between sobs she whispered, "Yes, Papa," and went to picking as fast as she could.

Nothing was said at dinner or supper about the whipping. Yet that night, after she had washed the caked blood off the welts on her legs, welts that burned like fire when the water touched them, Mama rubbed coal oil on them, shaking her head in silent sympathy.

The memory of those welts was still clear in her mind later in the month as she let Bob and Emma each give her fourteen slaps on the back for her birthday, plus one to grow on.

"Mattie, you better watch your step next year," Bob teased, "or somethin' bad's liable to happen to you."

She wanted to say that nothing worse than leaving Bear Creek and drowning Tommy could ever happen to her, but since so many grown-up ears were listening, she pretended to smile and said nothing.

Chapter 9

On the very same day they finished the first picking for Mr. Carpenter, Papa led them across the road to the south for half a mile to the Sparks farm. Here most of the other hired cotton pickers were Negroes, who came driving out from Kickapoo hours after sunup in rickety carts and wagons pulled by crowbait teams. One family had a donkey and a horse hitched to the same wagon.

She felt sorry for these people because they looked half starved, and were dressed in the raggedest clothes. As the days went by, she noticed that most of them were even slower cotton pickers than she was, but for a different reason. They never stopped talking. They were always doing more talking, laughing, and arguing than picking cotton, especially the men. With them it was a constant hullabaloo all day long.

She and Bob kept track of how much cotton each picked during the day, and at night she wrote it down in her school tablet. They were earning money faster than she ever thought they could, and she wanted to make definite plans with Bob about going back to

Bear Valley before winter set in. Yet every time she tried to bring up the subject, he had some excuse for not wanting to talk about it.

Most important of all, she was anxious for them to actually get their hands on some of the money they had earned. She knew Papa had been paid for the picking at Carpenters, because she heard him talking to Mama about it one night. She passed the news along to Bob, and from then on she kept expecting and hoping that any day Papa would say something about giving them their part of the money, but he never even hinted at it.

They had finished the first picking at Sparks and started on the second picking at Carpenters, when one day the long hot dry spell was broken by a thunderstorm and a sudden downpour. By the time they got out of the cotton patch and up the hill to the dugout, the ceiling there was leaking like a colander, and Mama was having a busy time trying to keep everything from getting soaked.

After such a violent start, the rain calmed down to a steady drizzle that went on for three days, getting a little colder each day. Papa and Bob spent the days out in the weather, helping Mr. Carpenter and his boys dig a storm cellar in the rain-softened ground back of his house. They had the big oblong hole finished by the fourth morning, when the wind picked up from the north and the drizzle ended in a burst of sleet that dropped the temperature to near freezing within an hour.

At dinner, Mama said, "Jim, you jist got to do somethin' about shoes for these children. They're goin' to ketch their death in this weather."

"Well," Papa said, "they ain't nothin' stoppin' us now we got that cellar dug. You git their feet measured, Mandy. Ain't no reason why me and Alice cain't go to town soon's we've et. Is there, Alice?"

Alice shook her head, and right after dinner she and Papa rode off in the wagon, Alice carrying a rolled-up piece of newspaper with the right footprint of each one of the children traced on it.

Watching them leave, Bob turned to her and said, "Come on, Matt. This is jist the chance I been waitin' for to git me some of them wild grapes Vernon's been tellin' me about."

"I'll get the buckets," she said. She would rather have stayed inside the warm dugout like Emma, but she saw this as a good chance to talk Bob into asking Papa for their money.

She carried Bob's bucket as well as her own, so he could have both hands free to use the shotgun if he saw something to shoot. The first thing they found was a grove of persimmon trees, but the persimmons were not ripe enough yet. It would take a frost or two to sweeten them up until they tasted like candy. They tried to eat some anyway, and the persimmons puckered their mouths worse than green plums.

Pretending that the persimmons made them sick, she and Bob walked away from the trees, stretching their lips in outlandish shapes and making wild faces at each other. Laughing and playing along, they almost stepped on a covey of quails, and a dozen or more birds burst out of the weeds at their feet and whirred away in as many directions.

Bob was so flustered he fumbled getting the shotgun up and cocked before the birds were out of range. "Damn me for a slow poke," he said, and went on ranting and raving at himself for failing to get a shot off. But she kept silent, secretly pleased the quails all got away unhurt. After mockingbirds, bobwhites were her favorites, and she never tired of hearing the clear, sharp whistle they made in calling to each other.

She and Bob came to the creek beyond the Indian land, and turned down it towards the river. They passed lots of pecan trees, the grass under them covered with fallen nuts, but since they were looking for grapes, they only stopped long enough to eat a few and then went on.

Soon they found masses of grape vines crushing down bushes and climbing high up in the trees. The purple grapes were smaller than the ones they were used to on Bear Creek, and from the looks of things, birds or coons or something had already been eating on them. But there were still plenty of juicy bunches left, and they ate all they could hold. Then they filled their buckets up to the bails, and turned for home, leaving many a bunch of grapes for another day.

Right away she started trying to talk Bob into asking Papa for their money. "It's only fair you should do it," she said. "After all, you're older. And besides, everybody knows Papa never pays attention to anything a woman says, unless it suits him."

But in spite of all her arguments, Bob still wanted to wait. Finally he admitted, "I'm skeered to ask 'im, Mattie. Skeered of makin' him mad, so mad at me he'll give me a whippin' fer even bringin' it up."

"Huh," she said, flinging up her head. "Then I will. The worst he can do is give me another whipping. And that won't hurt long."

"I say wait."

"I'm not afraid," she said, but she knew that was a lie. She was more afraid of Papa than Bob was, but they had to have money or they would never get back to Bear Valley.

All the way home she kept trying to change Bob's mind. When she finally realized if Papa was going to be asked she was going to have to do the asking, she got so nervous thinking about it her hands began to sweat.

At first she thought it might be best to ask Papa when she was alone with him, because she was afraid he might somehow make fun of her in front of the rest of the family. But since Alice and Emma had also earned money, maybe she should bring it up when they were all together. She didn't see how Papa could say no to all of them at the same time.

When they got back to the dugout, she still had not made up her mind about what to say to Papa, or where to say it, and she was relieved to find that he and Alice had not come back from town yet.

Mama was so pleased with the grapes, she said, "You all jist go right back tomorrow—if it's still too wet to pick cotton. Git all you can, and I'll put us up some good grape jelly."

It was nearly dark before she heard the wagon stop outside the dugout, and the mares and colts start nickering to each other. While Bob hurried out to help Papa put the team away, she stayed near the cookstove and tried to find something to do to help Mama with supper. Even in the half-dark outside, she was afraid to face Papa just yet, afraid he would read in her eyes what she was thinking about doing.

From behind the cookstove she watched Alice come through the door with an armload of packages. At first she hardly recognized her sister. Her face was half hidden by a hat that looked like a big pancake curled up around the edges, laid on her head and tilted down low in front. She had never seen Alice wearing that hat before, and her heart gave a leap.

Alice had bought a new hat! That meant Papa had given her her money for picking cotton. In an instant the whole world looked different. Having nothing to be afraid of now, she rushed from the stove to help arrange the packages on Mama and Papa's new bed. And when Alice said there were more to bring in, she hurried outside to help carry them.

Now her heart was light as nothing, and she went skipping barefooted over the wet, cold ground without feeling it, asking one question after another about the trip without waiting for an answer. She could hardly believe that after all her arguing with Bob, neither of them would have to ask Papa. All they had to do was be patient a little longer. Papa would probably hold off giving them their money until after supper, for he was bound to be cold and hungry.

And then he would take his pocketbook out of his pocket, unsnap one side of it and slide the coins out on the table, unsnap the other side and shake out the folded bills. He would count out loud the amount for each one and make a little pile of it—at least that was the way he always did it when they picked blackberries for Mr. Barngrover—and he would push it over to them, one by one, saying, "There you are."

When she and Alice got back in the dugout with the rest of the packages Mama told them not to open anything until after supper because Papa would be starved and want to eat right away.

Papa came in ahead of Bob, huffing and puffing from the cold, and filling up the doorway in his patched old jumper buttoned up to his chin. He greeted them all in a louder voice than usual, circled past table to the back door of the dugout and held his hands out to warm them over the cookstove.

"I'm starved, Mandy," he said.

"Well, set down then," Mama said. "I reckin it's ready." She eased Papa to the side of the stove and pulled a pan of cornbread out of the oven, turning it upside down and steaming on a platter.

Setting the cornbread on the table, Mama said, "Bob, you washed your hands?"

Anxious to pass the good news about their money on to Bob, when he came back inside she tried to catch his attention by lifting her eyebrows and smiling towards Papa. Bob only shrugged at her and sat down. She was too excited to think about eating, but she lowered her head and waited silently along with the rest of them for Papa to return thanks.

When the food was passed, she took some without thinking about what it was. While the others ate, she toyed with her supper and tried again to catch Bob's eye so she could signal the good news to him. But Bob was hanging on to every word of Papa's account of seeing Mr. McDermit in town.

The McDermits had not been able to get a place of their own either, and they were still living with her cousin. But the biggest news was that the outlaws had returned Prince. Mr. McDermit went out to feed the stock one morning and there was Prince, fat and sleek as a town dog, standing in the lot with the rest of the horses. Beauty was gone.

After a moment of silent wonder around the table, Mama asked how Mrs. McDermit and the children were getting along. Papa said Mr. McDermit never mentioned them, and went on with more talk about Beauty and Prince. She had never known it to take Papa so long to eat, and she kept her eyes on him, watching for the first hint of what she was waiting for.

Finally she saw him take out his watch, look at it and put it back. Here was the moment she had been expecting for weeks, and she held her breath as she waited for him to reach in his hip pocket and pull out his pocketbook. Instead of doing that, Papa put his hands against the table, ready to push himself back and stand up.

He paused and said to no one in particular, "Mister Carpenter told me on the way in that it's still too wet to pick cotton. But he wants us to hep gather that high piece of corn next to the Indian land tomorrow. We can sure use some of that corn, so you all better git them shoes and thangs tried on in a hurry and git to bed."

Seeing Papa about to stand up for sure this time, she jumped to her feet without thinking and said, "Don't we get our money, too?"

Slowly Papa sat back down on his stool and looked up at her. "How's that, Mattie?"

Seeing everybody's eyes on her, she was suddenly too scared to say another word. Her glance fell on Bob, and for some reason his wild-eyed look brought words tumbling out of her mouth. "Our money for picking cotton. Aren't we getting ours? We picked hard as Alice. Specially Bob. He picked hardest of all."

Papa frowned and shook his head. "You ain't makin' sense, Mattie."

"Didn't Alice get a new hat?"

"New hat? What's that got to do with anythang?"

"Why, yes, I..." Alice stammered and blushed and didn't seem to know what Papa wanted her to say. But when he kept on frowning at her hat, she put her hands up to it and said, "The flowers had come off it here. And the little man—I guess he saw me tryin' it on. Anyhow, later he said seein's how I'd bought so many other thangs, why he'd throw the hat in for nothin'. So I jist thought I'd wear it."

As Papa turned back to her, she looked again to Bob to help, but she could tell by the sickly look on his face he was now too scared to say a word. She hated him for being such a coward. He didn't want to go back to Bear Valley. That was the truth of it.

"So, Mattie?"

The edge in Papa's voice started her trembling, and she wished she had never opened her mouth in the first place. But there Papa was, frowning up at her, waiting for her to go on. The only thing she could think of was the awful whipping she was going to get when this was over with.

Finally she was able to say, "Are we...," and had to look away from Papa's frown before she could go on. "Are you ever going to give us any of the money for the cotton we're pickin'?"

After she got all the words out, she looked back at Papa and saw that his face had gone redder than Alice's.

"Give you any money?" he roared, and she flinched as if he had slapped her in the face.

"Now, Jim," Mama said, but Papa paid no attention to her.

"Give you any money?" he roared again. "Ain't them shoes and thangs I bought today money? Ain't them vittles you jist et... ain't they money?"

Tongue-tied with fear by Papa's furious words and looks, she tried to speak, but she could not get a word out. Again and again she wet her lips. At last she was able to say a little above a whisper, "You always gave us our money when we picked berries... for Mister Barngrover."

"Hah!" Papa said, but his face softened a little. "That was different. The ox wasn't in the ditch then. Now we all got to pitch in and hep git it out. So don't let me hear no more talk about money. You hear me?"

She wanted to say she did, but she was shaking so hard she couldn't speak. It flashed through her mind that she would never see Aunt Sis again—that she would never be a schoolteacher—and a long wail broke from her and hot tears streamed down her face.

"You hear me, Mattie?"

Half blinded by the tears, she turned to the door and fumbled it open.

"Mattie!" she heard Papa roar again, but by now she was out of the dugout and running through the dark.

End of Part One

Chapter 10

After crying herself out, crumpled against a post at the horse lot fence, she lay in the dark listening to the horses chomping their fodder and sniffing around in the feed trough for another stalk. Her thoughts slipped away through the night past Oklahoma Territory and Indian Territory, and across Arkansas to Bear Valley. Grandma and Aunt Sis would be asleep now in their house in the neck of Hale's Bend, not knowing she and Bob had planned to come back and live with them—and not knowing now they never would.

She thought of Tommy and wished she could be lying beside him in his little coffin, even if it would be way too short for her. Then she remembered Tommy was not in his coffin, only his overalls and his old double-bladed barlow, and she wished wherever he was she could be there to tell him she did not mean to drown him, and she was sorry.

She felt her legs and feet getting numb with cold where they were touching the wet ground, and she pulled her feet up under her dress and wrapped it around them the best she could. She had not had even a peek at her new shoes yet. Thinking of her new shoes reminded her that Papa might still come out of the dugout any second and give her a whipping. She didn't know why he had not already done it. He usually never put off a whipping to the next day, or even to the next minute. But since she could not go back to live with Grandma and Aunt Sis, she didn't care what happened to her now.

When the dugout door did open and let a strip of light out through the dark, she was surprised to hear Mama instead of Papa call her name. She answered and listened to Mama coming towards her, scolding her for staying out in the cold night air for so long.

"I'm not cold," she said.

"Well, you come on in and go to bed anyway."

"Is Papa goin' to whip me?"

"No, they're all asleep in there. But he ought to. You oughtn't to have said what you said."

She tried to protest, but everything she started to say made her realize she could not say it without giving away her and Bob's secret. Even though that was over and done with now, she was still too scared to say anything about it.

"Never mind, Child," Mama finally said. "You done wrong shamin' your papa in front of us. Don't ever do such a thang again. You git on in there now and go to sleep. You got a purty pair of shoes waitin' for you tomorrow. If they fit."

The shoes did fit, just fine, and she laced them up snug around her ankles. The new black stockings and garters felt itchy on her legs as she walked around the dugout helping Mama and Alice with breakfast, all the time listening to Emma complain because her shoes were too big for her.

When Papa and Bob came in from the chores, and they all sat down to breakfast, she was surprised there was no hint of last night's roaring anger in Papa's voice. Yet it was still so fresh in her own mind that she kept her eyes on her eating, afraid to look at him.

It was not until she was alone with Bob in the corn patch later in the morning that last night's fight with Papa came up, Bob saying, "I told you to wait. Jist the same, Matt, if I'd'a said to Papa what you did, I'd'a been skinned alive."

"Maybe not. He didn't skin me."

"Cause you're a girl."

"So?"

"So you're different than me." Reaching out with the nubbin of corn he had been tossing from hand to hand, Bob touched it to one of her breasts. "That's what I'm talkin' about."

She slapped the nubbin out of Bob's hand. "Is that the way you used to act with Lena May?"

"Now don't git huffy, Matt. You know I'm right. Didn't Papa stop whippin' Alice after she started growin' up? I see Vernon lookin' at you. And I guess it ain't by accident that he always picks the row next to you."

"Well, it's the Carpenters' cotton patch," she said, suddenly so hot in the face she hardly knew what she was saying. "I reckin he can pick any row he wants to."

"Huh."

"And you're a fine one to talk about looking at girls. Over at Sparks you always had your eyes on Gladys."

"Gladys Sparks! That cow." Bob tried to shrug off her meaning, but she noticed he was blushing just the same. "She's got cantaloupes where most girls got apples." And he burst out laughing.

For an instant she laughed, too, and then she sobered up and said, "That's a mean thing to say."

"It's true, though. But all this ain't what I started out to say. I didn't tell you this yesterday, but me and Ralph Sparks are goin' out to the wheat harvest next sprang. He says we can make oodles of money. And when I come back we'll run off and go to Grandma's!"

Bob went on talking, but she only pretended to listen. For the first time in her life he had made her think of him as something other than her older brother. She was mad at him for that, and ashamed of herself at the same time for thinking it. Yet what he said about Papa whipping Alice was true. He had not done it in years.

Naturally she knew she was beginning to grow up, but she never thought Bob or Papa or anybody else was noticing. Lately Vernon did seem to be always picking the row next to hers, but she had never thought anything about that either. It wasn't as if she didn't like him. Everybody liked Vernon's happy face, all freckles and a big grin. She talked and joked with him the same way she did with Bob and Emma.

Now she could never feel free and easy with Vernon ever again, or with any other boy. The touch of that nubbin against her breast had made her think of boys in a way she had never thought before. If this was what they meant by growing up, she wished she could go back to the way she used to be.

They finished the upper field well before sundown. The men scooped the corn through the high door of the corncrib, while she and the other children picked up all the ears that had missed the little door and threw them back up in the wagon. When all the corn was in the crib, the men leaned on their scoop shovels, resting and talking about the crop.

Mr. Carpenter admitted that so far it hadn't been too bad this year, but he was worried because there was more smut in the corn this year than last, and the year before that. "I dunno, Jim," he said, shaking his head. "Seems to me like this new land is gittin' old mighty fast."

"Jist the same, Ed," Papa said, "I wish I could git my hands on a quarter section of it. Or even eighty acres."

The next morning it was dry enough to pick cotton again, and as she shuffled sleepily down the hill in her new shoes, she was brought wide-awake by the new sun sparkling on patches of mist scattered across the fields. Even as she started picking, the patches were fading away. She would be watching a white patch getting fainter and fainter, blink her eyes to see it better and it was gone.

Vernon was picking next to her, and they were talking along as usual, but in the back of her mind she now suspected he was thinking of her body even when he was looking her in the face. Talking to him was not the same as it used to be, but she still laughed and joked as usual.

When Indian summer came she was happy to go barefooted again. The days were not really hot now, and nights out under the wagon sheet again were just cool enough for good sleeping, although she was often awakened by noises in the night.

Sometimes it was hoot owls in the cottonwoods below Carpenter's barn, or whippoorwills in the blackjacks up back of the dugout. The whippoorwills' shrill, singsongs seemed to go on forever without a stop, or even a change of tune. The yapping of coyotes was a nuisance every night, but she was so used to it she paid it no more attention than she did to the barking of the Carpenter's dog, Rusty, unless the yapping got too close to the tiny chicken house Papa and Bob had built next to the horse lot.

Papa had traded two loads of firewood from the Indian land to a family in town for a red rooster and a dozen hens, and it was her job to bring in the eggs at night and close up the chicken house. More than once when she heard the coyotes getting near, she crept out in the dark to make sure she had remembered to close and fasten the door.

Yapping coyotes were one thing, but she could never get used to the howling of a wolf, a real wolf and not the whistle of the railroad trains that ran up and down the bottom along the river day and night.

No matter how many times she heard a real wolf howling, the next howl sent the same shivers through her bones and made her thankful she was safe here under the wagon sheet. From whichever direction the howl came, it spread all through the dark, rising higher and higher and pushing all other sounds out of the way until it filled the whole night.

Then the howl would hang there in the dark, thin and quivery, scary and lonely at the same time. As it faded away, the scary part seemed to fade with it, but long after the sound was gone and all was silence again, the loneliness of it would still be with her, like an old tune she couldn't get out of her mind.

Even lonelier at night, but in a different way, was the sound of wild geese flying overhead. During the day she did not pay much attention to the long lines of them heading south, unless the geese came circling down over the cotton patch. Then she would stop picking and watch the big, snake-headed birds droop their wings like arms, and flutter to the ground in the nearby cornfields. She did not like Bob sneaking up on them with his shotgun, but whenever he brought one home slung over his shoulder, she was as pleased as everyone else to eat the meat and talk about its wild taste.

In spite of this, when she heard wild geese at night, sounding lost way up there in the dark and calling for help, she wanted to be up there with them, leading them to some green sunshiny place where they would have plenty to eat and be happy. The next thing she knew, Alice or Mama would be shaking her awake, it would be morning, and it almost seemed she had only dreamed about the wild geese.

The only day she looked forward to now was Sunday, even if it did mean a hard morning's work helping with the washing, for after Sunday dinner she had the rest of the day to herself. Sometimes she would go with Bob and Emma to try to find more wild grapes, or to pick up buckets of pecans or hickory nuts. But since she was no longer so close to Bob, she often went up the hill behind the dugout by herself to read a schoolbook, or just sit and look around the countryside.

Although nothing else was ever said about the time Bob touched her breast with the nubbin of corn, she knew by the more serious way he treated her that he had not forgotten how mad it made her. On the surface they were as friendly as before, but the old Bear Creek days of telling each other their problems were gone. She kept hers to herself, and she supposed Bob now told his to Vernon and Ralph, since he was usually running around with one or both of them, all carrying guns or fishing poles and always trying to find something to kill or catch.

Most Sundays Papa was gone. When he didn't go to town, he would saddle Nellie after breakfast and be off all day looking at farms. In a stray copy of the newspaper, he had read that a rick of firewood would buy a year's subscription to the paper, and within two weeks he and Bob had cut another load from the Indian land and hauled it to town to the editor.

Now once a week Papa's copy of the Kickapoo Chronicle was delivered with Mr. Carpenter's mail. After supper she would wait while Papa went through each of the four pages, clearing his throat and reading the headlines about the Spanish War aloud and criticizing the President every chance he got, still mad because Bryan had not been elected. He would shake his head and complain out loud to Mama as he read about the latest train or bank robbery in the Territory, or the latest shooting scrape in Kickapoo or elsewhere in the Territory. But Papa seemed to give his closest attention to farms for rent or lease or sale or trade. Only when he had read all of these notices to Mama, and torn out and put in his pocket the ones he intended to look at, did he leave what was left of the paper on the table for the rest of them to read.

Since Mama and Bob almost never looked at the paper, and since Alice only looked at the advertisements that had to do with women, she had the newspaper mostly to herself, and she got in the habit of reading all that was left of it every week. It seemed a miracle to her that she could sit in a dugout way off out here in Oklahoma Territory, listening to coyotes yapping a couple of hundred yards up the hill, and read about something that happened yesterday, or a few days before, to unknown people in places hundreds or even thousands of miles away. Before, places like New York, Washington, London, Paris, Chicago, and even St. Louis—where Papa said he had been once—had only been names on the maps in Aunt Sis's classroom. Now she thought of them as places where actual people lived and had all kinds of things happen to them.

One day Vernon brought the news to the cotton patch that Valley View School, over south of the Sparks farm, was going to start the next Monday. According to him, all country schools had a six-week summer term after the 4th of July, closed for cotton picking in the fall, took up again for several months, and ended at cotton chopping time in the spring.

She was so excited by the chance to start to school that for the rest of the evening she had more trouble than usual keeping her mind on her picking. After they weighed up for the last time, she ran all the way through dusk to the dugout by herself to tell Mama the good news.

Right away, Mama started shaking her head. "Why, Matt," she said, turning from the hot cookstove, "you know your papa ain't goin' to let you all out of that cotton patch long's they's money to be made."

Her excitement collapsed, and she turned and walked slowly out to the chicken house to gather the eggs and close the chickens inside. At supper, Papa said, "Mandy, I hear the Valley View School's startin' Monday. But Bob and the rest of them cain't thank of startin' long's there's any boll of cotton hereabouts left to be picked. Winter's comin'. And we got to make ever nickel we can fore it gits here."

As unhappy as the news made her, in the days that followed she tried to put school out of her mind and get on with picking cotton. From habit, she still picked as fast as she could while thinking about picking, but she kept losing herself in daydreams of going to school, from which Papa's shouts would wake her up and start her picking. Also from habit, she was still afraid of Papa's threats to give her a whipping.

Yet after a time, when he no longer carried out his threats, she realized her days of being whipped were over. She could remember when knowing this would have made her happy every waking hour of the day. Yet now she was unhappy almost every waking hour of the day, wishing she could be going to school.

Gradually the beautiful Indian summer turned to raw, cloudy days, and cold nights that left a film of ice in the water bucket outside the dugout door. One night at supper, after they had been picking and shivering all day in spitting flurries of snow, there was so much coughing and sniffling at the table that Mama said, "Jim, these children are goin' to come down with pneumonia if they don't git some warm clothes."

"I know, Mandy. But they got to hold out till Saturday before Christmas. Then I'm planin' on takin' us all to town."

From that night on, even though Christmas was still many days away, the trip to Kickapoo was the main topic of conversation between her and Emma. One topic she never mentioned to Emma was the beautiful lady with snow white skin and red red lips. She would have been ashamed to have anyone think she would take an interest in such a bad woman as Mama had told her about. Even so, she now spent more time than usual each night scrubbing her own face with hot soapy water.

At supper the night before the trip to Kickapoo, Papa gave Bob and her and Emma a dollar each to buy Christmas presents, and she went to her pallet thinking about how she was going to spend the money.

First, she thought of a pretty comb for Mama to take the place of the one she lost somewhere on the trip. And for as long as she could remember, Papa's suspenders had been fastened with a safety pin at the place where they crossed in the back. As for Alice's present, no ideas came to her before she fell asleep. She woke the next morning and, wearing her one good dress, was the first one at the breakfast table. For once, she wished Papa would hurry everyone along the way he usually did, but this morning he stayed at the table, sipping a second cup of coffee while Mama was having Alice make a list of what to buy.

Yet the sun was hardly an hour high when they left Mama at the dugout door, holding Ben wrapped in her old red shawl to keep the cold out, and drove off to Kickapoo.

Chapter 11

Kickapoo had even more people and horses and dust than she remembered, but it was far from hot this morning. The cold north wind that had blown on them since they left the dugout seemed to be coming from every direction now. But she was so excited to be there she paid little attention to the weather.

Secretly she was looking for a black buggy, pulled by a high-stepping bay horse, driven by a beautiful lady in a big yellow hat, but she did not see anything like that among the horses and wagons and buggies in sight. People in every kind of garb were hurrying by, but she noticed it was mostly farm families crowding the sidewalk. It was the papa out front, then the mama dragging along one or two red-faced runny-nosed little children, with the bigger ones strung out after them, everyone hunching over against the cold, and nobody looking as happy as she felt.

Now that she had a whole dollar of her own, she was more interested in buying presents than in getting new winter clothes, but she followed Alice happily to the dry goods store where their shoes had been bought last month, and the hat thrown in for nothing.

A foreign looking little man came smiling and bowing out to wait on them. He turned out to be the little Jew man who had given Alice the hat. But even with that to recommend him, she felt uneasy with him because he looked so strange, and never stopped smiling. A black beard covered his face up to thick glasses that seemed to be keeping his bulging black eyes in his head.

When her turn came to look at clothes, she still had her mind so much on the Christmas presents she was going to buy that she tried on whatever Alice showed her. Before long she was walking around the store in a yellow stocking cap with a blue tassel, a long blue coat as thick as a horse blanket, and a pair of red mittens. Dressed in these new clothes, she felt like another person.

Out on the sidewalk once more, she followed Alice and the others along crowded Main Street to a place called Hodge's Racket—Cheap Cash Store! It had more things to buy than she had ever thought of. She wandered up and down the aisles, dazed by all the things she saw. She found dozens of combs for Mama, and settled on one the man said was imitation tortoise shell—whatever that was—and cost twenty-five cents. This was a little more than she had expected to pay, but it was the prettiest comb there and, after all, it was for Mama.

Next to the combs, she found oval-shaped looking glasses with handles, just the thing for Emma, and only a dime. While looking for something for Bob, she came across piles of suspenders of every color, and decided on a blue pair for Papa that cost a quarter. She had forty cents left, and she still didn't have anything for Bob or Alice.

Going around the end of a counter where she had not been before, she met a tall, blue-eyed girl coming towards her. She stopped. The other girl stopped and they exchanged surprised smiles. Thinking how pretty the other girl looked, she noticed the dark widow's peak sticking out from under a yellow stocking cap, and with a sudden tingling realized she was looking at herself.

Startled, she looked again, but now all she could see was the surprised look on the other face. For a long time she stood in front of the big looking glass, turning this way and that as she looked herself up and down from scuffed shoes to yellow cap. What surprised her most was that her face was not as skinny as it used to be, and that pleased her.

Finally, she tried to give herself another pretty smile like the first one, but every time she tried it the smile looked sillier. Giving up, she made a face at herself and turned away from the looking glass. Yet that first smile warmed her heart as she circled through the aisles again to where she had seen some pocket knives.

She picked out a black-handled one that had a long blade on one end and short one on the other. She knew Bob wanted a hunting knife, but the only ones she saw cost ten times as much as she could pay. Now with a quarter left for a present for Alice, she looked and looked until she came across a pale blue fascinator. It would look scrumptious draped over Alice's light hair and tucked under her chin.

Going around and gathering up all the presents she had picked out, and then looking to see that no one in the family was watching her, she put them on the counter with her dollar bill, and was very happy when they were paid for and the man hid them away in a paper sack.

They stayed in that paper sack until the night before Christmas when she took them out and wrapped each present in the thin white paper Alice gave her. She put the presents under the little cedar tree Bob had cut the day before on the Indian land. She and Emma had popped popcorn and made strings of it for the tree, and Alice had cut out a white paper star and tied it to the top of the tree.

At Shades Crossing they always went to church the night before Christmas, where a big Christmas tree would be standing behind the altar. After they had listened to a prayer and sung some Christmas songs, Santa Claus would come whooping in at the front door, throwing candy to everyone as he romped up the aisle. Then he would go to the Christmas tree, empty his sack on the floor in front of it, and start handing presents up to Reverend Farthing, who would call out the names.

But there was no church to go to this Christmas Eve, and it was the next morning after breakfast before they were allowed to open their presents. Then with much oohing and aahing the presents were passed around for everyone to see. She felt a touch of guilt when she unwrapped a hairbrush from Alice—whose brush she had been using—but her last present made her forget all the others.

The little red package was not much bigger than her thumb, and not until she undid the ribbon could she see her name written on the paper. She was about to ask Bob how he knew this present was for her, and then she noticed Vernon's name in the other corner. To try to stop her blushes, she called out his name and began fumbling at the paper. Out slipped a little box, and when she opened it she found a thin gold chain.

She lifted the chain, and from it a tiny golden heart dangled in the air.

"Matt's got a beau!" chanted Bob, and Emma took it up. "Matt's got a beau! Matt's got a beau!"

Clutching the present to her chest, she ran outside to get away from their teasing. The cold air felt good on her hot face as she stood there wishing she could give the present back to Vernon and never have to think about it again. She did not want him or any other boy for a beau. The cold drove her back inside, where Mama made her put the necklace around her neck, saying she could not give it back without hurting Vernon's feelings.

As the family gathered around the table for Christmas dinner, she forgot Vernon's present for the time being, pleased to see that Mama was wearing her comb and Papa his new suspenders. Alice had put on the fascinator earlier, and it did look scrumptious on her—just the color of her eyes—but Alice said she would save it for an extra special occasion.

They usually had a turkey gobbler for Christmas dinner, but that day they were having to make-do with the red rooster. Papa said the rooster wouldn't be needed until spring, when the hens began to get broody and ready to set, and by then he would get hold of another rooster.

That night before going to sleep, she thought about her new clothes and her other Christmas presents, especially about the golden heart on the gold chain. When she had gone over to thank Vernon for it, and told him it was the most beautiful thing she had ever seen, his freckled face turned so red it made her forget about her own hot blushes.

Early in the new year, Papa rode off on Nellie one morning without saying where he was going. Before suppertime he was back and announced they now had a farm. She was tempted to yell, "Hooray! Now we can go to school." But she knew better than to interrupt Papa. He said when the bids on the school-lease farm were opened this morning, his was the highest, and now they had a hundred and twenty acres of land with a house, a barn and a well already on it. Papa said until a homestead turned up by and by, which it was bound to do the way so many farmers were moving around, this farm would make a good place to live.

She soon realized from Mama's questions and Papa's answers that they had a farm for as long as they paid the lease every year, but the land would never belong to them. She had the feeling that Mama was disappointed they were not moving to a place they could call their own, although not a word was said by anybody about that. Mama just nodded at Papa's answers and started talking about the move itself. At one point, she said, "Jim, you find out if the Carpenters'll sell this stove. I'd jist as lief have it as a new one."

The next day as soon as they had the first load on the wagon, which included the old cookstove, the family all went over and said good-bye to the Carpenters and thanked them for the use of the dugout. Later, as they drove by their house, Vernon yelled to Bob that he would ride out and see him some Saturday or Sunday. Feeling herself blushing, she pretended not to hear.

The new home was miles south and west of the dugout, a lonesome looking unpainted frame house facing east on the side of a hill, with a bucket hanging out of the well in the backyard. Beyond it was an outhouse with the door swinging in the wind, and then the barnyard with a log barn and cow shed, and a scattering of blackjack trees.

She and Emma were the first inside the house, and as they clattered through the empty, strange smelling rooms, it seemed as big and cold as a barn. A kitchen and three other rooms were downstairs, and upstairs it really was just like a barn loft, open from end to end, and the bare rafters bumpy with dirt dauber nests.

Mama wanted to give the kitchen a good scrubbing before the cookstove was moved in, but Papa said, "They ain't no time fer that, Mandy. Looks like snow on the way and me 'n Bob got another trip to make." And as soon as he and Bob set up the cookstove, they drove off to the Carpenters without waiting for dinner to be cooked.

At supper she was sad to hear Papa say he had traded the colts to Mr. Carpenter. But she listened quietly while he explained to Mama that out of the trade he got a wagonload of corn and two shoats, one fat enough to butcher and the other one already bred. He also said he got some cash to boot, but he never said how much, and Mama never asked.

The next morning a solid mass of clouds hung low over the hillside, but the snow still had not come. Papa said they had better get going while the going was good, and warned Mama and Alice to bundle themselves and Ben up warm. They all squeezed together on the spring seat, wrapped a heavy quilt over them for a lap robe, and headed off to Kickapoo to buy furniture.

As soon as she finished doing the dishes, she and Emma went out to help Bob, who had been told to get plenty of wood cut up for the cookstove, and for the new heating stove Papa was going to buy. The Thorpes had left lots of blackjack limbs and logs at the woodpile, and she and Emma spent the morning at the sawhorse, sawing them up with the crosscut saw, while Bob did the splitting. By noon they had enough firewood sawed and split to last at least a month, and Bob said that would do.

That evening he led them around for a look at the farm, scaring up jackrabbits and cottontails in the fence lines, and squirrels once they got in the woods. Late in the evening it started to snow, and they hovered around the cookstove to keep warm. By the time they heard Papa call "whoa" to the mares in the driveway it was after dark and snowing hard.

The wagon was loaded with furniture—most of it secondhand— including a Singer Sewing machine like the one they sold at their going away sale. The heating stove was new, and Papa and Bob set it up in the living room and Bob built a fire in it. As it got hot for the first time, it began to stink up the whole house with the smell of burning paint, but Papa said they would just have to put up with the smell for a few days.

She felt strange that night sleeping in a bed again after all those months on a pallet, but even the comfort of bedsprings and a mattress could not make up for the drafty attic. From the way the cold wind poured through the cracks, she reckoned this attic might make a cool place to sleep in summer, but for warm sleeping in winter it was no match for the dugout they had just left.

Two mornings later she was happily following Bob to Oakridge School through six inches of snow, and trying not to listen to a grumpy Emma following her. Dressed in her warmest clothes, she carried a new book satchel hanging from her shoulder, one of three Mama made out of the leftover canvas bought for the cotton sacks. In her satchel, along with her pencil box, was her dinner wrapped in a page of the "Kickapoo Chronicle"—a fried egg in a biscuit, a baked sweet potato, and a piece of gingerbread.

She expected Oakridge School to be on or near a ridge of oak trees, but it was on a flat, open space next to a thicket of scrub blackjacks. The building looked as if it had started as a one-room school, and recently had a second room stuck at a right angle on the back. A hundred yards to the rear, and well apart from each other, stood two snow-covered outhouses.

Leaving Bob to watch boys in a snowball fight, she opened the schoolhouse door and came face to face with a wave of hot air from a potbellied stove, and silent stares from a circle of girls standing around it. At the far end of the room she saw a woman writing on the blackboard.

"Come on, Em," she said, "let's go this way." And while walking up the aisle, she took off her red mittens and yellow cap, opened her blue coat and shook her loose hair until it slipped off her shoulders.

She stopped near the woman and eyed her gray wool skirt and striped shirtwaist with its big puffy sleeves. When the woman looked around at her, she said, "I'm Mattie Lane. And this is my sister,

Emma."

"Oh, yes," the woman said, smiling. "And you have a brother. Your papa was by here a few days ago. I'm Miz Reese."

Mrs. Reese sent Emma on to a Miss Rogers in the other room, and called to one of the girls to ring the bell. School began with Mrs. Reese reading a few verses of scripture. Then she put the Bible aside and asked them to stand and sing the first and last verse of "America." Then the old pupils were set to work on a reading assignment, and she and Bob were called up to Mrs. Reese's desk.

"Oakridge is not a graded school," she heard Mrs. Reese begin in a half-whisper, and her happiness at being here was gone in nothing flat. She felt heartsick to hear that instead of separate classes, pupils were grouped by how well they could recite in a subject. She was afraid she would never learn enough this way to ever become a schoolteacher.

Yet for the rest of the day she did her best as she and Bob were moved from group to group while Mrs. Reese watched and listened and questioned. On her way home she did not say anything to Bob about her disappointment—nor later to anyone at home.

In the following days she found that Mrs. Reese was kind and helpful to everyone, raising her voice only when one of the oldest boys tried to make a nuisance of himself. Then it was easy to see why those pupils called her Bulldog Reese behind her back. She was a big woman anyway, and when a boy made her mad she bristled up even bigger.

A wrinkly scowl would come over her face. If that and a few sharp words did not bring the boy around, he had to wait after school, which meant a whipping or being expelled for a week. Since a whipping at school usually meant another one at home if the papa found out about it, most of the time even the roughest boys kept as quiet as in church.

Chapter 12

Although she did not want it to happen, the last day of school arrived. She made up her mind she was going to spell down Jenny Hubbard in the final contest of the term. Yet she was so anxious to do it that she made a silly mistake on an easy word—putting the "i" before "e" in seize—and had to sit down early in the contest and watch Jenny win as usual.

When it came time for the foot racing, held out in the road in front of the school, she was so mad at herself for her spelling mistake she could think of nothing else. Yet she took off her shoes and stockings and, feeling light as a feather, outran all the other girls without trying her hardest.

After Fred Dawson beat Bob in the boys' race, nothing would satisfy the boys but that she run against Fred. She didn't want to, but when all the boys—including Bob—starting calling her a cowardly cat, she finally said she would.

The whole school lined the road near the finish where Miss Rogers and Jenny were holding the string, while she and Fred stood in the center of the road a hundred of Mrs. Reese's long steps away. Once Mrs. Reese had everyone quieted down, she bellowed, "On your mark! Get set! Go!"

Away she flew ahead of Fred, scared half to death with excitement. Yet by the time she got close enough to the finish to notice little Miss Rogers jumping up and down and screaming her name, she heard Fred puffing almost in her ear. She never knew what happened to her then. Losing all sense of running, she felt like she was skimming over the ground without her feet touching anything. Not until the screaming girls swarmed around her and began slapping her on the back did she realize she had outrun Fred and was the fastest runner in Oakridge School.

Yet it was neither her victory in running nor her loss to Jenny in spelling that was on her mind as she walked home from school that evening. After the footrace, Mrs. Reese had told her to come to the classroom. Once all the other pupils and the visiting parents had gone, Mrs. Reese told her how pleased she was to have a pupil who always paid attention in class and always did her best. Then she pulled a book from those at the back of her desk, and said, "Mattie, I want you to have this dictionary as a present."

Too surprised at first to say anything, she finally found her tongue and thanked Mrs. Reese again and again. But since that did not seem like thanks enough for such a fine present, she confessed she wanted to be a teacher herself one day, if she ever could.

"Why, of course you can, Mattie, if you want to bad enough. But let's see how you feel about that in a couple of years or so. Most likely you'll be thinking of something else by then."

"No, I'm not ever going to get married."

Mrs. Reese laughed and said, "Neither was Jenny. She was all fired up to be a teacher herself. And you're twice as pretty as she is."

She felt herself blushing at this, but Mrs. Reese went right on. "Oh, I see the boys making sheep's eyes at you, Mattie. I'll be surprised if Fred, or another one, doesn't get you by the time you're as old as Jenny is. In the meantime, come by my house this summer if you want some books to read. If you're going to be a teacher, you have to do a lot of reading."

At supper, Emma told about her winning the footraces, and everyone had a good word to say to her. She herself told about Mrs. Reese's gift of the dictionary, but she said nothing about the other compliments.

The vacation began with winter coming back without any warning. She had taken Ben, who was walking now, out to the barn lot to see Old Blackie's brand new heifer calf. Seeing the old cow's bag swelled up fit to burst, she thought how good it was going to be to taste some milk and butter again. They had not had any since they turned Old Blackie dry a few weeks before so she could build up her milk for this new calf.

In the short time it took Ben and her to pet the drowsy calf, to scratch Nellie's nose a little, and to look at the spotted gilt—heavy with pigs and lying grunting in a shady corner of her pen—the warm wind from the south changed to a cold wind from the north. She hardly had time to notice the change before the sun disappeared behind swirling gray clouds.

A shower of sleety snow started Ben fretting, and then squalling. She picked him off the top log of the hog pen and hurried back to the house.

The norther was still roaring through the attic when she went to sleep that night, but when she woke up next morning everything was as still as the streak of snow slanting across the floor to her bed. Reaching out from under the covers she pinched up a taste. The instant her tongue touched the cold stuff she shivered all over. After she had dressed, she dropped a little snow down Emma's neck and ran downstairs.

In the clear sunshine, yesterday's green was now so sparkling white it hurt her eyes to look at it. Yet before noon, melting snow was running off the roof like rain, and in three days the country was greener than ever. A week later it was summer weather again, hot wind blowing from the south, and dust in the air.

With Kickapoo now too far away for an easy Sunday trip, Papa had to trade at Briggs, which was down south of Oakridge School. It was more of a wide place in the road than a town, but it had a few stores, a cotton gin and a blacksmith shop, along with a post office and an undertaker. On Sunday every place but the undertaker's was closed up tight as a jug, so the farmers did their shopping in Briggs on Saturday.

One day Mama had an answer to her letter to Aunt Sis, and after supper she read it aloud to the family. Aunt Sis began by saying how glad she was to get Mandy's letter and to know they had a farm at last. She had already heard about the drownings from Mrs. McDermit's letter to Reverend Farthing at Christmas. But even now with Mandy's letter in her hand, she found it hard to believe that Old Lady McDermit and Tommy were gone.

As she heard Mama read the word Tommy, she sat still as death and never heard another word Mama read. What must Aunt Sis think of her now? She didn't know if Mama had told Aunt Sis about her confession, and there was no way she could find that out without asking Mama, something she was ashamed to do.

One Saturday Papa came home from Briggs saying he had heard that some Methodists were holding services at the home of a farmer named Simpson, who lived east of them on the road to Kickapoo. The next day Papa took the whole family there. The service was held under the trees in the Simpsons' front yard, and a sudden shower of rain sent everybody crowding up on the porch, and the women on into the house.

She heard Papa say they would not have to worry about a little rain like this if they had their own church house, and maybe now was a good time to do something about one. Right then and there, he pulled out the pocketbook she remembered so well, took some bills out of it, dropped them in his hat and passed it to Molly's papa. When the hat got back to Papa, every man on the porch had put some bills in it.

After thanking the men and the Lord for the money, Papa held out the hatful of bills to Mr. Simpson. "Brother Simpson," he said, clearing his throat, "here's somethin' to start with. You find a piece of land fer us to put the Lord's house on, and I'll haul the first load of lumber out from Kickapoo fer it."

Mr. Simpson said, "I'm much obliged to you, Brother Lane.

And to all you other brethren, too." Then he bowed his head over the hat and thanked the Lord for bringing the rain just when He did. That done, he said, "Well, now. So far as findin' a place for a church house, I been thinkin' for some time about what to do with that corner of the farm up there where I buried my mama... God rest her soul. If that hilltop suits you all for a church house, I'd be proud to deed it over for one."

That was the start of the Calvary Methodist Church. Whenever any men could spare any time from their field work, they pitched in and helped with the building of it. In the meantime, they built a brush arbor in the churchyard to hold services under until the church house was ready.

When the church house was finished, a man wounded and back from the Spanish War was hired to be the preacher. They held a church supper, and after that Reverend Willis preached the first sermon in the new building, even though it would have been much cooler out under the arbor. The preacher finished his sermon by saying he had found God in the midst of battle and was going to spend the rest of his life in His service. He went on to set the date for the start of a revival, which he said was to re-enlist the veterans and fill up the ranks with new recruits.

She didn't know what all of this meant, so she let it go in one ear and out the other. She had been going to revival meetings all her life, and she liked them because they gave her a chance to be with her friends for two or three hours every night. Of course she had to listen to a lot of preaching and praying and hymn singing, but she never minded that too much. Anyway, she reckoned that part was mostly for the grown-ups.

The first night of the revival was just as she remembered them from Shades Crossing. Well before sundown, everyone all scrubbed and in clean clothes, started arriving at the church in wagons, buggies, and on foot, or horseback. The grown-ups stood around in little bunches outside the arbor, the men talking weather and crops, while the women mostly listened and kept an eye on their smaller children running around laughing and screaming and falling over each other in the grass.

Many of the young people were from Oakridge School. They stood in a circle of girls and a circle of boys, but she noticed from where she stood with Molly and Emma that while the boys talked and laughed and shoved each other around, they had their eyes on the girls much of the time.

At sundown, Papa and Mr. Wisdom went around lighting the coal oil lanterns hanging from the corners of the arbor and along the aisle. At the same time, Miss Rogers started warming up the organ. By the time she had fiddled with all the stops and had them pulled and pushed until they suited her, most of the people had moved under the arbor and filled up the benches, the grown-ups in front and the young people in the back.

After listening to the opening prayer and joining in the singing of a hymn, she went back to whispering with Molly about Jenny Hubbard, who was sitting across the aisle with her new husband. The next thing she noticed, the preacher was talking about Adam and Eve in the Garden of Eden, saying it was the very place where all the sin in this world got started. He went on to say that because of Adam and Eve—but mainly because of Eve, since she tempted Adam—everyone in the world was guilty of sin.

She stopped whispering to Molly. She had heard all this plenty of times before, but this was the first time in her life she ever thought it had anything to do with her. The preacher sounded like he knew all about her drowning Tommy. All ears now, she caught her breath when the preacher paused for a few seconds and then shouted out, "Ever last one of you under this arbor is a sinner!" A longer pause and he was off again. "Make no mistake about it. And there's no use tryin' to pretend to God you're not a sinner. You cain't fool God!"

The words leaped out at her as if the preacher had grabbed her and shaken her. "God can see sin in your heart no matter how hard your face tries to hide it. The only way out is to confess. Confess your sins! Accept Jesus Christ as your Lord and Savior! Let Him lift the burden of sin off your soul. Let Him set your soul free forever. Yes, forever! It's easy as that."

Leaning forward, she gave the preacher all her attention. Gradually she forgot all about the hot sticky air, the bugs circling the lanterns and smacking against them, the women fanning themselves and their fretting babies, but she never missed a word the preacher was saying.

Before long he had her feeling like a hemmed up animal, twisting and turning this way and that, looking for a way out. But the only way out was confession. The preacher kept hammering away on sin and confession, sin and confession. For years she had watched people go up to the altar and kneel down to confess their sins. She knew that was how you became a Christian. Yet until this very instant she had never thought it might be a hard thing to do. As sinful as the preacher made her feel, she still could not make herself move from the bench.

She had never listened to such a long sermon. It went on and on and on, and even when she thought it was over, it wasn't. The preacher stood still for a while behind the altar, looking as tired as if he had just run a long footrace in all this heat. He mopped his face again and again with a white handkerchief, and then dabbed his light skimpy hair with it. Eventually he stuffed the handkerchief back in his hip pocket and called the number for another hymn.

The organ fed softly into "Just As I Am." The preacher lifted his arms, and for what seemed to her to be the hundredth time he urged all those with a sin weighing on their soul to come forward and join those already kneeling at the altar. By now she felt so miserable she had stopped trying to join in the singing, no matter how much Molly and Emma kept looking at her. With sweaty hands she sat clutching the brand new hymnal, too choked up to sing, her eyes too filled with tears to even read the words. She could only sit and wait for this torment to get over with. When they sang the line "to rid my soul of one dark blot," she stiffened and was once more in the foaming water with Tommy.

The next thing she knew the hymn was over and the preacher was pleading once more for sinners to come forward and let Jesus lift the burden of sin off their soul. Right then she would have given anything to be free of her burden, but she was too scared and too ashamed to stand up and walk up the aisle past all those people. She looked at Mama and Alice up ahead and across the aisle, Ben asleep on Mama's shoulder in spite of all the heat and commotion, and then on up to Papa in the Amen corner with Mr. Simpson and Mr. Wisdom and some other men. She doubted if Mama had ever told Papa of her confession about Tommy, and at the thought of Tommy, again she had to bite her lip to keep from crying.

Lowering her head, she stared down at the withered grass between her shoes. She was afraid to look at the preacher now, afraid he would see the sin in her heart and say, "Come on, Mattie. Come on up and tell it to Jesus." Long after she had given up any hope of the singing ever ending, it finally did, and the preacher turned to the line of sinners kneeling at the altar. He kneeled down and talked in a low voice to each one. When he had finished with the last one, he stood up and strode down the aisle to the middle of the arbor and stopped.

Cautiously she looked up long enough to see the preacher lift his arms and throw his head back. And then while insects whirled and hummed around the lanterns, while babies fretted in their sleep and horses rattled their harness out in the dark, she sat with her stinging eyes shut tight and listened to the preacher's hoarse closing prayer. Not until his Amen rang out, echoed by others from the Amen corner, did she lift her head and take a deep breath.

Free at last, she whispered a quick good night to Molly and escaped to the wagon ahead of the others. She felt as worn out as if she had chopped cotton all day. On the way home she never said a word to anyone, thankful the night hid her burning eyes, and the moving air cooled her face. With half an ear she listened to Bob and Emma arguing over how many people went up to the altar to confess, and to Papa telling Mama her supper had not set just right with him.

"You must've et it too fast, Jim. T'was a good supper. Even if I do say so myself."

"Jist the same, Mandy, maybe you better git me a pinch of soda when we git home."

Mama only grunted at this.

Chapter 13

Night after night she agonized through Reverend Willis' long sermons, dreading his calls for sinners to come forward and be saved.

Every sermon made her feel miserable, yet she could never bring herself to go up to the altar to confess her sin. More than once she almost got up enough nerve to do it, but at the last second she couldn't make herself move from the bench.

Yet always later, as she rode home in the dark, she wished she had, and said to herself that next time she would. But the next night came and she was still too scared and too ashamed to do it. Tommy was always on her mind these days, just the way he had been for weeks after the drowning, but she still could not confess publicly what she had done to him.

Two nights before the end of the revival, she watched Papa leave his place in the Amen corner, look around until he spotted her, and then start walking towards her. Reverend Willis had finished his sermon and the nightly mopping and dabbing with his handkerchief.

He had just called for another hymn, and even as the first notes of "O Why Not Tonight?" rose from the organ, he lifted his arms and once again started urging sinners to come forward and be saved.

As she watched Papa come down the aisle past the preacher, her interest turned to fear when he stopped beside her. Before she could think what she might have done during the sermon to make him mad, he leaned over and said in a loud whisper, "Mattie, I know it would please your mama if you'd give your life to Jesus."

If Papa had slapped her face, she could not have been more surprised. Before she could say anything, Papa turned and walked back up the aisle. Emma leaned in front of Molly and asked what Papa wanted.

She couldn't answer. Her eyes were hot with tears, and her burning cheeks told her she must be red as a beet, but that was not why she was speechless. From far, far away the faint roar of the flood was filling her mind. The roar got louder and louder, shutting out everything else around her.

She found herself kneeling at the altar, gripping the wooden rail with both hands, trembling all over. She was surprised to hear the congregation singing as usual, as if no one had noticed her leaving her seat. She lowered her head and waited. If she could only stop trembling long enough, she thought she would be able to tell the preacher everything about drowning Tommy, just the way it happened.

Minute after minute she waited, but the trembling never stopped. The closer Reverend Willis came towards her the worse it got. And then, hot and smelling of stale sweat, he was kneeling in front of her, his black string necktie and damp white shirt only inches in front of her nose.

Glancing up, she saw the long red face hanging almost over hers, the lips moist.

Quickly she lowered her head. She felt his hot hand press down on her shoulder, forgot what she had planned to say, and blurted out, "I didn't mean to drown Tommy. I was just trying to keep him from drowning me.

The hot hand tightened a little, and before she could say anything else, she heard him whisper hoarsely, "Mattie, do you accept Jesus Christ as your Lord and Savior?"

This was not at all what she expected, but she nodded, and whispered, "Yes."

"Bless you, Mattie."

The hot hand was gone from her shoulder. Looking up, she saw Reverend Willis turning to the man next to her, and she wanted to call him back. Didn't he want to hear the rest of her confession? She kept looking at him as he kneeled down before the man, dazed that this was all there was to being converted. She was still the same as she was. Her burden had not been lifted at all. And he had promised!

On the way home nobody said anything to her about being converted, but that night in bed Emma asked her if she had been scared. She said she had been, although she never actually remembered leaving the bench or walking up the aisle.

Worried because nothing had happened to her at the altar, she lay awake hoping the change she had expected would come to her when she was baptized. She had heard it said you could not become a Christian without being baptized. And with her own eyes she had seen baptism bring out the Holy Spirit in people, starting them singing, shouting and praying out loud as soon as the preacher lifted their head out of the water.

She had never prayed, except to say the Lord's Prayer, and she wished now she could be more like Ramona, the girl in the novel she was reading, or like Papa. Praying seemed to come as easy for them as talking. This gave her an idea, and she slipped out of bed and kneeled beside it. Afraid of waking Emma, she whispered softly, "God, I'm sorry for what I did to Tommy. Really and truly I am. I didn't mean to drown him. All I was doing was just trying to keep him from drowning me. Believe me. It's the truth. So won't You please make something happen to me, God, so I'll know I'm saved? Please, God?"

Nothing happened. Yet Sunday evening, as she jolted along in the wagon to the baptizing with the rest of the family, a spare dress clutched in her lap, the hope that something would happen when she was baptized was still strong in her heart.

Bob had been fishing with Vernon in these sloughs down near the river, and as they drove along he was telling everyone in the wagon about the slough they were going to now. He said the farmer who let them fish in it, a Pottawatomie Indian, told them this slough was fed by springs coming up from a sandy bottom, and that was why the water in it was clear and not muddy red like the rest of the sloughs along the river.

They were among the first families at the baptizing, and as the wagon circled the south end of the slough, she guessed it was at least a hundred yards long and half as wide. Bushes and scrub willows lined the west side and far end, but all along the east side, dried up grass covered the ground all the way to the river half a mile away.

By the middle of the evening, dozens of wagons and buggies were scattered over the Indian's pasture between the slough and the river. The people had bunched up along the grassy edge of the water, visiting in the hot sun until everybody got there. A short distance away, a dozen or so Jersey cows and calves and a bull stood lined up facing the people, silently watching.

Reverend Willis drove up in his hack and got down. He took off his coat and collar and tie, handed them back up to his wife, and called for the people who were going to be baptized to gather around him. As she joined the gathering, she noticed that most of the people were barefoot like she was, but some had kept their shoes on. A few with bedsheets wrapped around them reminded her of Papa telling about the Ku Klux he had seen when he was a boy back in Tennessee.

When Reverend Willis started to pray, everything got so quiet she could hear a mockingbird singing somewhere on the far side of the slough, probably in one of the elm trees around the Indian's house and barn over there. Its chirps and whistles and warbles carried her so far away she did not realize the prayer was over until everybody started singing "Shall We Gather At The River?"

They had sung this hymn at church last night to get ready for today, and it never bothered her then, but by the time they finished singing it now, she felt trembly again the way she had felt that night at the altar. Reverend Willis told those being baptized to join hands and follow him. Slowly he led the line of people in a long curve out in the water towards Papa and Mr. Simpson, who had waded out ahead until they were waist deep, and stood waiting to help if needed.

Reverend Willis was big enough and strong enough that he probably would not need any help. Yet she remembered the time at Shades Crossing when a man who couldn't swim pulled Reverend Farthing under the water with him. It took three men to break the man's hold and keep him from drowning the preacher and himself. But usually the men's job was just to comfort the people who needed comforting, most often some of the women.

The warm water and sandy bottom felt good to her and made her think of swimming in Bear Creek and the river. It was not until the water rose above her knees, and she could feel the wet dress pressing against her body, that she thought of Tommy and was scared. The water was just sliding up over her hips when everybody stopped wading and let go of each others' hands.

No longer scared, she turned with the rest of them to face Reverend Willis, who was already saying something to young Dave Whittern. He had one hand in the small of Dave's back, and the other up to Dave's face.

"David Whittern," he said, now loud enough for everyone to hear, "I baptise you in the name of the Father, the Son, and the Holy Ghost." Over backwards Dave went, clear out of sight. In no time Reverend Willis brought him up blowing water and wiping his eyes with his hands.

She was not concerned about that part of it, but she looked hard to see if Dave showed any signs of being a different person now that he was a Christian. She was disappointed when all he did was look solemn and turn around and shake hands with Papa and Mr. Simpson. At the same time, Reverend Willis reached out to a woman and started all over again.

As she watched person after person rise up quietly from being tipped over backwards in the water, she stopped trembling and noticed that the mockingbird was still singing. And then a big fat woman, one of those wrapped in a bedsheet, came up from her baptizing, shouting, "Yes, Jesus! Yes, Lord!" and would have fainted right back in the water if Reverend Willis had not held on to her. Mr. Simpson took her off his hands until two of the closest women came up and put their arms around her, and the baptizing went on.

When her turn came, she waded forward the way she had seen the others do it, and stopped half-facing Reverend Willis, who by now was as wet as if he had been ducked in the water himself. He reached out his right hand to hers and lifted it to cover her nose and mouth. Feeling his other hand pressing against the small of her back, she started to tremble again.

"Martha Louella Lane," she heard him say, surprising her that he knew her full name. "I baptise you in the name of the Father, the Son, and the Holy Ghost."

As she felt the water close over her face, she suddenly clawed at the hand holding hers to her nose, but before she could pull it loose, her head was out of the water again. She was baptized! She stood blinking the water out of her eyes and felt nothing. Not a single sign of the Holy Spirit!

She wanted to look around at Papa, but she was afraid he would be able to see that nothing had happened to her and be unhappy with her. Feeling her dress plastered to her body, she tugged at the yoke to loosen it, and moved out of the way. She squeezed the water out of her pigtail and looked around at the others who had just been baptized. Not one of them looked as disappointed as she felt. She did not feel like a Christian, and she could not see how she was going to be able to call herself one.

When the last person had been baptized, they all joined hands once more, and Reverend Willis led them out of the water, the whole congregation singing "Bound For The Promised Land"—all except her. Since she had no reason to believe she was bound for the Promised Land, she couldn't sing a lie. Stepping out on the warm ground again, she stood with the wet dress still plastered to her body. Some men she did not know were staring at her as they sang, and she guessed they were wondering why she was not singing. She lowered her eyes until the hymn was over, and the closing prayer. Then she ran to the wagon and hid behind Molly and Emma to peel off her wet dress and put on the dry one.

The sun was low in the west when they hitched up and pulled out of the Indian's pasture and onto the road. While Papa waited for Bob to put up the barbed wire gate behind them, she watched a kingfisher come skimming low over the length of the slough, now smooth as glass. Without slowing its speed the kingfisher dragged its open bill through the water for a drink and left a long vee of ripples trailing on the surface. Watching the kingfisher soar up over the Indian's barn, she reckoned the bird got more satisfaction out of the slough that evening than she did.

That thought kept her silent all the way home.

Chapter 14

Her sore disappointment at not having her sin of drowning Tommy forgiven, even after her baptism, stayed with her as the days passed, and she didn't know what to do about her predicament. She couldn't complain to Reverend Willis. Since he wasn't God, it couldn't be his fault, although he had said time and again from the pulpit that confession was the cure for sinning. And she had confessed to God, too.

Yet within a week summer school was out, and she was too busy picking cotton to think about anything else. At the end of the day she was so tired that, after the supper dishes were done, she would wash herself and fall into bed to sleep until she was awakened for another long day in the cotton patch.

Weeks later, when the last boll of cotton had been picked and she was back in school, she grew so used to the daily scripture lessons read by Mrs. Reese that they no longer set her to thinking about Tommy. Yet the long Sunday sermons of Reverend Willis still left her sad for the rest of the day.

And then a simple, unthinking question to Alice one night renewed her worry. On her fifteenth birthday, Alice brought out a length of red and gray checked material after supper and offered to help her make her first dress. For the next several days she hurried home from school and spent every minute she could spare from her schoolwork, cutting and sewing.

One night while she was working in Alice's room and talking with her about the old days in Bear Valley, she happened to say, "Alice, did you feel any change in yourself the summer you were converted?"

"What do you mean?"

"I don't know." And she went on to tell Alice the misery she was in because she had expected something to happen at church or at the baptism that would show her she was now a Christian—but nothing had happened.

After a long silence, Alice said, "That's the way I was till I talked to Mama about it. She said to jist keep on bein' myself and try not to think about it. Said if the truth was told it prob'ly happened that way to most folks."

Jumping from her chair, she threw her arms around Alice, about to cry with relief when she was stopped by an awful thought. Afraid to say it, she turned from Alice and ran upstairs. She threw herself in bed next to the sleeping Emma and tried to put the awful thought out of her mind.

But she couldn't. She had been worried sick, ashamed that she was the only person converted at the revival meeting who had not felt the Holy Spirit. And here in a few seconds Alice had opened her mind to something she had never thought about.

Now she had a vision of thousands of people—maybe millions and millions for all she knew—living in the world as Christians when they had never felt any more of the Holy Spirit than she or Alice had. Yet they belonged to a church and there was no way anyone could tell by looking at them whether they were real Christians or not.

Unable to go to sleep, she slipped out of bed to the window. Kneeling on the hard floor, she looked out at the night. Again she went all through her talk with Alice, and once more the same awful revelation set her trembling. "Dear God, please forgive me. Honest, I didn't mean to drown Tommy. I was just trying to keep him from drowning me."

And then while waiting in the silent darkness for an answer that never came, she did cry, sick at heart that she would never again have a clean feeling inside her. She would have to carry the burden of that sin with her, and try harder not to commit any more.

As days passed and she got used to the idea that, like Alice, maybe she was one of those in church who never felt the Holy Spirit, and she no longer worried every day about it not happening to her.

One Sunday when the family drove in from church, Vernon Carpenter was waiting for them. He had tied his horse to a fence post and was sitting on the well curb. His straw hat was pushed to the back of his prickly blond hair, and he was playing tug of war with a stick and a gangly, brown puppy at his feet. She had not seen Vernon for months, and as he picked up the puppy and came towards the wagon, she noticed he already looked taller than his papa.

Vernon greeted the family by saying, "I brung you a present."

Everybody looked at Papa to see how the new puppy was going to set with him. He climbed down out of the wagon before saying, "Well, Vernon, has he got any houn' dog in him?"

Vernon looked doubtful. "I ain't sure what all he's got in him."

Quick as flash Bob said, "Don't worry, Papa. I can teach him to hunt easy as pie."

"And we can call him Reuben," she said. "It will be like having Old Reuben back again."

As if he had already forgotten the puppy, Papa said, "Vernon, how's your Pappy gettin' along?" And he went on from question to question, asking Vernon about the colts, the crops and half a dozen other things without letting up. Mama and Alice disappeared in the house with Ben, but she and Bob and Emma stood making a fuss over the puppy and looking at Papa now and then, waiting for him to come back to the point.

On and on Papa went until she was sure he had forgotten about the pup. Finally, and without a change of expression, Papa said, "Well, Vernon, I reckin we been needin' us a dog. Much obliged."

She would have been more pleased if Vernon had not handed the puppy to her, grinning his big grin as he did it. She knew Bob and Emma would have a lot to say about that once Vernon was gone, but she thanked him and took young Reuben in her arms. After a couple of minutes she passed the squirming thing on to Bob and dusted herself off as she went into the house to help with dinner.

At the dinner table the big news from Vernon was that he was not going to school anymore, and she could almost see Bob's ears prick up at this news. Vernon's papa had leased the piece of Indian land next to them, and Vernon said helping his papa farm that extra land would take up all his time.

Mama interrupted Vernon's farm talk to ask how his mama was getting on. Vernon said he guessed she was all right. She had a baby boy a couple of weeks ago. Then he turned back to talking farming, but news of a new baby reminded her of a new baby closer to home.

She had learned from Alice that Mama was going to have a baby of her own sometime next summer. Alice told her to keep the news a secret till everybody knew it, yet that had not kept her from hoping—every time she thought about it—that this baby would be a boy to take the place of Tommy.

On Christmas Eve the whole family bundled up in the wagon and drove through the cold to the church, just like the old days in Bear Valley. The Christmas tree before the altar had the same star at the top, was decorated with the same shiny ornaments, the same strings of popcorn, and the congregation sang all the same Christmas carols.

On the way home, wearing her new red scarf from Santa Claus—although she supposed Alice was the real Santa Claus—she joined Alice and Emma in singing the carols again.

Jolting along the frozen road under half a moon and a sky full of stars, they sang till they ran out of songs, finishing with "Silent

Night" twice. But when their last notes ended, the night was anything but silent. So many dogs had been roused up by people going home from church that the whole countryside sounded like one big choir of barking dogs. Even Reuben barked at them till Bob whistled to him from the lane and brought him running.

As happy as she was at home during Christmas, she was happier when she started back to school. She liked her studies even more than the games they played outside at noon and recess, and was never happier than when she had her nose in a book—history, civics, geography, any book. She liked them all, but most of all she liked stories and poems.

More and more as the winter term of school went on, she found herself answering questions no one else in her group could answer, although some of the pupils were two or more years older than she was and had studied these same books before. The boys did not seem to mind having someone younger recite better than they did, but she began to notice some of the older girls looking at each other in a smirky way whenever she answered a hard question. This did not bother her, even when these girls stopped acting friendly and started choosing her last when they chose up sides for games out on the playground.

The leader of these unfriendly girls was Bonnie Stevens, a big redhead from Briggs, who wore a different dress to school every day of the week and was always hovering around Fred Dawson, who had grown into the handsomest boy in school. Having done nothing to harm Bonnie, she didn't know why Bonnie seemed to want to pick on her. Molly told her it was jealousy over Fred, but she doubted this. She was no more friendly with Fred than she was with any other boy at school.

Yet she was surprised one Friday morning to hear Fred take up for her. It was after geography class during which Mrs. Reese had tried to get someone to volunteer to go to the board and draw a map of the states east of the Mississippi. When no one else would, she said she would try. She thought she had done it right, but Mrs. Reese pointed out that she had switched places with Vermont and New Hampshire.

"Well, now," Mrs. Reese said, writing in the corrections, "since no one here is from Vermont or New Hampshire, nobody's feelings are hurt. But let's all remember which way they go."

Later when the class was crowding out of the door for recess, she heard Bonnie call, "Hey, Clara. That's what some people git for tryin' to show off."

She never let on in any way that she knew Bonnie's gibe was meant for her, although Molly gave her a knowing little poke in the ribs.

Then she heard Fred ask, "Bonnie, I reckin you could've done better?"

Looking back, she saw Bonnie's face flame as red as her hair. For the rest of the morning she could not help noticing that Bonnie sat quiet and stony-faced in her seat, taking no part in the reciting and never once looking at Fred. In the Friday spelling bees she sometimes lost to Bonnie, but that evening Bonnie seemed to have her mind somewhere else. She missed an easy word and had to sit down early, staring at her desk while the lively contest went on around her.

On the way home from school that evening, Bob told her she should have punched Bonnie in the nose for her mean remark, but she disagreed, saying, "From the cowed way Bonnie looked when she left school, maybe she won't make fun of me anymore."

Yet all the next week Bonnie and her friends were at her more than ever, although they always took care to keep Mrs. Reese from seeing them making fun of her. When Friday came, and the weekly spelling bee got under way in the evening, she could see that Bonnie—unlike the week before—was all attention and determined to win. Finally she and Bonnie were the only two left standing. Turn and turn about they spelled word after word with no mistakes, until Bonnie was given a word from their study of poetry.

When Bonnie finished spelling the word, Mrs. Reese shook her head and said, "Mattie?"

Remembering what Mrs. Reese had cautioned them about when teaching them the word weeks before, she put an "s" in the middle of the word where Bonnie had put a "z." Mrs. Reese nodded, repeated the spelling of "caesura." The visiting parents clapped, and the spelling bee was over.

Later when she was leaving the schoolhouse, she was surprised to see Bonnie and her friends bunched up near the foot of the steps as if waiting for someone. She was even more surprised when Bonnie smiled very friendly-like at her and said, "Mattie, I don't mind you beatin' me in spellin'."

Stopping uncertainly before Bonnie's big smile, she had started a smile of her own when Bonnie went on in the same sweet voice, "At least I ain't got an Indian face."

For an instant, the burst of laughter from Bonnie's friends paralyzed her. Then across her memory flashed Aunt Sis's dark skin and hooked nose, and her hand lashed out and slapped Bonnie smack on the mouth. Bonnie gasped as if a dipper of water had hit her in the face. Then she lunged screaming and purple up the stone steps at her, grabbed her hair, jerked her head back and forth in a frenzy, and threw her down.

When she came to, she was lying on her back looking up at Mrs. Reese, who was washing her face with cold water. A ring of blurred faces was staring down at her and she heard far away voices saying, "She's coming to." "She's all right."

But she was not allowed to sit up till Bob had put Mrs. Reese's horse to the buggy and driven it up to the schoolhouse. Then, wrapped up in the lap robe, she rode off with Mrs. Reese, Molly, Bob and Emma all crammed into the buggy.

Every now and then she would slip a hand out from under the lap robe to feel the pain where her head had hit the stone steps. She was hearing that Mrs. Reese knew all about Bonnie picking on her and was just waiting for Bonnie to make a mistake, such as her remark today, so she could call her on it.

"That's why you shouldn't have slapped her," Mrs. Reese said. "Now she will just say you hit her first. But when I was your age, Mattie, I would have hit her long before you did, and not with my open hand, either.

"Well, we'll see what happens."

At home she was put to bed, but by suppertime, in spite of the goose egg on her aching head, she said she felt well enough to come down for supper, and Mama let her. She had never said anything at home about Bonnie picking on her, and now when the whole story came out, everybody agreed that she had done the right thing. Papa said that even though the Bible did say you should turn the other cheek, no one had the right to slur her that way.

She did not know how to explain to Papa that she had taken Bonnie's slur as an insult to Aunt Sis instead of to herself, so all she said was that she had read in the Bible where it said you could take an eye for an eye and a tooth for a tooth.

"Oh, yes," Papa said, suddenly looking stern. "That's the Old Testament. But you got to remember they done heathenish thangs back then. Our Lord wanted to change all that. That's why the Jews crucified Him."

Everybody around the table was silent for a moment, and then Emma started telling how Bonnie's friends led her—her all bent over and blubbering—down to the pump to wash her bleeding mouth.

Monday morning as she was leaving for school, Mama stopped her at the kitchen door and ran a hand over the spot where the goose egg had been, and then took her face between her hands and looked at her. "I ain't never seen this Bonnie Stevens," she said softly, "but try not to thank too mean of her, Child. I reckin you wouldn't of had no trouble with her in the first place if she had a face perty as yourn."

Too choked up to say anything, she gave Mama a hug and hurried out the door to catch up with Bob and Emma. At school everything went along as usual during the first part of the morning, except that the usual smiles and smirks from the girls were missing when she recited, and Bonnie even tried to keep her hand over her own bruised lips.

Yet at recess and noon the fight was all the talk on the playground. She heard that Bonnie's papa had stormed over to Mrs. Reese's house Friday night, hollering about her taking Mattie Lane home in a buggy when his own daughter was hurt worse and had to walk home bleeding every step of the way. Mr. Reese got in the argument and ordered Mr. Stevens out of the house. Mr. Stevens went, but on Saturday he was heard saying around Briggs that the school board would have the last say about Mrs. Reese.

What she heard made her scared for Mrs. Reese, and when school let out that evening she stayed behind to tell her how sorry she was that she had caused her trouble.

"Oh, I had my troubles with Mister Stevens over Bonnie long before he got on the school board," Mrs. Reese said. "Of course George, my husband, should have stayed out of it. But he was taking up for me."

While she stood shaking her head, not knowing what else to say, Mrs. Reese smiled across the desk and said, "Don't you worry, Mattie. We have only three more weeks to go, and I don't expect anything will happen between now and then."

Chapter 15

On the Monday morning after the Fourth of July, while she was out in the backyard cleaning her teeth with a pinch of soda and salt, she saw Bob headed for the woods in the wagon with Papa. He had talked Papa into letting him quit school, and the two of them were on their way to clear more land to plant more cotton next year. Reuben circled ahead of the wagon, looking to scare up a rabbit, or something.

Even though she and Bob had grown apart since they left Bear Valley, his going his separate way this morning reminded her of all the years when they were close to each other—the long talks in the mulberry tree down on the creek, and especially the months of secret plans for running away from Oklahoma Territory to live with Grandma and Aunt Sis. But now, all that was gone.

Nothing lasts. That was what she was beginning to realize, and for the hundredth time this summer she thought of Mrs. Reese gone from Oakridge School, fired by Bonnie Stevens' papa. She had felt so guilty about it she tried and tried to get Papa to do something, but he said there was nothing he could do.

On the opening day of summer school, she and Emma found Molly waiting at her corner, and Molly picked up their yesterday's conversation at church about whether they were going to like their new teacher as much as they had liked Mrs. Reese.

When they arrived at school, little Miss Rogers was standing on the schoolhouse steps next to a tall, slender woman who was talking to a half circle of pupils. The woman broke off what she was saying and stepped forward.

"Good morning. I'm Missus Whitaker," she said, smiling and reaching out to shake hands with her, and then with Molly and Emma. She hadn't expected this kind of greeting, having never had Mrs. Reese or Miss Rogers offer to shake hands with her. But she liked it, and felt friendly toward Mrs. Whitaker right away. She also liked the alert, gray eyes even as she was noticing that the brown hair—pulled straight back and rolled in a ball at the nape of her neck the way Alice sometimes fixed her hair—had strands of white in it at the temples.

Listening to Mrs. Whitaker going on in a low voice with what she was saying to the other pupils, she noticed her speech was different from any she had ever heard. The words came out faster, yet each was so clear it was easy to understand. She had never heard such a pleasing voice, and she took to Mrs. Whitaker even more.

Later in the week when she thought about it, she felt guilty that she had let Mrs. Whitaker take Mrs. Reese's place so fast. To ease her conscience she rode over on Sunday evening on Nellie to see how her old teacher was getting along.

At first it seemed to her that Mrs. Reese had suddenly grown heavier and older, and slower in her speech, but after they had talked a little while she realized it was just that she had become used to a slender, younger teacher with a faster way of speaking. Mrs. Reese was teaching at a school out at Little Axe, which was several miles away, and she said that except for the longer buggy ride she liked it fine.

As the weeks passed, she came to like Mrs. Whitaker more and more. Yet Fred Dawson and some of the other pupils did not like her at all. Behind her back some made fun of what they called her prissy way of talking, some complained because she made them work harder, and almost all of them were unhappy when she announced she was going to turn Oakridge into a graded school. At the end of each year a pupil would either pass to the next grade, or fail to pass and be kept in the same grade for another year.

Mrs. Whitaker did not seem to let any of the pupil's complaints bother her. At least her friendly voice never changed. In two weeks she had given them examinations in all their subjects and placed each pupil in a grade.

Along with six other pupils, she was placed in the eighth grade. She was sorry that Molly was put in the seventh grade, but Molly did not seem to mind, saying, "I'm having enough trouble keeping up as it is."

As usual, it seemed to her that summer school had hardly got good and started before it was about to be over. She hated to see it come to an end. This time she hated it more than ever because she knew she might have to stay out till nearly Christmas before they finished picking all of this year's big cotton crop.

Apparently Mrs. Whitaker overheard her talking about this with some other pupils one day, for she called her aside later and said she would be willing to urge her father not to keep her out of school for so long.

"Please don't do that, Missus Whitaker," she said, knowing it would only make things worse at home. If Papa thought anyone—especially a woman—was trying to tell him how to handle his children's schooling, he would be fighting mad. He might even keep her out of school for good, and make it impossible for her to ever become a schoolteacher, something she had already talked to Mrs. Whitaker about.

Mrs. Whitaker agreed not to say anything to Papa, but she offered to help her on Sunday evenings to keep up with her studies while she was still picking cotton, even though the winter session of school had started. Mama and Alice said it was mighty obliging of Mrs. Whitaker, but Papa grumbled around about the offer for a few days, mainly about the ten-mile round trip on Nellie to

Mrs. Whitaker's house. Yet he finally gave in, saying, "Well, Matt, if you're dead sure you want book learnin' that bad, I reckin you can give it a try."

She left school the next day feeling happier than she had felt all summer. Fred was walking home with her again, something he had been doing regularly that summer. He only came as far as Molly's corner. There he would say good-bye, swing up on his sorrel horse, Carrots, and lope off towards home, leaving her and Molly and Emma to stand to talk and talk.

Later, before she and Emma got home, she would remind Emma not to say anything about Fred walking with them. She liked Fred better than she did Vernon, but he was still just a friend, and she didn't want Bob teasing her about having two beaus at the same time, when she knew that she didn't even have one.

That Sunday, Reverend Willis announced the day for the start of the revival, and once more Papa and Bob helped set up the framework for the brush arbor in the churchyard covering it with fresh willow branches. This year she had no trouble listening to the long sermons, and the calls for sinners to come forward and be saved, although it did make her think of Tommy, and that always made her sad.

The day after the end of the revival, at the very hour when all the family except Mama and Ben was dressed and ready to go to the baptizing, Mama complained of feeling sickly. Right away she offered to stay home and look after Ben, but Alice said that in the circumstances, she had better do the staying at home herself, and Papa quickly agreed.

Leaving Alice in the backyard with Ben and Reuben, who had learned to stay home when Bob told him to, the rest of them started the long dusty ride to Clear Pond in the hot sunshine of early afternoon.

At sundown, when they got home from the baptizing, Dr. Williams' horse and buggy was there, and before they reached the back door, she heard a groan coming from the house.

She had always been sent away to Grandma's when Mama was about to have a baby, but she had heard enough about it to know what was going on in the house, even before Mr. Watson stepped out of the kitchen door to say the baby was coming. He told them about Alice cutting through the woods to his house for him to go get the doctor, and his wife going back with Alice while he jumped on a mule and rode to Briggs for Doc Williams.

Before the day turned completely dark a weak little cry took the place of Mama's groans, and in a few minutes, Alice came out to where she was waiting with Bob and Emma on the well curb to say they had a baby sister. Later that night, when she saw it, she was surprised at how skinny and wrinkled the puny little thing was. But what scared her half to death was the way Mama's looks had changed since dinner. Her face was yellowish brown and hollow-eyed, and so filled with pain she couldn't get the look out of her mind that night no matter how hard she tried.

Dr. Williams came the next two mornings to look at the baby, but it just seemed to pine away. The third night it died. Alice told her she heard the doctor tell Papa he was lucky Mama hadn't died too, that she was done-in from too much hard work in all this heat. That was why the baby came early, and that he had better make Mama rest up for a spell or he could lose her yet.

After the funeral, as she stood with the others around the little heap of red dirt in the graveyard, she thought of Tommy's empty coffin back in Indian Territory—his bones picked clean or worse somewhere along that creek—and of the three other coffins in the graveyard up at Shades Crossing with Mama's babies in them. That made ten babies Mama had had, and her hardly forty years old.

Later, when she asked Alice why Mama wanted to have so many babies, Alice said that she didn't and explained to her how Mama had no say in it if she wanted to keep on living with Papa, or with any other man, for that matter.

When Alice finished, she wanted to say, "But what about the beautiful lady we saw in the buggy—the one you said looked like she had stuck her head in a flour barrel? Why doesn't she have babies?" But to ask that question she would have had to bring up what Mama had told her about scarlet women and she was ashamed to talk to Alice about that.

Once cotton picking started, the only thing making it a less miserable time for her than usual was the happy thought of seeing Mrs. Whitaker every Sunday evening as soon as school took up again. When the great evening came, she rode off on Nellie on the back road to Kickapoo, looking for a blue house. Since most of the houses she passed were not painted at all, she had no trouble deciding that the first blue house she came to was the house Mrs. Whitaker had described.

She turned Nellie up a lane that had an orchard on the right, and sheep in a pasture on the left. As she got closer to the house, she noticed the roof slanted lower down in the back than in the front, making the house look lopsided. She supposed they had built it that way on purpose, but she didn't know why.

Mrs. Whitaker, pretty as a picture in a shirtwaist the color of lilacs, and a gray skirt, met her at the door and invited her in to the nicest front room she had ever seen. A reddish flowered rug covered much of the polished floor, real pictures hung on the walls, and the soft chairs had arms of dark, shiny wood. Mrs. Whitaker introduced her to her parents, whose name was Weston. They also talked as fast as Mrs. Whitaker.

After a little talk, Mrs. Whitaker took her into a room lined with books. She had never seen so many books in one place before in her life, and said so. Mrs. Whitaker said they were mostly her late husband's, and nodded toward a picture on the desk of a man all dressed up and wearing glasses—a handsome face, but skinny.

Nothing else was said about him until Mrs. Whitaker had finished laying out her schoolwork for the week and walked out with her to where she had tied Nellie to an orchard fence post. "My husband is buried there," Mrs. Whitaker said quietly, dipping her head towards a narrow mound of red soil just over the fence. "And our son."

Already startled by the first piece of news, she looked a second time and noticed a little green mound next to the long, bare one. "My husband was brought up in a city," Mrs. Whitaker went on, speaking as if answering a question in the classroom. "He gave up being an English professor because he wanted to be a pioneer. He had no idea how hard farm work was."

Not knowing what to say to all of this, she nodded and said nothing. After a long silence, she thanked Mrs. Whitaker again for her help and rode away down the lane past the grazing sheep. From the pleasant way Mrs. Whitaker acted in the classroom, no one would have thought she had ever been through such problems as these, and she was glad she had never caused her any trouble.

On Sunday evenings afterwards, worn out from another long week of pulling a heavy cotton sack, she would ride up the lane past the sheep in the pasture and think what relief it would be to sit in the shade and watch the sheep get bigger and fatter, and her not ever have to pick another boll of cotton. She could hardly wait till she got to be a schoolteacher and put cotton picking behind her forever.

One Saturday evening Papa and the others came back from Briggs with an old buggy tied to the back of the wagon. Alice said it was a way for her and Bob to get to church Sunday nights to meetings of the newly started Epworth League without having to walk or hitch the mares to the wagon.

She had not thought having a buggy in the family would change the way she went to Mrs. Whitaker's house, but the very next Sunday Mama said, "Matt, now that you're fifteen you're too big to be straddling a horse out in public... and on Sunday of all days."

Yet she only had to use the buggy once, for before a second week had passed, they finished picking a cotton crop of almost eleven bales and she and Emma were back in school again. As if that was not enough good news, Papa took the whole family to Kickapoo on Saturday to buy winter clothes.

———————◆———————

Hodge's Racket Store was as full of people as she remembered, but she hurried past them to the long looking glass. Even though she knew she was going to be seeing herself, she was surprised by the half-stranger staring at her, grown-up looking and bigger all over. It was several seconds before she started nodding to herself that, yes, she looked like she was fifteen. She was almost old enough to wrap her pigtail on top of her head the way Mama and Alice sometimes put their hair up.

Pleased by how grown-up she looked, she went off in good spirits to find the others, ready to get new shoes, material for a new dress, and Christmas presents, too.

Later, down at Jenkins Feed and Seed they ran into the McDermits and had a good visit. It seemed to her that Mr. McDermit had not changed at all, but Mrs. McDermit—nursing a baby boy—had lost weight and grown a lot of wrinkles. The yellow hair of the girls had turned almost white, and they, like Junior, had grown so much she hardly recognized them. The grown-ups had so much to talk about that it was past the middle of the evening before they headed west up Main Street for the long stretch home with the sun in their faces.

As they started down the hill towards the river, a contraption that looked like a cross between a topless buggy and the running gears of a grasshopper came lurching up the road towards them. She had never seen anything like it, but she knew what it was even before Papa called, "Hey, lookee there!" and pulled the mares to a stop.

Hunched over the top of the sputtering grasshopper, like a pair of strange bugs themselves, sat two men covered in brown coats and little caps, their faces half-covered with great big goggles. As their noisy contraption bounced past the shying mares, the two men waved and smiled.

She and Emma waved and turned around to look back. There was not much to see except dust, but the idea of seeing their first horseless carriage was all the talk in the wagon for some time. Yet before they got home she was thinking of her schoolwork again and looking forward to Monday.

On the evening of the last day of school before Christmas, she walked home with Fred and Molly and Emma—Carrots clip-clopping along behind as usual. At the corner, after they wished each other a Merry Christmas, Fred pulled a flat package out of his book satchel and said, "And, Mattie, a special Merry Christmas to you."

Surprised, and a little embarrassed—since she wouldn't have

thought of a present for him even if she had had any money for one—she thanked him, and silently hoped it was a book. She was surprised again on Christmas morning when she opened the present and found it was not a book, but a box of chocolates. This time it was Emma who led the teasing about her having another beau. Only Bob joined the teasing, but each one in the family accepted a piece of chocolate, shaped like a thimble with a cherry in the center.

Reuben's barking said someone was coming, and Bob went to the back door and brought in Vernon, looking grown-up in a new hat and new boots. He wished everybody a Merry Christmas, and then held out to her a present about the size and shape as Fred's box of chocolates, now open on the table.

She thanked Vernon, unwrapped a box of similar chocolates and stammered more thanks, afraid Emma or Bob was going to accidentally, on purpose, let out that this was the second box of chocolates Santa Claus had brought her. She could see they were itching to do it, but Mama and Papa were too close.

Chapter 16

That spring she was working so hard to make sure she was well prepared for her final examination that she never thought about hoeing corn or chopping cotton. Yet one Sunday on the way home from church she saw Papa dip his head at a field of their corn next to the Hartleys—who had the school lease just east of them—and heard him tell Mama that the children had to start hoeing that patch on Monday.

Not until that moment had it crossed her mind that field work might take her out of school before she could graduate from the eighth grade. Scared half to death, she gave Alice a wild look and started to call up to Papa to remind him that this spring school was going on longer than usual, but Alice reached out and put a finger on her lips.

Once they got home and out of the wagon, Alice told her that she would talk to Papa alone and tell him that she and Bob could hoe out the corn by themselves, with maybe a little help in the evenings from Mama, if Mama felt like doing it.

In the kitchen when Mama agreed this was a good idea, her hopes rose. Yet when she heard Papa and Bob come back from putting the team away and start washing up outside the kitchen door, she felt scared again. She couldn't believe Papa didn't already know that to graduate she had to pass an examination from the County Board of Education. Maybe he didn't care whether she passed it or not.

She looked closely at him as he came in and sat down to eat, but his brown face—lighter across the forehead down to where his hat came—gave her no hint of what he might say to Alice, not even when he smiled across at Ben, who was already in his special chair next to Mama's.

She sat down with the rest, anxious to get dinner over with so that Alice could talk to Papa. Yet as soon as Papa finished returning thanks, he brought up the field work himself and repeated what he had said in the wagon. "I know you all ain't through with school yet," he finished, looking calmly at her and Emma, "but them crops won't wait."

She saw Alice start turning red, probably from the thought of having to argue with Papa in front of everybody, but before Alice could say anything, Mama said, "But, Jim, Alice and Bob can git that corn hoed out. I can hep in the evenin', if they need me."

Papa shook his head. "They ain't no way all the hoein' and choppin' around here can git done without Matt and Em. So they ain't no use talkin' about it. He looked around as if that settled the matter. Then he finished helping himself to a second slice of ham, passed the platter to Mama and dropped his glance to the table to see what he wanted next.

"I won't mind missing school," Emma said, looking cheerfully around at everybody.

Papa paid no attention to her, but the instant Alice started to speak, he said, "Alice, I'll thank you to stay out of this." When Alice looked like she still wanted to say something, he stared at her until he was sure she had changed her mind.

Mama said, "Jim, maybe you've forgot that if Mattie's to git a diploma she's got to pass—"

"I could hoe on Sundays," she said, looking directly at Papa.

Papa bristled and said, "We ain't come to workin' in the field on the Lord's day yet. And we ain't likely to if I have anythang to say about it."

"But, Jim, Mattie has got to graduate."

"Yes, Papa," Emma said, looking at him as if she had an exciting piece of news. "Mattie's goin' to be a schoolteacher!"

Papa's frown showed that all this talk was upsetting him, but before he could say anything, Alice turned her red face in Bob's direction and said, "I jist know me and Bob could hoe out that corn."

"Sure," Bob said. "Easy as pie."

Smiling and nodding, Mama started to speak, but Papa slapped the edge of the table with both hands, scaring Ben and making him wrinkle up and start to whimper.

"Now you all listen to me," Papa said, raising his voice above the whimpering. "I done said all they is to say. Tomorrow mornin' you all are goin' to be in that corn patch. And that's the last I want to hear about it." He stopped to let that sink in, and then in a calmer voice he said, "So lets us git on with our dinner."

She kept her eyes on her plate as Papa started to eat. She was determined not to cry, and she was afraid to look at Mama or Alice for fear she wouldn't be able to keep from it. She took a bite of cornbread and chewed it slowly, but the cornbread stayed scratchy in her mouth until she washed it down with a swallow of sweetmilk.

Papa tried to start a conversation about Reverend Willis's sermon, but only Mama helped him out, calming Ben down at the same time by giving him a piece of ham and helping him cut it up.

As soon as dinner was over, she slipped away upstairs, but instead of crying she sat on the bed with her head in her hands, scared and mad at the same time. Now she knew why boys ran away from home, and her thoughts flew to her older brother, Jimmy.

But she was afraid to do what he'd done. She had no money and no way of getting any. Besides, running away would put an end to her chance of becoming a schoolteacher, although it looked to her like Papa was already trying to put an end to that himself.

When Emma came upstairs and started saying how mean

Papa was to keep her out of school, and how she ought to tell Mrs. Whitaker on him, she had an idea. She changed out of her church dress, wrote a note to Mrs. Whitaker telling her what had happened and asking her if she would send the daily lessons home by Molly.

Then she went downstairs to the front porch, where Mama sat with a lap full of mending while listening to Papa reading from the Bible, and asked Mama if she could walk over to Molly's.

The next week she spent her days with the rest of them hoeing corn, but every night she worked on the lessons Molly left for her at the oak tree. For as long as she could stay awake she studied and wrote and did her arithmetic, thankful that Mama never once called up for her to blow out the lamp and go to bed. Sunday evening she was at Mrs. Whitaker's house as soon after dinner as she could get there in the buggy.

She was thankful that Mrs. Whitaker never mentioned Papa's keeping her out of school, for as mad as she still was at him for having done it, she didn't want to have to agree with anything bad anyone said about him. But Mrs. Whitaker kept the talk on the lessons, asking questions and listening to her read and recite, usually praising her for all of her work except the arithmetic, and there quietly showing her how to do the problems she had missed.

When they had finished, Mrs. Whitaker asked her to stay and have a cup of tea. A cup of hot tea on such a warm day was the last thing she wanted, but she thanked her and said "Yes" to be polite. She had always thought the sassafras tea she used to drink at Grandma's was the best in the world, but this turned out to be even better.

At first she was almost afraid to pick up her cup because it was so beautiful—thin and pure white with a chain of blue and yellow flowers running around the rim. She was afraid that somehow she might drop it and break it.

When she did raise the cup to her lips, a faint spicy smell came to her nose before she could sip the tea. Later, on her way home in the buggy, she closed her eyes again and again to bring back the wonderful smell and taste of that tea.

Three weeks passed and they finished hoeing the corn and were chopping cotton now in weather hot as summertime. By the end of each day she was tired out, but she never failed to do her lessons. If Papa knew about her staying up late at night to do them, he never said anything about it.

No one mentioned her lessons except Alice, who tried to help her with arithmetic one night and gave up, saying, "Matt, you've done passed me."

Although Papa had never said he was going to let her out of the cotton patch to take the examination, she felt almost sure that he would. Just the same, she was relieved when Mama told her a few days ahead of time that Papa said it was all right.

And then on the big morning itself, Papa went even further. A heavy rain had come during the night, and at breakfast he said the roads would be so muddy that she had better take the buggy, adding that he had harnessed Nellie and had everything ready for her.

"Thank you, Papa," she said, trying to sound calm in spite of her heart pounding with excitement at what lay ahead of her.

Yet once she got to school and started talking with Lelia Couch and Sally Tarbox, the only other pupils in the class taking the examination, her excitement faded away. She felt like she was back in school again, and she wasn't nervous at all, even when Mrs. Whitaker handed out the long sheets of paper and explained what they were to do.

The questions were easier than she expected, except for two arithmetic problems she couldn't make sense of even after she came back to them again and again. She was still working on one of them when she heard Mrs. Whitaker's watch case click shut and then her announcement, "Time's up, girls."

It seemed to her that only a few minutes had passed since they started, and she could hardly believe she had been sitting in one place, writing and figuring, for such a long time.

On the way home, she noticed that the hot sun was already turning the ground dry in the ruts. At this rate, by Monday they would be back chopping cotton again, but that didn't bother her now. She started humming a tune about nothing and looking at the familiar countryside as if seeing it for the first time.

In the air ahead of her, two scissor-tails broke into a fight, turning and swooping at each other until they were almost down to the ground. At the last second they flew apart and sat on the barbed wire fence a few feet from each other and watched her pass.

She hadn't felt so good since she left Bear Creek. Maybe she would write Aunt Sis a letter and tell her about today. That would please Aunt Sis. On second thought, she decided to wait until she heard from Mrs. Whitaker, just in case.

The fear that she might have failed the examination gave her an uneasy pang that came back often in the next two weeks. The biggest pang came the Saturday evening Alice brought home from Briggs a letter from Mrs. Whitaker. She took the square, pale blue envelope from Alice's hand and stood looking at the Miss Martha L. Lane written there in Mrs. Whitaker's perfect handwriting.

As anxious as she was to know what the letter said, she was scared to open it with everyone watching her. What if she had failed the examination?

Emma's urging her to hurry up and see what the letter said only scared her more, and she turned and ran upstairs so that she could open it alone. Once there she was in such a hurry to get the suspense over with, whatever the outcome, that she quickly slit the envelope open with the edge of her ruler and pulled out a single, folded sheet of the same pale blue paper.

"Dear Mattie," she read, "I'm pleased to tell you that you passed your examination handsomely and...."

Her mind went into a whirl and she sat down on the bed before she could get control of herself and go on reading. "I have your diploma for you if you can come over for it some Sunday afternoon. I would have sent it to you in this letter but I didn't want to spoil such an important document by folding it. I shall hope to see you soon."

And then there was "yours truly" and the perfectly written signature of Anne W. Whitaker.

During the excitement at supper over her good news, it was agreed that she could go to Mrs. Whitaker's the next evening for her diploma, but Sunday morning Papa came back from the barn saying that when he whistled up the stock to feed the mares and fasten them in the lot so he could harness them later for church, the fillies didn't come up.

He sent Bob, who was in the cowshed doing the milking, to take a run down through the pasture to see if they were all right, but the fillies were not to be found. What Bob did find was a stretch of sagging fence where someone had pulled the staples out of all the wires on two posts.

Papa hurried back with Bob to look, and this time they saw tracks where the fillies had stepped over the wires and gone out in the road.

"It must've took at least two men to do it," Papa told them at breakfast. "One to hold the wires down an one to lead 'em over. Cause them fillies is skittish. Well, they been stoled. Mandy, I guess I got time for jist a sip more coffee."

There was no church for them today. As soon as Papa finished his coffee, he saddled Nellie and rode off to the sheriff's office in Kickapoo. It was noon before he got back, and he wasn't hopeful. The sheriff said the fillies were probably already out of the county by now. He would spread their description around, but he reckons that without a brand on them they were as good as gone.

Papa was in such a bad mood at dinner that she didn't dare bring up the subject of going to get her diploma. She knew Papa would say Nellie's trip to Kickapoo was enough for one day, and he was also bound to think she wasn't showing much concern about their losing the fillies if she still had her mind set on going for the diploma. So she didn't mention it.

Papa spent the next week riding Nellie around the county trying to find a trace of the stolen animals, while she spent her time chopping cotton and counting the days, and then the hours, until she had her diploma in her hand.

When she did, it was pretty as a picture, a big sheet of stiff white paper with greenish black curlicues spread around in each corner, the words "Certificate of Diploma" arched across the top like a rainbow, and underneath that her full name in fancy writing. Down to the right was a signature she couldn't read, but in the same place on the left was Mrs. Whitaker's signature clear as day. When she looked closer she found that her name was in the middle of a sentence that said this was a diploma of honor certifying that Martha Louella Lane had completed the course of study of the Oakridge School, Pottawatomie County, Oklahoma Territory.

She was so excited that if she had been alone she would have cried with happiness. After reading the diploma over again and again, she let Mrs. Whitaker roll it up in a page of newspaper and tuck in the ends so that it couldn't come unrolled.

"There you are," Mrs. Whitaker said, handing the diploma back to her. "Don't lose it. Now about next year. Since you don't seem to take to mathematics, I think you better prepare yourself in literature. I have all the books you will need, most of them my husband's, but he would have been pleased to have you use them."

Mrs. Whitaker went on talking about next year while she walked around the room, now and then pulling a book from a shelf and putting it on her desk. When she finished, she sat down and examined the pile and then leaned back in her chair.

"That's enough to get you started. Spend the next year doing as much reading as you can. In the meantime, come to school and help me with the teaching. Good experience for you. Next year we'll find a way for you to go up to the Normal School at Edmond for three months. That will be enough to get you started teaching. You can always go back for more schooling later. Well, what do you think?"

She didn't know what to say. All of these things coming one right after another were more than she could take in—the diploma, the pile of books to read, helping Mrs. Whitaker teach and, finally, going away to Normal School.

It was her dream coming true, and she was afraid to do more than nod at that smiling face across the desk, afraid if she said a word she would break the spell and wake up and find it was only a dream after all.

Chapter 17

The very next night after bringing home her diploma and having everyone in the family look at it and exclaim over it—all except Papa, who still seemed too worried about losing the fillies to take much interest in anything else—she started reading the novel Mrs. Whitaker had told her to begin with. Yet before she opened the cover she had to look up a word in her dictionary.

She knew well enough what pride was, she had even heard preachers preach about "pride" going before a fall, but she wasn't sure about "prejudice." As she was studying the definition, it crossed her mind that most of the people she knew were prejudiced against Indians—and that went for Papa, too, in spite of his being part Indian himself and being married to someone who was even more Indian.

As she tried to get interested in the novel, the thing that made it hard reading for her, and tempted her again and again to give it up and go on to another novel, was that she couldn't feel much sympathy for people who had plenty to eat and a dry roof over their heads, and still weren't happy.

And where did all the money come from to let them loll about with nothing more important to do than going visiting or having tea or going to balls, with servants around to do all the work? She had never known a family that didn't have to work for a living—even Mr. Barngrover with his three farms and a sawmill worked every day except Sunday. Worst of all, though, she couldn't stand that silly Mrs. Bennet.

She thought the novel about Emma Woodhouse was easier to read. She also thought Emma was too stuck on herself, and she doubted that Mr. Knightly was going to find her easy to live with for very long. But it was Heathcliff who made her shake her head most often. She couldn't believe such a queer person would be welcomed any place, and she was sure that if he tried to settle around here people wouldn't put up with him for very long. He would either have to start acting like everybody else or he would be in for trouble.

She was beginning to think Mrs. Whitaker's husband had been interested in some strange stories, until she started reading "Tess of the D'Urbervilles" and changed her mind. Her heart went out to that poor girl. Here was a person she felt at home with, and it was just too bad that Tess fell in love with such a wishy-washy man as Angel Clare. In spite of the sad ending, she turned right around and read the story again.

She was able to spend more time reading once the cotton was all chopped, for now all she had to do was tend the chickens and turkeys and help Mama in the garden. Soon she had read all the books Mrs. Whitaker had lent her and gone back for more.

The books were filling her mind with all kinds of interesting things about people and places and making Oklahoma Territory look smaller and smaller. She couldn't understand why more people didn't read books—Alice for instance, and Bob. Of course Papa read the same book all the time, the Bible, and so did Mama now and then.

Two of the new books in the second batch from Mrs. Whitaker's were about half the size of the regular novels, and when she got home with them she found that each one was a Shakespeare play. All she had read of Shakespeare's writing were the pieces of his plays in her Readers, and of those the only one she could remember well was the "to be or not to be," which they had all memorized and recited before the class.

She was surprised to find that even though the first play she started reading took place a long, long time ago, the people back then already seemed to be very hard on the Jews. She didn't think that Shylock was such a bad man, except for the pound of flesh. But that was too awful to think about.

She had grown up hearing people talk about Jews being so stingy, yet the only Jew she had ever seen was the foreign looking little man in the store, and he had given Alice a hat for nothing. As for lending money, before Mr. Barngrover lent Papa the money to buy Nellie and make the Runs for a homestead in Oklahoma Territory, he took a mortgage on the farm.

Anyway, Romeo and Juliet helped her to forget about Shylock. She had heard about these two before, but she had never run across any boys or girls like them. She tried to put herself in Juliet's place, but she couldn't see herself falling in love with Vernon or Fred after only one look at them, much less slipping off the next day to marry one of them. Yet, for the first time in her life, the excitement of the lovers aroused the same kind of feeling in her and made her even sadder for their death than for Tess's.

On the morning before the Fourth of July, Mama told her she would have to put her reading down for the day and help them get ready for the trip to Kickapoo for the big celebration. The program in the newspaper listed a barbecue dinner in the park after the reading of the Declaration of Independence, but Papa told Mama not to count on that.

"They's bound to be more people than eats," he said. "Besides, maybe the eats ain't meant for the likes of us."

So there were fryers to catch and kill and pick and singe and cut up; potatoes to get from the barn loft and peel and cut and boil for the potato salad; beans to pick and shell and cook; summer apples to gather and peel and slice for pies; a cake to mix and bake; and a dozen other things to do that kept her and Mama and Alice busy late in the night. They wanted an early start next morning in order to get to Kickapoo before the heat got too bad, and in time to see everything there was to see, beginning with the parade.

It seemed to her that she had barely fallen asleep before she was awakened in the near dark by Papa calling up the stairs that it was time to get up. On her way to let the chickens and turkeys out, she could tell by the close, sticky air that it was going to be another sweltering day, but everybody hurried through the chores and breakfast without mentioning the weather.

After breakfast when Papa drove the wagon down near the house for them to load up the food and things, she was unhappy to notice the youngest pair of mule colts running back and forth along the fence, making the strangest bawling and squalling noises she had ever heard as they tried to find a way to follow their mamas. But there was no help for it today. The colts had to stay home, and without a second look, she hurried back in the house for another load.

While Papa wandered round and round the wagon and team, fidgeting with the neck yoke, the harness, the double tree, and the spring seats—and finally checking his watch against the sun low in the clear sky—Bob and Ben filled the water jug at the well, wet it down and put it in the wagon, and she finished helping Mama and Alice carry out the food, and quilts, and pillows.

At last they were all settled in the wagon and ready to pull out, Bob driving, with Papa beside him. During the winter Papa had bought a second spring seat for the wagon, and she was sitting on it between Mama and Alice, while behind them Emma and Ben sprawled in the back of the wagon bed on the quilts and pillows covering the hay for the mares.

Just then Reuben started barking and running towards the lane, where sure enough, someone had turned in. Bob held up the mares, and they all watched a hack load of people pulled by a span of brown mules that came trotting up the lane with their big ears cocked towards the barking dog, ready to shy away if Reuben got too close.

"It's the McDermits," Bob said.

"What in the world is Ed McDermit doin' way off out here this time of day?" Papa wanted to know.

The hack turned in next to the wagon and everybody started calling greetings and piling down. She had never seen the McDermits in such good humor, everybody talking at once. But it was Mr. McDermit who caught her attention especially. He pumped papa's hand as if he hadn't seen him in years, and said, "Shore glad I got here in time, Jim. Thought I might have to chase you all the way to Kickapoo."

"You jist about did. Five more minutes and you'd 'a missed us."

"I got holt of a new field hand for you a couple of days ago, Jim. And knowin' you like I do, I jist knowed you'd want me to git him to you soon's I could."

"Field hand, Ed?" Papa slanted his head over one eye as if he wasn't sure he'd heard right. "You know I ain't got no money to pay no field hand."

"Oh, he'll work for nothin'. Ain't very big, but a great worker. You'll like him. He used to be a blacksmith's helper, but he wanted to come and live with y'all and—"

"Live with us? Well, now...." Papa hemmed and hawed and didn't seem to know what to make of all this talk, but Mr. McDermit kept right on telling him what a big help the new hand was going to be on the farm.

By now everybody else had stopped talking to listen to Mr. McDermit going on and on about this great new field hand. The funny thing was that except for Junior, who was driving the mules, the only other person in the hack was a bushy-headed boy about half his size sitting next to him.

Dressed in a brand new blue work shirt and blue striped overalls, the boy didn't seem to be paying much attention to all the talk. He just sat there looking around at everybody and smiling an easy smile. Yet when Mr. McDermit reached a hand up to him, the boy grabbed the hand and jumped to the ground in the middle of the two families.

Suddenly her ears were split by a shriek and she saw Mama and the bushy-headed boy rushing together, Mama calling, "Tommy! Tommy!" and both of them crying.

She staggered, felt like she was going to faint, and then she was on her knees beside Tommy, clutching him, her body shaking with great sobs. The others, calling Tommy's name and trying to get their hands on him, swarmed over her and pushed her aside.

Getting to her feet, she leaned against the wagon bed, still crying and so weak she could barely stand. "Tommy is alive!" she sobbed again and again to herself, feeling the fear of hellfire and damnation lifting from her heart. Something touched her arm and she turned to find Mama smiling at her out of a tear-stained face.

"Don't cry, Mattie. Tommy's alive!"

She tried to squeeze her eyes tight against the hot tears, but the relief of knowing she hadn't drowned Tommy after all was too much. She smothered her head against Mama's shoulder and let the tears come.

"Mattie," Bob called. "What're you cryin' for? Look here!"

She didn't answer, but when Bob said, "Look at Tommy," she turned and saw a grinning Tommy sitting straddle of Bob's neck, just the way he used to ride in the old days.

"Swin' me," Tommy said, holding out his hands. She caught hold of his wrists and pulled him off over Bob's head to the ground. But Tommy had grown too heavy to lift and swing around. She gave up trying and they stood face to face, laughing.

Papa announced that the trip to Kickapoo was off. He said they would have their own celebration right here, and Mr. McDermit agreed. The wagon and hack were unloaded and everything carried to the house, and the menfolk, including Tommy, went off to the barn with the two teams.

In the house, Emma and the McDermit girls disappeared up the stairs, but she hung around the kitchen with Alice, waiting on pins and needles to hear what Mrs. McDermit had to say about Tommy. As they unpacked the dinners on the kitchen table, Mrs. McDermit started by talking about the flood.

According to her, Ed had always felt a lot worse about being the cause of his mama's drowning than he ever let on, and had told her even before they got to Oklahoma Territory that when he got settled, no matter where at, he was going to go back and get his mama.

So last week when he had finished laying by his first crop on his own place, he bought a ticket on the railroad train at Kickapoo and rode to as near as he could to the little Indian settlement where his mama was buried. From there he hired a team and wagon for the rest of the way.

The Indian blacksmith who had preached the funeral and made the coffins was still there, and helping him in his smithy was a white boy. What a surprise that was having the boy look up from the anvil and say, "Howdy, Mistuh McDermit." And what a shock to find out it was Tommy Lane. The preacher said that two days after the funeral an Indian man and his son rode up with the boy, hoping they might be in time to catch up with his parents, and he took him in.

"Ed he dug up Tommy's coffin same time's he did his mama's," Mrs. McDermit went on, "and Ed said Tommy grabbed that old rusty pocket knife and kept it. I betcha he's got it right now in one of the pockets of them new overalls. Wasn't Ed a caution, Mandy, makin' a joke with Jim about the new field hand?"

Mama barely grunted by way of agreement, and she could tell that Mama was still too stirred up by Tommy's being alive to laugh along with Mrs. McDermit about the trick played on Papa. So was she, and as she stayed around the rest of the morning listening to them catching up on each other's news, she had to remind herself every few minutes that she had not drowned Tommy after all, that he was alive and out there somewhere in the barn lot right now with Bob and Ben and Junior, probably playing around with the mule colts. It was almost more than she could believe.

At noon everybody gathered on the front porch to eat the basket dinners they had planned to eat in Kickapoo. After Papa returned thanks—with special thanks to God for sparing Tommy—Mr. McDermit started talking about his trip, but even he didn't know how it came that Tommy was still alive. He said all Tommy could tell him was that the water washed him and Mattie away at the same time, but when he woke up in the Indian's house Mattie was gone.

And now as Tommy sat there while Mr. McDermit was telling the story, he didn't say anything himself, just went on eating and playing across Mama's lap with Ben as if he didn't know the grown-ups were talking about him. She had already noticed that Tommy still talked in a slurred voice the way he used to and he still seemed to be a little hard of hearing, but nobody let on about those things.

By the end of the day, it seemed to her that Tommy was already one of the family again, and he and Ben had taken to each other like old friends. When it came time for Ben to go to bed, he wanted Tommy to come in and lie down with him in his little trundle bed, but after Ben fell asleep Mama sent Tommy upstairs to sleep with Bob.

She went to bed that night thinking this was the happiest day of her life—even happier than when she got her diploma in her hands. Yet for the first time in months she had her old dream about the flood and Tommy. Over and over they tumbled in the foaming water while she struggled to tear his arms from around her waist.

Finally, as she lay alone in the plum thicket, crying because she had drowned Tommy, she heard Mama say as clear as anything, "Don't cry, Mattie. Tommy's alive!"

She woke up and lay without moving, listening, but all she could hear in the dark house was Emma's breathing.

Slipping silently out of bed, she crept towards the door. Bumping into the doorframe, she eased by it and kept going until she reached the banister at the head of the stairs. She crossed to Bob's door, went in, and walked slowly towards his bed, holding her hands out in front of her.

When her fingers touched the iron rim of his bedstead, she reached out and gripped it with both hands and stood listening in the dark. Gradually she could make out the two sets of breathing coming from the bed, a heavy rising and falling sound from the right, a lighter sound on the left. It went from one to the other, back and forth.

For a long time she stood there in the dark, smiling and crying at the same time as she listened to Tommy and Bob sleeping side by side.

The next morning at breakfast, watching Tommy trying to chew with his mouth too full of egg and biscuit, she thought how silly she had been to doubt that he was really still alive, but lying there in the middle of the night with that old dream fresh in her mind, it hadn't seemed silly at all.

Chapter 18

More than once during the next few days whenever Tommy's name passed across her mind, as usual her heart would start to sink with guilt. Then she would suddenly remember that Tommy was alive and such a flood of relief would come surging up that tears filled her eyes.

Yet on the following Monday when she was walking to school with Emma and Tommy, she was worried about him for another reason. He had never been to school, and knowing his trouble in speaking and hearing, she was afraid he might not be able to catch up with the other pupils his age.

Last week, without saying anything to anyone about her worry, she dug out an old primer, which had the McGuffey's marked out and the word Jimmy's written in its place.

For a moment her thoughts flew back to the day Papa gave Jimmy his last whipping, and then she put the picture of his bleeding welts out of her mind and asked Tommy to say the alphabet for her. She knew he used to know it by heart because she had taught him to read it, say it, and write it. But she found that he had forgotten most of it, and now even had trouble reading the letters.

Remembering that Aunt Sis said pupils learned something easier the second time around, she didn't fuss at Tommy for what he had forgotten.

She merely turned the page and started talking about the cat pictured there looking up at a bee—if it was a bee—and then on to the rat on the next page.

Before Tommy lost interest in those two animals, she had him happily reading "A cat and a rat. A rat and a cat." Then she let him look through the rest of the primer at the pictures of animals and people, pointing to the word for each one and spelling it out with him.

The next day Tommy wanted another look at the picture of the cat with the rat in its mouth, and asked her to read what it said underneath the picture. After that he was willing to try to read the alphabet with her over and over again.

They were at the big oak tree that evening, and as they walked home along the road and up the lane in the hot sunshine, they sang the alphabet together up and down the scale. Later when they went out to gather the eggs and close up the chicken house for the night, they sang it some more, and Ben tried to sing it with them. In two days Tommy was once more able to recite the alphabet and read it from A to Z in his primer.

Each morning during the rest of the week—for as long as she could keep him interested—she showed him how to make his letters, and each evening she read with him in his primer. She had crossed out Jimmy's name in the front of the book and helped Tommy write his own name there.

She had also given him Bob's book satchel and pencil box for his own. Tommy's pride in his new possessions was great, but no greater than hers in him when she introduced him to Miss Rogers. She spent the rest of the day in Mrs. Whitaker's room watching closely everything she did, and how she did it while keeping an eye on Tommy who seemed to be settling in fine.

Within a week Mrs. Whitaker was letting her take classes

outside in the shade of a blackjack tree to recite their lessons. There she learned quickly that it was harder to keep the attention of her pupils when they were outside the schoolhouse than when they were inside. Yet teaching was still as much fun as she had thought it was going to be, and the summer term of school flew by. Even Emma, now that Tommy was setting such a fine example for her, seemed to like school.

One Sunday as they were finishing dinner, Vernon showed up in a shiny black buggy with red spokes. Alice set a place for him at the table, and he sat listening wide-eyed to Bob tell about Tommy being found alive, saying from time to time, "Well I'll be," and looking around at everybody.

After Vernon had wolfed down a helping of peach cobbler and a glass of sweet milk, and told all the Carpenter news, he offered to take Bob for a ride to tryout his papa's new buggy, and in the same breath he asked her if she would like to come along.

She had planned to go out to the big oak that evening to read, but she looked at Papa, and Papa looked at Mama, who said, "I don't see why not, if you ain't gone too long, Vernon. It is such a fine day today."

Tommy wanted to go, too, and then Ben set up a howl to ride in the new buggy. While the others waited, Vernon gave the two boys a ride down the lane and up the road a ways, and came back with Tommy driving the horse at a fast trot, his face holding a grin as big as Vernon's.

A few minutes later she felt happy enough to grin as she went floating along towards Briggs, wedged comfortably in the swaying seat between Vernon and Bob, while the springs of the new buggy smoothed the bumps out of the road she was used to jolting over in the wagon.

Several times that summer she took a buggy ride with Vernon and Bob, and once with Vernon and Alice when Bob was sick. She also started going to Epworth League meetings. Alice had been after her for a long time to do it, but she had always said she would rather stay home and read a book. Yet a Sunday night came when she had finished all her books from Mrs. Whitaker, and she decided to go.

From the talking and laughing going on when they walked in the church house, it seemed to her more like a social gathering than a meeting of a religious group, especially when she saw Molly with another girl and a boy from school arguing loudly in the corner.

Noticing that most of the people there were as old or older than she was, she came to realize that all the older ones but Alice were married. Bob had once hinted that Alice had a beau here, and now out of curiosity she kept a close eye on her sister to see who it might be, but from the easy way Alice was talking and acting with everyone, she began to doubt that Bob was right.

The meeting was started by Marvin Cole, a sandy-haired widower who had the farm next to the Simpsons on the west. He began with a prayer and then led them in singing a hymn. After that, he read a passage of scripture from Mark about the kingdom of God being like a man casting a seed in the ground, letting it grow, and then cutting down the grain when the fruit was brought forth.

Marvin said this was supposed to be one of the parables of Jesus, and everybody started talking at once about what Jesus might be saying. Just a few did most of the talking. Some thought it was no parable at all and meant only what it said, that it told what a farmer did every year of his life—except that anyone knew you had to cultivate what you planted or the crop wouldn't amount to much.

Others argued that if the passage only meant what it said, Jesus wouldn't have taken the trouble to say it. Back and forth and around and around the talk went, and Marvin was forced to read the passage over and over again to clear up this or that point.

After hearing all the talk and listening closely each time the passage was read, she came to think Jesus might be saying that once a seed has produced a seed, its purpose is finished, and she was unhappy to think that was all there was to life. It didn't seem right to her that no matter how good she and Aunt Sis might be at teaching school, unless they had children they wouldn't be fulfilling their purpose on earth. She wanted to say something to the others about what she thought, but since this was her first meeting and since Alice and Bob hadn't said anything, she kept her opinions to herself.

The discussion wore itself out, with no general agreement on what the passage meant, and Marvin turned the talk to raising money to help support a missionary in the Philippines. It was soon agreed that the best way to do this was to hold a pie supper later in the fall.

Now that the business of the meeting was finished, one of the married women passed around fresh baked sugar cookies, while another served the men hot coffee she had made on the little coal oil stove up in the corner behind the organ. She noticed without saying anything about it that Bob drank a cup of coffee, something Mama didn't allow any of the children to do at home, telling them that coffee was bad for you.

She liked the meeting more than she expected to and decided to go the next Sunday night. This time she was surprised to find Fred there. He looked more grown-up in a dark coat and shoestring tie than he had when he sat beside her in his shirtsleeves at school. He came right over to talk to her, sat next to her during the meeting, and spent most of his time with her afterwards when everybody stood around talking and eating sticky gingerbread.

Fred's attention to her was not lost on Bob, and the first thing he said on the way home in the buggy was, "Say, Mattie, looks like Fred Dawson is tryin' to beat Vernon's time with you."

"No, he's just being friendly."

But Bob wouldn't settle for that. "Better watch your step, Mattie. You know him and Vernon are both Baptists. That wouldn't set too good with Papa."

She told him Papa had nothing to worry about, insisting she and Fred were just good friends. Knowing this was true, and since she was having fun at the meetings, she saw no reason to stay home just because Bob thought Fred Dawson was paying too much attention to her. Nor did she see anything wrong when Fred started walking out to the buggy with her after the meetings.

They would stand and talk until Alice and Bob came, and it seemed natural enough to her that Fred always took her arm to help her get in the buggy, although he must have known she didn't need any help.

One night they walked out as usual, the lamplight from the windows pushing the warm dark ahead of them just far enough that they could see where they were going. When they got to the buggy and she turned to say good night, she felt Fred's arms going around her, and then his lips were touching hers.

Surprised, she jerked away, felt her cheeks burning and hurriedly got in the buggy. She was too flustered to know what to say, but thankfully she could hear Alice and Bob coming and didn't have to say anything but good night.

She had no idea what they had seen, but on the way home she tried to talk and act her usual self, even though her thoughts kept coming back to Fred's lips touching hers. She wished he hadn't tried to kiss her, yet each time she thought about it a warm feeling tingled her cheeks in spite of herself. She was surprised at this, and puzzled that something in her seemed to like the feeling. At the same time she was a little scared without knowing why.

Last year at school when the girls had been talking about whether or not they would let a boy kiss them, most of them agreed with Molly, who said, "Sure, if I liked him."

She had no interest in kissing then, but in thinking about it now, she decided that even though she did like Fred, she didn't want him to kiss her. So she guessed she wouldn't walk out in the dark alone with him any more, if he ever asked her again.

He did ask her the very next Sunday night, but she put him off until Alice and Bob were ready to leave and they could all walk out together. From then on she found one excuse after another for not walking out alone with Fred. She felt ashamed for making these excuses, yet she didn't know how to tell him that even though she liked him she didn't want him to kiss her. She kept hoping he would figure this out for himself, but he didn't seem to.

Instead, he made things worse by asking her to go to a dance with him. She had heard about the dances that took place down around Briggs, but it never crossed her mind that Fred went to them, or that she would ever be asked to go to one. Since she had read about dances so many times in novels, she would have liked to go just to see what it was like, but after thanking Fred for asking her, she didn't have to think twice about sayin', "No."

She told him that in the first place Papa wouldn't let her go anywhere alone with any boy. Immediately Fred offered to get another couple to go with them, friends of theirs from school last year, but she had to tell him that wouldn't help a bit.

For in the second place, Papa didn't approve of dancing—anywhere, anytime, by anyone, under any circumstances. It wouldn't make any difference to Papa if the whole school—teachers and all—went with them, his answer would still be "no."

Fred listened politely enough to her reasons, but she could tell he wasn't satisfied to have her refuse him again.

Still, he kept on sitting with her in Sunday school and spending more of his time with her at the Sunday night meetings. Finally she reckoned that not going to the meetings would be the best way to keep from having to worry every Sunday night about how to put Fred off again without hurting his feelings. Yet it was not until cotton picking season came along, and she found she no longer had enough time to keep up with her reading, that she could do it with a clear conscience.

At Sunday school one morning she told Fred she wouldn't be at the meeting that night and told him why. He didn't say anything right away, but after the sermon, as they were walking out of the church, he said, "So you're not coming to any more meetings?"

"I don't have time," she said, and she started telling him about a history of England that Mrs. Whitaker had given her to read. Usually Fred took an interest in what she was reading, but today he surprised her by cutting her right off.

"What's the matter, Mattie, ain't the people in this part of the world good enough for you?"

"Sure, Fred, but I already know about us. If I'm going to be a good teacher, I have to learn about other people, too."

"Is that what Skinny Whitaker tells you?"

She had heard him make fun of Mrs. Whitaker before, but usually with a smile on his face. Now it was a sneer. She didn't understand why he was suddenly trying to pick a fight—and right here in the churchyard with people all around—but she just laughed and said, "If Mrs. Whitaker was heavy as Mrs. Reese, would you like her any better?"

"Not with her prissy way of talkin'."

"I don't reckon the people back East think it's prissy."

"Then she should've stayed back there with her own kind."

"Maybe we need some of her kind out here, too."

The more Fred ran Mrs. Whitaker down, the more she took up for her, even though she could see he didn't like it. After a few more jabs at each other, during which Fred stared at her as if he hated her, he turned and walked off in a huff without even saying, "Good-bye."

Sorry that she had riled him up so much, she watched him cut across the churchyard, looking from the back like a grown man. She kept her eyes on him while he jerked loose the slip knot tying Carrot's reins to Ben Center's fence. She half expected that any second he was going to look around and give her a big laugh to show her the whole thing was put on, but he rode off without a hint of a glance in her direction.

After that Fred stopped coming to the Calvary Methodist Church, and when Bob asked her why, she said she didn't know why. She guessed to herself that taking up for Mrs. Whitaker was one reason, and not walking out with him was the other, but she couldn't tell Bob this. She was sorry Fred had stopped being her friend, if he had. Maybe if she hadn't kept him from kissing her, it wouldn't have turned out this way, but she had, and she wasn't sorry she had.

Here it was only a short while since Tommy had returned from the dead and made her so happy she vowed never to be unhappy again, and already she was. Even having Tommy right here in the cotton patch with her as a reminder of how happy he had made her was not enough to keep her from feeling unhappy about her last meeting with Fred.

A turn in the weather only added to her unhappiness. The usual dry hot days for this time of year came to a sudden end. One night a norther blew in bringing ice to the water trough, and after that, cold rains started coming every week or two. Sometimes it was impossible for them to work in the field for days at a time. When the cotton did dry out enough to pick, they couldn't keep warm at it. The raw north wind chilled them to the bone and kept them shivering from morning till night.

Yet nobody complained, for they knew if they didn't pick every boll of cotton they could before the weather got even colder, and snow came, they would have to pick it later. Some farmers might give up after a time and leave a little of the cotton crop in the field, but not Papa.

Her reading for Mrs. Whitaker helped keep her unhappy thoughts about Fred out of her mind and made her think of better days ahead. Each night after supper, tired but warm now for the first time all day, she would get ready for bed, stick her nose in a book, and lose herself in another world. She couldn't help noticing, however, that people in those other worlds had their problems, too, mostly with other people. She was learning that everybody had problems.

When their problems did make her think of her own now and then, she could remind herself that one day she wouldn't have to worry about picking cotton or making a boy mad at her for not letting him kiss her.

Maybe as an unmarried schoolteacher she wouldn't be fulfilling her purpose on Earth according to the parable Marvin Cole had read at the Epworth League meeting, but if she could be as happy as Aunt Sis seemed to be, that would be enough.

Chapter 19

The bad weather didn't get any better as the weeks passed, but one Sunday night Alice and Bob came home from the League meeting with a piece of news that made her pay less attention to the cold and rain from then on. The pie supper was going to be held in two weeks, and even though that was before her sixteenth birthday, she immediately set her heart on going and taking a pie of her own. The next day she could hardly wait until she caught Mama alone and asked her.

Mama said she could, adding with a little laugh, "You thankin' Fred Dawson might come back and buy your pie?"

Startled to find Mama teasing her about something she didn't think Mama knew anything about, she quickly denied any such idea. Then, figuring that Mama must know all about her trouble with Fred anyway, she went on to say, "I liked Fred as a friend, but I didn't like it when he tried to kiss me."

Mama shook her head. "Oh, Child. All of 'em try to kiss you. And some try more'n that."

She blushed and didn't know what to say, but Mama went on. "It's the way men are. So don't let it go to your head. Jist the same, I wisht one of 'em would take some interest in Alice."

Letting that go by, she said, "Reckon I could borrow your big comb for that night? I was thinking of putting my hair up."

"I don't see why not," Mama said, and turned back to the stove to move something boiling over. "Now you go call the children. We're ready to eat soon's your papa and Bob come in. You know your papa don't like to be kept waitin' around."

With rain coming so often, it wasn't surprising that on Thanksgiving Day the ground was too wet to pick cotton. She was thankful for that, and while Papa was returning thanks at dinner, she started calling up all the things she had to be thankful for.

First of all, she was thankful the family was well and had a roof over their heads and plenty to eat. A cellar full of food—canned and dried—that Mama and Alice had put up. Several gallon buckets of new molasses down there, and more than enough Irish potatoes from the fall crop to last till spring. Bushels of turnips still in the ground, too, if you could stand to eat turnips.

More chickens than she could count. Eleven turkeys—nine hens and two gobblers—besides the gobbler on the table in front of her and another one she was still fattening up in the coop for Christmas dinner. Two brood sows, and plenty enough fat shoats—thirteen to be exact—to fill the smokehouse at hog killing time and have several live ones left over to sell when the man came around. Three cows milking, two heifers coming on, and a bull calf fat and ready for Papa and Bob to butcher when the weather turned really cold. All the milk and butter they could use and some spare butter to sell each week.

Oh yes, and eggs, the basket of eggs Alice sold each week along with the butter.

And for Babe and Doll and Nellie and the two spans of mule colts out in the lot—though she was not thankful that they had never seen hide nor hair again of the two stolen fillies. And enough corn in the cribs and hay in the loft and stacks to see all the stock through to grass, so Papa said. Seven bales of cotton already picked and sold, and several more bales in the field if it ever stopped raining long enough for them to pick it.

And Tommy! How could she forget Tommy after all she had been through with him? She should have put him first. And Reuben. And her sixteenth birthday coming up. And the pie supper. And her diploma. And Mrs. Whitaker for all her help.

She was still thinking of things to be thankful for when she heard Papa say, "Now, let's see what this turkey looks like." She opened her eyes in time to see the butcher knife cutting through the golden brown crust of the turkey breast and suddenly remembered she was thankful for Vernon's golden heart on the gold chain she was going to wear for the first time to the pie supper.

As the slice of white meat fell away from the blade of the butcher knife, Papa said, "Well, Tommy, what do you thank?"

Tommy answered with quick nods and his easy smile, while Ben clapped his hands and shouted "eat" so loud he scared himself and hid his face in Mama's lap.

It turned out to be the best Thanksgiving dinner she could remember, and it made her think of that first fall when they didn't have a Thanksgiving dinner, just a quick meal of cornbread and beans and then right back to the Carpenters' cotton patch. Now as she toyed with a piece of pumpkin pie, for which she barely had enough room left for a taste, she started thinking about the pie she was going to make for the pie supper.

Mama had offered to help her make her own favorite, a chocolate cream pie, and Alice had offered to make a second pecan pie and let her take it, saying two could be made as easy as one, but she said, "No, thank you," to both offers. She wanted whoever bought her pie to know she had made it herself, and since she had never made any kind but apple, it had to be an apple pie.

That made her think of something else. Would anyone buy it? From what she knew about pie suppers in Bear Valley, it was usually the girl's beau who bought her pie. If he didn't, he really didn't think much of her. Knowing this, men would sometimes bid on the pie of a pretty girl just to beat her beau out, or bid him up so high he would have to pay through the nose for it.

Since she didn't have a beau, and since the pie supper was open to the public, she knew the chances were good that she would have to eat her pie with a stranger, if anybody at all bought it. This was only one of the many things she had to worry about these days, and it was no wonder that while she was in the cotton patch every day it was fit to pick, her mind was usually somewhere else.

For a week she spent every night after supper cutting and sewing her new dress, and most of the days thinking about it. She liked the feel of the soft material Alice had bought, and the color, too, a reddish purple like wild grapes, but she was so nervous about getting it finished in time that she made mistakes that Alice had to help her fix.

When the dress was finished, she was afraid it wasn't going to fit right. She wished she had a long looking glass—like the one at Hodge's Racket Store in Kickapoo—to see for herself what it really looked like, but Alice raved about it and Mama told her it just suited her, so she was satisfied with that. She also wished she had a new pair of shoes to go with the new dress, but there was no chance of getting them, so she didn't ask.

Once the dress was finished and ready to wear, she started fussing with her hair, having decided to put it up for the first time in her life. She took hours from her reading each night practicing how to do it, and again she had to have Alice help her.

The first time she saw herself in the looking glass with her hair loosely drawn back from her forehead, coiled on top and held there by Mama's beautiful comb, she hardly recognized herself. Alice and Emma agreed that she looked scrumptious, and Alice made her go downstairs and show Mama.

Sometimes when she stopped to think about all the trouble she was making for herself over going out for the first time as a grown-up, she had to admit it really wasn't like her, and she didn't know what had got into her. Even worse, here she was all bothered about the way she was going to look, scared that no one would buy her pie, and acting as if she wanted to catch a beau, when what she wanted most of all in this world was to get the cotton picked as soon as possible so she could start back to helping Mrs. Whitaker in school.

Whenever she had doubts like this, all the bother seemed so silly she was tempted to call everything off and stay home. But she didn't, and by the time the day of the pie supper rolled around, she wasn't thinking about much else but it.

Since it came on a Saturday, they had to pick cotton only till noon, and in the evening while the rest of them went to Briggs—except for Mama and Ben—she spent the time making her pie and getting herself ready for that night. Even so, she was still struggling with loose ends of hair when Alice came home from Briggs and showed her in a few minutes how to start all over again and do it right.

Later when she rode down the lane between Alice and Bob in the buggy, Mama's shawl over her head and a spicy smell coming from the warm apple pie on her lap, she was too happy to talk. She was thinking of her last look of many in the looking glass, and in her mind's eye she could still see Mama's tortoise shell comb shining in her hair, her sharp widow's peak not so noticeable now that the hair was not pulled back tight, her eyes shining bluer than she had ever seen them. A rosy tinge showed through her cheeks—probably because she was so nervous—and the golden heart stood out like a jewel against the high, dark neck of her new dress.

She felt like a fairy princess going to her first ball, and it didn't matter in the least to her that instead of being in a carriage drawn by four prancing horses, she was riding in a rattletrap buggy pulled at a slow trot by Nellie.

When they got there, the church house was almost full of people, all in their Sunday best and even noisier than at Christmas time. A good many in the crowd were strangers to her, although she had seen some of the men in Briggs at one time or another. Alice found a place for them to sit up near the front, and they left their coats there with Bob and took their pies up to the altar, where two long tables had been placed end to end.

Already rows of pies—and a cake here and there—had been put on the tables for everyone to parade around and look at—the women looking to see what the other women had brought. She had no idea what the men were doing wandering around there, except maybe hunting for a likely looking pie to bid on later. After she and Alice had handed over their pies to a couple of the League women, and had been told a number and reminded to remember it, they walked around the tables doing their own looking.

When they got back to where they had left Bob, Vernon was sitting with him. She had never once thought that Vernon would be here tonight, although she suspected that Fred might. At first she couldn't think how Vernon, from way off down in the bottom where he lived, could have heard about a pie supper way out here, and then she remembered that Bob had gone goose hunting with him Thanksgiving morning.

"Mattie!" Vernon looked her up and down a couple of times before bursting out again. "Well I'll be! I swear I wouldn't 've knowed you if I'd met you in the road."

She took this to mean that he liked her hair, and she was relieved to think it wasn't falling down, something she had suspected from the number of men looking at her as she and Alice were walking back to their seats just now. Suddenly remembering that she was wearing Vernon's necklace, she put her hand up to feel if it was still there. She hoped Vernon liked it, but if he noticed it at all he didn't say anything about it.

In a few minutes Marvin Cole appeared in the pulpit and introduced the auctioneer, Rufe something or other, a bald-headed fat man with a red face as round as a pumpkin. Many of the men seemed to already know Rufe. At least there was a lot of loud joshings going back and forth as he peeled off his coat, loosened his necktie, rolled up his sleeves, and patted his big belly.

He waited for the laughter to die out, and then in a voice that shook the rafters he got down to business. "Aw'right, men. Unlimber your pocket books and get ready to start shelling out for a good cause. Y'all ready?"

Whistles and shouts answered him as he took a pie from one of the League women and called out, "Now lookee here! The number one pie of the night!"

With one hand he swung the pie high above his head so that everybody could see it, bringing gasps from some of the women afraid he was going to drop it or turn it upside down. But Rufe just grinned at their gasps and gave the pie another swing.

He then pretended to examine it from every angle, hefted it, shook it, smelled it and held it up to the light. "Looks good. Smells good. And you can bet she tastes good. Mmmm, hunh! I tell you, a gal can turn out a pie like this is bound to be a mighty fine filly herself. So what am I offered? Two dollars? Do I hear two dollars?"

"Yeah," sang out a man behind her.

Quick as lightning, Rufe stabbed his finger at the man and shouted, "Got two dollars! Now who'll make it THREE?" Sweeping his glance across the church, Rufe chanted, "Three, three, three! Got TWO! Who'll make it THREE? Three, three, three! Got TWO! Now who'll gimme THREE?" The pie supper was under way.

The first pie sold for four dollars and twenty-five cents, but most of the ones coming after it sold for less than half of that. The final bidding on each pie usually moved slowly up by dimes and then nickels as Rufe carried the bidders along with jokes and jibes to get every cent he could out of them.

Now and then when the bidding stalled, he would get a scornful look on his round red face and threaten to bid on the pie himself, declaring, " Y'all better come on now before I git in on it. Cause if I buy it, you're likely to have a lot of explainin' to do to the little woman that made this pie."

She had been to more public sales in Bear Valley than she could remember, but she had never seen an auctioneer like Rufe for keeping everything in a big hurry and moving the bidding right along at the same time. Vernon told them that Rufe ran a mule barn down south of Kickapoo where he held an auction once a month, and that he was even funnier selling mules than he was selling pies.

She was surprised when Bob started bidding on a pie, and even more surprised when he kept bidding until he bought it for two dollars and fifty cents—his wages for two and a half days of work when he could find a farmer who needed a hand and Papa could spare him.

As the number of her own pie got closer she began to get nervous, but when Marvin Cole bought Alice's pie, he gave her something else to think about. Maybe Marvin was Alice's beau after all, but if he was, he was mighty quiet about it, and so was Alice.

At last Rufe held up her pie and started saying the usual silly things about it, embarrassing her as much as if he had been saying things about her. She couldn't think which was going to be worse, no one bidding on her pie or having it bought by one of the strange men she had seen bidding on other pies. While she was fretting about it, Rufe started the bidding at two dollars.

She was relieved when she heard some one way in the back say, "Yes." Immediately Rufe looked at her and shouted, "And THREE!" Before she could think what to make of this, he lifted his look to the back of the church again and called, "Got THREE! Do I hear FOUR?"

She didn't hear any answer this time, but apparently Rufe saw one, for he called, "Got FOUR!" and once more turned his red face towards her. This time she caught Vernon ducking his head just a fraction, and when Rufe shouted, "And FIVE!" she realized it was Vernon that Rufe was looking at and not her.

Back and forth the bidding went, with more and more people shifting their looks from one bidder to the other as if watching two men walk towards each other playing "burn out" with a baseball, the watchers anxious to see who was going to drop the ball first. Rufe was no longer calling anything but the bids, his voice getting more excited with each bid.

"And EIGHT!"

"And NINE!"

"And TEN!"

The bidding was going so fast she hardly had time to think what was happening, but when she saw Vernon dip his head and heard Rufe call out, "And ELEVEN!" she grabbed Vernon's arm to stop him from bidding any more. No pie was worth that much money. The crowd had become so quiet that her whispered "no" to Vernon filled the church and brought a scattering of laughs.

But it had no effect on the bidding, or Rufe. Up and up the bids went, Rufe shouting them out dollar by dollar. She had no idea who the other bidder was, and she was too embarrassed to look around and find out.

She still wanted to stop Vernon from wasting his hard earned money, but when he kept on dipping his head no matter how hard she squeezed his arm, she finally took her hand away. Thinking that all this was somehow her own fault, she dropped her head and wished she had never come to the pie supper in the first place.

By now there wasn't a sound to be heard except Rufe's voice. When he announced a twenty-dollar bid from the back of the church, she looked up at Vernon, hoping he would have the good sense to stop now, but down snapped his head and Rufe boomed out, "And twenty-ONE!"

At this there was a commotion in the back of the church and then a sound of boots clumping on the floor. As one person the crowd turned to see what was happening, and she saw Fred Dawson storming out the door of the church, leaving the door swinging open after him.

Rufe didn't waste any words over that disturbance. Nodding at Vernon, he said in a quiet voice, "Sold for twenty-one dollars to the young man with the porkypine hair cut."

He then took a cake handed to him, and instantly he boomed out, "Awwwright! Jist lookee here at the CHOCOLATE CAKE! Ain't it a jim-dandy? Who'll say five dollars?"

But she was no longer listening. She was thinking how miserable Fred must be feeling riding off alone through the dark out there. Yet even while she was sorry for him, she was thankful that he had run out of money when he did, otherwise there was no telling where the bidding would have stopped.

Later, as she was cutting the pie, she thought of the ball of pie dough, the five apples, the sugar, butter and cinnamon, and she shook her head at Vernon's twenty-one dollars gone. No pie was worth that much money, and she could still hardly believe Vernon had paid it for this one.

Yet when she started to scold him for doing it, he stopped her, his freckled face lost its happy look and turned serious. "Mattie, no matter what it cost, I come to buy your pie."

To keep from bursting into tears, she had to turn her head away and bite her lip. Yet later that night when Vernon stood with her at the door of the dark house, after holding her hand under the lap robe during the ride home in his buggy, she felt nothing at all as she let him kiss her good night.

Chapter 20

The morning after the pie supper, she still felt embarrassed at having been the cause of such a to-do between Fred and Vernon, and she hoped it would soon be forgotten. At breakfast she seemed to be listening while Bob told the story at length, with Mama and Papa now and then clucking their disapproval, but she was thinking mostly about Vernon kissing her, and how it hadn't been exciting the way the girls at school were always making kissing out to be. It hadn't been exciting at all.

Later that morning at Sunday school some of those same girls were full of talk about the stir raised over the bidding on her pie. Molly, who had been at the pie supper, went so far as to say she would have just loved to have two boys fighting that way over her pie.

Then Molly wanted to know if she was going to marry Vernon, and she had to remind her that she was going to be a schoolteacher and never get married, to Vernon Carpenter or anybody else. At this, Molly and the other girls looked at each other and rolled their eyes as if to say, "Tell us another one."

So much was said about her and Vernon and the pie supper that she got tired of hearing it and was glad when Sunday was over and she went back to the field on Monday to help finish the cotton picking. Since she had thought of the pie supper as the real celebration of her sixteenth birthday, when her actual birthday came along she paid no attention to it, although Alice did make a cake for her. Just the same, being sixteen years old made her feel very grown-up.

One Saturday she had the satisfaction of seeing the last sack of cotton weighed up and knowing she could now start back to school with Emma and Tommy.

After dinner the next day she had just settled down to an evening of reading when she heard Vernon downstairs. Closing her book, she stood up and took a quick look in the looking glass. She hadn't seen Vernon since he kissed her good night after the pie supper, and she was a little nervous about meeting him in front of the family, afraid they might notice something.

Yet Vernon's friendly greeting was the same as usual, and so was his grin as he sat listening to Bob teasing him about being rich enough to pay nearly a month's wages for an apple pie.

It was too cold to go for a buggy ride, and she was thankful that the family was there to keep the conversation going. As much as she liked Vernon, she found it hard to talk to him for any length of time by herself because he gradually left it to her to do all the talking.

On Christmas day Vernon was back again with a present for her. As she lifted the lid of a black leather case lined with white satin, she saw half hidden below in the dimpled red plush a fingernail file, a pair of shiny little scissors, and several other shiny things she didn't know the use of. But she did know that this was a manicure set, and even though it reminded her of how awful her hands looked after months of picking cotton, she was happy to have such a present and told Vernon so.

She had expected that he might come today with a present for her, and she had a gift for him already wrapped and under the tree—a pair of red tassels for the bridle of his horse. She had Alice buy them for her one Saturday evening at the harness shop in Briggs, thinking then that she might give them to Fred some time for his horse, but it hadn't worked out that way.

She was a little surprised that Vernon wanted her to go right outside in the cold with him to put the tassels on his horse's bridle, but she was shocked out of being cold when he finished tying the tassels on the headstall and turned to her and said, "Mattie, I reckin' you know I want to marry you."

When she thought about it later in her room, she didn't know why she should have been so shocked, especially after what he had spent for pie, but she was. Even so, she had enough gumption left to thank Vernon and tell him she liked him as a friend, before she told him she was going to be a schoolteacher and never get married.

At the same time she was talking to him, she was thinking that all of this would never have happened if Mama had let her give the necklace back to him that first Christmas the way she wanted to.

Vernon had listened calmly to all she had to say, and then he told her he was ready to wait for as long as it took for her to change her mind. This made her feel more miserable than ever, and when they got back in the house she could hardly wait for him to go home, although at the same time she was ashamed of herself for having such a mean thought.

In the following days, she had too much else on her mind to think a lot about Vernon, what with being back at school and busy helping Mrs. Whitaker with the children during the day and reading her books at night. Yet now whenever she read about someone falling in love, it would remind her of Vernon, and she would start feeling sorry for him again. At the same time she couldn't help thinking about how much she liked teaching the children, and how she was sure to enjoy it even more when she got to be a real teacher. She usually ended up believing that everything had worked out for the best after all.

As the weeks passed and Vernon didn't come back to the house, now and then someone in the family would wonder out loud what had happened to him, but she never said anything. One day Alice asked her outright if she and Vernon had had a falling out, and she told her sister what had passed between them.

Alice said that Vernon would probably make her a better husband than most, but she didn't blame her for wanting to be a schoolteacher.

Alice confessed that she wouldn't mind getting married herself, but one thing she was certain of was that she would rather die an old maid than marry a man who already had children.

Remembering that Marvin Cole had bought Alice's pie but that he did have two children, she was tempted to ask Alice if Marvin was her beau. Yet she let the chance go by, afraid of making Alice feel bad if the answer was "no" and maybe even worse if it was "yes."

One Saturday evening in Briggs, she ran into Fred. She tried to be friendly, and with her doing most of the talking they did pass the time of day a little, but it wasn't the easy kind of talk they used to have before he said those hateful things about Mrs. Whitaker that day in the churchyard.

She made no mention of the pie supper, yet all the time they were talking Fred was fidgeting a chip around in the dirt with the toe of his boot, and as soon as he could he tipped his hat and hurried off.

She walked along slowly towards the feed store. It was strange that Fred and Vernon were both mad at her, when so far as she knew she had never done an unfriendly thing to either one of them. Maybe it wasn't possible to be friendly with a boy the way she was with Molly, and her thoughts went back to Bob touching her breast with that nubbin of corn to hint at why Vernon liked her. Maybe Fred had liked her for the same reason, but whether he did or not she hoped there wouldn't be any more boys to worry about.

In spite of being uneasy whenever she thought about Fred and Vernon, she was having the best time at school she had ever had. Her greatest enjoyment was coming from teaching the children about those things in their books that she liked when she used to read them.

She didn't mind that most of the pupils weren't as interested as she was in a story or poem, or whatever else they were studying. From her earliest days in school she was used to hearing boys and girls say they didn't like this or that or the other thing, and she had gone on liking it just the same.

Now when some of her own pupils said the same things to her, or acted as if they thought school was something bad that had to be put up with—like having measles or picking cotton—it made her want to try even harder to show them what they were missing. Yet she found out that with some she failed no matter how hard she tried, and this worried her until she had a talk about it one day with Mrs. Whitaker.

Mrs. Whitaker finished by saying, "Do the best you can for your pupils, Mattie, but don't feel hurt if they fail to learn as much as you'd like. If you do, you only make things worse. Always remember that what children need most of all is encouragement."

By the time winter gave way to spring, she was so pleased with her teaching and studying that she would have been happy to go on this way forever, but one day Papa took her and Emma and Tommy out of school to start hoeing corn and then chopping cotton. She didn't complain with the others about the usual hot sun and blistered hands, because she now appreciated more than ever how much one day she was going to like being a schoolteacher all the time.

In early June, she got a letter from Mrs. Whitaker asking her to come and see her. Once there, she listened with increasing interest to Mrs. Whitaker tell her about a family that had a son laid up from an accident and wanted someone to teach him during the summer. Mrs. Whitaker said if she would take the job she could earn enough money to pay her way to Normal School in the fall.

She was almost beside herself with excitement. Her dream was coming true faster than she expected. Carrying a fresh supply of books out to the buggy, she put Nellie to a fast trot for home in spite of the heat, and her thoughts leaped ahead to going away to the Normal School up at Edmond. In her mind she was already there, until she happened to notice a green field of cotton she was passing and her heart sank. What if Papa made her stay home this fall to pick cotton?

Scared now, and her excitement gone, she waited with her news when she got home until she could talk to Mama alone. Mama was sure Papa wouldn't mind her doing the teaching once the cotton was all chopped, but said it would be best not to say anything about Normal School until she had the money in her hand, and then they would see.

She cheered up a little at this, and at supper when Papa said he supposed it would be all right for her to take the job, she was almost as excited again as she had been when she left Mrs. Whitaker's house. Papa went on to remind her not to drive Old Nellie too hard in this hot weather, the first time she had ever heard him call Nellie "old."

Her new pupil was a ten-year-old boy much like the feisty, tousle-headed boys she had been teaching at Oakridge, although this one walked with crutches and had one leg wrapped in something that kept it stiff as a stick.

Orin had come that spring with his papa and mama and little sister, Amy, on a railroad train from Indiana. His first day at the farm he had broken his leg "in a few places"—as he put it—when his new horse bucked him off against a feed rack. Once he asked and found out that she had never been bucked off a horse, he seemed to take to her right away. Noticing this, she didn't think it necessary to tell him that Old Nellie and the work mares were the only horses she had ever ridden.

About nine each morning she would drive in between the big stone pillars at the entrance to the Marlowe farm, go past the yellow two-story house and leave Old Nellie tied in the shade of a pecan tree back near the horse lot fence.

Behind this white plank fence stood a big red barn with a shed on either side, all trimmed in white. In a separate lot to the left was a red dairy barn, and to the right was a red chicken house with the south side all windows. Way off behind it, farther than Orin wanted to hobble the day he was showing her the farm, was a hog pasture with a scattering of little red houses not much taller than the sows themselves. Back of all of these red buildings and white fences, level green fields of cotton, corn and alfalfa shimmered in the hot sun.

She had never seen such a farm, and she wasn't surprised when Orin told her it used to belong to a banker, adding, "But he died." It was even fancier than Mr. Barngrover's home farm, but

Mr. Barngrover did his own farming while Mr. Marlowe had a family living in a little house back towards the river that did his.

Orin told her that his daddy had grown up on a farm, but he was a lawyer now and usually drove into Kickapoo each morning in a buggy before she got here. Yet she did see him one morning, a big, heavy, red-faced man who looked much older than Mrs. Marlowe and talked very loud through tobacco-stained teeth. He was a man of big gestures liking to laugh and smoke a cigar while he talked.

Everything inside the house was so rich looking it made her want to whisper. All the rooms, except the kitchen, had dark furniture, thick carpets, and heavy curtains, which seemed to smother noises. She liked that because when she was upstairs with Orin in his study room she couldn't hear anything else going on in the house.

But what opened her eyes widest was an outhouse inside the house—the first one she had even seen. And that wasn't all. In the same room, which they called the bathroom, was a white bathtub almost as long as a horse trough. It made the round, galvanized washtub they bathed in at home seem almost as little as the pan they washed their hands and face in.

After the first day, Mrs. Marlowe insisted that she must eat dinner with them, although for some reason she called it lunch. The table was set with the prettiest dishes, all the same looking and not one chipped or cracked. The knives and forks and spoons were silver, and by each plate was a starched white cloth you unfolded and put on your lap—napkins they were called—in case you spilled something while you were eating.

One day Mrs. Whitaker came to lunch. She and Mrs. Marlowe had gone to college together back in Connecticut. As they sat talking and laughing about their college days—calling each other Anne and Thelma—she thought Mrs. Whitaker looked years younger than Mrs. Marlowe, who had a puffy face and had grown fleshy all over.

She didn't see how this could be, for from what she knew, it was Mrs. Whitaker who had done the hard work and the suffering. Mrs. Marlowe even had a Negro woman to do all her cooking and housework.

She started Orin's lessons each day with arithmetic, and for almost the same reason that she first ate the food on her plate she liked the least—to get it over with. Next came what she liked best—reading, which she followed with writing and then spelling.

In the evening, penmanship was first and history after that. Last came geography. She had learned from Mrs. Whitaker that getting and keeping a pupil's attention was the most important part of teaching, so it seemed to her that by putting Orin's favorite subject last she could keep his attention longest. Some days it worked better than others.

One evening after Orin's geography lesson in the breezy corner room, she drove out in the hot sun towards home and saw a tall man walking in the road ahead of her. Overtaking him, she called out asking if he would like a ride. As she spoke she noticed he was carrying a bulging knapsack on his back and wearing a soldier's broad hat like the ones she had seen so many times in the newspaper.

The man stopped and turned to answer. His quick smile caught her by surprise, and she found herself smiling back at a young man whose eyes were as blue as her own, his face sun-browned and shiny with sweat.

"Thanks," he said and hesitated a moment, seeming as surprised as she was. "It is getting a little warm."

Once the young man was seated next to her, and she had Old Nellie moving again, the two of them sat there as silent as if the cat had their tongues.

Eventually thinking it was her place to say something, she started to speak just as the young man did. Laughing, they were soon at ease and talking away. She told him her name and where she lived and what she was doing way down here in the bottom.

His name was Roberts, Hamp Roberts, and he lived on the other side of Briggs, but he knew the Thorpe place where she lived, mainly because it was close to old friends of the family, the Wisdoms. The Wisdoms and Roberts were a part of the bunch that came up from Texas together for the Run. Yes, he knew Molly Wisdom, had known her since she was a baby.

She liked Hamp's voice without knowing exactly why, but maybe because it was so alive. After walking all the way from Kickapoo in this hot sun, most people would have sounded half done in, but there he sat as fresh as dew. He was saying that his family was originally from Georgia and had come out to Texas after the War. "The War between the States, that is. I'm just getting back from this last one myself."

She asked where all he had been, and as he talked of Florida, San Francisco, Hawaii, and the Philippines she wished Orin could be here. This was much better than her own geography lessons.

When they passed her church she pointed it out to Hamp, but he shook his head and said it wasn't there when he went away to the army. Since she couldn't remember any Robertses connected with the church, she guessed they must not be Methodists.

As if reading her mind, Hamp said, "Mama's a Baptist, and Papa's not much of anything. I used to belong, but lately I seem to be takin' more after Papa."

When she reached her driveway, she wished she had an excuse for driving Hamp on home and keeping the geography lesson going, but she didn't. She pulled Old Nellie to a stop and Hamp jumped down. Smiling again and giving her a half-salute, he thanked her and struck out up the sandy road.

Without a word, or tug on the lines from her, Old Nellie turned off the road and went slowly up the lane and past the house to stop at the front gate of the horse lot fence. Only then did Hamp Roberts' parting smile fade out of her mind.

That night as she went over Orin's lessons for the next day she had trouble keeping Hamp Roberts out of her thoughts. Too bad he wasn't a Methodist or she might see him in church sometime.

No sooner did this thought cross her mind than she started scolding herself. What was she doing wanting to see Hamp Roberts again? Suppose they did get to be friends? He would probably wind up being unhappy with her the way Fred and Vernon had.

Besides, in the meantime he would just be taking her mind off her studying and schoolteaching. "Don't be a fool," she said to herself and went to sleep.

Chapter 21

The rest of that week, without trying to or even wanting to, she often thought about Hamp Roberts. Each time she drove by the place where she had stopped to give him a ride in the buggy she was reminded of his quick smile, and the blue eyes looking up at her.

She had Orin studying the geography of South America these days, but in their talks about the rainforest of the Amazon or the pampas of Argentina she would often find herself thinking about the coconut palms of the Philippines. Hamp Roberts would appear, smile and all, whacking the end off a green coconut with his bolo knife the way he had told her about, and drinking the milk. Suddenly she would realize where she was and hurry back to South America before she was missed.

Sunday morning when she walked into her Sunday school class and saw Hamp sitting next to Molly, a flash of warmth touched her cheeks. During the lesson, instead of taking part in the discussion as she usually did, she caught herself giving her attention to the way a tuft of light brown hair at the nape of Hamp's neck slid back and forth over his white shirt collar as he moved his head.

Once the Sunday school classes were over and the curtains on the wires crisscrossing the church were pushed back against the walls so that everybody could visit around until time for the sermon, there was no polite way she could get out of moving out in the aisle and talking with Molly and Hamp.

She noticed that he was taller than she remembered, even taller than Bob. But when he smiled warmly down at her he was the same friendly person again.

"Mattie," he began, "I bet you're surprised to see me here after what I said about not going to church."

Before she could admit that she was, Molly spoke up to say that Hamp was going to talk about the Philippines at the League meeting that evening. "You just have to come," Molly exclaimed. "After all, you've got a twenty-one dollar interest in that country. You bring her, Bob. You hear?"

She smiled at Molly but didn't say she would or wouldn't come, and that evening while trying to read at the big oak tree, she changed her mind several times about going. At supper Bob was so full of talk of going to hear a soldier tell about killing savage Filipinos armed with spears and bows and arrows that he got Tommy all excited and wanting to go, too.

Papa scolded Bob for thinking he would hear that kind of talk in the house of the Lord. "After all," Papa said, "you're a Christian, Bob. By now you ought to have learned enough to know Jesus was agin' killin'. He told the Jews they was suppose to love one another."

She finally decided to go, yet even as she was dressing with more care than usual, she didn't really know why she was going. She told herself that maybe by getting used to seeing Hamp he would no longer take her mind off her school teaching.

He began his talk by saying he hoped the Epworth League hadn't wasted its money by helping send a missionary to the Philippines. Yet he was bound to say that from what he had seen of the natives in the back country there, anyone trying to make Christians out of them might have a longer row to hoe than he was used to hoeing. He spent the rest of the time painting such an awful picture of the heat, the rain, the insects, and the people in the jungle that he made Oklahoma Territory seem like a paradise beside it.

Somewhere during the talk she found herself paying more attention to what Hamp looked like than to what he was saying. She noticed the curve of his lips when he smiled, the blue eyes that came to rest on hers now and then, and the mass of tawny hair that fell over his right ear. His nose was too long for him to be handsome. Yet there was something about him that had caught hold of her and wouldn't let go.

Afterwards when everyone was having lemonade and cookies, and a crowd—including Bob—was surrounding Hamp, she stood in the back with Alice, and Marvin Cole listening to them talk about whether it might not have been better to send the missionary to Africa.

Yet in a few minutes Hamp was at her elbow greeting her and telling her he was glad she came. It wasn't her nature to hide what she felt, but as she introduced Hamp to Alice she kept under control the little tug of excitement she had begun to notice going on inside of her and wouldn't let go.

On the way home Alice had nothing but good things to say about Hamp Roberts, which made up for Bob's disappointment that—as Papa had predicted—he didn't say a single word about killing Filipinos.

She listened and said nothing, determined not to let her family know that she had any opinions about him, much less give them a hint that she liked him. She had already had enough teasing about beaus without having Hamp Roberts brought into it.

Days passed without her seeing Hamp again. He didn't fade out of her mind as she expected he would, but she was so busy working with Orin all day and reading for Mrs. Whitaker after supper that she didn't mind not seeing him. He didn't come to church again, and even though Molly kept bringing his name up, she was careful not to ask her anything about him. She was sure that before long she would stop thinking about Hamp Roberts.

One Sunday evening after dinner she had just got herself settled in her favorite spot under the big oak and opened her book when she heard voices coming along the road below her. Sometimes she crept out to the edge of the knoll and spied on people she heard going by, noticing that they never looked up her way as they passed—unless a horse caught her scent and threw its head around. Today she stayed sitting against the tree, more interested in her book than in finding out who was passing by.

The talk got louder and louder and in a few seconds she looked up and saw with mixed feelings that Molly and Hamp Roberts were climbing the knoll to where she sat.

Molly said they had come to pay her a visit, and for the next hour or so they sat around in the shade and talked about whatever crossed their minds. When the subject came around to the war, Hamp told of hearing about the Spaniards blowing up the "Maine" and said he decided that very day to run off and join the army. It didn't take him long to find out that he liked farming better than soldiering, and now he was happy to be alive and well and back on the farm again.

But it wasn't all visiting. Molly finally got around to the real reason for their being here. Next Saturday she was going to have a party for her sixteenth birthday, and since her papa had been sick this morning and she had to stay home from church, she had come over to invite her and Bob to come.

In the middle of the talk about the party, it crossed her mind that Hamp must be Molly's beau, and a pang of jealousy struck her. She was immediately mad at herself for being so dumb she hadn't realized this until now, especially since Hamp had told her the day they met that he had known Molly all his life.

For the rest of the visit, she didn't enjoy Molly's conversation as much as she had before. When they left, it was easy enough for her to give Hamp a good-bye that was more sober than her greeting had been.

She picked up her book again, but the sight of Hamp holding Molly's arm as they went down the knoll stuck in her thoughts. Finally she said to herself, good, now there wasn't the slightest excuse for Hamp Roberts being a distraction anymore. She could put him out of her mind once and for all.

Slamming the book shut, she got up and walked home with long strides. When she got there she started an argument with Emma over nothing. Mama put a stop to it and later told her privately that maybe she was spending too much time on her books and it might be a good idea if she put them down for a spell.

Looking at Mama's worried expression, she couldn't tell her that reading wasn't the reason she was upset, so she just nodded and walked out to the barn lot fence and rubbed Old Nellie's nose when she came over to be petted.

From then on, in spite of putting Hamp out of her mind again and again, she found herself thinking about him more than usual, and about Molly, too. As much as she liked Molly, she thought if Molly had been as true a friend as she ought to be, she would have said long ago that Hamp was her own beau, instead of leaving her to figure it out for herself. She was put out with Molly Wisdom.

At Orin's, for the first time since she had started teaching him, she found herself getting short-tempered over his mistakes, and she raised her voice more than once to him about little things that wouldn't have bothered her before. One day after lunch Mrs. Marlowe took her aside, asked her if she felt all right and told her she could take the rest of the day off if she wanted to.

Feeling guilty, she thanked Mrs. Marlowe but stayed on. She was ashamed that she had let a personal problem get in the way of her teaching and she made up her mind not to let it happen again.

When the day came around for Molly's birthday party, she wasn't excited about it as much as Bob seemed to be. Hamp Roberts was on her mind all right, but she told herself this didn't mean she was looking forward to seeing him again.

Yet when she was dressing for the party she kept Bob waiting out in the backyard playing catch with Tommy and Ben while she primped and primped. Finally she called Alice up to help her fix her hair, and all the time she was thinking about Hamp.

Since Molly's house was only half a mile away, she and Bob were going to walk over. They went down the lane a little before sunset and turned west up past the big oak. The sun was in their eyes and a slice of moon as pale as skim milk was riding in the sky behind them.

They walked without talking, Bob whistling a snatch of a tune every now and then and her fretting silently along beside him. Knowing she was going to come face to face with Hamp Roberts in a few minutes, she wished she wasn't so nervous, but wishing didn't calm her down.

Papa had said he knew Sam Wisdom well enough to know there wouldn't be any dancing at the party, and by the time they reached Molly's corner the sound of singing voices and a strumming guitar came floating through the twilight.

"Jay Jay," Bob said, but her mind was elsewhere.

It was J.J. Barnes, seated at the top of the steps to the front porch, head bent over his guitar, while below him a cluster of boys and girls stood swaying slowly as they sang "My Old Kentucky Home." Other boys and girls stood around on the grass talking and laughing.

She knew them all, and seeing some of the eighth grade pupils she had taught this last spring, she suddenly felt older than her sixteen years.

One of the singers broke away from the rest and turned to her. It was a smiling Fred Dawson, dark curly hair falling over his forehead and all, and he greeted her with his friendliest voice from other days.

Taken aback for a second, she got hold of herself and was about to tease him a little by saying "My, my, Fred, how you do change." But thinking that would be a mean way to start a conversation, she caught herself in time and was as friendly as he seemed to be.

In a few minutes Molly came out of the house followed by Hamp, each of them carrying a lighted lantern.

"That's Hamp Roberts jist back from the war," Fred said. "Him and my brother Jake used to fight all the time over Jenny Hubbard when they was growin' up."

Suddenly thankful that Jenny was married, she watched Hamp climb up on the rail at the far corner post of the porch and hang one of the lanterns up at the top of the post. Taking the other lantern from Molly, he came over and did the same thing with it on the near corner post. That done he looked around at everybody for a moment and then jumped down on the grass near where she and Fred were standing.

Before she had time to catch her breath, Hamp was holding out his hand to her. As she felt the strong hand close on hers and looked up to meet his smile and warm hello, everything she had been thinking about him and Molly for the last few days faded away to nothing.

She had the strangest feeling that if Hamp leaned down and kissed her right then it would be the most natural thing in the world for both of them, and she wished he would do it. The thought made her pull her hand away from his before he could feel it starting to tremble.

Noticing Molly making her way down the steps past the singers, she suddenly felt so guilty for wanting to try to take Hamp away from her that she wished she could crawl in a hole and pull the hole in after her, but it was too late for that.

They gave each other a long hug and Molly half-whispered in her ear, "Be friendlier to Hamp."

Abruptly letting go of Molly, she gave her a fierce look. Molly's two nods put her in a lovely dream for the rest of the party. She joined in the singing and the games, sometimes near Hamp and sometimes not, but always near him in her mind. Even when spin the bottle took her around the house with Sally Tarbox's brother Billy for a kiss in the dark, it was Hamp's smiling lips she pressed hers against.

The pale slice of moon was yellow and way down in the west when she and Bob started back along the road towards home. This time Bob was not whistling nor was she fretting, for Hamp was walking between them, leading his horse and answering Bob's questions about the war.

Earlier while she and Fred were side by side on the porch, eating a piece of birthday cake and drinking fresh cider, Fred had asked her if he could walk home with her. As ashamed as she was to do it, quick as a wink she told him a lie, saying she already had an invitation, even though Hamp hadn't asked her yet.

At the well curb at home, after a couple of minutes of talk, Bob said good night to Hamp and went along the walk to the house, sweet talking to Reuben as he went.

Although she didn't want her dream to end, she also said good night, but Hamp held on to her hand. "I'm not letting you go, till you say I can come see you tomorrow."

After she had told him she usually read at the oak tree Sunday after dinner, he still held on to her hand, but she didn't mind now. He bent his head, his lips touched hers and his arms were around her and she was close against him. A surge of warmth swept through her, setting her all atingle before she finally broke away, breathless and scared at something stirring in her she had never felt before.

She heard Hamp half whispering, "I love you, Mattie," but she was already slipping out of his arms. Hardly trusting her voice, she said good night and hurried into the house.

The next morning she woke before Emma and lay without moving, letting her glance wander idly around the room and listening to Hamp say, "I love you, Mattie."

She never imagined such a feeling as his kiss had stirred in her. Just thinking about it spread the tingling warmth through her again, but this time without scaring her. Her eyes stopped at the stack of books on her desk. While she was thinking that no man in any of those stories had given her such a feeling, it flashed across her mind she hadn't thought once the whole night about school teaching.

She threw herself upright in bed and her hand flew to her mouth as if to wipe Hamp's kiss away. It didn't matter that she had wanted him to kiss her. She was sorry now that it had happened. Suddenly remembering that she was going to see Hamp again this evening, she groaned and shook her head. She had been a fool last night but she wouldn't be again.

At breakfast she ate little and said less, thankful that in talking about the birthday party Bob didn't say anything that could start Emma teasing her about having another beau.

Between Sunday school and the sermon, she thanked Molly for the good time she had at her party, but she purposely didn't mention Hamp. She reckoned that standing in the middle of the church surrounded by people was no time or place to explain to Molly why she wasn't going to see Hamp Roberts again, and anyway she knew she had to tell him first.

Home again, she forced herself to eat some dinner and tried to talk and act as usual. Yet afterwards when she and Alice had finished doing the dishes and she went upstairs to her room, she dropped down on her bed and lay without moving. For a long time she stared up at the rafters, her mind a jumble of school teaching and Hamp and Aunt Sis.

After all that she had written to Aunt Sis about her plans for teaching school, how could she ever go back on them? And what could she say to Mrs. Whitaker? And to her own family?

Eventually her thoughts came around to Hamp waiting for her even now under the big oak, waiting and no doubt wondering where she was. She could stay home, but it would be wrong not to show up at all after as good as promising him she would.

Without changing out of her church dress, and without a single glance in the looking glass, she went downstairs with a book in her hand and was soon climbing the knoll up to the big oak tree, resolved to tell Hamp why she couldn't see him anymore, and then leave.

Chapter 22

She saw his horse tied to the fence in back of the big oak, but Hamp was not in sight. She stopped and was looking around when a loud hello came from high up in the tree. Answering, she craned her neck and looked up through the leaves trying to find Hamp. He called out again, telling her he had been watching her all the way from her house.

"You can almost see Kickapoo from up here, Mattie. What do you think of that?"

By now she could see him climbing down, talking and asking questions as he came. She was reminded of the old days on Bear Creek when she and Bob used to play follow the leader. In those days she could climb any tree Bob could, and as fast, too. Now she couldn't remember how long it had been since she had climbed one bigger than an apple tree.

As Hamp neared the ground, scrambling down from one big limb to the next, he began telling her how much easier it was to climb coconut palms than this oak because the Filipinos cut notches, like little steps, up the trunk of their palm trees.

"You can go up and down a palm tree fast as climbing a ladder. Course you have to be barefooted to do it. Don't you hate bein' too big to go barefooted on a hot day like this? You can't believe how hot these old boots are."

Even though she was in no mood for light talk, she had to laugh at his rattling on like a child without giving her a chance to say anything. When he reached the ground, instead of coming over to her, he said, "Wait, I have a surprise for you." Disappearing behind the big tree, he called out after a moment and told her to close her eyes.

Without a second thought, she did as she was told and stood listening to his footsteps rustling through the leaves towards her. When she was allowed to open her eyes, Hamp was smiling down at her, and cupped in his hands a few inches in front of her nose was a peach, a big yellow-brown peach turning rosy red across the top where it was already cracking open just ready to be eaten.

As she gasped out her surprise and thanked him, their eyes met and last night came rushing back to her. Suspecting that he was thinking the same thing, she felt herself turning as rosy as the peach and forgot where she was.

It was the peach under her nose that brought her back to herself, and she took it from Hamp's hands, relieved to have something to do to take her mind off last night. Letting him take the book, she split the peach open the way she had done it all her life and offered him his choice of halves. They quickly ate the juicy peach, talking between bites about how good it was.

"Eat every time you get a chance," Hamp said. "That's one thing I learned in the army."

He darted behind the tree again and came back carrying two more peaches in his hat. As they sat eating them, he told her about all the strange fruit he had eaten in his travels—breadfruit, papayas, oranges, pineapples, bananas, and best of all, mangoes.

She had seen oranges and bananas in the stores in Kickapoo, but she had never eaten any, and except for pineapples, she couldn't remember having ever heard of the others.

She had come to the oak tree ready to say what she had to say, but she had been put off by Hamp being up in the tree. Then the peaches got in the way, and now that they had finished eating them she thought it would be too ill-mannered to just up and say, "Good-bye. Thanks for the peaches. I came to tell you I'm going to be a schoolteacher and never get married."

Besides, as she sat there in the shade talking with Hamp, she felt more than ever the excitement of being around him. She hadn't counted on this when she was making up her mind back there at the house. She had only been thinking about doing what she had to do, and she never thought she would have any trouble telling him. After all, she hadn't been nervous telling Vernon why she couldn't marry HIM, and this was almost the same thing.

Arguing with herself even as she sat listening to Hamp talking about having to go away to New Orleans for a few days, she finally got up her nerve and stood up to say good-bye and all the rest of it.

Yet before she could get more than his name out, Hamp had jumped to his feet and said, "I'll walk home with you, Mattie. I brought a bolo knife I promised to show Bob."

The result was that she walked home with him without telling him what she had made up her mind to tell him. At the well curb she said good-bye and left him standing in the shade surrounded by Bob and Emma and Tommy and Ben, who were passing the awful looking bolo knife back and forth and asking questions faster than Hamp could answer them.

The days that followed were miserable for her. She made a special effort to be friendly with Orin, and at night spent every spare minute reading Mrs. Whitaker's books, but now even all of this wasn't enough to keep her mind off Hamp. She didn't need Emma's daily teasing about him being her new beau to be reminded of him. Many times she wished she had never met Hamp Roberts, for she was coming to realize she had to put him out of her mind for good if she was ever going to be a schoolteacher.

It seemed to her that her life had been nothing but ups and downs ever since she left Arkansas and now just when she thought everything was going along smooth and easy for her, Hamp Roberts had come along and upset her plans.

Yet even as she blamed him for her misery, she had to be honest with herself and admit that he made her feel a kind of excitement she had never felt before. When he kissed her she had turned into another person and she couldn't pretend to herself that she hadn't.

She was used to all the teasing that went on about beaus and sweethearts, and she had read about men and women falling in love, but since she never wanted it to happen to her she had never thought much about it. Maybe this exciting something that kept Hamp on her mind so much of the time was what they meant by falling in love. If she dared she would have asked Mama how she knew when she was in love with Papa, but she was too embarrassed to bring up the subject.

Instead, to strengthen her determination to get on with her schoolteaching, one evening on the way home from the Marlowes she drove by Mrs. Whitaker's house to talk to her about applying to the Normal School.

Mrs. Whitaker said she had heard good things from Mrs. Marlowe about her teaching, and while they were having a cup of tea she questioned her about her reading. It was a relief to have someone to talk to about this side of her life, and she left Mrs. Whitaker's house with her spirits lifted.

Only before she got home her thoughts had drifted from books back to Hamp. What worried her most in thinking about him was that she didn't know if she was happy or sad that she hadn't told him good-bye for good when she had the chance. Sometimes she felt one way and sometimes the other. What was even worse—if anything could be—she still didn't know what she was going to say to him the next time they met.

Once it crossed her mind that if he never came back from New Orleans that would solve her problem. But at the thought of never seeing him again, a new fear took hold of her, and if he had appeared in front of her right that minute she couldn't have told him she was not going to see him anymore.

A few days before the annual supper celebrating the founding of their church, she noticed as she drove by the church one morning that the brush arbor was being put up. From that day on, the arbor was a twice daily reminder of the first revival there and of her nightly struggle to confess her great sin against Tommy. This brought up all the worry she had over believing she was the only one converted who hadn't felt the holy spirit, and her great relief when Alice told her she hadn't felt it either. That had put a happy ending to months of misery, but she couldn't see a happy ending to her misery over Hamp's not turning up again.

The Sunday for the church supper came, and even though there was no church service in the morning, she was busy all day helping Mama and Alice make the food for the supper, as well as helping them get breakfast and dinner. In spite of the rush all around her, her thoughts were as much on Hamp—who had been gone for two weeks now—as on what she was doing. More than once Mama had to hurry her along, just the way Papa used to have to hurry her along in the cotton field when she was lost in other kinds of daydreams.

The sun was still two hours high when everything was ready and loaded in boxes and baskets and pots and pans in the wagon—the usual fried chicken, scalloped Irish potatoes, candied sweet potatoes, butter beans, creamed carrots, sliced beets and onions in vinegar, sliced tomatoes, coleslaw, pickles, cantaloupes, watermelons, two apple pies and a chocolate cake, along with all the knives, forks, spoons and plates needed for the family and a few extra people.

It seemed to her that there was always enough food at these suppers to feed an army, and by the time it was ready to go she had seen enough of it for the time being.

Restless all day anyway, after she was dressed she felt more like being alone than seeing a lot of people eating and then listening to a long sermon. By telling Mama she had a headache and didn't feel like going, she had no trouble getting permission to stay home. She hated telling Mama a lie about the headache, but it was true enough that she didn't feel like going.

Once the others had driven down the lane, she changed out of her church dress, took the hairpins out of her hair, brushed it out and let it hang loose down the back. She started looking through the stack of books she had brought home last time from Mrs. Whitaker, but not finding anything that especially appealed to her she reckoned she didn't want to read either. For the first time she could ever remember she couldn't think of anything she wanted to do.

She went downstairs and sat in the swing on the front porch for a while, not swinging but just sitting and looking out across a field of cotton on the other side of the fence. After a while she walked around the house to the backyard, talking to Reuben who came up to be petted.

She noticed the colts up in the lot sticking close to Old Nellie now that their mamas were gone, but today she didn't feel like going up to the fence to rub Old Nellie's nose and tell her what a good horse she was.

Wandering around out near Mama's rose bed, she came across a molty old red hen stepping slowly towards the chicken house, crooning a scratchy singsong and cocking her head from side to side as she peered at the ground for anything she could peck up for food.

For no reason she could think of she had a sudden urge for a juicy cantaloupe from the garden and was just on the point of going out to pick some when she heard the call of a bobwhite from somewhere down the lane towards the road. Forgetting about the cantaloupe, she drifted down the lane towards the clear notes of the bobwhite cutting through the late evening air, and when they stopped she wandered up the road to the big oak.

The sun was so low now it was slanting under the tree, dazzling her eyes until she had to turn away from it. Looking up she could see great streaks of sunlight flashing through openings in the branches, shimmering off some leaves while others stayed dark. She thought of Hamp saying he could almost see Kickapoo from up there, and remembering the climbing she used to do down on Bear Creek, she quickly slipped off her shoes and stockings and looked around for a good place to start up the big oak.

Out where a limb crossed the fence into Watson's pasture she was able to use the strands of barbed wire like a ladder and was soon standing on a big limb and holding on to another one above it. The bark was much rougher against her feet than she remembered.

Then she realized it was because her feet were tender from her not having gone barefooted this summer. Carefully she worked her way up two more limbs; her feet hurting fit to kill every step she took. At this rate she would never get to the top, and she was put out with herself because she could no longer climb up a tree without stopping.

Reaching an opening in the leaves, she looked out to the east hoping she could see Kickapoo. Instead, on the top edge of a green line of trees the full moon stood like a gold plate. With the moon rising in front of her and the sun setting behind her, she thought about making a wish, but her feet were hurting too much for that.

Hurrying down, she jumped to the ground from the lowest limb, skirts flying, and went tumbling through the leaves. That was more fun than all the rest of it, except for seeing the moon.

A clapping of hands startled her and she jumped to her feet and looked around to see Hamp walking towards her, the last of the sun full on him as he called, "Well done, Mattie."

Instantly filled with happiness, she answered, "Hamp!" and rushed to meet him, her heart in her throat.

The full moon had moved but a little way up the sky when she rushed in the back door at home carrying her shoes and stockings, half blinded by tears and unable to believe what had happened. The last thing she remembered clearly was kissing Hamp and feeling so happy to see him she could have kissed him forever.

That was all she wanted, just to tell him how glad she was to see him again, but before she knew it a rush of excitement had drowned everything else out. The rest was a hazy fumbling confusion until she found herself crying, with Hamp trying to kiss her and tell her it was all right, and her so ashamed of herself she hated him for thinking about kissing at a time like this.

Upstairs in bed she kept asking herself between spells of sobbing how was it possible for her to do such a disgraceful awful thing when she hadn't meant to at all. Yet she had done it, and no matter how sweet Hamp had talked afterwards, she knew in her heart he would never want to see her again.

As for teaching school, that was out of the question now even if she didn't have a baby. And she was sure to have a baby. She thought of Molly once telling her that her papa said he would kill any man that got her with a baby before he married her, but here she was already too scared to think about what Papa might do to Hamp if he found out.

She was ready to kill herself right then if she had an easy way to do it. The shotgun was downstairs behind the kitchen door, loaded. But she could never kill herself that way.

After she had cried until she couldn't cry any more, she lay staring up in the dark, waiting for them to get back from church and wishing the night would never end. For in spite of the agony she was in now, she couldn't bear to think what it was going to be like when tomorrow came and all the days ever after that.

End of Part Two

Chapter 23

She opened her eyes and lay looking at the naked shoulder and head of rumpled hair. Even after waking up every morning for many weeks with Hamp lying next to her, she sometimes needed a few seconds to remember she was married.

This morning, however, the naked shoulder reminded her of how she had tried to change Hamp's habit of sleeping without pajamas on. She had picked out a blue-striped nightshirt for him at a store near their hotel in Norman. Hamp just smiled and paid the man for it, but that night he hung it on the bedpost and said, "Thanks a lot, Honey. I'll give it a try when cold weather comes."

Yet for the most part, she was getting used to being Mrs. Gordon Hampton Roberts, although she was still ashamed of what she had done with Hamp before she had his name. Not even the legal ceremony that gave his name to her could wipe out that shame. The words of the justice of the peace had eased her mind, but not her conscience.

Mama and Alice had made it possible for her to run away with

Hamp, riding a horse sidesaddle for the first time in her life. Hamp had brought the saddle—which had a purple velvet seat—back from New Orleans. He said it, and a few silver dishes, were all that was left after the lawyers got through with the estate of his sister and her husband, who had died in some kind of epidemic down there in the spring.

The only trouble she had getting away from the house that evening came from Tommy, who had not gone to Briggs that Saturday with Papa and Bob. Tommy somehow got the idea that Hamp was forcing her to go, maybe because she could not keep back her tears when she said good-bye to Mama.

Tommy came running down the lane behind the horses, crying himself, and calling, "Brin' my sistuh back. Ham, brin' my sistuh back." This time she told him she would bring him some candy when she came back, and then he smiled and waved goodbye.

Recalling how quickly she had changed Tommy's unhappiness made her think how quickly her own unhappiness was changed the morning after her shameful conduct at the oak tree.

Having tossed and turned in shame and misery all that night, she was in no condition to face young Orin Marlowe or anyone else. Yet she still had two weeks of teaching left, and she felt obliged to go on with it no matter how little she felt like doing it. So she drove down the lane determined to be cheerful with Orin no matter what.

At the foot of the lane she was astonished to see Hamp sitting in the shade of his horse, waiting for her. He stood up and stretched, walked over to the buggy and said with a smile, "Good morning, Mattie. Do you want to get married in church, or elope?"

His words lifted such a weight off her mind that if she had not already loved him she would have after he said them. When she got home that evening and had a chance to get Mama alone, she told her everything. Mama seemed less surprised than she expected and never said a single hard word to her.

Instead, Mama said, "Best thang is for you two to git married soon's possible without saying anything to anybody. Specially to Papa. Once that's done, ever thang else'll take care of itself."

She was still scared to death of what Papa might do if he found out before she and Hamp could run away, but Mama calmed her down by saying she would take care of Papa. "If worse comes to worst, I'll remind him of a few thangs about his own courtin' days. Thangs he might of forgot."

She didn't know what Mama meant, and she didn't ask, just kept quiet while Mama went on talking to the rose bushes she was pretending to be hoeing around. "You may thank now, Mattie, that you two cain't git enough of each other, but they'll come a time—"

"Mama! You know that's not the way it was."

"Jist listen to what I'm tellin' you. Men ain't like us. Seems like they cain't never git enough of us—'cept for a short spell—no matter what. And they ain't nothin' we can do about it. Remember that."

"Oh, Mama—"

"No 'O, Mama' about it. You don't satisfy Hamp in bed, and he ain't never goin' to be satisfied with you nowheres else for long. Makes no difference if you work your fingers to the bone for him. It's jist the way men are. And we got to put up with it."

It had been Alice's idea that she stop teaching half a day early so the two of them could drive on to Kickapoo that last Friday evening and buy some wedding things—the new night gown she was wearing right now, for instance, using some of Mr. Marlowe's money—the most money she had ever had in her hands at one time.

A couple of weeks after the wedding, when she had gone to see Mrs. Whitaker and told her how guilty she felt for having wasted so much of her time and effort, Mrs. Whitaker put her at ease right away by telling her not to give it another thought, saying she had followed her heart and that would give her the most happiness in the long run.

"I like teaching school, Mattie—like it very much—but it's not the same thing as being married and having children."

That was the only time she had ever seen a sad look on Mrs. Whitaker's face, and thinking of the two graves out there in the edge of her orchard, she felt sorry for her all over again.

She had seen a similar look on Hamp's mama's face when they met for the first time. Hamp had already told her not to pay any attention to the way his mama took on over him. Yet she never expected his mama to dote on Hamp as much as she did.

A little woman with grayish red hair and bright blue eyes, his mama bustled around fretting over how peaked Hamp looked and asking him if he was eating enough and things like that. His mama seemed to have forgotten how long he had survived in the army without her being there to look after him. At first his mama seemed stand-offish with her, although the rest of the family was as friendly as could be, surprising her with even more of a Southern accent than Hamp's or Molly's Texas drawl.

Mr. Roberts, with his long white beard, looked much older than she expected, even though she remembered Hamp telling her that his papa had fought in the war and had been taken prisoner at Vicksburg. Mr. Roberts greeted her with a kiss—a greeting unheard of in the Lane family—and so did Hamp's old maid sister Lizzie, who walked with a limp and had a bad scar slanting down across her left cheek.

Brown, an older brother of Hamp's, still lived at home with his wife Rissy and their two boys and a girl so far. Brown was shorter and heavier than Hamp and didn't look anything like him, having a round face and brown hair—what there was left of it.

Gradually during the visit, Hamp's mama seemed to warm up to her, taking her in the kitchen and telling her what Hamp's favorite dishes were and just how he liked them cooked. She came away from the visit feeling more at ease with her in-laws than she had expected.

On her first visit home, the only person she had been uneasy about was Papa, but before he came in from the field that day Mama set her mind at rest about him. "He never raised too much sand when he learned you two had run off," Mama said. "Once he got over bein' surprised, he ended up sayin' he reckined gettin' married was sight better'n bein' an old maid schoolteacher any day."

That opinion had made her think of a similar one from Hamp when they were looking around Norman one day on their honeymoon. She had stopped and was gazing at a big building with lots of boys and girls coming and going, feeling sad for the moment that here was a kind of life she was never going to know anything about.

Hamp must have read her thoughts, for he took her hand and said, "I know you had your heart set on bein' a schoolteacher. But, Honey, you're too much of a woman to spend your life like that."

She was not sure she knew what he meant, but because she loved him she gave his hand a squeeze and said nothing. She had made up her mind before the wedding never to complain to Hamp, or to anyone else, about what might have come of her school teaching plans but for him.

Besides that, being married for three days and nights had already made her feel more grown-up than all the living she had done so far. It was as if she understood for the first time what the world was all about. And as for being happy, she didn't see how she could be happier, and she had squeezed Hamp's hand again to let him know it.

Until they had ridden back to Briggs from their four-day honeymoon, she didn't know where they were going to live. Hamp told her he had found them a place, but the rest was to be a surprise.

The surprise was a two-room log house on an eighty-acre farm two miles south of Briggs. Chinked with red clay and shaded by a blackjack tree in front and two in the back, the log house stood on high ground close to a creek—dry this time of year.

Down the creek some fifty yards away, past a weedy, burned up garden, she could see the rusty, sheet iron roof of what she took to be the barn. But what held her eyes longest as they rode around to the back of the house was a lilac bush on either side of the back door.

While Hamp was untying their gripsacks from the saddles, she stepped inside the house and stopped beside the washstand. Beyond it, and against the north wall, a shiny new, black cookstove stood facing her. A row of empty shelves ran along the rest of the end of the cabin and along the east wall to the window. In the middle of the room a pine table with four chairs around it held a coal oil lamp.

She crossed the kitchen to the other door and pushed it open to see an empty fireplace dead ahead in the south wall. The only furniture in that room was a bed in the far corner away from the front door. Going back to the kitchen door, she called, "Hamp, it's just fine."

That evening, Hamp rode home to leave the extra horse and borrow a wagon and team, bringing back with him his big brindle dog, Jack. They left Jack tied in the backyard to get used to his new home, and drove to Briggs for a few more pieces of furniture and a supply of groceries.

Later in the week, Brown brought over a milk cow, and a heifer to keep her company. Bob and Alice came with the wagon crowded by a dozen hens and a rooster, two shoats to be killed when it turned cold, a tow sack of Irish potatoes, a bushel basket full of jars of Mama's canned fruit and vegetables, and a gallon lard bucket of new molasses. In her lap, wrapped in a couple of pages of the Kickapoo Chronicle, Alice was carrying two loaves of Mama's light bread still warm from the oven.

Nothing made her feel more married to Hamp than cooking for him—not even sleeping with him—although her thoughts about that had changed a lot since her disgraceful conduct at the big oak tree. She could hardly believe that such an all-powerful feeling, which she had known nothing about while she was growing up and studying to become a schoolteacher, had suddenly become a regular part of her life.

Nor could she understand why this feeling was made out to be such a bad thing that nobody talked about it, except maybe to warn against it in sermons about Eve beguiling Adam—as if any man needed beguiling.

When she thought of how ignorant she had been about all this, she had to shake her head, because now it seemed to her that a man and a woman living together was the most natural thing in the world. Maybe it was the only purpose of people living at all—to be fruitful and multiply, as the Bible said—yet no one she knew bet that might be so.

Thinking of sleeping with Hamp reminded her of the shivaree. They had known it was going to come because friends always surprised newly married couples with a shivaree. The purpose was meant to surprise them, get them out of bed and have a party. For his part, Hamp had laid in a box of cigars for the men. The cigars would keep, but she could not keep a fresh cake on hand all the time.

Yet this was not what bothered her, the night guns started firing over the roof, tin pans banging against the walls and windows, and shouts calling for them to open up in the name of the law. As she found out from Alice later, the folks had all waited up the road until the house had been dark for a while, hoping to find Hamp and her just the way they did find them.

This did not bother Hamp a bit. He was out of bed and putting on his clothes in nothing flat, lighting the lamp and calling for everybody to come in, even while she was still whispering to him, "Hamp, wait a minute!"

She had at least a little something on before the folks came pouring in, Jake and Jenny Dawson in the lead, and then Bob and Molly and Fred and the others, everybody talking and laughing at the same time and all the men hurrahing Hamp. Last of all came Alice, and Marvin Cole, Alice carrying something covered with newspaper, something that turned out to be a fresh-baked chocolate cake.

She didn't know why she wasn't mortified by all the teasing and jokes and knowing looks from the men, but she wasn't, not even the ones from Fred. She supposed it was because she was too busy hurrying around half-dressed, stirring up a fire in the cookstove to make coffee and trying to get enough cups and plates and forks and spoons together for everybody, her hair streaming loose down her back until she found a free second to rush back to her little dresser and get a clip for it.

Although the night was warm already, Hamp lit a small fire in the fireplace to give everybody something to sit around while they talked and told stories about other shivarees and ate the cake, drinking coffee or milk with it. Afterwards they sang old songs until the men gradually filled the house with cigar smoke, and the front and back doors had to be opened so folks could breathe.

Finally at a late hour, she and Hamp were left standing arm in arm in the front doorway listening to the noisy bunch going off through the dark, someone firing a last shot from up the road a ways towards Briggs.

After watching the steady rise and fall of Hamp's naked shoulder and listening to his even breathing for a time, she heard the milk cow bawl from down at the barn. After hearing it again, she realized the cow was reminding them that it was past her milking—and feeding—time. But it was Sunday and even though the sun had been up for some time, she decided the cow was going to have to wait until Hamp got his nap out.

Easing herself out of bed, she picked up her comb and brush from the dresser, paused a moment to look at their wedding picture, and slipped out to the kitchen in her nightgown, softly closing the door after her.

After a trip to the outhouse, she returned to the kitchen, took the water bucket from its stand, carried it outside, emptied the water around the lilac bushes, and drew a fresh bucket of water from the well.

Once back in the house, she washed her face in the chilly water and looked at herself carefully in the looking glass above the wash pan. "The prettiest face God ever made," Hamp told her the first morning of their honeymoon—and at many such times since—but she hadn't believed him. Yet that was not what was on her mind right now.

Checking the calendar hanging next to the towel rack, she stopped a second to admire her gold wedding band. Then counting the months on her fingers, she reckoned that early in the spring, if things went the way they were supposed to, Gordon Hampton Roberts was going to become a papa.

Chapter 24

As month followed month and fall gave way to a new year, she realized she had never been so happy for such a long time since she was a little girl. Every day except Sunday she and Hamp were up at daybreak, and while Hamp went whistling down to the barn to do the chores, a bucket of slop for the shoats in one hand and the milk bucket in the other, she made breakfast.

After breakfast, Hamp left for work, riding off on Shorty to his papa's place to help gather the crops there. Once those crops were in, he brought home a span of half-wild mules that had run away so many times that the family was glad to make Hamp a present of them.

Hamp's first step in gentling the mules was to throw Shorty's saddle on them and break them to ride. He told her he had learned that trick the year he worked on a ranch in Colorado, having run away from home at sixteen after a fight with Brown.

It worked with the mules, and when the weather was at all fit that winter, she would walk out in the evening to where he was plowing and talk with Hamp while he let the now gentle mules take a rest.

Yet by the time spring came, she had grown so heavy she gave up the walks. Now each night as she got ready for bed she would look at herself and think her stomach was as big as it could possibly get, yet the next night it seemed to be even bigger. These nights an ache or a cramp would keep her awake, and as she waited silently in the dark for it to go away, her mind would fill with the awful stories she had heard about women dying from trying to have a baby, especially their first baby.

Yet the next day as soon as Hamp went off to the field and she got busy doing whatever had to be done—cooking or churning or mending or cutting and putting together the pattern for the cover of the first quilt she had ever tried to make—she would remember the fears of the night before and think how silly she was to worry.

Just the same, she was always pleased when Mama and Alice drove up in the buggy every few days to see how she was getting along, bringing with them something to cheer her up—a jar of her favorite pickled peaches out of the cellar, a loaf or two of fresh light bread or a pie, and always another new piece of sewing to add to the pile of baby clothes.

Mama would examine her, feel all over her swollen stomach and make her tell about every ache and pain and kick of the baby since the last visit. One day after looking at her as usual, Mama said that since her time was getting close it might be best if Alice stayed with her, so that Hamp would feel free to go for the doctor at the first sign. She thought Mama was rushing the time, but she never said so. Instead, while Alice was getting her things out of the buggy, and Mama sat holding Old Nellie's lines, she stood quietly by the buggy listening to more last minute advice. "Now mind what I say," Mama repeated. "Don't make a pain worse by tryin' to hold it in. Groan and holler all you want to."

Since there was only one bed in the house, she and Alice slept in it while Hamp slept on a pallet on the kitchen floor. Sometime during Alice's second night with her, a pain so sharp it took her breath away brought her sitting up in bed. When a second and third pain came along before she could get back to sleep, she had Alice wake Hamp. He rode off to Briggs for Dr. Williams, while Alice built a fire in the stove to heat water, and waited and waited.

At first the pains came only now and then and lasted for just a few seconds. As they started coming closer together, got worse and worse and hung on and on, she would twist and groan and try to break away from Alice holding her on the bed. When a spasm did finally let go she would sink back, too worn out to even open her eyes. And still no Doctor Williams.

One time the pain was so bad she had to scream, and her screams ended with her fainting. She woke up feeling a cool damp washcloth sliding over her face and hearing Alice saying softly, "You're doin' fine, Mattie. Jist keep on pushin' hard as you can. You're doin' fine." After that the pains and screams and pushing gradually blurred together until she no longer thought about a doctor, or Hamp, or anything else.

This torture went on and on so long she lost all sense of time. Once after the longest and worst pain of all, she woke up seeing daylight at the window. Her eyelids drooped shut again and she lay in a stupor waiting for another pain to come, dreading it, but too weak to move. A long time seemed to pass before she realized maybe the pains were not going to come anymore.

She tried to say something to Alice but her mouth was so dry she could only make a whispering sound. Yet she heard Alice answer from the kitchen, heard her come in the room and stop by the bed. "Well, Matt, you've got a pretty girl here, and she's anxious to see you."

Her eyes flew open, her stupor gone in an instant. At first she was so surprised she could only stare. Then with trembling hands she reached up and cautiously took the fretting bundle. Forgetting she had hoped for a boy, she studied the wrinkled red face frowning at her, the eyes shut tight and a tiny fist clenched against a tiny chin. It was the most precious thing she had ever seen. She looked up teary-eyed to thank Alice and saw tears in her eyes, too.

The baby was asleep in her arms when the kitchen door burst open and Hamp came rushing in full of apologies and explanations, the doctor close behind him. The doctor examined the baby and then her, praising Alice all the while for what a fine job she had done.

As the days passed, she thought less and less about the pain of giving birth. Now her main concern was naming the baby. Having expected it would be a boy and take Hamp's name, she and Hamp had not even talked about a name for a girl. Hamp left that to her. Learning one day from Hamp's mama that her mama's name was Sarah, she leaped at the name because Sarah was also Aunt Sis's real given name.

One Saturday morning in April, she and Hamp took little Sarah Alice Roberts, her red face and wrinkles faded to a pink skin smoother than satin, for her first visit to Grandma and Grandpa Lane.

"Well, Matt," Papa said at his first and only look at the baby all day, "I think I see a mite of Lane in her. Jist around the eyes. Yourn, yes, I'd say so," he went on, turning back to Hamp to continue their conversation. The rest of the family made more of a fuss over Sarah, especially Alice and Emma, and one or the other had the baby in their arms most of the day.

That spring and summer Hamp wouldn't let her go to the field with him to hoe corn or chop cotton, although he did let her put in a late garden after he had plowed the ground and harrowed it smooth as a flower bed. Yet when fall came, she insisted on helping with the cotton picking, and took Sarah to the field with her, letting Sarah ride on the cotton sack or sleep under the wagon.

At midmorning she would leave the cotton patch to hurry home and make dinner. Except for that, she and Hamp picked "from can see to can't see" every day but Sunday. At night when she got in from the field she would put a kettle of water on the newly made fire, throw together a batch of cornbread and stick it in the oven to bake while what was left of dinner was being warmed over.

After this she would bathe Sarah in a pan of warm water set on the kitchen table, get her ready for bed and let her nurse. Usually by the time Hamp had done the milking and the other chores, and come in carrying a bucket of milk, a hatful of eggs, and his lantern, Sarah would be asleep in the wicker crib all the Roberts children had slept in—and all the Kent children before them, so Hamp's mama told her when she lent her the crib.

After she and Hamp had finished eating supper, and she had washed up the supper dishes and then herself, she was too tired to think of anything but sleep, even when Hamp was not. Yet tired as she was, she remembered what Mama had told her about men in bed, and she never failed to let Hamp have his way there, nor ever hinted by word or deed that at the end of these long days she often was merely letting him have his way.

With only the two of them to do the picking, it went on and on until Christmas was almost on them before Hamp hauled the last wagonload to the cotton gin in Briggs. The next week he started his winter plowing, but not until she borrowed Mama's quilting frame and had Hamp hang it from the ceiling in the kitchen. After dinner she would tuck Sarah in bed for a nap, let the frame down from the ceiling and go to work stitching on her first quilt, a pinecone pattern of Mama's.

Two days after Sarah's second birthday, she had an easy time giving birth to another yellow-haired blue-eyed baby, a boy the image of Hamp from the start. She had expected the pains of Sarah's birth all over again, but after the first pain gripped her, Dr. Williams had her drink something that kept the next ones so far away she could barely feel them.

She wanted the baby to have Hamp's name, but because it was not the first born in the family, Hamp named it James Monroe after his own papa. Since this meant the boy had two grandpas named James, he would be called Monroe. Once more the wicker crib was set where she could reach down and touch Monroe during the night, and Sarah did not seem to mind having her trundle bed rolled out to the other side of the fireplace at her bedtime.

One morning in late June as she was cooking dinner, churning, nursing Monroe and keeping half an eye on Sarah playing in the backyard in the shade of the near blackjack, she heard Sarah call, "Howdy, Grandpa." Stopping her churning and Monroe's nursing, she went to look out the back door and saw Hamp's papa tying his horse to the far blackjack. After a little talk with Sarah, he came onto the kitchen door, taking off his old black hat to fan himself, and speaking of the hot weather even before he greeted her in his usual friendly way.

As soon as she asked after him and his family and learned that everybody was "just fine," she offered to pump a bucket of fresh water from the well so Mr. Roberts could have a cool drink, but he would not hear of it. Instead, he drank two full dippers from the water bucket, declaring after emptying each one that it was mighty fine water. After some small talk to her, Mr. Roberts said, "Hamp in the field?"

"Yes, he's laying by corn. Down in that creek bottom piece."

"Guess I bettuh go see if he's doin' it right."

It was close to dinner when Hamp's papa came back from the field, and she was pleased that he could stay and eat with them. During dinner nothing was said about the purpose of his visit, but when he had ridden off, Hamp came back in the house where she was clearing the table and said, "Honey, how would you like to move to the home place?"

She had no idea what he meant until he went on to say that Brown had taken over a lease on some Indian land near Kickapoo and was going to start a dairy. "He's had that dairy bug in his ear for years. To me, milkin' that many cows every day would be worse than havin' to pick cotton year round." He clucked his dislike of such an idea and went on with more life in his voice. "So Papa wants me to come and farm the home place. I'd be workin' the whole hunerd and sixty... except for his orchard. I think we could make us a good livin' out of it, Honey. And maybe more'n that. If we farm it right, we ought to be able to make us some money, too."

She set the stack of dishes back on the table and stood listening as Hamp hurried on to layout the changes he would make in the farming. Plant more corn and less cotton. Plant a field of alfalfa. Raise more hogs. When he finished and went off to the field, it seemed to her these were changes he must have been thinking about for some time. Yet she had never heard him speak about them before.

And he had failed to mention the most important change of all. They would be living under someone else's roof. No matter how well they got on she realized she must say something now or forever keep her mouth shut about it.

After supper when she had the children put to bed for the night, she went back into the kitchen where Hamp was looking at an old newspaper. Stopping across the table from him, she took hold of the chair and said, "Hamp, I've been thinking all evening about papa's offer. It is a wonderful chance for us. But the—"

"Good for Papa and the others, too," Hamp cut in, folding the newspaper and smiling up at her.

"I was about to say... the only drawback is that I want us to live by ourselves."

"But, Honey, the family is crazy about you."

"It's not that."

"And there's plenty room."

"It's not that either. I just want our own little family to be together. Don't you see?"

"We'll be together."

"I mean... alone... together."

"But, Honey!"

No matter how many ways she tried to say it, Hamp could not seem to understand why she was raising such a fuss about living by themselves when a few miles up the road a big house and good farm were waiting for them. By now they were standing face to face, their voices raised, and she had forgotten all about not wanting to hurt Hamp's feelings.

Finally Hamp threw up his hands and said, "But I done told Papa we would!"

"Well!" she said, mad as hops at this. "Why didn't you say that in the first place?"

Hamp reached out to her and started to answer, but she pushed aside his hand and turned away, went into the other room and started getting ready for bed. Not another word passed between them, but she lay awake for hours, scared of what was going to come of this. She thought of the fights between Mama and Papa she had listened to over the years, and remembered Mama saying, "The menfolks always git their own way."

The next morning there was no mention of last night's fight.

She and Hamp were civil to each other in saying what had to be said, both answering as usual to the chattering of Sarah. After breakfast, Hamp went silently off to the barn. As usual Sarah played with Monroe in his crib while she washed the dishes, and when she brought Monroe into the kitchen to change his diaper and nurse him, she let Sarah go outside to play under her tree.

In a short while Sarah came running in to say, "Papa went away."

"Thank you, Sarah. Papa goes away every day down to the cornfield."

But Sarah shook her head and pointed out towards the road. To humor her, she picked up Monroe and followed her outside, where Sarah pointed to a horse and rider so far along the road to Briggs that she could not tell if it was Hamp or not. Going down to the barn, she found the mules harnessed and tied in their stalls, but Shorty was missing and so was Jack. She guessed Hamp had changed his mind after getting the team ready for the field and gone off somewhere.

More scared than ever now, yet puzzled, too, she walked slowly back up the hill to the house, shading Monroe's eyes with her hand, unable to answer Sarah's questions about where did Papa go and when is he coming home.

For the rest of the morning, she had Hamp on her mind every second as she went about doing her housework and taking care of Monroe, who by refusing to nurse, and fretting about nothing, seemed to be as upset as she was. She wished now she had not spoken out against going to live with Hamp's family. Still, he might have at least talked to her before he told his papa they would come. He had made her feel like he thought her opinion not worth having. Yet she could hardly wait for him to come back so she could admit she had been wrong and tell him she was sorry.

She had Monroe finally nursed and asleep, and everything ready for Hamp to eat at his usual time, but noon came and went and he was still gone. After keeping Sarah waiting until she became cranky, she let her eat alone and then put her down on their bed for her nap.

Unable to eat anything herself, she put the dinner in the

warming closet and walked out to the road. She came to the end of the driveway and stood looking and looking up the empty road towards Briggs. The glare of the sun on the bare road kept her eyes squinted to slits. It was the hottest part of the day, and the whole countryside was as still as death, not a single blue jay or crow complaining anywhere.

Many times she had been here at home all day while Hamp was off working on his papa's place, but she had never felt so alone before. It was not because Hamp was gone from the farm but because he was gone from her. Trying to get her mind on something else, she was idling back to the house when her eyes stopped on her hoe hanging on the garden fence. Without realizing she was out in the sun with no bonnet on, she opened the gate and took her hoe off the fence.

Starting with the crab grass between the poled beans, she soon lost herself in a cloud of sticky dust. By the time she reached the end of the row she was thinking only of her hoeing.

"Honey, what ARE you doin' out'n this heat?"

She gasped and looked around. Across the garden fence, Hamp sat on Shorty, his smile reminding her of the first day they met. Yet instead of running to him, or saying all the things she had planned to say, she was suddenly shy, or something she didn't know what. All she did was pick up her hoe and say, "I'll go get your dinner ready."

But Hamp slid off Shorty and was waiting for her at the gate. "We're not goin' to live at Papa's after all," he said. "What do you think of that?"

She hung her hoe carefully back on the fence as she said, "I think I was wrong to raise a fuss." Then she turned to face him. "And I'm—" Before she could finish saying she was sorry, Hamp's arms wrapped around her.

Chapter 25

It was after dinner before she heard everything about Hamp's visit to his family. He began by saying he had gone there to tell Papa they had changed their mind about moving in with them. This brought tears to her eyes, but she blinked them away while Hamp went on to say he had explained to his papa that they would still work the farm. They would just find a place to live as close to it as possible, maybe in Briggs.

She was brought to tears a second time when Hamp told about his mama scolding him for what he had done to his wife and saying, "Of course a woman wants her own home!"

Then Hamp said that after a lot of talk back and forth his mama flabbergasted him by saying he ought to build his own house, over by that big cedar on the south eighty where she had wanted theirs put. "Well, Honey, what do you think about that?"

She reached across the table and put her hand on his. "Oh, Hamp, I'm too happy right now to think about anything but you and me."

"There's plenty of good timber on the farm I can cut for the sawmill," he went on. "Why, Honey, we can build us a house for almost no cash at all."

For the rest of the summer she waved good-bye to Hamp every morning as he rode off to cut trees along the creek on the home place and haul the logs to the sawmill on the running gears of the wagon. He had to stop this work when the time came to get his own crops in. Once again she helped with the cotton picking, sweating through the heat of September with the two children and finishing it in freezing November weather.

After all the crops on both farms were gathered, and Hamp had helped Brown and his family move to the Indian lease near Kickapoo, she and Hamp got ready to move in with his parents until the new house could be built. When the last day of moving came, she felt sad to be leaving their little log house. In spite of the pain of Sarah's birth and the long hours in the cotton patch, most of her days here had been the happiest of her life.

For the last wagonload, she took a spade and from under one of the lilac bushes dug up two shoots she had had her eye on for some time. She wrapped the roots in a tow sack, wet it down, and put the shoots in the wagon. She already had the spot picked out in the backyard of the new house where she was going to set them out.

Everything Hamp had said to her about living with his family turned out to be true. Yet she was never quite at ease there, not even when she and Hamp were alone in their room. Having heard that some women caught a husband by doing on purpose what she had done without thinking, she could not help feeling that as friendly as Hamp's mama seemed, she might believe the same thing had happened to her favorite son, and resent it.

Even so, she never let on to Hamp's family that she was not as happy to be there as the family seemed to be to have her. She tried to help around the house in every way she could, but Hamp's mama insisted on doing all the cooking—said Jim couldn't abide anybody else's—and Hamp's sister Lizzie seemed to like nothing better than looking after the children.

She was pleased to find that Lizzie had read most of the books she had read, and would probably have been a schoolteacher herself except for what she called "this thing on my face." One fall from a horse had ruined her chances of getting a husband or becoming a schoolteacher, yet she limped around the house doing what she could with never a complaint.

Hamp's mama kept up with the families that had come up from Texas with them, and one Sunday Molly came with her mama for a visit. Molly was still as plump and friendly as ever, and told her privately she had two fellows on the string, that she liked both of them and was going to marry the one who asked her first, declaring, "I'm going on eighteen, and I'm not going to take a chance on bein' an old maid."

A few weeks after hearing Molly say that, she was not surprised when Hamp's mama brought home the news one day that Molly Wisdom was engaged. But she was so surprised she could have been pushed over with a feather when, as an afterthought, Mrs. Roberts added, to Fred Dawson."

On Christmas Eve, she felt right at home with Hamp's family in the Baptist church, listening to the manger sermon and later watching Santa come up the aisle calling to the shiny-eyed children and tossing candy to them.

After Christmas it was easy for Hamp to get lots of help building their house because it was the slack season for farmers. Not only was his papa there to show him how to build it, but Jake Dawson and a couple of other friends came to give him a hand. Even Papa and Bob took to coming over in the buggy every morning and working all day, and sometimes having dinner with the Robertses.

One especially fine sunny evening, she decided to leave the children with Lizzie and walk across the corner of the farm and see how the work on the new house was coming along.

After she had said hello to everybody and talked to Bob awhile, Hamp showed her where the kitchen and other rooms were going to be, and where he would add on to the house when they needed more room. She took him to mean when they had more children, and she didn't say anything. Yet as they walked out to look at where the well was going to be dug, Hamp went back to that subject himself.

"Cain't get the most out of a hunerd and sixty acres with only one son," he said, adding with a twinkle in his voice, "Less you can take to drivin' a team of mules yourself."

She just smiled back at Hamp. She knew as well as anyone that it took a big family to do all the work that had to be done on a farm, especially if you raised cotton. But her mind kept slipping back to what Bob had just told her about going out to the western part of the Territory in the spring to try for a homestead, saying he had not been able to find any land anywhere closer.

She could see that maybe a few farmers like Hamp and Vernon might be lucky enough to get a place to farm, but she couldn't see how Bob and Tommy and Ben, as well as her own children, could ever hope to find enough land around there to raise a family on.

Later when she was walking back home, she still had Hamp's hint about having more children on her mind. They had never talked about how many they would have, but knowing now what it was like to have a baby, and how much work it was to take care of even two of them, she hoped she would not have too many more.

Yet from what she saw around her, a wife kept on having babies until she couldn't have any more. Mama had had seven that lived, Hamp's mama eight, and she knew of women who had twelve or more. There didn't seem to be any way to keep it from happening if you wanted to hold on to your husband, and she did want to hold on to Hamp. Their fight last summer had shown her that.

When she had been studying to be a schoolteacher, she thought she knew that was her purpose on this earth. And then she fell in love with Hamp. Now her purpose was to have his babies and help raise them until they grew up and went off to have babies of their own. And on and on.

One morning a month later, when the warm air was heavy with the smell of sand plum blossoms from the bushes behind her new garden, they moved into their new house. Except for the kitchen and their bedroom, no rooms had any furniture yet, but she forgot about that for the moment when she saw that the two lilac shoots near the kitchen door had both lived and were greening up.

Hamp, carrying Monroe and leading Sarah, led the way up to

the top of the rise towards the unfinished barn to show them the new pump. He said the well-digging machine had spent three weeks pounding a hole through sixty feet of sandstone to a steady flow of good water. He said someday he would put a windmill here like the ones he had seen in Colorado. She looked around at the new house and new garden and was happy.

But a month later cotton chopping was putting the same old blisters on her hands.

On a visit home in July she found Bob back safe and sound from his trip to western Oklahoma Territory looking for a homestead. He had not found any, but he had followed the wheat harvest all the way north to Canada, and was full of the places he had seen and the money he had made.

Noticing at dinner that Alice took no part in the talk, she asked Mama later if anything was wrong and learned that Marvin Cole had married that week. "Poor thang," Mama said. "She's took it real hard. I don't know what's to come of Alice. Way thangs is goin', Emma'll be married 'fore she is."

A week later she saw Alice driving up to the house in the buggy, bringing her out of the garden with the sad news that Grandma Hale had died—just up and died in her sleep, Aunt Sis's letter had said. Maybe it was that bad news that loosened Alice's tongue a little later to the old news about Marvin's marriage.

Alice said now, since she had time to think about it, it was bound to happen sooner or later, and she was just happy she had not done anything with Marvin to be sorry for.

Meeting Alice's eyes on this, she said, "I reckoned mine happened before I knew what I was doing. I guess the real truth, Alice, is you've just got more will power than I have."

"Well, maybe," Alice said slowly, and after a pause, added, "But then Marvin's not Hamp." Looking away, she changed the subject.

As soon as Alice drove off, taking with her a mess of new black-eyed peas from the garden for supper, she went in the house and wrote Aunt Sis a letter, telling her how sorry she was to never have a chance to see Grandma Hale again, and reporting how her namesake Sarah and the rest of the family were getting along.

That fall they made an extra good crop of cotton and corn, and had the best weather for picking and gathering it that anybody could remember. Indian summer came early and the warm days and cool nights went on and on—the nights so clear the moon and stars seemed almost in reaching distance.

The cotton crop brought in some cash money, and Hamp said he was thankful to be able to pay some of his bills, just which ones and how much she didn't know, since Hamp never talked much to her about such things. Yet he must have had some money to spare because he borrowed his papa's hack and took her and the children to Kickapoo to buy new shoes and other things for winter.

The first thing they noticed was an automobile parked on Main Street. Hamp pulled up for a look, saying, "Honey, we'll have us one of them gasoline buggies for ourselves someday."

She doubted they would ever have that much money, but she didn't say so, mainly because her mind was already on her shopping. At the first store she tried on several pairs of fancy slippers and button shoes in various styles and colors before she bought a pair of high-topped leather shoes that laced up the front and had double soles.

A week before Christmas, Indian summer ended with a rainy spell that stopped Hamp's work on the cow barn, but sent him to Kickapoo with a wagon load of hogs to sell. He got back, wet and cold, long after dark. Yet he happily wolfed down a hot supper while he told her the news of his day, the most important piece being that he got his asking price for his hogs.

She had some news of her own she been putting off telling him until she got a little more used to it herself, hoping in time she might become almost as pleased by it as Hamp was bound to be. After all, she had so much to be thankful for that year that she would have to be pretty ungrateful not to be happy in the face of all their good luck.

Now as she watched Hamp enjoying his second piece of pecan pie, she asked herself who else had a husband that could spend the whole day out in a cold drizzle, jolting twenty miles over rough roads in a wagon, and get home at nine o'clock at night wet and cold and still be in a good humor?

She found it easy to smile as he finished the last bite. Then she told him they were going to have another baby. He jumped up with a whoop and turned to his wet coat, which she had hung over the back of a chair to dry out in front of the open oven door. She watched with raised eyebrows while he pulled a little brown paper package out of a pocket in the coat and handed it to her, his smile now a grin.

"I was going to give this to you for Christmas. But after news like that, it can't wait."

Without a hint of what was in the soft package, she slipped the string off the damp brown paper and found underneath it a white package tied with a red ribbon. Inside this, wrapped in tissue paper, was a pair of silk stockings just like the ones she had looked at the week before without once thinking she would ever in her life have a pair of her own. She sat for a moment, feeling her rough fingers against the slippery silk.

Now she found it even easier to smile as Hamp swallowed the last bite. Then she told him "I hope it's a boy."

Chapter 26

Yet on a sunny morning the following summer, after being in labor all night, with Dr. Williams in charge—and Hamp and Alice hovering around—with the painkiller not killing the pains, and eventually her too worn down to care whether it was a boy or girl, just as long as the pains stopped, she finally gave birth to a big baby girl.

As soon as Hamp's mama saw the new baby, she said it looked like Agnes, her firstborn daughter, now living in Texas, and that became the baby's first name. The middle name came a few days later when Emma, all dressed up and wearing a hat, arrived at the front door with a young man who looked vaguely familiar. He turned out to be Glenn Watson, the older of the two neighbor boys who used to walk to school with them.

Glenn was just back from his homestead way out in the panhandle of the Territory to marry Emma and take her away the next day. All of this was a surprise to everyone, even to Emma, until last night.

The visit was short, and she and Emma were soon giving each other tearful good-bye hugs. As she was waving to the excited couple, whirling out the driveway in a livery buggy from Kickapoo, she decided she would call the baby Agnes Emma.

Some six weeks later while Agnes Emma slept in her crib and Sarah and Monroe played school in the living room, she was sitting sideways against the kitchen table, reading and churning at the same time, one hand holding the folded newspaper, the other raising and lowering the handle of the dasher. From the stoneware churn on the floor beside her, the steady, muffled plunk-kerplunk filled the kitchen.

To hear the "Kickapoo Chronicle" tell it, thousands of people were up there in Guthrie, the new capital of the new state, drinking and dancing and whooping it up. When she looked at the picture of the pretty Indian girl and handsome cowboy standing together in what the paper called a mock wedding ceremony uniting Indian Territory and Oklahoma Territory as the State of Oklahoma, the cowboy reminded her of Hamp.

Last night as he had finished reading the account to her, Hamp joked, "Instead of making it a state, maybe we should give the Territory back to the Indians. The way the boll weevil is movin' in on us from Texas, the end of cotton raisin' in this part of the country is in sight."

She took another look at the picture of the cowboy and was reminded that before long Hamp would be coming in from gathering corn, cold and hungry and in a hurry to sit down to a hot dinner.

For a moment she could hear the older children playing "school" in the front room, something they had been doing every day since her recent visit to Oakridge School with Sarah. She had promised Sarah that as soon as they finished the cotton picking she would take her for a visit to her mama's old school, and last week while Lizzie came over to look after Monroe and baby Agnes, she and Sarah walked the nearly two miles to the school.

Once inside the schoolhouse, she left Sarah with Miss Rogers, while she spent her own time in the next room with Mrs. Whitaker and the older pupils. Mrs. Whitaker had not changed since she had last seen her years before. Maybe her brown hair had a little more white in it at the temples, but she was still alert and cheerful and as friendly as ever.

Putting the newspaper down, she lifted the dasher clear of the churn and saw from the very few specks of butter on the milk that she would have to finish her churning after dinner.

She got up and peeked at the cornbread and sweet potatoes baking in the oven, smelling the sweet potatoes even before she opened the oven door. Using a corner of her apron, she lifted the lids from the pots on the stove, stirring and tasting to see how everything was coming along.

Then, finding Agnes was still asleep in her crib, she quietly brought Sarah and Monroe to the washstand in the kitchen to wash their hands and faces before their papa came in.

She expected that somehow their lives were going to be changed by Oklahoma becoming a State, but nothing changed. Life on the farm went on as before. She and Hamp both worked as hard as ever, early and late, day after day except Sunday, which had become a day of rest so far as work in the field went. Sometimes they had Sunday dinner at his family's house or at hers, now and then they went to one church or the other, and once in a great while she had one of the families over for a Sunday dinner at home.

The seasons slipped into one another—wet springs, long and hot dry summers and unpredictable winters—one generally so much like another that she all but lost track of them. Yet she would never forget the surprise on a hot July day when having given birth to a tiny son she had another tiny son within an hour, making Hamp more excited than she had ever seen him. He was in and out of the bedroom, giving her another kiss and then carrying on around the house, laughing and joking with Alice and Dr. Williams.

"Two boys! Can you beat that?" she heard him say again. "Have to build onto the house for sure now."

That had not crossed her mind. Instead, as she lay in bed trying to look as pleased as Hamp, she was worried because she knew she could not possibly have enough milk to satisfy two hungry boys. She guessed she would have to put both of them on bottles.

No one would have taken the twins—Otis and Arthur—to even be related, much less twins. Otis was a dark-haired, rosy-faced angel, while sandy-haired Arthur was a skinny, frowny child from birth.

He turned out to be a sickly one, always out of sorts, the one she had to walk the floor with night after night trying to ease his colic—if that's what it was—to stop him from crying and keeping Hamp awake.

When the twins were two years old, she had another son and had to get used to nursing a baby again. They named him Harold after Hamp's mama's favorite brother, who had been killed in the battle of Shiloh.

More and more Sarah was becoming her right hand, helping her with the cooking, washing, ironing, and sewing, as well as doing any outside chores she was asked to do. Besides all this, at church Miss Rogers told her more than once that Sarah was the best pupil she had ever taught.

As for Monroe, he was so jealous of Sarah at home because she never did anything to get Hamp mad at her—Papa's Pet, Monroe called her—that when he found Sarah also a favorite at school, he fought against school work the way he fought against everything at home he didn't want to do—he tried to get out of doing it.

At home neither she nor Hamp had to ask the other children more than once to do something, but it sometimes took more than words to get Monroe to do what he was supposed to do. She did not like it when Hamp whipped him now and then, hitting him with whatever was handiest, his belt, a switch or even his hand, but she had to tell Monroe when he came crying to her, and she held this living picture of Hamp in her arms, that he brought most of his troubles on himself.

Remembering that her own fear of Papa whipping her had made her try harder to do what Papa wanted, she would beg Monroe to do his chores on time, stop picking on Agnes or the twins, or whatever he had done or not done that had brought on the whipping.

"Aw' right, Mama. I will," Monroe would promise, looking up at her with teary eyes and wiping his tears off on his sleeve as he went sniffing away. But she noticed that his promises did not last long.

Yet in spite of the children's tears now and then, and the big fights among them that went from screams to laughter in seconds, she was thankful to them for their help in making the farm prosper. And it was beginning to prosper beyond anything she had ever imagined.

It had become the land of milk and honey she used to hear Papa predict to Mama back in the old days when he was trying to talk her into leaving Bear Valley and moving to Oklahoma Territory. Year after year there was more of everything.

Hamp not only had more mule colts, which he broke to work when they were old enough, and then sold them for a good price. Now that he had three extra milk hands in Sarah and Monroe and Agnes, he kept more cows. He built a new milk house between the new windmill and the new smokehouse, bought a cream separator and had the cream picked up and carried off to the creamery in Kickapoo. The skim milk was fed to the many hogs he raised to eat or sell.

He had pens for sows with pigs, pens for shoats being fattened to be butchered or sold in Kickapoo, and an extra strong pen for a big red boar that hemmed chickens up in a corner of his pen whenever he could and ate them, feathers and all.

She kept a few turkeys and more Rhode Island Red chickens than she could count. In laying season Sarah and Agnes would gather as many as six dozen eggs a day, most of which went off twice a week with the man from the creamery. Fryers kept them in fried chicken all summer, and for the rest of the year whenever she wanted a chicken, she culled one or two hens out of the flock.

Because Hamp liked them, she also kept a dozen or so bantams. The flashy-colored little roosters ruled the barn lot. They out-fought red roosters several times their size, fought rats for the loose grain in the stalls, and fought off hawks swooping down to try to carry off their baby chicks.

"There's nothin' a banty rooster's afraid of," Hamp would say, "and that's why I like 'em."

Along with more of everything else on the farm, there was more money—just how much more she didn't know and didn't ask. All she knew was that Hamp never said "no" when she ordered something from the catalog for herself or the family, or bought material in Kickapoo for a new dress for herself or the girls.

The farm was doing so well that Hamp had bought the south eighty from his papa, paying it out year by year. His papa had offered the land to Brown first because he was the older son, but Brown wanted to stay close to Kickapoo where he had running water and electric lights in his house and was soon to have—of all things—a telephone, something she had never seen close up.

When she mentioned Brown's telephone to Hamp, he shook his head and said, "Well I hope to God it heps his dairy business. Mama says he's way in debt cause it costs them so much to live. No wonder! Him now with seven mouths to feed. No orchard. No garden. No hogs. And not a chicken on the place."

At the time, except to sympathize in her mind with Brown and Rissy, she never thought anything more about Brown being in hard shape until one year at Thanksgiving when he came out to greet them as they arrived in the Roberts' backyard. Then she did notice that he had a worried look about him.

She had come close to staying home that morning. She was going to have another baby soon and she had been sick so much with this one—sometimes having to take to her bed for a week at a time—that she would much rather have stayed home and rested. But the trip over there was short, it was a chance to visit with Rissy, and most important of all, it was a chance for all the cousins to play together for a day.

The minute Brown laid eyes on the spic and span hack he reckoned out loud, even before greeting them, that he would like to have a rig like that if he could afford it. This was all she heard him say about the hack until he brought it up again while they were eating dinner.

When Hamp explained it was just their papa's old hack fixed up a little, Brown seemed even more put out than ever to hear it. He frowned down the table at his papa and said, "Well, Papa, if you'd only told me you wanted to git rid of that hack, I'd a been glad to take it off your hands."

Mr. Roberts only smiled, but the edge in Brown's voice stopped the talk among the grown-ups until Hamp laughed and said, "Why, Brown, if you really want that hack, you can have it for just what I give Papa for it. We'll forget about the paint and the new seats."

Seeing Brown bristle at this, she guessed he must be thinking Hamp was showing off his money, and she was relieved when his mama put her hand on Brown's shoulder and said, as if talking to a child, "Now, Son, remembuh yoah mannuhs." The talk went on to something else, but she could see that for the rest of the meal Brown was still fuming.

After dinner she and Rissy were helping Lizzie wash the dishes when two of Rissy's girls came bursting in from the outside, shouting, "Papa is hitting Uncle Hamp!"

While Rissy and Lizzie looked wild-eyed at each other and rushed out the kitchen door, she leaned against the counter to hold off a sudden sick feeling; afraid she was going to vomit. Slowly she put down the plate she was drying and made it to a chair at the kitchen table.

She felt that if she took another step she would throw up for sure, so she sat with her head lowered, listening to the commotion of crying children and voices until Hamp came looking for her.

When it was all over, and Brown and Rissy had gathered their family and ridden off home, and she and Hamp and their big-eyed children were on the way home in the spic and span hack that had caused all the trouble, only then did she learn there had been no hitting, just Brown ranting and raving at Hamp and throwing his arms around, mad at what he saw as more proof of his old, old feeling that the family always played favorites with Hamp.

At the time Hamp shrugged it all off in his smiling way, saying it was nothing to worry about. Yet less than a month later when her baby was born dead, he blamed its death on his so-called fight with his brother. She reminded him of how often she had been sick while carrying this baby and Dr. Williams said that from the looks of it the baby girl had been in trouble all along, but Hamp still blamed himself.

With just the three families and Reverend Willis present, they buried the unnamed baby girl in the Methodist graveyard a week before Christmas. Afterwards, she noticed Hamp's easy good humor was a long time coming back. He was as thoughtful as ever with her and the children, but he no longer joshed with them the way he used to.

One Sunday morning at breakfast for no reason that had anything to do with what they had just been talking about—at least as far as she could see—Hamp turned the conversation to Reverend Willis, saying what a good man John was. He ended up by saying, "I been thinking maybe we ought to start taking the children to his church every Sunday... instead of just now and then."

"That's fine with me," she said, and knowing how long it took to get a house full of children washed and dressed and ready at the same time to go anywhere, the next Sunday morning she got up earlier than usual.

Chapter 27

Now that she was back in church seeing the old familiar faces again every Sunday morning, it was almost as if she had always been there. Even so, some of the boys and girls had grown up so much she sometimes could not place them until she saw them with their parents.

Once more she got used to Miss Rogers fiddling with the stops as she warmed up the organ, to Reverend Willis mopping his face with a handkerchief after his hour-long sermon, and to hearing the same solemn "Amens" from the same solemn faces in the Amen corner, Papa's among them.

It was sad to see Molly, fat now and never smiling, come into church carrying a child on her arm, leading another one and a third one trailing, all girls. It was even sadder to see the bright, and once pretty, Jenny Hubbard surrounded by children and looking as scrawny as if she had been dragged through a knothole.

Behind these two weary looking mamas and their children, Jake and Fred Dawson strolled along, seeming as pleased with the world around them as if they had made it themselves—which, in a way, they had.

She never doubted that going to church was good for her soul, but after getting all the children scrubbed and dressed, and kept dressed until Hamp called from the hack, and after trying at the same time to get as much of dinner ready as possible before she left the house so the family would not have to wait such a long time to eat when they got back from church, and after rushing at the last minute to put on her church dress and hurry out the door before Hamp called a third time—after all this, she felt like she had already done half a day's work before she left home.

Yet when she was finally in the hack and spinning along the road at a fast trot with Hamp in charge of the children as well as the team, she would start thinking about seeing the family in a few minutes—all except Mama, who never came to church anymore—and this would make her forget about all the effort it took to get there.

She and Alice usually had visiting time before and after their bible class—and sometimes after the sermon—to stay caught up on the family news and gossip.

One day Alice told her that soon after Bob had gone out to the wheat harvest that spring the girl he had been sparking for some time married another man. Remembering that Bob had lost his first girl because he had to leave in Arkansas, she hoped that sooner of later he would get himself a good wife.

Some mornings after Sunday School was over, Tommy, whose every appearance always made her think for an instant of their long-ago struggle in the flood, would come and sit next to her during the sermon just to be near her, able to say little or nothing because it was so hard for him to speak in a whisper or hear a low voice.

But later, out in the churchyard, they would talk, although then she mostly listened and kept her eye on Sarah riding herd on the children until Hamp finished his conversation with Papa.

She was unhappy that Papa had not taken Mrs. Whitaker's advice and sent Tommy to a school for the deaf. Yet Tommy never seemed to mind that he had been unable to finish school. He liked farming, especially driving a team and using farm machinery, and whenever he was with her where he could talk, she heard all about the new riding plow they had now and the new riding cultivator, the new riding hay rake, and so forth.

One Sunday Alice brought word to church that Bob was due back in a week from what had become his yearly trip of working the wheat harvest north to Canada, and that she and the family were to come Sunday for his homecoming dinner.

She expected Bob would be unhappy that his girl had married another man while he was gone, but if he was, he didn't show it. He was his old self during the meal, and afterward out in the barn lot bragging up the great saddle horse Vernon had sold him for his trip to the broomcorn harvest down south of Norman.

Two weeks later Bob was back home from the broomcorn harvest, lying in his coffin. From what Papa learned when he went to get the body, Bob and another man rode under an open shed to get out of a rainstorm. Lightning struck the sheet iron roof of the shed, killing Bob and his horse—melting the bridle bits in the horse's mouth—without touching either the other man or horse.

She was so saddened by Bob's death that for weeks any thought of him would bring tears to her eyes. Yet long after she had worn her sorrow out, whenever she thought of Bob she would remember Papa in the churchyard telling Bob's story to a neighbor, shaking his head as if he still couldn't believe Bob had been so foolish, and finishing in a broken voice, "He ought to knowed better."

More than once, as she struggled to get everything done, she thought about how her idea of work had changed since coming to Oklahoma Territory. The first year she picked cotton she didn't think she could ever work any harder. Yet once married, she found out that looking after the house and taking care of the children as well as spending every spare minute in the cotton patch was twice as hard.

Often she thought the only thing that could make the situation worse would be for her to be pregnant. Yet since she was well into the second year after losing her baby and not pregnant yet, she hoped she might be like Mama after losing her nearly stillborn baby and not have any more.

The possibility of not having any more babies gave her spirit a lift every time she thought about it. Seven babies—six that lived— were more than enough for any woman to have, although right now it would have been a godsend to have twice as many hands helping her with the cotton picking, the milking, and all the other chores that had to be done every day.

This was especially true now that Hamp's papa had become so feeble she had to send two of the children every other evening to help him and Lizzie pick the fruit and load it in the wagon so that he could drive it to Kickapoo at daylight the next morning.

Every fall of the year the work went on at fever pitch, everybody helping, and they always managed to get the crops all gathered in before Christmas, even the cotton picked for the last time except maybe for a scattering of late-opening bolls that Hamp would let the stock trample down as they browsed the fields.

With each new year came the days she liked best, the season when for a few weeks she had a little time to recover from the rush of gathering the crops in the fall and the rush of planting and cultivating them in the spring. Chores and housework and looking after sick children still had to be done, but during the week after dinner, with all the children, except Harold, away in school and Hamp working outside—usually breaking land—she had a little time each day she could call her own.

Before she was married she would have used this time to read, but for years she had never had time to ready anything but the newspaper, and often she didn't have time to look at it from one week to the next.

From one year to the next, the trouble of women she had read about in Mrs. Whitaker's book and cried over never crossed her mind—not Emma, or Ramona, or even poor Tess, the one she had shed the most tears over.

Now, once dinner dishes were done, she would let her quilting frame down from the ceiling in the front room, and while Harold played on the floor near the stove, she would spend an hour or two stitching on her quilt and thinking about the things she hadn't had time to think about for months—Jimmy never coming back home,

Bob killed by lightning, Emma and her family way out in the Panhandle where the wind never stopped blowing, and always, Alice getting a little more rawboned each year and less likely to find a husband.

After a while, her thoughts would always drift back to the years of growing up in Bear Valley, where it seemed nothing bad ever happened to any of them until Jimmy ran away from home and Papa and Mama started fighting over moving to Oklahoma Territory.

By then she already knew she wanted to be a schoolteacher like Aunt Sis and never get married, for it seemed to her that Aunt Sis was the most exciting person in Bear Valley. She read books, and no matter what kind of a question you asked her she could give you an answer. Now and then Aunt Sis would even correct Papa when he was quoting scripture, which always made Papa fume.

And then when her dream of becoming a schoolteacher was so close she could taste it, one evening without warning—while a full moon was standing like a gold plate on the top of the green ridge to the east and the last rays of the setting sun were flashing under the big oak tree on Hamp's laughing face—she started a different future by running into his arms.

She had relived that instant a thousand times, going over everything leading up to it that day which made it look like it was meant to happen, asking herself what might have happened if she hadn't felt like staying home from the church supper that evening; if she hadn't heard the call of the bobwhite that started her wandering down the lane to the big oak tree; if Hamp hadn't got back from New Orleans and come from the church supper looking for her; if she hadn't climbed a tree and leaped down from the limb in a whirl of skirts in front of him; and, most important of all, she asked herself what might have happened in spite of all that, if she had known then about the powerful hidden feeling, urge, or need, or whatever it was, that sent her running innocently into his arms.

Since then she had heard Hamp laughingly say every once in a while about a friend of his getting married, "Well, it's better to marry than to burn." Now, even though she didn't know where in the Bible it came from, she did know what it meant, something she hadn't known that evening under the oak tree. If she had known she was burning without being aware of it, she might not have thrown away without a thought, the school teaching career she had dreamed of for so many years for a man, and the children, and work that came with him.

Not that she ever complained about the work. Complaining wouldn't have made it any easier, and besides, she saw Hamp working just as hard. She loved him even more now, although for her the burning was mostly gone, and she was proud of him, thankful for the roof over their heads, food to eat and clothes to wear. Yet she did miss having so little time to look forward to anything but the work that had to be done day in and day out, with no end in sight.

Chapter 28

At first she thought Hamp was talking a lot about the outbreak of war in Europe because of his experience in the army, and since her main concern this summer was to keep the drought from burning up her garden, she didn't pay much attention to what he said about war. Yet when the fighting in Europe got worse, she did pay more attention to the news, although she still didn't think a war way over there would have much to do with them here on the farm.

Hamp disagreed, saying a war would hike the price of everything, especially cotton because soldiers had to have uniforms, and he started thinking out loud about which pastures he would plant in cotton the coming year.

They were chopping cotton in one of those old pastures the next spring when a passing neighbor stopped to tell them that a German submarine had sunk a British ship with a lot of Americans on it. That Saturday Hamp came back from Briggs, newspaper in hand, and saying we were sure to get in the war now that Germany was sinking our ships.

But the sinking of ships and the fighting in Europe that summer brought no changes in the country that she could see, although closer to home there was one sad change. Mr. Roberts died suddenly. Seemingly well one day, except for a little fever. Two days later he was dead from what Dr. Williams said was pneumonia—and this in the middle of a heat wave.

Only just that week she had let Hamp know she was pregnant again, and he was so afraid the shock of his papa's death might bring on another stillborn baby that he made her stay home from the funeral. More than this, he put his foot down on her wanting to help with the cotton picking that fall, and since she herself was a little worried about the baby, she stayed out of the field without raising a fuss.

Careful as she could be all winter, early in the spring she was more relieved than she ever let on to Hamp when she gave birth to a healthy baby girl. She thought this one was the prettiest of the three girls, and right away Hamp told her they should name the baby Martha Louella.

But she wanted it named after the two grandmas, since they hadn't had any of the children named after them yet. Finally Hamp gave in and the new daughter became Edith after his mama's middle name and Ellen her mama's middle name, and all three families were pleased.

That spring Hamp outdid himself in planting every acre in cotton he could, even plowing up more pastures to plant in cotton. In the fall she once again found herself exhausted every day trying to keep up with all the work she had to do, and she was thankful she had Harold to look after baby Edith somewhere in the shade around the cotton field while she picked.

Sarah was now doing a woman's work, both around the house and in the field. She was going to miss this help when Sarah went away to high school in Kickapoo in the fall, but she was so happy for Sarah that she did not give the extra work for herself a second thought.

Ever since she had first mentioned to Hamp last year about Sarah's going to high school and got a "We'll see," for an answer, she was afraid he was not going to let Sarah out of the cotton patch, even though she was the apple of his eye—so much so that when he bought a saddle horse for Monroe he bought Sarah a piano just because Miss Rogers was teaching her how to play.

Yet from the way Sarah's going away to school finally came about, it looked like all of Hamp's doing. He had insured their new house with a Mr. Billings, a laughing, red-faced man who sold insurance and real estate in and around Kickapoo.

After that, Mr. Billings would stop by the farm to visit with Hamp now and then, and next he started bringing his family along for a Sunday visit, driving up the driveway on a Sunday evening in his flivver, making the boys' new dog, Tige, go rushing out to bark at the noisy machine until it sputtered to a stop.

Among the Billings' children was a girl Sarah's age, and over the years Sarah and Elsie had become friends. One Sunday while the families were eating watermelons on the front porch—after they had worn the election and the war talk out to a frazzle—Mr. Billings asked Hamp if it wouldn't make good sense for Sarah to come live with them and go to high school with Elsie.

Hamp said he'd think about it, and Grace Billings promptly said, "Good, that's settled," and never once hinted that the two mothers had talked it over before.

A funny thing about Mr. Billings' invitation was that for some years he had been after Hamp to give up farming and move to Kickapoo, saying the only sure future in a farmer's life was a bad back, and you couldn't buy insurance for that. Having grown up on a farm himself—until he ran off to the Spanish War like Hamp—Andy Billings knew farming firsthand, and he was always saying it was a shame farmers had to work themselves to death just to make a living.

At the end of every visit, as the Billings family got ready to go back to Kickapoo—their flivver loaded with apples or peaches or "rosen ears" or cantaloupes or whatever was ripe just then on the farm—the last thing Mr. Billings would do—after he had cranked some life into the flivver and was standing by the fender of the quivery thing ready to climb up in it—he would take Hamp by the

232

hand and thank him for all the groceries and then he would say, "Hamp, still wish you'd stop balkin' about comin' to work for me. Remember, reveille don't come so early in town."

Hamp would always give him a smile and a shake of his head and say, "Thanks, Andy. But farmin's all I know. I'd be a fish out of water round all them townsfolk."

Surprised at how easily Hamp had agreed to Sarah's going to school in Kickapoo, she started worrying about what might happen to Monroe when his turn came. Already he had gone from having trouble with Miss Rogers to having trouble with Mrs. Whitaker, although Mrs. Whitaker did tell her that once Sarah was no longer there to set such a perfect example for him, Monroe would probably cause less trouble.

"I hope so," she said, but she had her doubts. Her other worry was the war. She believed President Wilson would keep on keeping the country out of the war, while Hamp kept saying it was bound to come.

And then one day when she was planting in the garden with Harold—Edith asleep in a basket at the garden gate—she heard the children coming in from school talking much louder than usual. Right away she guessed the loud talk might be about the war. Her mind leaped to another ship sunk, but then her thoughts finally settled on a more likely happening: Monroe getting another whipping at school.

Unable at the moment to think of any other possibilities, she looked up to see the twins running towards her, calling over and over again something she couldn't make out. They rushed up to the garden fence, their caps in their hands, each trying to be loudest as they shouted out together, "The President declared war today!"

Before she had time to catch her breath, Otis and Arthur turned and ran towards the house. Speechless, she watched them go, knowing how anxious they were to be on hand for whatever there was to eat in the warming closet. Then she slowly shook her head, trying to think of what a war was going to mean for the family.

At supper that night—and every meal afterward, it seemed to her—all the talk was about the war. Monroe gave her a pang of fear by repeating, "All I hope is, it lasts long enough for me to get in it."

At church the next Sunday, Papa told her he was afraid the Army was going to take Tommy and Ben both, but it took Ben only and sent him off to a training camp in Texas.

After listening to gloomy talk all summer, when fall of the year came, she found the brightest spot in her life was following Sarah's progress at high school in Kickapoo. She kept up with it from Sarah's Friday letters, thinking as she read each one aloud to the family at suppertime that they were just the kind of happy letters she might have written if she had gone away to school. Each Sunday night she wrote back to Sarah, making sure to say something about each one in the family.

It was not until Sarah came home for Christmas of her second year that she learned Sarah had been so miserable during her first weeks at school—because some of the other girls made fun of her clothes and the way she talked—that more than once she was on the edge of running away and coming home.

"And then you'll never believe what changed it all," Sarah said. "One day I helped them pass their Home Economics test by making their biscuits for them. And we've been friends ever since."

Knowing that Sarah did not have a mean bone in her body, she was not surprised Sarah had done this, but at the same time she had to smile because she also knew that Sarah's biscuits were usually heavy as lead.

One morning in early January, she stood with Hamp in the kitchen, straightening the knot in his tie and giving a wifely look at his white shirt collar, one of several she had washed and starched and ironed for him the day before. He was dressed in his church clothes, and on the floor beside him was his old gripsack, the first time it had been used since their honeymoon. After years of talking about buying an automobile, he was on his way to get one.

In a few minutes Hamp was going to town on the creamery

wagon. Then he was going to ride on the railroad cars to Michigan and drive home the touring sedan he had bought in Kickapoo in December.

"I better go," Hamp said, giving her a hug and a kiss, but a kiss so different from last night that she suspected his mind was somewhere else. Sure enough, as he let go of her he said, "You keep after Monroe now. I told him I want that barn cleaned out and the manure spread in the near cornfield by the time I get back."

The next time she heard from Hamp it was a letter from St. Louis saying he would be home Saturday, and here it was Friday already. From Saturday noon on, one or more children waited out in the driveway to be the first to see the new automobile, while she set about making a big supper to celebrate this great occasion.

When the new automobile still had not come by the time the children had done the chores and waited an hour for their supper, she fed them and then let Monroe and the twins wait with a lantern out in the cold to listen for the first sound of it. More than another hour passed before she heard a shout and rushed out the kitchen door along with the children.

"Listen," Monroe said.

A sound like a steady growl was coming out of the night from the east, then a roar that got a little louder each hill it came over. When the roar died down at the south corner and then started again louder than ever as it turned along the road towards the farm, the children started jumping up and down shouting, "Here it comes!" "Here it comes!"

A pair of far-reaching lights swept the road into the driveway and started Tige barking. She grabbed Edith and Harold and told the others to stand back. The big two-eyed monster roared up the driveway and stopped a few feet from them, roared a final blast and turned dark and silent.

A door flew open and Hamp called, "Hold'er Newt! She's a rearin'." Laughing and shouting, the children swarmed towards the black monster.

At church time the next morning the black monster was still silent, and remained silent in spite of Hamp cranking and cranking the handle at the front end of it, and in spite of her heating kettle after kettle of water to a boil and watching Hamp pour it in the black monster's engine—or maybe on it—for a reason she was not told, did not understand, and did not question.

After that—and all of Hamp's other efforts—failed to bring back to the black monster the roar of last night, he finally quit trying, harnessed a team and put it to the hack. Instead of the freshly washed big, shiny black automobile carrying them to church in style, which had been all the talk at the breakfast table, the family rode at a fast trot in the hack, but when they got there Sunday school had already started.

Yet she forgot about the trouble with the new automobile when she learned from Alice at church that Ben had already been shipped to France and was somewhere on the Western Front, which his letter said was muddier than Texas and Oklahoma put together.

Chapter 29

One Sunday morning at church the war was brought closer to home for her when she learned that Lester Watson had been killed on the Western Front. He was the younger brother of Glenn, and as Mrs. Watson was telling her the news she could see the towheaded little boy wearing his brother's handed-down overalls—knee patches and all—as he trailed after them to and from school and never said a word.

Her own sudden tears were also for Ben, said to be somewhere on the Western Front, wherever that was. Ashamed that she hadn't written Ben, she got his address from Alice and wrote to him that very night.

Ben's answer was like from a stranger. He complained about everything, the mud and stink in the trenches, the body lice he couldn't get rid of and how dirty the French people were. Instead of the happy brother she used to know, it was as if some old grouch had stepped out of Ben's letter and started telling her how disgusting everything about the war was.

So saddened was she by this great change in Ben that she could not keep her mind on the sermon the Sunday after she heard from him. When Reverend Willis closed the service by asking them to pray for all the soldiers in the war, the living and the dead, she found herself with her head bowed, crying and thinking of Ben as already one of the dead. After that not even the fast ride home in the black monster, with the air blowing fresh on her face, could take her thoughts from Ben and the mud and lice and the stink of the dead all around him in that foreign land so far away from Oklahoma.

Yet in her weekly letter to Sarah, she did not say a word about Ben and all the sadness she felt. Instead she forced herself to talk about things on the farm that would make Sarah happy, knowing Sarah would have plenty of time later on for sad things.

She had a fresh worry about the war when the President announced a new Draft requiring all men eighteen to forty-five to register for military service. "Don't fret, Honey," Hamp told her the day he drove off to register. "Uncle Sam needs my high-priced cotton more than he needs me." Whether this was the reason or not, it turned out that he was not drafted.

The only good thing she could see coming from the drought this year was that the cotton crop was so skimpy the picking was not taking as long as usual. This meant the children would not have to miss as much school as usual. One November morning they were picking in the last field when a passing neighbor stopped his team and came to the fence to shout out that the war was over.

She was sure this was false news. It couldn't be true. American troops were still being sent to France. Yet as suddenly as lightning striking the cotton patch, the twins and Harold threw off their cotton sacks and began to shout and jump around.

But not Monroe. "The war's over?" he called back, as if he didn't want to believe it. "You kiddin'?"

Hardly believing she was hearing right herself, she hurried over to the fence with the children to hear it again, her mind on Ben every step she took. All Mr. Stapp had heard in Briggs was that Germany had surrendered, but that was enough to make her grip the top wire of the fence as she choked back stinging tears of joy and hoped that

Ben was still alive.

True or false, the news put a stop to their cotton picking. They weighed up and went to the house, the boys full of war talk as they rushed ahead, while she, still concerned about Ben, walked slowly along with Agnes and Edith. It didn't seem possible to her that the war could be over when the Americans had been fighting over there for such a short time. There must be a catch to it that Mr. Stapp had missed.

Yet before noon Hamp came riding home on a mule from one of his peanut thresher teams. He had heard the news, too, and had quit for the day to come home and celebrate with the family.

"It's too good to be true," she and Hamp kept saying to each other, and after dinner they all piled in the car and drove first to his mama's house and then on to Mama's to rejoice over this good news, shed tears over it, and shake their heads as if they still could not believe it was true.

She had hardly grown used to the war being over when the newspaper started carrying headlines of thousands of people dying in Europe from Spanish Influenza. When she realized they meant the flu, it didn't seem so bad, yet her first thought was of Ben, whom they had now heard from. He was not only alive and well, he seemed to have forgotten all the awful things he said earlier about soldiering, for he wrote this time that he had decided to stay in Germany with the Army of Occupation. About the outbreak of flu, he never said a word.

A few weeks later when she read in the newspaper that the flu epidemic had appeared in Boston and New York City and was moving on west—killing people right and left—she realized she had been wrong in thinking it was ordinary flu. They said that in some cities people were dying faster than they could be buried, and the worst part was that the doctors did not seem to know what caused the flu or how to cure it.

According to what she read, it was just a matter of time until the plague—as they were beginning to call it now—would spread all across the country. The night she read this, she was so alarmed for Sarah that she told Hamp they should go right to Kickapoo in the morning and bring her home before it could reach this part of the country. Whatever was to happen she wanted the family to all be together.

But Hamp laughed at her for getting herself so concerned about something so far away, and said they would have to wait until Sunday to make the long trip to get Sarah. He was too far behind with his plowing to stop on a work day.

Yet before the week was out, Andy Billings appeared at the farm with Sarah. He said the Superintendent of Schools in Kickapoo had closed the schools as a precaution in case the flu did spread this far west. Sarah had a long vacation at home while the rest of the children, except Harold and Edith, had to go to school each morning, with Monroe complaining every day—just the way Bob used to— about having to go to school at all.

By the time Christmas arrived, she was greatly relieved that the flu epidemic seemed to have passed through Kickapoo, taking only a few lives and had completely skipped them out here in the country. Brown was the only person she knew who came down with it, and he was up and around in a week. A Christmas letter from the Billings said they were all well.

As she sat in church with Hamp and the children on Christmas Eve, listening to Reverend Willis repeat the old words about peace on earth and goodwill toward men, her eyes brimmed with tears of happiness. Year after year as far back as she could remember she had heard those same words, but they had never touched her heart the way they did tonight here among their friends and neighbors, the war over, Ben alive, and all the family well.

She still had the happy feeling next day as she and Alice helped Mama put Christmas dinner on the table, while Papa and Tommy and Hamp sat talking by the stove in the front room, and the children filled the house with happy sounds. After a year filled with so many unsettling events, it was a relief and a comfort to celebrate this holiday.

In January, on a sunny morning so mild it could have passed for October, except for the leafless trees and bare fields on either side of the road, she and Hamp drove Sarah to the Billings' house in

Kickapoo to start to school again after her extra long vacation.

On the way back home, while Harold and Edith were in the back seat making a noisy game of counting the animals they saw on the farms along the road, she was sitting silently next to Hamp and thinking now was a good time to bring up again something she had been trying for the last year to talk him into doing—sell the farm, move to Kickapoo, and go to work for Andy Billings selling insurance. That way they could keep the family all together and give them a good education at the same time.

After a while she turned to Hamp and said, "From what Sarah says about what she's learning, high school might be just what Monroe needs."

"Maybe," Hamp said, his eyes staying on the washboard road.

"I know he makes trouble at school. But Mrs. Whitaker does say he's smarter than Sarah."

"Oh, in some ways Monroe's too smart for his own good. He knows how to git someone's goat. Trouble is, he don't seem to realize that's no way to git along in this world."

"He may grow out of that. Once he gets where he can start learning something he likes,"

"Likes?" Hamp said. "Seems to me the first thang a person ought to learn is to do what has to be done. When it has to be done. Whether he likes it or not."

"Haven't I heard you say many a time what a good worker Monroe is?"

"Sure," Hamp said, taking his eyes off the road for a moment to smile around at her. "When I'm breathin' down his neck. Or when he takes a notion to work. But look at Sarah. Put her off in a cotton patch with him... jist the two of 'em. She'll pick more than Monroe every time. But if I was there, she couldn't pick fast enough to beat Monroe if she had four hands."

"But, Hamp, that's just it. You'd be there if we lived in Kickapoo."

"If we lived in Kickapoo," Hamp muttered. "Honey, we aw' ready plowed that ground so many times we 'bout wore it out."

"But it's true."

"So's what I keep tellin' you and Andy about me. Farmin's all I know."

"You can learn to sell insurance."

"Maybe. But I'd still be a fish out of water round all them townsfolk."

"Why, Hamp, everybody who meets you likes you. Andy thinks you'd do fine. And so do I."

"Suppose I don't. Who's goin' to feed us? And keep clothes on our back?"

"I'm not worried about that," she said, but Hamp kept his eyes on the road and didn't say anything else. After a little, she said, "We've got to think about the rest of the children, too. They've got to have their chance."

When Hamp still didn't say anything she had to let the talk die where it had died so many times before. The two of them rode in bumpy silence until Edith got tired of the game with Harold and climbed in the front seat and was put down for a nap.

It was nearly noon when Hamp turned into the driveway at home and surprised her by driving the car on past the house, past the car barn, past the milk house and smokehouse. Followed by the barking Tige, he drove to the barn lot gate near the windmill, where the noise of Tige and the car raised a commotion among the chickens and turkeys around the barns. Roosters started crowing, and the two turkey gobblers began gobbling and strutting among the turkey hens to let them know they were still in charge.

The horses and mules standing in the lot pricked up their ears and turned their heads towards the car, but over in the cow lot, where most of the cows were lying on the sunny side of their barn, one cow standing near the windmill went on sipping and sipping water from the trough as if she didn't see or hear anything around her.

Harold jumped out to play with Tige, but she sat watching Hamp looking straight ahead. She knew this was a picture he had seen thousands of times and she could not imagine what he was looking at. Finally he took a deep breath, slowly let it out and said, "I'd sooner have this farm than the best job in Kickapoo. And the best house to live in, to boot."

Struck by the sadness in Hamp's voice, she reached over the sleeping Edith and touched his arm. "I know," she said, and through her mind went the years and years he had worked summer and winter to turn a bare pasture into the farmstead around them, and to make the whole farm prosper.

Yet as much as it hurt her to make Hamp unhappy like this, she could not make herself say, "Then we'll have to stay here." For if they didn't sell the farm and move to Kickapoo, she couldn't see how they could ever get the children educated.

They sat in silence, Hamp barely shaking his head. After a while he hunched his shoulders and said, "Well, I guess I better git a team ready for plowin'. This weather's too good to last."

"I'll get some dinner ready," she said, and gently shook Edith and lifted the sleepy head out of her lap.

Chapter 30

She was a little worried when no letter came from Sarah on the first Friday after they drove her back for the start of her second year at Kickapoo High School. This was the first time they had ever not had a Friday letter from Sarah, and she could not believe it was because Sarah had simply forgotten to write.

Fretting silently through the weekend, she asked Hamp at dinner on Monday if he would go get the mail instead of having to wait until the children brought it on their way home after school.

When Hamp came back without a letter, she was sure something was wrong, and she wanted him to drive them to Kickapoo that very evening. He still smiled at her worries, said the letter would probably turn up in a day or two, and went back to his plowing.

The next day she felt a little guilty about being pleased to see a cold rain come on and drive Hamp out of the field before noon, but her guilt did not keep her from prevailing on him during dinner to drive to the mailbox once more. This time Hamp brought home a letter, and one look at his face told her that he was not carrying good news.

Grace Billings wrote that Sarah was in bed with a fever. They had the doctor looking after her. She would write again soon, and in the meantime she hoped they wouldn't worry. Anxious to have Grace explain more than was written there, she read the few lines out loud again and offered the letter to Hamp.

"Never mind," he said. "I'm goin' to Kickapoo."

As much as she wanted to go with Hamp, she knew this was out of the question and she did not even bring it up. The children would be home from school in a few hours and there were chores to be done and supper to make.

She watched Hamp down another cup of coffee. Then he put on his coat and hat, threw his slicker over his arm and gave her hand a hurried squeeze as he called good-bye to Harold and Edith playing in the front room.

Afraid to mention Sarah's name, she followed Hamp to the kitchen door and kept it open a crack so she could see him and still keep out of the rain, which was now mixed with sleet. She watched him turn the car around, slipping and sliding back and forth, in spite of the chains on the rear wheels, before he had it headed down the driveway and roared away.

Within an hour, Hamp was back. The car had slid off the road on the hill this side of the church and he left it there in the ditch. "Let the damn thang stay there tilt sprang," he said. "I'm goin' to take the hack."

With the day so far gone and the rain now all sleet, she tried to talk Hamp out of going. She urged him to wait and get an early start in the morning when the sleet would most likely be over, saying the delay could not make that much difference, but Hamp would not hear of it.

While he went off to the barn to put his steadiest team of mules to the hack, she fried some ham and put it in a lard bucket, along with some of the children's cornbread and baked sweet potatoes from the warming closet. In this weather, and with the roads already so slippery, there was no telling how many hours it might take him to cover the ten miles to Kickapoo in the hack, and he might need some food to keep him going.

Once Hamp had gone a second time, she started making a pan of gingerbread to take the place of the children's snack she had sent with him. Sleet rattling against the kitchen windows was a constant reminder of what it was like outside, and she worried about Hamp forcing a team along in such weather. She wasn't too much concerned about the children coming home in it because they were dressed for bad weather, and besides, the sleet was out of the north and they would be walking south all the way.

Even so, when she heard a fumbling at the kitchen door, she was relieved to know the children were home so early, and she hurried to welcome them to the spicy smell of gingerbread that filled the warm kitchen.

But it was Hamp, big as a bear with his slicker on over his heavy coat, the lard bucket in one hand and a tow sack from the barn in the other. While Hamp thawed out in front of the open oven door, drinking fresh coffee and bolting pieces of the children's fresh gingerbread, he told her about the mules slipping and falling down, one after the other, trying to go up the icy hills, until Samson fell across the tongue of the hack and broke it. After that there was nothing to be done but tie the tongue back together the best he could by wrapping it tight with the butt lines and come on home feeding the mules, the hack weaving every which way behind them.

She was so happy to have Hamp back home safe and sound she never asked why he had brought a tow sack in the house with him until he asked for her big scissors and sat down and started cutting the tow sack into strips. "This sackin'll give me footing on the ice. Looks like I'm goin' to have to walk to Kickapoo."

"No!" she said, catching her breath, and then she told Harold and Edith to go back in the front room and play. When she had closed the door after them, she said, "Hamp, you can't do it. It'll be pitch dark before you could get half way there in this weather. What if you fell in a ditch? Nobody will be out. You could hurt yourself and be there all night. You could freeze to death. This time you have to listen to me."

"I'm listenin'," Hamp said quietly, but he went on wrapping the strips of tow sack around the foot of his boot and up his trouser leg, and tying them below his knee like leggings.

In spite of all her pleading with him, Hamp would not change his mind. He admitted he was being stubborn, but he said it was all his own fault they hadn't gone to see about Sarah sooner. "If anythang happens to her, I'll never forgive myself. So let's not talk about it anymore."

After watching Hamp out of sight a third time, again carrying the bucket of cornbread, fried ham and baked sweet potatoes, she closed the kitchen door, dried her eyes on her apron and started making supper. She wanted to have it mostly ready by the time the children got home from school so she could go out with them to do the chores.

She usually never had to help with the chores this time of year, but with Hamp gone she could not trust Monroe to take charge and get the job done. He could do it if he wanted to, and he might do it, but no one could predict when he might take a notion to put the chores off while he egged on a fight between the twins, or got the boys in some other trouble only he could think of.

Out in the freezing, sleet-covered barnyard, while Monroe and Otis and Arthur were in the cow barn, each one with two cows to milk, and Agnes and Edith were gathering the eggs and fastening the chickens and turkeys in their house for the night, she and Harold fed the horses and mules and hogs, and then went to the milk house and got the cream separator ready for the buckets of steaming milk coming soon from the cow barn.

In less than an hour, with Harold turning the separator—a job he liked to do—the milk from the cows had the cream spun out of it and drained down the spout into the can for the creamery. The skim milk had been carried out to the hog trough where the big boar and the sows, now all in the same pen until all the sows were bred, squealed and slurped and fought over it to the last drop before turning back to root around in the dirty sleet once more for their shelled corn.

It was dark before she and the others were back in the house, washed up and ready to eat their own supper. She had purposely said as little as possible to the children about Sarah being sick and their papa walking to town to see how she was, and only Harold showed any concern.

After supper when he came back inside from feeding the scraps to Tige, he turned his usually happy face, now solemn and wide-eyed, up to her and worried out loud about his papa being all alone out there in the cold dark.

"Maybe Papa is already at the Billings by now," she said, smiling down at him, but that did not keep her from worrying about Hamp herself as she washed and scalded everything from the separator, cleaned up in the kitchen and kept the children busy at their studies.

It wasn't that Hamp couldn't walk the ten miles to Kickapoo, even in this awful weather. Every day he was used to walking from morning till night behind the plow. But as she had warned him, on a black night such as this if he should fall hard on the ice or slip in a ditch and hurt himself, he might freeze to death lying alone somewhere in the dark waiting for help.

The children went to bed at their usual time of eight o'clock— after noisy dashes out and back through the night to the outhouse. The fire in the front room slowly burned itself down. When the room began to get cold, she didn't build up the fire or go to bed herself. With the lamp turned low, she sat worrying and dozing, only to be brought fully awake again and again by the clock striking.

Eventually she went to the bedroom and came back with a quilt, which she wrapped around herself and sat down again in Hamp's big chair, waiting for she didn't know what. All she knew was that she didn't feel like going to bed while Hamp might be somewhere out there in the cold dark night.

Yet her thoughts always came back to Sarah. While thinking about Hamp, she would be reminded of something she had read during the recent flu epidemic. She tried to tell herself Sarah was most likely well by now. She remembered reading that some folks got well in a few days, even without a doctor, and she felt better until it crossed her mind that she had also read that in three days some of them were dead.

After that, whenever she dozed she dreamed Sarah had died and they were burying her in a hole in the red ground next to Bob's grave. The strange thing was that even though the coffin was open and she was standing beside it, she could not see if it really was Sarah inside. Each time she leaned towards the coffin for a closer look, she would be awakened by the clock striking before she could see anything.

Finally determined to find out if it was Sarah in the coffin, she had put her hand on the coffin and was starting to lean over it when the clock woke her again. Stiff and cold she jerked upright and sat rubbing her eyes and counting the strokes while her dream faded away. Once she opened her eyes she noticed the gray dawn at the windows and heard a rooster crowing.

Now that she was fully awake, anxiety about Hamp and Sarah flooded her mind again and stayed with her as she stood up and went to work. She built a fire in the heating stove and one in the cook stove. Then when she was starting breakfast she called to the children to get up, repeating her call until all of them but Edith were dressing around the warm heating stove.

Leaving Agnes, who was yawning in the looking glass at the washstand and braiding her hair, to finish making the breakfast, she bundled up and led the sleepy boys out into the early light. The sleet storm had passed and the pale sky was cloudless, but the freezing air still took her breath away as she walked along the icy path to the barnyard, carrying the lantern and trailed by a line of sleepy boys.

They had the chores all done by the time the first gray light had turned to rosy dawn, and the blood-red sun sliding up out of the dark horizon had grown to a ball of fire that blinded them as they shivered back to the kitchen.

Later when the children left for school, blowing smoke with every breath as they slipped and slid down the driveway calling warnings to each other, that same sun was blinding white and still dazzling to the eyes as it glinted and sparkled off the ice-coated limbs of trees, and posts and barbed wire and everything else in sight.

Holding Edith's hand, she stood between her and Harold, shivering and squinting until the other children reached the end of the driveway and turned to wave goodbye. Yet before she got back to the house, Hamp and Sarah were on her mind again.

She worried through a long day and another near sleepless night, this one in bed, without any word from Kickapoo. Yet desperate as she was to hear from Hamp and Sarah, she said nothing about it because she didn't want to scare the children by mentioning her fears to them. They were used to having Sarah gone, but already they were asking her what could be keeping Papa in Kickapoo for so long.

On the second morning, when she went out in the dazzling sunshine to see the children off to school, water was dripping from the eaves and the heat from the sun was cracking the ice on the trees and sending pieces of ice tinkling against lower limbs and on to the ground.

After worrying through the morning and making do with a bite of dinner for herself, she worked on a newly started quilt in an absentminded way as she waited and waited through the evening. The first hint she had that someone might be coming was Tige's bark. Harold jumped up from his play with Edith by the stove and ran to look out the front door.

"It's Mister Billing's car!" she heard him shout, and was relieved and scared at the same time.

Chapter 31

The instant she heard that Andy Billings' car was coming up the lane she dropped her needle and was out through the kitchen to the back door in one rush. There she stopped, suddenly too scared to go on in case it was bad news.

As the barking Tige led the nose of Andy's mud-splattered flivver past the back corner of the house, she saw Hamp and Andy in the front seat, but instead of feeling relieved by the sight of Hamp alive and well, she was more scared than ever.

Watching Hamp step to the ground, muddy to the waist, she held onto the kitchen door, ready to run to him but too anxious for news of Sarah to say a word. Not until Hamp turned and saw her, gave her a tired smile and called, "She's all right," did she have the strength to let go of the door and hurry out.

Andy, as muddy as Hamp, got out of the car and came around to say he could only stay long enough to say hello and goodbye. In between he added several times that he had been stuck in more than enough mudholes for one day and that he wanted to get back through all of them before dark.

In the kitchen Hamp joshed with Harold and Edith about his muddy clothes while he washed up, making light of his long sleety walk to Kickapoo, except to tell her above their heads that it was worse than any march he had ever been on in the army.

He had found Sarah with such a high fever she was out of her head and didn't know him. He sat holding her hand for hours while she babbled on about everything and nothing.

At this point in his story, Hamp turned from the towel rack where he was drying his hands and face, and said, "Honey, you'll never guess what that Sarah said over and over again." A sheepish smile came to his face and he paused before going on. "She was worried that you'd be worried because she didn't write."

He went on to say that when Sarah's fever broke towards morning she seemed to get well all at once. She wanted to come home with him that day, but the doctor said to wait another day. So he went to Brown and Rissy's for the night, but finding how muddy the roads were in the morning he was afraid to bring Sarah home until they dried still another day.

"Tomorrow mornin'," Hamp said, "I aim to git Tipsy and Topsy to pull that car out of the ditch. Then tomorrow evenin' we'll go git Sarah. Harold, maybe we'll take you and Edith with us if y'all've been good while I was gone."

Two pairs of big blue eyes turned from Hamp to look up at her with the same question on the solemn faces.

"Oh, yes," she said right away. "Very good. They both helped with the chores, too."

"Well, we'll all go bring your sister home and let her rest up for a few days," Hamp said, and when the children had gone out of the kitchen, his joshing manner dried up and he shook his head at her. "Sarah could've died."

The thought of it kept them both silent for a time.

The next morning at breakfast Monroe seemed more than pleased to learn he was going to be kept out of school to go with his papa to help get the car out of the ditch.

Later she saw him going side by side with Hamp past the house, him already within two inches of Hamp's height and only fourteen. He was all smiles driving Tipsy and Topsy and watching them prance along dragging the doubletree and a log chain to pull the car out of the ditch.

At dinner, however, Monroe looked put out when he heard he had to go to school that evening, but he didn't argue with Hamp about it, just silently finished eating his meal and left the house.

That night, during supper, the excitement of having the pale looking Sarah at the table and telling them about her awful experience was suddenly interrupted when Arthur, on being teased by Monroe for spilling some buttermilk on himself, let out that Monroe had hid out in the woods all evening instead of being in school. Monroe's look of rage at Arthur was cut short by Hamp's rising voice. "Is that so, Monroe?"

When Monroe looked down at his plate and mumbled, "I guess so." She was afraid of what Hamp might do.

She had seen him take Monroe straight outside from the table and give him a whipping for playing hooky, but it had been a long time since he had done that. Now, once Hamp repeated his question to Monroe and got a clear "yessir," he turned back to Sarah as if nothing had happened and asked her to go on.

That night in bed Hamp told her that at last he was going to give Monroe the punishment he had promised him if he ever caught him playing hooky again—sell his saddle horse, Whiskers. More than once she had talked Hamp out of doing that, always after first getting Monroe's word that he would never play hooky again. Now, as much as she hated to have Monroe lose his horse, she agreed that it had to happen.

A few days later Hamp did sell the horse, and kept Monroe in his chair after Saturday dinner to explain that he had done it because of his string of broken promises not to play hooky any more. When she saw Monroe looking at his papa fit to kill, she was a little scared that he was going to make things worse by trying to argue himself out of trouble, as he was able to do now and then with her. But Monroe never denied a thing, never even said a word.

Hamp finished by saying, "Don't ever give your word less you mean it, Monroe. But when you do, by God stick to it."

"Yessir," Monroe said. He got up from the table, walked slowly out the kitchen door and started running towards the barn lot, apparently to see if Whiskers really was gone.

Afterwards she was sorry to see Monroe sullen around the house, out of sorts with her and everyone else for days. He never spoke to his papa unless Hamp said something to him first, and for the rest of the time Sarah stayed home he was so bad tempered to her—even making fun of her piano playing—that she accused him of being jealous because he had to go to school while she was having a vacation. He denied that, yet after she went back to school he was a little friendlier around the house.

Hamp never let on to her that he was bothered by or even noticed Monroe's sullen behavior, but as days passed into weeks she began to see a change come over Hamp himself. He seemed to have lost his easygoing humor. He no longer joshed so much with the children, and when he did say something it was usually to be short with them, or with her.

She couldn't help noticing how he had changed towards her, even in bed. Now as soon as she blew out the lamp and lay down he would say goodnight in a matter-of-fact voice, never offering to so much as kiss her goodnight, and turn facing away from her. Yet though he stayed silent there beside her until she fell asleep, she knew he was not sleeping.

These days the only person he seemed his old self with was Andy Billings, who had paid him several visits since bringing him home through the mud that time. Yet even with Andy, after a long visit with him in the field one morning, Hamp seemed strangely upset for the rest of the day. When he only fiddled with his supper, she asked him if he felt all right and he said he did, but he still ate only a few bites.

In bed that night after a longer than usual time of silently lying awake, she was almost asleep when she was surprised by Hamp's voice coming out of the dark as if they had just been talking to each other.

"Andy may be right, you know. And not only about Sarah and

the family bein' together. He swears good times for farmers are over. He says sell out right now while the prices are still up. I keep tellin' him I'm not interested, but I do think about Sarah. And the others. This mornin' Andy told me he's got a sure buyer for the whole hunerd and sixty. For more money than I ever thought about. God!" he finished and let out long sigh, almost like a groan.

Unable to believe what she was hearing, she lay there tongue-tied. Before she could think of something to say, Hamp went on in the same low, dream-like voice. "One thing, Mama's sure to be happy livin' in a town again. And Andy keeps after me to come and work for him. So I guess if the man likes the farm, I'll give Kickapoo a try. I'd sooner lose an arm than move, but I reckon you're right. If we're goin' to see the children educated we got to let the farm go."

In spite of all her hopes of moving to Kickapoo, in her heart she had never thought she would ever hear what she had just heard, for she never believed Hamp would be willing to sell the farm. It was on the tip of her tongue to tell him how happy his news made her, but at the sudden thought of what it had cost him to say what he had just said, she lay beside him silent and almost breathless, afraid to say or do anything to make him feel worse.

As she tried to think of what she ought to say, her sorrow for him got too big for words and she found herself crying for the misery he must have been going through, him trying to decide between staying on the farm and doing what he really wanted to do, or giving up the farm and doing what he had to do for her and the children.

She wanted to comfort him, to say that maybe they could find another way out, but she didn't think there was another way, and she couldn't make herself lie about it. Even when his hand drew her head softly against his bare shoulder to let her know he understood how she felt, she could only cry harder.

After the tears had washed her grief away, she was happy to have Hamp's arms around her and his lips against hers, and later when she was falling asleep she knew she had never loved him so much as right then, not even in those unforgettable weeks of the honeymoon in the little log house when he was on her mind morning, noon and night.

Chapter 32

Once Hamp decided to sell the farm, move to Kickapoo, and go to work for Andy Billings selling insurance, the changes started coming so fast she could hardly keep up with them. Yet with Hamp and Andy making all the buying and selling arrangements, she was able to spend her spare time getting everything in the cellar and the house packed and ready to move when the time came. Andy sold the farm for them, and sold to them a two-story house on the far edge of Kickapoo—a house whose backyard ran up against the backyard of the little house he had already sold to Hamp's mama. Now all that had to be done was sell the livestock and farm machinery, and then the family would be ready to move to where her dreams for the education of the children could come true.

One day when she walked to school to say goodbye to Miss Rogers and Mrs. Whitaker, she was surprised to hear that maybe a high school was going to be built somewhere out here in the country in the next couple of years. She knew such a piece of news would only make Hamp unhappier; but she felt she had to tell him anyway.

He took the news with a shrug. "What's done is done," he said, but that did not keep her from thinking she might have been too outspoken about moving to town for the sake of the children's education. Yet that, too, was already past undoing.

Standing in the kitchen one morning in late February, reading the Bill of Public Sale listing their livestock and farm machinery to be sold at auction, she was made unhappy all over again because so many of the animals listed there tugged at her heart, calling up a string of happy memories.

A matched pair of Percheron mares, 10 years old, good mouth, said nothing about the pleasure she often had seeing the dappled Tipsy and Topsy coming along the driveway, necks arched and heads nodding as they picked their big hoofs up and put them down like dancers, or watching the mares drowsing head to tail in the summer shade, or watching their tails switching flies for each other. But most of all, she thought of the soft nickers coming from those huge mothers as they talked to their tottery, baby mule colts.

As she read on, every mule, every cow, almost every animal there called up similar memories. Reading "one Duroe boar" reminded her not so much of that mean old red hog out there in the pen—now half as big as a cow and eating every chicken it could catch—as it did of the sleek little red pig Hamp brought home in a tow sack one day and lifted it out and put in her arms for her to admire, calling it his prize pig.

Old Jack was still alive then, and when the prize pig squirmed loose from her and started to run away, Hamp told Jack, "Git him." In a couple of leaps Old Jack caught the pig and held it by an ear, squealing for its life until Hamp grabbed its hind legs and dropped him back in the sack. Yes, she would miss even the mean old boar that little red pig had grown into.

The morning was starting out cold and drizzly, not the best weather for folks to be standing around outside looking to buy something, but good for selling coffee and she was waiting for the Ladies of the Calvary Methodist Church, who would soon be here to make it by the gallon on her cookstove.

The first of those Ladies to open the kitchen door was Alice, not looking well but always in better spirits out in public than when she saw her at home. Following Alice through the door came Papa and Tommy, rubbing their hands together against the cold—Papa's gray hair when he took off his hat reminding her that he was getting old.

By noon a weak sun breaking through the clouds had dried up the drizzle, and the men ambling down from the auction in the barn lot, a few with wives, seemed to find it pleasant enough eating their dinner in the backyard at tables made from doors laid across sawhorses.

At the center of much laughter at one table sat a fat man whose sagging round face and loud voice seemed familiar to her, but it wasn't until he took off his hat, pretending to cool his chili by fanning it, that he showed off his shiny bald head and she recognized him as the auctioneer who long ago had sold her apple pie to Vernon Carpenter.

That had been more years than she could remember right off, but she would never forget that the pie had cost Vernon twenty-one dollars, and would have cost him no telling how many more if Fred Dawson had not run out of money.

After what happened to her later at the big oak tree, she always thought Vernon must think she had told him a straight-out lie when he proposed and she said she was going to be a schoolteacher and never get married, even though she did believe it at the time. She hadn't seen Vernon since Bob's funeral, and she sort of expected he might come to the sale, but so far he hadn't shown up.

After dinner Molly seemed to want to talk to her, and the two of them wandered out past the parked cars and wagons and teams to the garden, talking about the old days at Oakridge School. The garden was still a tangle of dead vines and stalks, just the way it had been left last fall after the second crop of Irish potatoes had been dug.

Normally Hamp would have had it plowed and harrowed by now, and she would have already planted her Irish potatoes—sprouting right now in a bushel basket down in the cellar. But this year she would have to wait until they moved to town, and Hamp made her a new garden out of his mama's backyard and their own. Then she hoped to make time to get those seed potatoes cut and in the ground before they all shriveled up or rotted.

Molly turned the talk to Fred—who was not here today and who had not been coming to church with her for sometime. Molly said she was having trouble with him because she didn't want to have any more children. It was easy for her to sympathize with Molly, because she was tired of having children herself. Yet she had long ago resigned herself to having to keep on having them for as long as it happened, because she had no real choice. Her only other choice was denying herself to Hamp, which was what Molly was doing to Fred, and she knew she could never bring herself to do that.

"Course you know men," Molly was saying. "Now Fred's gone every Saturday night. He don't say where and I don't ask. Fact is, we don't talk much anymore."

She looked at Molly's face, still pretty in spite of the sad expression on it, but so different from the happy face she used to see years ago that it hardly seemed like the same person. Out of nowhere came the thought of what Mama had told her about satisfying Hamp in bed, or else.

Yet as sorry as she felt for Molly, she still could not bring herself to pass along Mama's advice about such a personal matter. She listened until Molly had talked herself out, and they walked back past the cellar to the house, remarking along the way on how nice the weather had turned out.

The end of the sale did not put an end to her being saddened at leaving the farm, and over the next couple of days as she saw the last of the animals led or hauled away she felt sadder and sadder. Knowing that Hamp must be feeling even worse, she could hardly look him in the face, but he seemed not to notice anything but all the work that was keeping him busy.

Today he was hurrying around with Papa and Tommy helping load their wagons with furniture and bedding, filling every space in-between with boxes of canned goods from the cellar—fruit jars of peaches, vegetables, sausage, pickles and the like, along with the shoulders and hams and sides of bacon from the smokehouse—and then driving off to Kickapoo in the car with Monroe to be there to help unload the wagons. Brown had promised to help out with a wagon and team, but he never showed up either day.

Yet Brown had showed up at the farm the day before the sale wanting to buy Hamp's peanut thresher. He said he didn't see why he couldn't make the same good money with it Hamp had made, and Hamp had said, "Oh, it can make you some money, Brown, if you work at it." Later as they stood watching Brown towing the thresher down the driveway behind his wagon, Hamp said, "Honey, don't hold your breath till we git the money for that thrasher."

The day and the hour came when everything was gone from the farm but the family and the car-all the farm machinery and livestock, every last turkey and chicken, even Hamp's banties.

When she closed the kitchen door behind her on the freshly scrubbed floor, the only sound of farm life around was the groaning of the shut-off windmill as the tail of the fan swung the blades away from the shifting breeze and the sound of the children playing with Tige while they waited to get in the car.

Once upon a time she had looked forward to this moment as a happy event, but now as she took a last notice of the lilac bushes greening up and the fruit trees around the house budding out, and heard the birds going on as if nothing had changed, she was as sad as if headed for a funeral.

At the last minute Hamp made her feel worse when he brought the children to tears by telling them he was leaving Tige behind for the new family coming to live here. He said the dog would be happier in the long run, since the farm was his home. "Besides," he said, "town's no place for a dog to have to live." The children still cried and carried on, but Hamp had his way.

Putting the tearful Edith in the front seat beside her, she closed the door and silently added her own good-bye to Tige to the mournful ones around her, Hamp let the car coast down the driveway to the road, where it started with a pop and a roar as he turned it towards Kickapoo and picked up speed. Like the children, she had tears in her eyes, but her tears were for Hamp. When she heard him say that town was no place for a dog to have to live, she knew he was thinking of himself.

Yet once the children saw their new home, they were so taken by it that they seemed to forget how unhappy they had been about Tige. They ran from room to room upstairs and down, calling, "Come and see!" to each other. In the kitchen, at the turn of a little handle, water spewed into a big metal bowl and disappeared out the bottom when you took the plug out of the hole there. From the center of the ceiling in every room hung a black cord with a dear glass bulb screwed into a metal socket at the end. Pull on the little chain dangling beside the bulb, and the room was instantly filled with more light than you ever got from a coal oil lamp. Pull again and the light went out like magic, leaving the little wires inside the bulb glowing red for a second or two.

But the most astonishing room of all for the children was the little room at the top of the stairs, which was much like the room she remembered from her days at the Marlowe house when she was teaching little Orin. The room had a round white sink, on a pedestal, for washing their hands and face, and a long white tub for bathing in. What caused the most commotion among the children was the contraption that took the place of an outhouse—a seat with a cover that lifted up. Attached behind the seat was a pipe that ran up the wall to a small, flat, water tank, from which a long chain hung down. A pull on the chain brought water rushing down the pipe, through the contraption and out the bottom. It was almost as magic as the light bulbs.

Although it had not been for these newfangled things in the house that she had moved to Kickapoo, she was pleased to have them, and as the days went by she grew more and more used to them. Gradually she came to realize that while her reason for coming to Kickapoo had been to give the children a better education, in moving the less than a dozen miles from the farm to town the family had moved from one world to another.

Chapter 33

She wasted no time getting the children started to school in Kickapoo. She had Sarah take Monroe with her to enroll him in his school downtown. She left Harold and Edith with their Grandma Roberts—now so handy out the back door and across their two vegetable gardens—and walked with Agnes and the twins the few blocks to their school.

She had not expected so many pupils, and finding herself jostled along the hall in the midst of a crowd of boisterous boys and girls, she felt as cowed as Agnes and the twins looked. Yet later when she talked with their teachers, the two women were as friendly as Miss Rogers and Mrs. Whitaker.

As the days passed, she came to see that Andy had been right about reveille not coming so early in town. Instead of following Hamp out of bed before daylight and making breakfast while he and the boys were out in the barnyard doing the chores, now she and Hamp both got up later.

Hamp started a fire in the cookstove for her, and with the rest of the family still sleeping, she made breakfast while he shaved upstairs in the bathroom. Because of his new job, he had to shave every day now, and not when he felt like it, or for some special occasion such as church.

About church, she didn't know what to make of the Methodist church they started going to. It did have a Sunday school, but the sermon that followed was nothing like Reverend Willis's long hellfire sermons that gave the grown-ups something to chew on. And there was no Amen corner of old-timers like Papa to back the preacher up.

Reverend Brinley—new from a religious school back East, so she learned—took only a few minutes to deliver his mild sermon, which he read without ever raising his voice or losing the smile on his soft, jowly face. Seconds later he was standing at the front door of the church, still smiling as he gave a limp handshake to the grown-ups and thanked them politely for coming. His whole performance was one long smile from start to finish.

Along with Hamp's shave every morning went a fresh, starched collar, one of his two neckties and his new suit of clothes, although he never put on his collar, necktie and coat until after breakfast. Leaving the rest of the family still at the table, he would go back upstairs and finish dressing, come down and stick his head in the dining room door to say good-bye to the children.

After she had said good-bye to him at the kitchen door, he would put on his new brown hat, which she thought made him look as handsome as he was the day she saw him for the first time in his soldier hat, and go out the door with a little squeak in his shiny new high topped town shoes. Soon from the car barn—or garage as it was called here in town—would come the noise of the black monster's engine starting and usually coughing and stopping a time or two before it settled down to a steady roar.

Not until Hamp had backed the car out past her at the kitchen window, and was on his way to the Billing Realty and Insurance Company on North Kickapoo Street, did she feel free to turn her complete attention to getting the children off to school.

At first she was little concerned that since the twins had been used to doing chores several hours each day they would not have anything to do with their spare time after school. But she quickly found out she had no need to worry about that.

Before the week was out they were rushing in the house from school for a bite to eat from the warming closet, and then rushing off to an open field a block north of the house where they played baseball with a lot of other boys until suppertime.

When Harold started going with them, she stopped him one day and told him she was afraid he would get hurt playing with the bigger boys.

"But, Mama!" he wailed "I'm the pigtail!"

She took hold of one of his spindly arms, not much bigger than a real pig's tail, and looking at it closely, said, "Pigtail!" as if she didn't know what he was talking about.

"Yeah! And when I get bigger Otis says I can be the real catcher." Otis nodded to her, and off the three boys ran, Harold in the lead.

Only Agnes moped around the house saying she had nothing to do. This went on for a few days until Sarah set about teaching her to play the piano. Next, Edith wanted to learn, too, and from then on, every evening until suppertime, there was no shortage of noise coming from the living room.

Yet from the first day of school, her main concern was Monroe. Without trying to make a nuisance of herself, she asked him questions about his new subjects and new teachers, for unlike the other children, who had something new for school to talk about every night at supper, Monroe never volunteered any news from his school day.

After enough short answers and shrugs her questions got made her realize Monroe thought she was making a nuisance of herself, she stopped asking. But she did keep on asking about the rips and tears to his jacket and the bloodstains on his shirts now and then. Monroe always denied he had been in a fight, saying these had come from wrestling or playing. She never mentioned her suspicions to Hamp, afraid of what he would do if he learned that Monroe had been fighting.

One night at suppertime when Monroe came to the table with a bruise on his face and Hamp asked him about it, Monroe did admit he had a fight with a boy after school that day. "But it wasn't my fault," he said. "One of the big boys was picking on me. You can ask Sarah if he didn't."

Before Hamp could say anything, Sarah said, "I've told you a dozen times, Monroe, you can't fight 'em all. The sooner you stop trying to beat up every boy that calls you a hick, the sooner they'll stop calling you one."

At first Hamp seemed a little taken aback by Sarah's outburst, which was so unlike her. Then instead of continuing questioning Monroe, he surprised everybody by cocking his head at no one in particular and saying, "That makes sense, Sarah."

Hamp then smiled at the ferocious look Monroe was giving Sarah and said, "Monroe, you keep your fists to yourself from now on. No matter who calls you a hick. You hear?"

Quickly Monroe said, "Yessir."

"If it'll make you feel any better," Hamp went on, "ever day I see folks eyein' me like they thank I'm a hick. I try to smile and not to let it bother me. I guess to them, I am... and maybe they're right."

As the heat of spring came on and the doors and windows were kept open, the noise from the piano was not all she had to listen to every day. Cars were always roaring and sputtering by in front of the house, and half a block south towards town a streetcar squeaked and groaned by every hour from early morning until midnight, its bell jangling now and then to warn people to get out of the way.

Even louder noises came from two blocks down the slope to the west, where railroad trains clanged slowly by several times a day, their whistles tearing the air with long drawn-out yowls like the ones that had scared Alice and her and Emma so much the first time they heard them in the tent that night long ago, way back in Indian Territory.

She had never expected to find so much noise way out here in the edge of Kickapoo—more noise in a day than she was used to hearing on the farm in a month. Neither had she thought she would miss the comforting sounds of roosters crowing at dawn, birds waking up peeping and chattering to each other, a horse nickering or a cow bawling, wild geese honking their way across the sky day and night, or even the shivery night sounds of owls and whippoorwills making the dark mysterious and spooky.

She had not heard one mockingbird since she left the farm. Once she thought she did, but when she hurried to the front door so she could hear better, it was only a boy going by and playing with a whistle.

At night as she tried to go to sleep, she would even have welcomed the noise of yapping coyotes to that of the neighbor's tied-up dog breaking into a fit of barking every time it heard the streetcar squeaking and groaning by the corner. Hamp had been right about town being no place for a dog.

Although she did not like it that she was always surrounded by noise and people, and strangers at that, she was thankful that those long days in the cotton patch were over and done with.

While she liked having less work to do, she did not like having to buy every mouthful of food the family ate. Used to having more milk, butter, and eggs than they could eat, she had to think now about having enough to go around. Milk came in quart bottles to the back door before she got up in the morning, and even though she kept ordering more and more bottles, for the first few days they were always running out of milk.

The same was true of butter and eggs, and there was no cream in a milk house out in the backyard to churn into more butter and no bushel basket of eggs to reach into for as many as you wanted, knowing that more were waiting for you in the nests out in the henhouse. Neither was there a cellar with plenty of apples and Irish potatoes and sweet potatoes, and fruit jars full of every kind of food from pickled peaches to sausage, nor a smokehouse with hams and shoulders and bacon hanging from the rafters.

As easy as it was to understand, it was very hard for her to get used to the idea that, once they had eaten what they brought with them from the farm, every last mouthful of food the family ate had to be bought.

She had started trading at a big grocery store three blocks away towards town. She was careful to buy only what she had to have and to make it go as far as she could, but the grocery bill was always bigger than she expected. Without ever mentioning the size of it, Hamp would take her signed slips to the store and pay Mr. Freeman.

Having to spend so much cash money week after week just to live, made her also worry for Hamp's mama and Lizzie. His mama's war pension wouldn't go very far these days, and even though she knew his mama had some money in the bank before she got her part for the sale of the farm, that and what she had left after she bought her house in town would not last her forever.

Hamp borrowed a team and plow and harrow from Browny, and by plowing up most of the two backyards, he had made her a garden about half as big as her garden at the farm. She planted every foot of it in vegetables, including the shriveled up Irish potatoes, and spent many an hour, with Harold and Edith helping, hoeing and watering the growing plants, trying to hurry them along to the table.

In spite of all the things she was finding about living in town that she did not like, she never complained about anything to Hamp, or to his mama and Lizzie, whom she saw several times a day now that they lived in hollering distance of each other. With five of the children in school right where she had wanted them for years, she was determined not to complain about anything, no matter how much it bothered her.

No, if Hamp could only come to like his job with Andy, she would not ask for anything more, but it was too soon to tell how well he was going to get along as an insurance salesman. After a few days he did come home one night joking that he was now worth more dead than alive, explaining that Andy had made him take out an insurance policy on himself.

"You know, Hamp, if you're goin' to sell the stuff you got to believe in it," Hamp quoted Andy, imitating his drawling twang and little grin exactly, and then he added in his own voice, "God knows I need to sell some, if I can jist ever learn how it's done."

Chapter 34

At first Hamp ate dinner downtown with Andy at the Kickapoo Club, which Andy had wanted Hamp to join because he said it would be a good way for him to pick up business, but Hamp was soon coming home for dinner, saying he couldn't stand all the whiskey drinking that went on there in spite of Prohibition.

At night Hamp started going out after supper two or three times a week, telling her it was the only chance he had to talk to some of his prospects—as he called the people he was trying to sell an insurance policy—the men he could not talk to on their job during the day. One night he came home smelling of whiskey, mad that a man who drank half a bottle of the stuff between supper and bedtime would then say he could not afford the cost of a life insurance policy.

As the months passed, she had no way of knowing from Hamp whether he was making a good or bad insurance salesman, because he never said much about what he actually did all day, although now and then he would let drop that he had sold another policy. One day while Grace Billings was showing her the best places in

Kickapoo to shop, Grace told her Andy thought Hamp was a natural born salesman.

When she passed this along to Hamp that night in bed, he sighed and said, "Oh, Honey, I guess I wish it was true. You ought to see Andy workin' on a prospect. You wouldn't believe it. He gits so fired up about all the reasons why that policy is jist right for that man... the man would have to be deaf, dumb, and blind not to sign up."

"But you'll learn how to do it."

"As far as that goes, I can already do it. It's jist that I cain't git worked up over a prospect the way he can. Yet he thanks I worry too much when I let one git away. I never told him this, but sometimes I do it on purpose. If I find out from his wages and the size of his family that he's already got more mouths to feed than he can put food in, I let him go. But if I ever told Andy this, why he'd go right through the roof."

It was on the tip of her tongue to ask Hamp if he was making enough money yet to pay for the food they were putting in their own mouths, but she let the moment pass, afraid the answer might be "no" and he might take her question as a criticism.

When school let out for the summer, she had not realized what it was going to be like having a houseful of children underfoot and nothing to keep them busy from breakfast to bedtime. She could find enough for Sarah and Agnes to keep them busy, more or less, around the house, but after she had finished having the boys take turns hoeing the garden until not a live weed or sprig of grass was left in it, she talked to Hamp about sending Monroe and the twins out to her family to live for a few weeks and help with the farm work.

This was all right with Hamp, but Monroe didn't want to go, mainly, she suspected, because he never got along with Tommy, whose slurred speech put a lot of people off. Hamp said maybe it would be better if the boys worked for Brown, who always needed help. Besides, they could walk the two miles out there in the morning and walk back home at night.

Brown's oldest boy and namesake had been expelled from school the year before for drinking whiskey, and she was afraid a summer in his company might not be good for the boys, especially Monroe. Hamp shrugged off her worries, saying Brown had told him Browny had learned his lesson, and it was settled that the boys would start to work the first of the week.

Before Monday came around, Otis, without saying a word to anybody, got a job working for Mr. Freeman down at the grocery store, a job he was paid for, while Monroe and Arthur started spending their summer days working for their Uncle Brown for nothing.

As the long hot summer drew on, she came to realize that while Andy thought Hamp was a born salesman, Hamp would never be happy in town. His heart was back on the farm.

———————————◆———————————

She had gone for so long without a baby that she thought the first sign of one must be a mistake, and she put off telling Hamp until she was sure. The night she did tell him, he turned over and gave her a kiss and said, "Good. We'll have it in Colorado."

He had threatened to move out there before, but Andy had always been able to talk him out of quitting, arguing that business in Kickapoo was bound to get better before too long. But this time Hamp quit his job after Christmas and went by railroad to Colorado looking for a farm to buy.

Every day from then on, Monroe pestered her to let him spend Saturday night with Browny, but she refused, not wanting him to be away while Hamp was gone. Yet on Friday she gave in when Monroe said, "I'll make a bargain with you, Mama. Let me go and I promise to do better in school."

Monroe came home on Sunday saying he had a wonderful time, and all the next week he was so cheerful around the house she let him go again the next Saturday. Early Sunday morning an unhappy Brown was at the door with Monroe, who shuffled in red-eyed and with a hangdog look on his face.

After she shooed the other children out of the kitchen and closed the door, Brown said Rissy had been awakened during the night by shouting coming from the barn. When he rushed out to find out what the matter was, he found Monroe and Browny drunk and singing to the cows. "What bothers me the most" Brown said, "is that Monroe brought the whiskey."

She doubted this because she knew Monroe had no money, but since Monroe never denied it, she had to believe Brown. Yet when Brown left, she said, "Monroe, where did you get any money to buy whiskey?"

Without looking up, Monroe said "It was Browny's whiskey."

"But you didn't tell your uncle that."

Still not looking up, Monroe said, "I didn't want to get Browny in more trouble."

She stared hard at Monroe but said nothing. At last he looked up as if surprised that she might be doubting him and said, "Honest, Mama."

"All right, you'll have to settle this with your papa. Now go to bed. You're in no condition to be seen in church."

She didn't feel like going to church herself, but she got everybody ready at the usual time, put a penny for the collection plate in each child's hand, and walked out into the sunshine. Silently she and Sarah led the way, followed by Agnes and Edith, with the three noisy boys last.

When Hamp came back from Colorado, he was as cheerful as he used to be in the old days, joshing with her and the children and saying again and again how great it was going to be back living on a farm. She didn't have the heart to spoil his good humor right away with the bad news about Monroe, and she kept putting it off.

Hamp had found several farms for sale and wanted to sell the house and go right back and get settled on one before the baby came. She reminded him that she was pretty far along with the baby for such a long move, and besides, maybe they should not take the children out of school this time of the year.

Hamp agreed to wait, saying he would find some kind of job in the meantime to help pay the mortgage. The first night that he came home without having found a job he remarked at supper he reckoned jobs in Kickapoo were scarce as hens' teeth. Harold and

Edith laughed so hard he had to repeat the saying each night.

Funny as it was for the children, she knew it was not funny for Hamp, so she still kept putting off adding to his worry by not telling him about Monroe's drinking. At the end of the second week he came home saying a man he had once sold a life insurance policy to told him of a job as a streetcar conductor, and he took it. At supper the joke about jobs and hens' teeth died, and this time Hamp laughed as much as the children.

That night she told Hamp what a fool she had made of herself letting Monroe visit Browny. After she told him the whole story, he said he had already heard it from Brown, and that Brown found out the boys had been drinking during both of Monroe's visits. And that wasn't all. Brown was convinced Monroe furnished the whiskey both times.

Hearing all this, she felt like even more of a fool, yet it also made her mad that Monroe would treat her this way. His promising to do better in school and not doing it would have been bad enough, but to beg for a favor and then lie to her about the whiskey was being too sneaky to talk about. She could hardly believe he had done it, and she said she would face Monroe herself with the story, but Hamp said to let him handle it.

The next night after supper, as she was excusing the children from the table, Hamp asked Monroe to stay, and started telling him about his trip to Colorado. He talked about the many changes since the year he lived there, and went on to tell Monroe of the hard time he had here in Kickapoo trying to find a job, any kind of job at all except manual labor. "Not that I'm too good to dig ditches," he said, "if that's all the work there is."

Wondering what Hamp was leading up to, she listened with much interest as he went on to say that his trip, and the trouble he had just had trying to find a new job in Kickapoo, had made him realize how much the West had changed since he was a boy. The time of free land where a man could start with nothing but his two bare hands and make a go of it was over and gone. To get ahead today you had to have an education.

"Your mama's right about this," Hamp said, lifting a hand

towards her and causing Monroe to turn questioning eyes on her sitting watching him. "That's why we're in Kickapoo instead of still out there on the farm. The trouble is... I ain't got the education to make us a decent livin' in town. But you'll be able to do it, Monroe... if you git an education. That's why you got to start doing your best in school."

Hamp turned the talk to Monroe's poor grades and asked him what he thought the trouble was. Apparently so relieved that the word "whiskey" didn't seem to be coming up, Monroe surprised her by not repeating a word of what he always said to her about hating school and hating living in town. Instead, he talked easily about how hard he had been studying lately, and ended by saying, "I reckin I'll be doing a whole lot better real soon."

Nodding approval, Hamp leaned back in his chair and said as quietly as before, "It's a great feelin' bein' drunk, ain't it, Monroe."

Monroe's mouth dropped open and he broke out in a blush, but he never said a word as Hamp went on in the same easy tone. "When I was about your age, I got the feelin' many a time out there on the ranch in Colorado."

This was news to her, but she was so busy watching Monroe now fearfully watching his papa that she gave it only a passing thought.

"The trouble with whiskey," Hamp was saying, "is nothing good ever comes from gitt'n drunk. And it ain't like your hankerin' to play hooky. I cain't beat it out of you. You got to learn it for yourself. You believe that, Monroe?"

Suddenly looking relieved again, Monroe quickly said, "Yessir," and started to rise again, more than ready to escape from his chair now.

"Well, we'll see. But remember this, Monroe. Till you git whiskey off your brain, you'll never amount to a hill of beans... in school or anywheres else."

"Yessir."

Monroe was half out of his chair when Hamp motioned him to sit down, and going to the foot of the stairs he called to Otis to bring down the toolbox under Monroe's bed. At the mention of the toolbox, Monroe started up and turned white as the tablecloth, but he settled back and never moved when it was brought in and placed on the table.

After thanking Otis and sending him back upstairs, Hamp said, "Now, Monroe, if you'll unlock this, I'll see for myself it there's anythang to what I been hearin'."

Moving as if in a trance, Monroe stood up and took a key from his pocket. He fumbled open the lock, raised the lid and sat back down.

Stacked next to a hammer and a couple of chisels were shiny new belt buckles, watch fobs and other such glittery things anyone could slip into his pocket in any store or harness shop if he had a mind to steal them; things easy to sell, or trade, too. At the end of the toolbox was something wrapped in a newspaper. Hamp unwrapped it and out slipped a flat bottle of whiskey with a smiling man on the label.

Poker faced, Hamp looked down at Monroe, and Monroe sat looking up at him, too flabbergasted to say a word.

"Here, Honey," Hamp said, handing her the whiskey, "better pour this out. As for the rest of them thangs, Monroe. You be in this house when I git home from work tomorrow. We're goin' to ever store in town till they're all back where you stole them from."

Head down and red-faced, Monroe hurried from the room without a glance at her, yet even with the bottle of whiskey in her hands proving him a liar, she still had an urge to grab him in her arms the way she used to when he was little, and try to make everything all right. Instead, she and Hamp watched him go, and then looked speechless at each other.

Yet they did have something good to say to Monroe when his report card came home next time, for not only had he not missed a day of school, he had raised most of his grades.

Hamp had been working hard himself, for the Kickapoo Traction Company moved him from one route to another until he had learned all the streetcar lines in Kickapoo. Sometimes he worked an early shift and was home by mid afternoon, as it was called here in town. Sometimes he started at mid afternoon and worked until midnight, although it was well after that time before he got his streetcar put away in the car barn and drove home.

After years of seeing Hamp do many things so well, she thought driving a streetcar around and around Kickapoo on the same track must seem to him like a childish way to make a living, but she never hinted as much. Whether Hamp thought it childish or not, she never heard him complain once about his work, his mixed-up working hours, or about the spasms of pain which had started again along the side of his head.

On wet and cold midnights when he came home to the hot supper she had waiting for him, if she said anything about the weather or asked how he felt, he made light of her concern by saying something like "It's not too bad out there," or "Oh, it could be worse," and ended by asking her how she was feeling.

Yet her main daily concern was not the baby she was carrying, but Hamp's headaches, which the doctor had started calling some kind of neuralgia that Hamp couldn't remember the name of. When the pills no longer kept the pain away, the doctor said an operation was the only cure, and it should be done at the Mayo Clinic, a hospital way off up in Minnesota that neither Hamp nor she had ever heard of.

Even so, she urged Hamp to go there, but at first he wouldn't hear of it. "Honey," he would say, "there's no use even than kin' about it. We cain't spare the money. Besides, maybe I'll git better like I did before."

After Hamp had been in daily misery for another month, with the pain getting worse all the time in spite of the medicine, she and the doctor were able to prevail on him to have the operation, and the doctor made the arrangements.

Not until the day before Hamp was to leave on the railroad did she realize there might be some danger to the operation, although Hamp never once used that word. He said he wanted to mention a few things, she ought to know, just in case, and went on to tell her how much they owed on the mortgage on the house, how much money they had left in the bank, and how much his life insurance policy was worth.

A week to the day after Hamp left for the Mayo Clinic, she was called to the front door about mid-morning by the loud hammering of the doorknocker. She found a skinny boy in some kind of uniform standing there with what he said was a telegram for Mrs. Gordon H. Roberts. She had never seen a telegram before, and the fact that she had to sign her name before the boy would give it to her made her think it was bad news.

Reminding herself she must stay calm for the sake of the baby, she leaned back against the stair post and tore the envelope open. As she puzzled out the lines of printed words, her fearful feeling turned slowly to a smile of relief that started her hurrying in her heavy way through the house and across the gardens to Hamp's mama and Lizzie.

OPERATION OVER STOP DOING FINE STOP HOME FRIDAY LOVE HAMP

The print on the yellow sheet of paper was read aloud and passed around even to Edith. Hamp's mama had been so dead set against his going that she still had her doubts. She shook her head at the telegram and said she would wait till she had seen with her own eyes how fine Hamp was doing.

When the children came home from school, she gave them the telegram to read, and later the twins and Harold went running off to play baseball, shouting, "Love Hamp!" to each other.

Lying in bed that night, she was so happy at Hamp's news she made up her mind to do what he had been after her for months to do. If the baby was a girl, she would call it Martha Louella. But first, she was going to make Hamp promise to let it be named after him if it was a boy.

Chapter 35

Several times Friday morning while she was cooking a dinner she knew Hamp would like—cornbread, baked sweet potatoes, spareribs and sauerkraut with pecan pie for dessert since this was such an extra special occasion—she left the kitchen to go to the front door and look out, thinking she heard him coming in that way.

She had put her hair up this morning and was wearing a dress Hamp especially liked—a flowered cotton she had made from material ordered out of the catalog way back when she was carrying Edith. Each time she passed the looking glass in the hall she would notice it as she paused to see if her hair was staying up.

Pictures of women with bobbed hair were becoming common in the newspaper these days, but Hamp had told her more than once that with her hair, it would be a shame to think of cutting any more of it off. She told him she had already decided against that, as handy as it would be to take care of. What she did not tell him was that her main reason was that the gray coming in her hair was starting at her widow's peak, and no hair style could hide that, even if she wanted it to.

It was long after noontime. She had fed Edith, had waited a while longer for Hamp, and was putting the special dinner away in the warming closet when she heard a noise behind her. There Hamp stood, just closing the door, his gripsack in his hand and his handsome brown hat still on his head. He turned to her and all she could see was a dark patch over his right eye.

She hadn't expected anything like this, and before she could get hold of herself she started back with a little gasp, and then rushed to him. Resting in his arms, she felt better when he said, "It's mainly to keep the light out, Honey. They say I can take it off after a while."

Just then Edith came running in to greet her papa, and when she saw the eye-patch she started laughing. "You look funny, Papa," she said, and as Hamp scooped her up in his arms she put out a finger to touch the patch and asked, "Is it a game?"

"No, it's to keep the light out of my eye."

"Why?"

"Because light's not good for it right now," Hamp said, and had to go on answering more questions before Edith was satisfied and slipped down and went back to her playing.

Nothing else was said about the eye-patch while they were eating their special dinner, Hamp praising the food as she tried to carry on a normal conversation when all she could think about was what was under the patch. She hoped his eye really was no worse than he made it out to be when talking to Edith, but it would be more like him to make too little of the problem on purpose.

Hamp's mama was so upset to see the eye-patch she started to cry. No matter how much Hamp smiled at his mama and tried to explain to her there was nothing to worry about, she would not calm down.

"I just knew something like this was going to happen," she said, shaking her head. "I said to Lizzie the very day you left, 'Mark my words,' I said. 'Before he's finished he'll wish he'd stayed away from doctors. He ought to let nature take its course,' I said. Doctors!"

After nodding agreement with her mama's statement, Lizzie tried to turn the talk away from Hamp's operation. Yet her mama was still shaking her head and muttering against doctors when they went out the back door towards home a few minutes later.

"Mama's never trusted doctors after all the arms and legs they cut off durin' her War," Hamp said. "I don't know how many times I've heard Papa try to make her understand the doctors was doin' the best they could to save lives. But no, all Mama can ever think of is her own papa hobblin' around on one leg and a crutch to the day he died."

As one after another of the children came in from school, she had to watch Hamp meet the same surprised stares and answer the same questions again and again. By suppertime it seemed all their questions about the eye had been asked. At least at the table Hamp was able to talk about places he had been, and sights he had seen, without anything being said about his operation.

He spoke of crossing the Mississippi River on a bridge more than a mile long and looking out the window of the railroad car and seeing patches of ice, no telling how long, floating in the black water.

When Hamp went on to tell about what a big city Chicago was, he said, "What would you say, Harold, if I told you I saw buildings maybe more than a block high?"

"I'd say maybe you was joshing me," Harold said, and they all laughed.

That night when she and Hamp were getting ready for bed, he slipped off the headband that held the eye-patch in place and said, "See, Honey. The eye's not so bad."

She had herself under control this time, and putting her hand to his cheek she nodded and pretended to examine the eyelid drooping half shut. Yet it was several seconds before she trusted herself to say anything, afraid her voice would give away the stab of sorrow she felt.

"It's supposed to git better soon," Hamp went on. "If it don't, I reckin' I'll jist have to put up with it."

Wearing the eye-patch, Hamp went back to work at the beginning of the week. When he came home that night she was relieved to hear him say he never had a sign of a headache all day long, and after that day there was no more talk about headaches.

Gradually she got used to seeing Hamp wearing his eye-patch, and she supposed the children did, too, since they no longer said anything about it. Yet in the bedroom she never looked at the drooping eyelid without a twinge of guilt at her part in making him have the operation.

One muggy evening in early April, after it had been threatening to rain all morning, it started pouring just as Hamp was leaving for work. Usually he was back in the house by shortly after twelve-thirty, but tonight as she listened to the rain still coming down, she guessed he would be a little late.

She was dozing at the kitchen table when she heard someone at the door, the front door. Finding a policeman in a wet slicker there, she was too surprised for an instant to say anything, or even invite him in. When he asked if she was Mrs. Roberts, fear took hold of her and she could only nod.

"You're to come with us, ma'am. Your husband's been hurt."

She held on to the door to steady herself. And thinking of the baby, she told herself to stay calm. After inviting the policeman to step inside, she turned to the foot of the stairs, but she still felt too unsteady to climb them. Holding onto the stair post, she called up to Sarah.

When Sarah came hurrying down, a long white ghost in her nightgown, she would not hear of her mama going out of the house alone, and rushed back upstairs to dress.

In a few minutes the two of them were holding on to each other in the back seat of the police car, riding through the wet night without saying a word, while up front the two policemen chatted about the rain.

In spite of the swish of the tires on the wet street, it seemed to her that the car was only creeping through the dark. She wanted to tell the policemen to hurry, but she was afraid they would not like her trying to tell them how fast to drive.

Ages seemed to pass before the car pulled up to a lighted building. She let Sarah help her out and they hurried inside. The strange smell scared her and made her more anxious than ever about Hamp. She held Sarah's arm as they crossed an open space to a counter where a scared woman looked up to greet them. Sarah told the woman who they were and the woman said, "Yes, if you'll just please take a chair over there in the waiting room." But she didn't want to sit down and wait. If Hamp was hurt, she wanted to see him right away. Turning back to the woman, she said "My husband's been hurt, and—"

"I know, ma'am, but you'll have to wait."

She wanted to say more, but Sarah led her to the closest chairs and they sat down facing the woman at the counter, who was now talking on the telephone.

The smell of the place, and having to sit here and wait to see Hamp after she had been sent for, so upset her that she fidgeted in her chair and wondered out loud what the matter could be.

Seeing a nurse come along the hall and stop to talk to the woman at the counter, she said, "Sarah, go find out why we can't see your papa now. Go on."

Sarah came back saying, "The nurse says in a few minutes."

Maybe it was the nurse looking back at her as she disappeared down the hall, but whatever the cause, she felt her irritation suddenly turn to fear. She stopped her fuming and sat looking down at her wet shoes without moving.

Finally, she heard footsteps coming and a nurse was standing before them, saying in a low voice, "Please come with me, Miz Roberts."

She took Sarah's arm again as they followed the nurse along the hall, with her holding onto Sarah's arm, smelling the strange smell and feeling more afraid with every step. At the end of the hall, they went into a large room and saw a man in a white smock—a doctor she supposed—standing in front of a narrow table. Behind him, a nurse was smoothing a sheet over something on the table.

The man turned a tired face to her and said, "I'm sorry Missus Roberts, but—"

"Hamp!" Pulling away from Sarah, she rushed past the doctor to Hamp lying face up on the table.

Even before she felt his cheek under her hand she knew he was dead, and she fell against him, crying and clutching at his shoulder, wishing she could die, too.

"Oh, Hamp," she whispered, lowering her head slowly next to his. "Dearest, dearest, Hamp. It's all my fault."

End of Part Three

Chapter 36

After a silent ride home from the hospital with Sarah and the two policemen in the police car, she spent the rest of the night in bed, silently blaming herself for Hamp's death.

If only she had not kept after him about the children's education, the family would still be out there on the farm. If only she had let him move to Colorado when he wanted to, they would be settled on a farm out there by now. And if only she had not kept urging him to have the operation for his headaches, the pain might have gone away again and he would still be alive and have all his eyesight.

Yet loving Hamp and the children as she did, she couldn't think how she could have done anything else. Even so, guilt plagued her as she woke Hamp's mama and Lizzie early next morning to tell them the sad news. Hamp's mama never shed a tear, just sat shaking her head and blaming the doctors.

After the children had eaten their breakfast, she took them into the living room, and told them about their papa's death, just as the doctor had told it to her. Sarah helped her answer their tearful questions and comforted them in their crying while keeping her own tears under control. In this they were soon helped by Lizzie, who had put her own grief aside and stepped right in to help run the household.

Later in the morning, with her eyes aching from crying and lack of sleep, she went over to talk to Hamp's mama about having Hamp buried in the Methodist graveyard. She broke into tears again when the old lady said, "Of course, Mattie. It's the right thing to do." They cried together.

As the day wore on, she wanted more to be alone. Yet she had to talk to everybody coming and going, family and friends offering to help any way they could, and others stopping to pay their respects. When her own family arrived from the farm in the secondhand car Papa had recently bought for Tommy, she arranged with Papa about where to put the grave, having it dug, and asking Reverend Willis to preach the funeral service.

The day before the funeral the undertaker came with the coffin and she had it put in front of the fireplace in the living room. That night long after she had gone to bed, worn-out from so much talking to family and other visitors, she was still wide awake. She listened to the clock strike hour after hour and thought of Hamp a few steps away down the stairs.

It crossed her mind how comforting it must be to Mrs. Whitaker— who had stopped by that day—having her husband buried so close at hand that she could step outside her back door and talk to him day or night.

She wished she could do this with Hamp, but it wasn't possible. She had already made up her mind to move back to a farm as soon as Papa and Andy could find one she could afford to buy, but she had no idea how close it would be to their church. The farm also had to be close to the new school which Andy said was starting up out there in the country in the fall.

Thinking of school, she was reminded of Sarah's graduation a few weeks away and made a mental note to get started making her graduation dress, which they had bought the material for several weeks before.

When the clock struck three and she was still wide awake, she got out of bed and eased herself down the stairs by holding onto the banister. The light from the hall left half of the living room in shadow, but she could see the coffin well enough.

Having no tears left, she stood holding to the edge of the coffin and looked calmly down at Hamp's face for a long, long time. She almost expected him to smile up at her the way he had the first time they met. It was easy now to realize she had fallen in love with him that first moment, and she would never understand why she had not known it then.

She pulled a straight chair up to the coffin and sat so close to it she could have reached over and touched Hamp's face, which in the shadowy light looked as young right then as it did when they were married. What a short time it seemed since that night in Norman when he slipped the gold wedding band on her finger and kissed her while the sleepy justice of the peace was smothering a yawn.

The fever of life—as she had heard preachers call it—was over for Hamp, cut off without any warning in the middle of the night and in the middle of his life. Yet as much as she would like it to be over for her, too, she knew it was with her now more than ever. The children would wake up hungry and needing her in the morning—and every morning—and in a few weeks so would the baby moving inside her at that very minute. She had to feed and take care of her family, and her with no sure way of even making her own living.

As full of grief as she was, she felt fear, too, as she sat there looking into Hamp's face and thinking of having to raise the family without him. She was afraid that even running a farm might be too much for her. She longed to put her hand in Hamp's and have him tell her it was going to be all right.

Reaching out, she touched the shoulder of his church suit. She knew he would laugh at her for being afraid, and she could hear him saying, "Come on, Honey, it's got to be done. So let's git at it."

At the funeral the next morning the heat in the church house was so bad, in spite of the wide-open doors and windows, she thought she might faint before Reverend Willis finished preaching that in the midst of life we are in death.

Once the sermon was over, and the hymn and the prayer, the congregation filed silently by the open coffin for a last look at Hamp, and shuffled down the aisle past her and the family on out into the scorching sun.

Having already said her good-bye to him the night before, she did not want to look into the coffin again, but she stood up and held onto Alice and waited dry-eyed while Hamp's mama, Lizzie, Brown and Rissy, and all the children went forward to gather at the coffin along with Mama and Papa and Tommy.

Wide-eyed, Harold and Edith soon scurried silently back to her, and she held them close and waited. After a long wait she watched Brown lead his mama, the last of the mourners, away from the coffin.

Reverend Willis closed it, and the pallbearers, led by Molly's father and Jake Dawson, carried it by within a few feet of her. Since she was too weak to follow the coffin out across the road and on out to the grave in this heat, she motioned for the others to go with it, and then sat down again.

She thought she was all through crying, but when Molly came looking for her and threw her arms around her, she cried again as if for the first time. Yet this time as much for Molly as for Hamp. Later, as she was getting in the car to leave the church, Grace Billings hurried up to remind her that she was sending Dr. Fortson by to see her that evening.

Dr. Fortson turned out to be a big, hearty man whose hand, when it took hold of her wrist to feel her pulse, looked and felt as if it could have lifted the handle of a plough just as easily. He told her that for her own sake as well as the baby's she was to go to bed immediately and stay there until the baby came. She didn't want to do it, but having already had one stillborn baby, she said she would.

Every night she went to sleep reliving her life with Hamp and thinking if it weren't for the children she would like to be beside him out there in the graveyard. The next morning she would wake up thinking of Hamp gone forever and be so overcome by the thought of living without him that she would close her eyes and wish she could die right then rather than have to go through another day.

Yet before long the sounds of Lizzie downstairs making breakfast for the family, or the noise of the children getting up, would take her mind off herself. By the time the children, all except Edith, had gone off to school, having run up and down the stairs and in and out of her room with this or that problem or just to say good morning or goodbye, she was ready to face another day. That day always began with Lizzie bringing her breakfast and was followed by reading to Edith.

She took an interest in Sarah's graduation dress, which Lizzie was helping Sarah make, and when it was finished and ready for inspection she was surprised at how grown-up Sarah looked in it, her hair done up and her wearing a wide-brimmed hat.

On Sarah's graduation day, she was tempted to forget the doctor's orders for a few hours, and to get out of bed and go to the ceremony, but Lizzie and Sarah both said "no" to the first hint of that.

A shiny-eyed Sarah came home with her diploma and the news that after one year in the nearby Baptist College she would have her teacher's certificate. "And guess what, Mama?" she hurried on in the same excited voice. "Elsie is going, too, and Missus Billings says I have to stay with them."

Summer had not yet arrived when the baby Dr. Fortson had been so careful to protect came into this world causing her no more pain than she expected. When she heard its first little squeak of a cry and asked anxiously if it was all right, Dr. Fortson's quick, "Yep, he's a dandy," turned her fear to joy.

Within a few days after Gordon Hampton Roberts, Jr. was born, looking much like his papa except that his eyebrows were as dark as her own, she went downstairs and picked up her life again. The demands of Gordon, as she decided to call him, put an end to her waking up in the morning wishing she were dead. Now from the instant she opened her eyes, she had too much to do to even think about herself.

Yet her guilt over Hamp's death was never very far from her thoughts, and one day when she was agonizing about that death to Andy, while he was showing her another farm for sale, he stopped in his tracks and said, "Mattie, you sound like the doctor never told you exactly what all happened that night."

Saying he was sorry to have to tell her such a story, he started by telling her what she already knew, that Hamp had been caught between two streetcars in the car barn. "They said the patch over his eye made him misjudge the distance of the car backing in," Andy went on, and when she heard this, she heard herself urging Hamp to go to the Mayo Clinic to have the operation.

She stopped and took hold of a fence post to steady herself. But after a little she asked Andy to go on, thinking nothing could make her feel more guilty or miserable than that piece of news. She leaned against the post and kept her eyes closed until he had given her the whole awful story.

At last she understood why no one had told her all that at the time, but when she and Andy walked on, it was a relief to agree with him that Hamp would not have wanted to live. With one good eye he would have made the best of it—and she heard Hamp saying this to her the first time she saw his drooping eyelid—but it would have been too much for him to try to farm with a bad eye and also have one leg sawed off at the hip.

Later in the summer Andy finally found a farm of the right size, location and price for her, but when she had looked it over with Papa and was ready to buy it, she found out she did not have as much money left in the bank as she thought.

Hamp had not told her he had signed a note at the bank for Brown, but the banker explained that now that Hamp was dead, the loan had to be—in his words—satisfied from the money in the G. H. Roberts account, unless B. M. Roberts was ready to pay it off. She had Andy drive her out to see Brown, and Brown said he was sorry but there was no way he could pay the loan off any time soon.

"Mattie, you know I'd do it for you in a minute if I could—and one day I will—but right now I ain't even makin' ends meet myself."

Disappointed but helpless, she left after visiting a few minutes with Rissy; who seemed more concerned about the loan than Brown did.

On the way back to town, she listened patiently as Andy explained that the banker was within his rights, and she would have to take out a mortgage on any farm she bought if she wanted to be sure to have enough cash left to buy all the livestock and farm machinery needed to get the farm going, and to keep the family fed and clothed until they could make a couple of crops.

Since she knew nothing about business, she could only put her trust in Andy. When Hamp had told her about their business affairs before he went away for his operation, she had been too much concerned about his operation to pay close attention to the amount of money left in their bank account, although at the time it seemed like a lot to her.

Now that she needed to spend that money, she was finding it much less than she had thought. The Mayo Clinic, Brown's loan, the hospital and doctor bills and the funeral expenses, all of these had eaten up the life insurance money as well as much of the bank account. She thought she would make some money from selling the house, but the best offer Andy could get for it in these hard times was less than Hamp had paid for it.

She took Andy's advice, sold the house, and bought an eighty acre farm west of Kickapoo known as the Old Koontz place. It was two miles from their Calvary Methodist Church and Hamp's grave, and a little less than that from the new red-brick Brinton Consolidated School the children would walk a mile and a half to each morning.

As she signed the mortgage, she made a silent vow that no matter how hard she had to work and skimp and save and do without, she would keep the farm going until every child had the same chance to graduate from high school as Sarah had—or she would die trying.

Chapter 37

"Are we going to live in this old house, Mama?" Edith asked again, as if she hoped the answer was "no." They were passing through a dingy, musty smelling little closet between the two bedrooms, and she waited until they came out to some more creaky floor boards and peeling wallpaper before she answered, "It'll look better once we give it a good cleaning. And get our furniture moved in."

Yet she remembered the happy noises the children made running through the house in town for the first time, and from the silence of Sarah and Agnes behind her she guessed they were as unhappy with what they were seeing as Edith seemed to be. Probably the small size of the house also had something to do with it—only four rooms, with a kitchen added to the back with a little screened-in porch off the south end of the kitchen.

"But, Mama, where we all going to sleep?"

"We'll have to see about that."

She paused at the door to the front room and looked around to see where she would put the couch and the piano. Then she walked out on the front porch where Harold was swinging in an old porch swing that had been left hanging from the ceiling. He slowed the swing by dragging his bare feet on the floor until Edith jumped on beside him.

The big, shady front yard, fenced with mesh wire, stopped thirty or so feet short of the road. Beyond the road a cornfield sloped up a tow hill, the south wind rippling the leaves of the tall stalks, making them flash and glitter in the sun, and swaying the yellow tassels sticking up out of the leaves. At the top of the hill stood an unpainted, one-story house in a bunch of trees.

She stepped off the porch and looked up in the elms for the orioles she had seen when she was here before. The orange and black birds were still busy up there, flashing through patches of sunlight and in and out of nests swinging from the ends of the branches like little gray gourds.

Strolling, around to the south side of the house, she pointed out to Sarah and Agnes the peach and plum orchard that ran down to the south boundary of the farm. That orchard, and the apple orchard north of the house, had been a big part of her reason for deciding to buy this farm. Having learned from living in town how expensive fruit and vegetables were, she was determined to have a place where they could have all they wanted in the summer, and she could can and dry enough for winter.

She stopped at a lilac bush and started idly breaking off the dried up blossoms, thinking she would move the bush closer to the house so she could smell the faint blossoms when they came on next spring. But since she had already decided to put a sleeping porch across the south side of the house, she had better wait until that was done.

Around at the back of the house she came again to the gravel path which slanted out from between the two mulberry trees at the kitchen door, out past a smokehouse rotting at the near corner, where notched ends of the heavy timbers met like crossed fingertips. At the back of the yard, a long-handled pump stood on a concrete weft curb about a foot thick and as long and wide as the kitchen table. Behind it a great big elm tree shaded the back corner of the yard like a gigantic umbrella.

Sarah and Agnes ran past her to see who could be the first to pump a drink of water from the well, reminding her that so far none of the children had seemed to notice there was no running water in the house, no bathroom and no electric lights, things they had come to take for granted but would now have to get along without. She did not look forward to having to scrunch up again in a galvanized tub in the kitchen to take a bath, but she would have to do it, and so would they.

Going past the noisy girls at the well to the car parked in the shade on the other side of the elm tree, she peeked in at Gordon asleep in his basket. She brushed away a fly and pulled the netting back over the top to keep them away from his face and his fat little arms and legs.

She was sitting on the weft curb drinking a dipper of fresh water when Monroe, Otis, and Arthur came up from the apple orchard, talking and eating apples at the same time, their pockets bulging with more apples.

Monroe stopped in front of her, and between bites said, "The barn's not much, Mama."

"I know. We're going to have to do something about that."

"And there's no cow barn, either."

"Maybe we'll have to build us a horse barn farther up the slope and use that old barn for the cows. When we get hold of some cows."

Just then Harold and Edith came racing around the house, looking for the rest of the family. As soon as they saw apples being eaten they wanted some, complained when the boys said they had already given Sarah and Agnes all they could spare, and then ran shouting off to the orchard to find their own apples.

A few minutes later she was holding the yawning Gordon on her lap as Sarah backed the black monster around and drove out past a long solid mass of rose bushes to the road. Mr. Koontz had put the entrance to the driveway next to a pair of huge blackjack trees standing so close to each other that their tops had grown together.

The road going north from the blackjacks ran down a gradual

slope to the corner of the section lines half a mile away, crossed the east-west road and rose slowly for another half a mile, going past a string of giant cottonwoods standing along a creek east of the road. At the top of this hill, once more the road sloped down to another creek and then rose up to another crossroads at the top of the highest hill for miles around. Here Sarah turned the car east towards Kickapoo four miles away.

Having packed everything ready to start moving to the farm on Monday, she had Hamp's mama and Lizzie over for supper on Saturday night. After supper the three of them sat out on the front porch talking long after the last of the children had gone to bed.

Sunday morning while she and the children were about to start breakfast, Lizzie, white as a ghost except for the vivid scar on her face, burst in at the back door and whispered to her, "Mama's dead!"

The end of Hamp's mama's visit last night leaped to her mind. His mama had stayed on and on at the back steps, chatting about nothing in particular long after praising her for a scrumptious supper and saying good-night a couple of times. And then the frail old lady took her leave only to turn back once more and draw her near for a kiss, the first time in all the years they had known each other this had ever happened. The bony hand kept its tight grip on hers. "Mattie," she said, "you made Hamp the best wife a man ever had. I want you to know that."

Thinking of that now, she made no connection between it and Lizzie's news. Yet later when she deemed death had come from a heart attack, she marveled that Mrs. Roberts might have suspected it was coming and wanted to let her know she had never—or at least no longer—blamed her for the way she had become Hamp's wife.

The move to the farm was put off until Hamp's mama had been buried beside his papa in the Baptist graveyard near Briggs, and Lizzie had left her house for Andy to sell and gone to San Angelo, Texas to live with an older married sister who had come with her husband to the funeral.

Once Lizzie had gone, the move to the farm was made the following day with Papa and Tommy furnishing two of the wagons. This time even Brown sent Browny over with a wagon, and as if that was not surprise enough, he sent along, tied to the back of the wagon by a rope around her horns, the lankiest milk cow she had ever seen—legs long as a deer's.

Later, back inside her empty house, she took Gordon from Edith and wandered through the empty rooms where she had left Sarah and Agnes sweeping up while they all waited for Andy to come by and get the key for the new owners.

A good thing about the new farm, she would not see a reminder of Hamp everywhere she looked. As this thought crossed her mind, her eyes met the blue-black eyes of Gordon Hampton Roberts, Jr. fixed on hers and realized here was a reminder of Hamp for as long she lived.

The new baby was a reminder of something else, too, and even as she felt a twinge of shame for thinking it, she was still filled with relief to know she would never again have to count the days every month while dreading she might be pregnant.

An hour later, with Gordon still in her arms, she was back walking inside the Old Koontz house trying to figure out what to put where. Looking out a north window at a pair of plum trees, she decided to put the boys' beds out there under them—until the sleeping porch was built—and was doubly pleased when the boys liked the idea. In fact, they were so happy to be living in the country again that they were like cattle turned into a new pasture, rushing here and there until they had seen it all.

Of all the neighbors they visited, the boys talked most about the Duncans, the family that lived across the road in the house at the top of the cornfield. They kept a great big yellow dog tied with a chain outside the kitchen door, where it barked and snapped and foamed at the mouth whenever you came near it. Even scarier, the dog was turned loose at night to guard the house.

The Duncans had come from Kentucky, and the boys grew wild-eyed talking about all the guns they saw up there. The two Duncan boys, Ralph and Ray, were always out shooting something—rabbits, squirrels, hawks, crows, and the like. And if that was not strange enough, the two Duncan sisters, Opal and Ruby, owned their own guns and often went hunting with their brothers.

She had known families like this in Bear Valley, the men carrying a rifle or shotgun to the field with them every day, and even carrying it to Shade's Crossing, except on Sundays. She remembered that even there in the early days it was common to see men carrying or wearing guns, but she was surprised to find herself living next to such a family.

At supper later in the week, a knock rattled the screen door to the kitchen, and when Harold jumped up to answer it, she heard a low voice say, "Is your mama here?"

Going to the door, she saw smiling up at her from under a worn out old black hat a little man in a sweaty shirt and overalls. The sun was still out and she took in clearly the sandy mustache and blue eyes as she stepped down off the doorsill, offered him her hand and said, "I'm Mattie Roberts."

The man's face reddened a little as they shook hands, but instead of saying who he was, he said, "Thought y'all might like some melons." He let his glance drop to a tow sack at his feet. "We got a right smart crop of 'em this year."

"Watermelons!" Harold said and started to push past her, but she put a hand on his shoulder and kept him where he was as she thanked the man and went on to show some interest in his melon crop.

After a little, the man chuckled down at the fidgeting Harold and said, "You like melons, do you?"

"Oh boy! Do I."

The man stooped and up-ended the sack. Out on the ground rolled three yellow cantaloupes and a long green and light striped watermelon.

She let go of Harold's shoulder and he was on his knees in an instant, thumping the watermelon and raving about how big it was, while the man folded his tow sack and went on talking to her.

It wasn't until he said, "I 'spect I better be git'n back," and reached towards the nearest mulberry tree with his free hand that she noticed the double barreled shotgun leaning up against it. Her first thought was that Mr. Duncan didn't look a bit like she expected.

Tucking the shotgun under his arm, he grinned down at Harold.

"Don't eat too much of that melon," he said and walked out of the yard with a funny little pigeon-toed stride.

As soon as the man was out of sight around the rosebushes, she said just above a whisper, "That's Mister Duncan, and wasn't that neighborly of him to bring those fine melons?"

Maybe Mr. Duncan wasn't as scary as the boys made him out to be. She smiled down at Harold hefting the watermelon, and already knowing what his answer was going to be, she said, "You have any room left for a slice of that?"

As the days passed, she was surprised at how fast she was getting used to living in the country again, in spite of having to go back to coal oil lamps, water from the pump, and an outhouse fifty yards from the kitchen door. At first the children grumbled a little about these inconveniences, but their grumbles didn't last long.

Chapter 38

She solved the sleeping problem for the boys, at least for the time being, by having them set up their beds out under the plum trees along the north side of the house. Since it was now the driest part of summer and not likely to rain very hard very often, she thought this would be better than trying to cram the beds into the hot little house.

The boys said they liked sleeping outside, and they bragged to their sisters about being able to lie in bed and eat ripe plums as they fell from the trees. What the boys didn't say was that they had been pestered all night by mosquitoes and by flies after daylight.

She learned this from Harold who asked her not to tell or Monroe and Arthur would call him a sissy. She was sorry about the mosquitoes, but she saw the flies as a help in getting the boys out of bed early. Too much work had to be done on the farm between now and the time school started for anyone to be lazying around in bed in the morning, except on Sundays.

Within a few days the boys had run all over the farm and the countryside in general, and they came back full of talk about what they had seen and heard. The white house to the north, which she could see from the kitchen window by looking down through the apple orchard and across a field, belonged to the Watkins. They had a big brindle dog, the mama looked Indian and the children they saw had black hair.

The Ricketts rented the one hundred and sixty acre farm to the south, but you couldn't see their house from here because it was set way back from the road on the far side of a creek bottom. They had two sons left at home, both older than Monroe, and one of them had a blazed-face sorrel horse that the boys had watched single foot like anything.

When Otis wished out loud at supper that he could have a horse like it, Monroe pooh-poohed the idea, saying he would rather have a car any day than a horse, and Arthur said, "Me, too."

She felt right at home again being able to put on an old farm dress and work in the yard without seeing strangers coming and going right by the front gate, or hearing any sounds louder than a bird singing—except for the children being noisy now and then. And always, after carrying a baby for months, it was good to feel light on her feet again and look slimmer, even if the looking glass showed her face thinner now than she could ever remember it. And more gray hair, too.

She was reminded of this in the mornings if she happened to glance at the wedding picture on her little table. Comparing it with the tired old face in the looking glass, she could hardly believe she had ever looked that young and alive. It was enough to make her want to break the looking glass and throw the pieces away. Instead, she would turn her mind to the day's work ahead of her and calmly finish braiding her hair.

Her one disappointment here on the farm was Monroe. Having listened to him complain for two years about how much he hated town and wanted to go back to the country, she thought he would be happy now and be her right-hand man. He knew how to do what had to be done and he was old enough and big enough to do it, but now that he was here he didn't show much interest in working.

These days Papa and Tommy were busy helping her get settled in, building shelves in the kitchen and the little screened in back porch, putting new screen in the doors and windows, fixing the crumbling logs in the smokehouse, and repairing anything else around the place that Mr. Koontz had to let go to pot.

Instead of trying to help them, Monroe would go straight from the breakfast table to playing baseball in the near south pasture with the other boys, or he might lead them off for another walk around the farm or the countryside.

After putting up with this for a couple of days without saying anything, she thought she might spur Monroe on by making him responsible for all the outside work. She called the boys together out at the well, explained that from now on Monroe was in charge, and finished by telling the twins and Harold that she expected them to work for Monroe the same way they used to work for their papa.

At the mention of their papa the boys were all silent for a time, and then Monroe spoke up. He was standing leaning against the pump, and she saw him give Otis a sly little poke with his boot as he said, "S'pose they don't mind me, Mama?"

"Oh, I think they will," she said, glancing around at the serious faces and finding Harold, always the sympathetic one, nodding at her.

"After all," she went on, "it's going to take all of us working as hard as we can to make a go of this farm. Everywhere you look there's something that needs to be done. See that lot fence, Monroe? Maybe it would be best to tear it down and build one high enough Old Hazel can't jump out in the apple orchard again."

What Brown had said about how much milk Old Hazel gave was true, but he hadn't said anything about her jumping fences like a deer. They would have to put a yoke on her if she jumped out into the neighbors' fields, otherwise they could get in trouble with them.

Now that Monroe was in charge of the outside work, she hoped she would be able to go about her own work with the girls—making apple butter, canning peaches, making curtains, putting in flower beds, as well as the usual washing and ironing and mending—and know that the farm work was getting done.

The meeting did put a stop to the daily baseball games after breakfast and the long walks around the countryside. Yet never a day passed without one of the twins—or more often Harold—coming to her mad or in tears, or both, to complain that Monroe had done this or that to him—usually hit him with his fists, something she had told Monroe more than once that he was not to do.

Stopping whatever she was doing, she would go out to where they were working and try to be a peacemaker, listening to all sides and urging them to try to get along with each other.

Where Hamp would have boxed a few ears and told them all to get back to work, she was careful to be fair, and especially careful not to make things worse by seeming to side against Monroe unless he was clearly in the wrong. He was quick to accuse her of taking the other person's side as he was to deny any wrong doing himself.

Hoping that his own team of horses might make Monroe feel more responsible and easier to get along with, she asked Papa to be on the lookout for a pair of mares and enough farming implements to make a crop with next year. Papa told her to wait a while, saying the best buys would come in the fall when some farmers would be selling out at a public sale.

In spite of his own advice, Papa drove up to the well one day with a team and a wagon with a plow in it, telling her when she came out that he had run across such a bargain he couldn't turn it down.

The family, including Gordon in Edith's arms, gathered at the well to see what he had brought, and while she could see that the bony mares—one light brown and the other a little darker—were not much to look at, she thanked Papa. When he told her the low price for everything, she could hardly believe it and thanked him again, glad to have one expense these days that was less than she expected.

Everybody seemed satisfied with the mares until it sank into Monroe that the new team was to be his. At once he got a sour look on his face and started looking the mares over again and shaking his head. Finally he came back to the well curb, where Papa was finishing a fresh drink of water that Harold had pumped for him, and said, "Mama, I hope you don't think I can make a crop next year with them worn-out nags?"

She was so hurt for Papa's sake that all she could do was call Monroe's name, but Papa didn't seem to mind. Swallowing the last of his drink, he waved the dipper in the direction of the team as he jerked his head around to Monroe with a little laugh.

"Oh, Maud and Kate won't take no beauty prizes, but they'll make you a crop aw'right, Monroe. Lots of 'em."

"But they're so old."

"Old? Why them mares ain't even smooth mouthed yet. Course you'll have to feed 'em up a little when you git Koontz's corn crop out of the field. But the main thang to remember, Monroe, is jist don't work 'em too hard next sprang when they are getting ready to have their colts."

"Mule colts, Grampa?" Harold asked, and when Papa nodded, he sang out "Oh boy! Mule colts!"

After Tommy had come in the car and driven off with Papa, she called Monroe to the kitchen where she had gone back to her canning. Asking him to sit down at the table, she tried to make him understand that it was an insult to say what he had said to his Grandpa, and especially in Grandpa's case since he was doing all he could to help them.

"You don't seem to realize, Monroe, that it's not like the old days down at Briggs. I wish I could afford to buy you a team like Tipsy and Topsy but I can't. Don't you see, Monroe, from now on we won't have a penny to spare."

"But I guess we got enough spare pennies to send Sarah to college."

That was the second time in the last few minutes that Monroe had surprised her with a sarcastic comment and it was all she could do to keep from slapping his face. But she stopped in time and glared at him while she got hold of herself.

For some reason his mean words made his drinking and lying and stealing flash through her mind. She had never said anything to him about them but she hadn't forgotten them either. The drinking she could understand and maybe the lying that went along with it.

But where had the stealing come from? Not from her. And not from the Hamp she had known. And not these smart aleck words.

There Monroe sat in Hamp's old clothes, the picture of Hamp when she first met him—except for the smirk on his face—yet no more like Hamp than the man in the moon. But she cut her thoughts off to answer him.

"I hope we'll be able to find enough to send you to college too, Monroe," she said evenly. "And the others when their time comes. But it can't be done if we don't make a go of this farm. Can't you get that in your head?"

Monroe just shrugged and said nothing. All he seemed to have on his mind was that he was expected to farm with a team he called nags, and she could tell by the abrupt way he left the kitchen and walked stiffly out to the wagon that he was still as unhappy as ever.

She noticed that after that Monroe had as little as possible to say to Papa whenever he came to the farm. Yet if Papa was put off by Monroe's coolness to him, he never showed it. One day when he brought them a milk cow, he made a point of handing the rope to Monroe, telling him that she was from Old Blackie's stock, the cow they had brought with them from Arkansas. "I hope you'll keep the line going, Monroe."

Monroe just nodded while she thanked Papa and recalled Old Blackie's running off from Bob and Tommy that time of the flood.

Another day Papa came with Mama and Alice and a wagonload of pullets just beginning to lay, also bringing a couple of tied-up shoats to be fattened for winter killing.

Harold asked his grandma if she brought any banties. "Lands no," she answered, "I ain't got one on the place and don't want one. All banties is good for is fightin' the big chickens and eatin' their feed. Their eggs is too little to amount to anything and their meat is too tough to eat, what little there is of it."

Mama didn't seem to notice Harold's unhappy look, but knowing that he liked bantams as much as Hamp had, she thought of something to take his mind off Mama's bad news. She told him and Edith that if he would run to the first tree beyond the crab apple tree and get a dozen of the best apples they could find, Sarah would make apple pies for dinner.

She caught up with Alice, who was on her way to the house with two killed, picked and singed fryers and some fresh smelling light bread. Alice wasn't looking at all well these days, but she said it was just the hot weather. Whether it was that or not, she didn't offer to help in the kitchen, something she could never remember her failing to do before. Instead she sat on the front porch talking to Agnes and holding Gordon while she and Mama, sweating in the hot kitchen, caught up on each other's news as they made the dinner.

During the meal, when Mama wanted to know where all the children were going to sleep when cold weather came, she said she aimed to put a sleeping porch on the south side of the house. She had already talked to Papa about it, and apparently he either hadn't told Mama or she had forgotten it.

On hearing it now, Papa cleared his throat and said, "If you're still planning on that, Mattie, better do it while me and Tommy got time to do the buildin'. First thang you know, it'll be cotton picking time."

Later when she talked to Monroe about going to Kickapoo for the first load of lumber for the sleeping porch, he said he would be ashamed to go out on the road with such a team as Maud and Kate. Surprised, she wasn't sure what to say, but as soon as Otis spoke up and said he would be glad to go, Monroe changed his tune and decided he would go after all.

She could remember when she would have been happy to go to Kickapoo with any kind of wagon and team, and in any kind of weather, just to see the buildings and the people. Now, for her, the happiest part of a trip to town was coming home to the cool shade of the elm tree, taking off her hat and sipping a drink of water fresh and cold from the well.

Chapter 39

One Sunday after church she and the children drove on out to Mama's for Ben's homecoming dinner. Having been warned by Alice at church that Ben had changed, she was not expecting to see the same skinny brother she had said goodbye to years ago when he went away to the War. But one glance at him coming out to the car showed her that size wasn't the only change Alice had in mind.

Dressed in town clothes, including shiny sharp-toed shoes, with his hair slicked down, Ben looked and talked and almost acted like a stranger. During dinner she was surprised to learn that he was going to be home only three or four days, and her heart sank for Mama. After Mama had worried for so long that her favorite might be killed in the war, and then waited more years for him to come home, now she would have him with her only long enough to do hardly more than say hello and goodbye.

She was so upset for Mama that she urged Ben to stay longer. He said he wished he could but he couldn't. A friend of his from the army had a job waiting for him in the Chamber of Commerce down in Lawton and he was anxious to get started at it.

She didn't know what a Chamber of Commerce did, and Ben admitted he didn't either, but since he seemed to be so set on hurrying off, she could only wish him well and turn the talk to someone else.

Yet gradually as the talk at the dinner table dragged along, she sensed that Mama and Papa and Alice all noticed that Ben no longer acted like one of the family. Usually at these gatherings everybody more or less talked at once unless Papa was talking, and in the old days Ben talked as much as anyone else, but today it was as hard as pulling teeth to get a word out of him.

When anyone asked him about the places he had seen, such as Paris, Germany and New York City, he gave the shortest possible answer and when anyone tried to stir the talk up a little with a story about him when he was a boy here on the farm, he would pass it off politely by saying, "Yes, I remember that," and go on eating.

She didn't mind so much that in the course of her visit Ben never mentioned Hamp's death, although she thought it strange that he didn't, not only for her sake but also because he had seemed to like Hamp so much. Even so, as they were leaving she asked him to come by for a visit. He said he would, but he didn't, and she had so many other things on her mind that Ben's strange behavior soon slipped to the back of her mind.

In getting ready to pick the first cotton crop, she had to buy new material in town and make the cotton sacks, including one for herself, just in case. As she ran up the sacks on her sewing machine she thought how she had hated picking cotton from the moment she pricked her fingers on the first boll she touched way back in the Creek Indian Nation long ago, and she hoped maybe she wouldn't have to use her new sack this fall.

Yet after listening for two days to complaints from Monroe about the others and from the others about Monroe, she didn't have any choice but to leave Gordon with Edith and go out there in the field and take charge of the picking if she wanted the cotton crop to ever get picked.

Once she started picking alongside the others she soon came to think that maybe she had expected too much of Monroe, for even to her the children complained constantly about the hot weather, the long day, their sore fingers and sore backs and every other imaginable ailment under the sun. It seemed to her that after being away from farm work for a couple of years they had forgotten how hard it really was, and they acted as if they didn't want to find out again either.

At one time or another she had to raise her voice to each one of them, even to Harold, who usually tried harder than the others to please her. If Sarah had been there she would have made a difference, because Monroe and the twins would have been ashamed to have her pick more cotton than they did, but Sarah was already away living at the Billings and going to college.

Once more she was reading Sarah's weekly letters aloud to the family at mealtime, letters full of excitement about what she was learning. Seeing Monroe and Arthur making eyes to each other over this excitement, she would keep on reading and pretend not to notice.

In her answer to Sarah, neither did she mention the trouble she was having getting the children to work the way they used to.

Fortunately for her peace of mind, the picking was soon finished because Mr. Koontz's crop made barely four bales. As she had done long ago, she got Monroe up earlier than early for each of the four long trips to the cotton gin, and he drove off before dawn, no longer ashamed to be seen on the road with the new team. Papa's prediction that the mares would be all right had proved true, and even Monroe was forced to admit that after a few weeks of corn had put some meat on their ribs and sleeked down their coats they no longer looked like nags.

Such a small crop of cotton from the two fields told her that the land was wearing out, and there wasn't anything she could do about it. She was grateful to have the money from the four bales, but she couldn't help remembering that during the war Hamp got more money from a single bale of cotton than she got for the whole crop that fall.

Since the cotton picking was finished so soon, Monroe and the boys had plenty of time to get the rest of the crops in before school started. When the corn crop filled the bin, and there wasn't enough room left in the little old barn to store the heads of the kaffir corn crop, Monroe asked her what he should do.

Kaffir corn was a new crop to her, and even though Monroe didn't want to do it, she sent him to Papa to find out the best way to store it. Papa came the next day with Tommy and showed the boys how to rick the crop outside—heads still on the stalks except for the top row—so that the grain would be protected from birds and the weather and still be easy to feed.

Instead of showing his appreciation for what they were teaching him, Monroe seemed to resent it, sulking around with a sour look on his face and doing as little as possible to help Papa and Tommy.

She pretended not to notice Monroe's bad manners, but when Papa and Tommy had gone, she turned on him. "Monroe, I'm ashamed of you! Here your grandpa and uncle stop their own work in the field right in the busy season to come help you. And what do you do? Do you pitch in and give them a hand? Show them how thankful you are? No. You stand around looking like you've got a stomachache. I never saw anyone so ungrateful. If I ever see that kind of performance again, you'll hear from me right on the spot."

As usual, Monroe shrugged her scolding off and left with the boys to cut and haul another wagonload of kaffir corn. In a few days they had the crop all cut and hauled in and picked up. Now all that was left to do was get in a supply of wood for the winter, and she knew the boys would have plenty of time to do that on Saturdays while school was going on.

In spite of the trouble she had had with Monroe, she was generally pleased with the way things had gone so far on the farm, and she was especially pleased that she had been able to plant a fall garden of turnips, beans, and Irish potatoes. The turnips for the hogs would grow in any weather, and if the frost held off she would have enough beans and potatoes to last the family all winter. They would cut down a lot on her food bill, something that was on her mind every time she made a meal.

The seed potatoes she planted had come from Mr. Duncan, who said, when he brought them to the back door one day, that these were some he had left over from his own planting and he hoped she could make use of them. He was always dropping by with something like that and making it seem she was doing him a favor by taking it off his hands—more watermelons and cantaloupes, lots of pumpkins which she canned or dried, new sorghum molasses from his own mill, and combs of honey from his bees.

Besides helping them with gifts of food and the like, Mr. Duncan kept a Jersey bull the boys took the cows to when the cows came in heat, and a boar hog they used to breed Papa's gift of a gilt instead of fattening her to kill.

Monroe had become good friends with Ralph, the older Duncan boy, who was already a head taller than his papa. The two of them spent a lot of their spare time together, hunting and fishing the way she remembered her brother Bob and Vernon Carpenter doing back in the old days.

From these adventures Monroe was always bringing home stories about guns and hunting from the Duncans, but it was from C.T. Watkins that Harold brought home the scariest story of all about Mr. Duncan. He said that C.T. said Mr. Duncan had been run out of Kentucky for killing a man, and the reason he carried a gun with him all the time, and kept a mean dog at his house and loaded guns in every room, was to be ready when one of the dead man's kinfolks came to get even.

Monroe said this was a lie, that the real reason the Watkins were spreading this story was that Mr. Watkins was a Ku Kluck and he was out to get Mr. Duncan because he had square dances up at his house now and then where people drank whiskey.

She didn't know how much of all this to believe, but it didn't change her opinion that the Duncans were the kindest neighbors she had ever heard of. She did notice that they never went to church anywhere, but she didn't hold that against them either.

At the very last minute on the morning the children, including Edith, were to start to school, she was astonished by Monroe's refusing to go. She even had his dinner made for him. Yet she sent the others off without raising the slightest fuss, and went back in the house to try to find out what was wrong with him, if he was sick or what.

The day before on the way home from church she had him drive by the school so they could see it. He parked next to the flagpole in front of the two-story red brick building and everybody but her and the baby got out and stopped to read aloud the big sign above the entrance Brinton Consolidated School.

Then while she sat holding Gordon and thinking how glad she was that they now had such a fine school out here in the country, Monroe ran around with the others, looking in at the windows and swinging on the swings. He gave no hint then or on the ride home that he was not going to start to school the next morning.

Back in the kitchen, before she could get a word out, Monroe stopped playing with Gordon strapped in his highchair and said, "Mama, no matter what you say, I'm through goin' to school."

To all her questions about why he was not going, he only shrugged, and as she gave him all the reasons she could think of to try to change his mind, he merely shook his head without ever looking her in the eye.

"I don't know. But I tell you one thang." And now he did raise his head and almost glared at her. "I ain't spending my life tailin' them mares around the field neither. Eat, work, and sleep. Git up in the morning and do it all over again. Is this all there is in this world? If it is, I ain't no better off than them mares."

"But that's just why you have to have an education. So you can get a good job you like."

Still staring at her, he shook his head. "That ain't so. Look at Uncle Ben. He's got a good job. Wears fancy clothes. And I already got more education than him."

She had no answer for this, but when the other children came home with the story that Ralph Duncan wasn't going to school either, she suspected the two were acting together. Yet Monroe denied it and again turned aside all of her arguments to get him to go to school the next day.

For a week she let Monroe loaf around the farm or go off with Ralph, but when a spell of cool weather came along she suggested that he start breaking land for spring planting. After she reminded him of this for a couple of more days, he said he would.

From then on, when watching Monroe leave the barn and go off across the hill with the team in the morning, she could almost believe that history was repeating itself, for how many times had she watched Hamp drive off just like that? But Monroe wasn't Hamp around the house. Instead of showing a friendly face, he was glum all the time and had little to say to her or anyone else in the family.

At supper the children's usual complaints about teachers and schoolwork went on around him, but he never asked any questions or tried to take part in this talk. Only when she asked him a direct question about the plowing or the team did he say anything about what had happened to him during the day, and even then he gave her the shortest possible answer.

Now that they had a sleeping porch that could hold at least three beds, she had put her own bed and two more out there and let Monroe have one of the bedrooms in the house for himself. As soon as supper was over he either went to his own room or disappeared towards the Duncans' house.

One day Papa and Tommy came by with the bantam rooster and hens she had asked Papa to get as a surprise for Harold. While she got some feed and water for them and Tommy put them in a coop where she could keep them for a few days until they got used to their new home, Papa said he would walk out to the field to see how Monroe was getting along with his plowing.

He was back in a short time, saying, "Mattie, Monroe seems a mite touchy these days, don't he?" He went on to say they had a few words when he told Monroe he was wearing out his team for nothing by plowing too deep, and offered to re-set the doubletree on the loggerhead for him.

She laughed off Monroe's touchiness with Papa and didn't think anymore about it until Monroe came in from the field at noon still fuming. He said he guessed he knew as much about how deep to plow a field as anybody and finished by saying, "I've had enough of Grampa Lane trying to tell me how to farm."

"I'm sure he thought he was helping you," she said and went on putting the dinner on the table.

"Is that what he told you?"

"Something like that."

"And I guess you agreed with him."

His tone accused her even more than his words, but she said quietly, "No, Monroe, I didn't. I could have. But I didn't."

Snorting at this, Monroe stopped drying his hands on the towel, opened the kitchen door and threw his wash pan of water outside and put the pan back on the stand. Running his fingers through his hair, he took his place at the table and wolfed down his dinner without saying another word, not even seeming to see Gordon looking at him silently from his highchair.

When Monroe had finished eating, he went back outside and she hoped that an evening of plowing would cool off his temper. But when she looked out the window a little later and saw Maud and Kate unharnessed and grazing in the near south pasture, she didn't know what to think.

She had no idea where or how Monroe spent the evening, but he appeared for the chores when the other boys got in from school and came in to supper with them. She carried on at supper as if nothing had happened and so did Monroe, but when he didn't answer her call to get up the next morning, she found that he was gone and his bed hadn't been slept in.

Three days later the children brought home from the mailbox a letter from Rissy. Monroe had spent the night there and left the next morning saying he was going out West. She read the letter to the children at supper, trying not to show how unhappy it made her. When she finished, the long silence was broken by Arthur.

"I knew it all the time."

"No you didn't," Agnes said. "You're just makin' that up."

"I am NOT! He told me a long time ago he was goin' to run off one of these days. Like Papa."

"Huh."

Instead of listening to their argument, she was thinking of something else. So far as she knew, Monroe had no money and she hated to think of his being hungry. The weather was still warm enough that he could sleep outside, but how would he get food? And how could he travel without money?

"Mama, don't worry," Otis said, bringing her thoughts back to the table. "I can do the plowing on Saturdays—and Sundays, too, if you want me to. Arthur, you and Harold can get the wood cut and we'll get along just fine."

"Just fine, Mama," Harold said, his teary eyes looking at her. Keeping her own tears to herself, she thanked the boys and went on with supper, but that night in bed, holding Gordon in her arms and remembering when she used to hold Monroe the same way, she did cry.

Otis meant well, but he still wasn't old enough to know how much work was ahead of them. They would get along without Monroe's help because they had to, but everything wouldn't be just fine.

The first thing she had to do was write Sarah about Monroe and tell her everything was going to be fine, for if Sarah thought she was needed at home, it would be just like her to quit going to college and come home to help out.

And another thing, they could get along without the car. She could put the money from it towards building a new barn next summer. Tomorrow she would write Andy and have him come and get it and sell it for her.

Thinking about cars, she was reminded that ever since Tommy bought a car she had seen the old buggy next to the lot fence at the home place. Papa would be glad to see her getting some use out of it. Nellie was dead, but Papa would be able to get her a buggy horse, possibly, she hoped, another bargain like the mares.

Putting Gordon back in his basket, she lay in the dark at her end of the sleeping porch with her old geography book map of the West in her mind. Maybe it was her fault that Monroe was sleeping somewhere way out there in that big country tonight. Maybe she had been too hard on him, and she started worrying about the hard words she had said to him—over the years as well as recently—for he had never been easy to get along with.

She remembered Hamp's mama saying once that Hamp's running away had been the best thing that ever happened to him, that when he came home he had learned how to get along with people. Maybe this would be true for Monroe, but this happy thought didn't keep her from missing him and worrying about him right then.

Chapter 40

At first she looked forward anxiously each day for the children to bring the mail on their way home from school, hoping for a letter from Monroe, but as days turned into weeks without hearing a word from him, she all but gave up hope. She was made even sadder by remembering that when her brother Jimmy ran away from home they never heard from him again. Yet her sadness didn't keep her from noticing that things were more peaceful on the farm now that Monroe was gone.

Like Hamp, Otis seemed to have an eye for whatever needed to be done around a farm, and he took care of it without ever complaining about the work or the weather or anything that went wrong. He and Arthur slept in Monroe's room now, and usually the first thing she heard in the morning was Otis coaxing Arthur out of bed, for Arthur never seemed to be able to get his eyes open unless someone shook him awake and got both of his feet on the floor.

Also like Hamp in the old days, Otis would make a fire for her in the cookstove as soon as he was dressed, and then he would hustle the sleepy Arthur and Harold out the kitchen door with him to do the chores. On Saturdays while he broke land with the turning plow, Arthur and Harold chopped wood over in the ten-acre patch of blackjack and post oak alongside the Rickett place. At the end of the week, Otis would hitch Maud and Kate to the wagon and haul home the wood that they had cut.

Having only one heating stove, she had it set up in the dining room, and when the weather turned really cold, she closed off the front room from the rest of the house. Since everyone but strangers came and went by the kitchen door anyway, the use of the front room was not missed.

As she had hoped, Papa found a horse for the old buggy, a tall dingy brown with a black mane and tail. After riding him bareback a few times, Otis said that Dan—the name the horse came with—had a rough gait and was a little spooky, but all right outside of that.

Ever since Monroe ran away, Papa had sent Tommy in his car to pick up her and the family for church Sunday mornings—after dropping him off at the church house first. Also, every Saturday at noon Papa and Tommy stopped by on their way to Kickapoo to see if she needed anything from town, or if she had any butter and eggs for Papa to sell for her at Jenkins Feed Store.

She could have stayed away from church with a clear conscience herself, but she felt obliged to give the children a chance to find out for themselves what the church stood for so they could join it if they wanted to.

When she thought of how different from Sarah Monroe was turning out, she felt a little guilty for not having urged him to become a Christian back in the days when he seemed to listen to her. Yet in light of her own experience with religion, she knew she couldn't have done that without being a hypocrite.

Sunday mornings at church were sad times for her now. Either Alice was there looking sick enough to be in bed, or Alice was absent and she sat with Molly, whose trouble with Fred had only become worse. According to Molly, Fred had now taken up drinking and was letting her papa's farm go to ruin.

Remembering how happy Molly had been during their school

days, she could hardly believe how bitter she had become. Yet as much as she sympathized with Molly, she also sympathized with Fred—whom she hadn't seen in ages—for she knew from her years with Hamp how much more that side of married life meant to a man than it did to a woman, and she would never have thought it right to deny herself to her husband. Molly's mess left her shaking her head to think where it would all end.

A cold wet Christmas came and went, and in a way she was relieved when it was over. It wasn't so much that she had to think twice about every penny she spent—and even then could only buy the children clothes for presents—but mostly that she couldn't help remembering that at the same time last year Hamp and Monroe were with them and they were all looking forward to starting a new life in Colorado.

Not even the Christmas Eve celebration at church that year could take her mind away from Hamp and Monroe for long, although nowadays it was usually Monroe she fell asleep thinking about. If she only had some way of knowing that he was alive and well, she would have stopped worrying so much about his not writing. It was the not knowing that grieved her most.

Yet she kept her grief to herself, and during Christmas, had many long talks with Sarah about her studies, aware when she listened to her talk about such things as psychology and philosophy that Sarah had already gone far beyond what she herself had learned down at Oakridge School from her reading and from Mrs. Whitaker. In these talks she hoped that Agnes would take some interest in what Sarah was learning, but Agnes only asked what the college boys were like and what kind of clothes the girls wore.

She was at least glad that Agnes was thinking of other boys, because it seemed to her she might be getting too thick with Ralph Duncan. When her brothers accused her of being sweet on him she denied it, and it was true that he never came to the house to see her. Yet she saw them talking to each other somewhere every day, leaning over the orchard fence or the front gate or at Duncan's lane where Ralph was often waiting for Agnes when she came home from school.

As for clothes, it seemed to her that Agnes was never satisfied with what she had to wear. In the mornings while Edith was waiting for her out in Duncan's lane with Opal and Ruby, Agnes would still be rushing through the house making last minute changes to what she was wearing and asking her to sew on a loose button or hook for her, or take a stitch in a torn place.

She would take her hands out of the dishwater, dry them on her apron and oblige Agnes, who would fret until the job was done and then run out the door without a word—her brown, bobbed hair flying, dinner bucket in one hand and book satchel in the other. Watching her go, and recalling her own school days when she wore the same dress every day, she hoped that one day Agnes would take as much interest in her studies as she did in her clothes.

Yet from what she could tell from the report cards, Harold was likely to be the only scholar among them, especially in arithmetic. Already she would notice as she was finishing up in the kitchen after supper, or sitting near the stove mending something—that if any of the others studying at the dining room table was stumped by an arithmetic problem, Harold would say, "Let me see it."

Then, fiddling with the pencil in his left hand while he read the problem, he would dab the point to his tongue and set to work and solve it.

Whenever she heard them arguing over something in history or a story or a poem, or when she was asked to listen while one of them recited a piece to be said in school next day, she was carried back to the excitement of her own school days. This would remind her of the time when she was teaching Orin, and reading at night for Mrs. Whitaker. Those days she was so sure she was finally on her way to becoming a schoolteacher that she could taste it.

The strange thing was that in spite of the memory of that wonderful feeling, and in spite of her present worries, she knew without a doubt that she would rather be here in this little old house trying to make ends meet and keep the children well and in school, than to be alone in a fine book-lined room like Mrs. Whitaker's, with nothing more pressing to think about than teaching her pupils the next day.

Having grown up used to walking to school in any kind of weather, she sent the children off in the morning for their mile and a half walk regardless of rain or snow or cold. As the winter passed, she was not surprised that the number of colds and sore throats she had to doctor was no more than she had last year when school was only a few blocks away.

In March, Otis borrowed a two-row planter from Papa, and on a windy Saturday morning she walked down through the apple orchard between rows of sweet smelling, pink blossomed trees to look over the fence and watch him planting his first field of corn.

Within two weeks the thin, forked blades had shot out of the ground in green rows as straight as if an old farmer had laid them off, and she made a point one night at supper of praising Otis for a good job.

This had been the last piece of work he was able to do with the mares for a while, for within a few days of each other Maud and Kate had the usual long-legged, wobbly-kneed mule colt that made everybody laugh as they watched them trying to scamper around the lot.

Right away Harold named the colts Dink and Seymour after his two best friends at school, and as funny as the names seemed to the rest of the family, she saw no reason to change them.

Towards the end of April, when the corn was more than a foot high and the cotton plants half as tall and needing to be thinned, Sarah came home from her first year of college, driven by Andy Billings. Andy also brought another passenger, a blackish looking puppy he called a German Police dog.

Andy sat for a white in the shade of the elm tree, drinking several dippers of water and talking about the latest doing of the Ku Klucks in and around Kickapoo: last week a man north of town whipped, and last night two men tarred and feathered on the South Beard Street bridge. He said the oil business was causing it, bringing in all kinds of riff-raft, men-and women drinking and carrying on, something the good people of Kickapoo were not going to stand for even if the police didn't seem to mind.

While she didn't hold with men and women drinking and

carrying on, the thought of them being whipped and tarred and feathered for it made her squirm. She was relieved when Andy went on to say that the good side of the coming boom was that it was already helping business.

"Make no mistake about it," he said. "One of these days soon the oil boom is goin' to bust wide open here in this county."

"You really think so?"

"Oh, it's bound to. Why, they say there's no tellin' how much oil is in the ground around here. So hold on to the farm, Mattie. Who knows? You may be a millionaire before you know it."

She intended to hold on to the farm as long as she could, but she thought so little of Andy's talk about it making her a millionaire that by the time he was out of sight the idea was out of her mind.

Yet later, as she sat in the shade listening to Sarah talk about her final examinations and watching Gordon rolling on the ground with the new puppy, she couldn't get out of her mind the picture of white-hooded men appearing out of the night, forcing people out of their own home and dragging them off to be whipped or tarred and feathered and left in the road.

That evening when the children came home from school, everybody wanted to hold the new puppy. When it came to naming the puppy, Sarah wanted to call him Jack, after her papa's old dog that she used to play with when she was a child. None of them could think of a better name and that one stuck.

The next morning Sarah drove off in the buggy looking for a job teaching school in the fall. For the next few days she went all around the county, talking to principals and heads of school boards, and each night she came home with the same story.

The schools were expecting no vacancies because times were still too hard. Any teacher lucky enough to have a job was holding on to it. Apparently not discouraged, Sarah said she would wait until summer came and then try all the schools again.

In the meantime, Sarah insisted that she be allowed to take charge of the cotton chopping—that it would-be good for her after so much studying—and on the first day after the children's school ended, Sarah led them off to the field.

She was afraid Sarah would have the same trouble getting them to work as Monroe had, but was happily surprised when Sarah seemed to have no trouble at all. At least not a complaint came from the cotton patch as they worked in the hot sun day in and day out.

One morning as she sat on the little back porch, churning and keeping her nose tuned to the dinner cooking next door in the kitchen, her eye caught the name LITTLE AXE in a headline of the newspaper she had spread under the churn in case milk splashed out on the floor. She hadn't thought of Little Axe in years, but at once her mind leaped back to her fight with Bonnie Stevens, which had caused the school board to fire Mrs. Reese, who got a job the next year teaching at Little Axe.

All of this had happened so long ago that Mrs. Reese was probably already dead and in her grave, but out of curiosity she tore off the paper, held it up in one hand and read that as a result of a feud with the school board, the teachers at Little Axe had been fired. Although she had never been to Little Axe, she knew about where it was, and she stopped her churning and made a rough guess as to how long it would take to drive there in the buggy.

Looking out to see where the sun was, she suddenly made up her mind, let go of the dasher and hurried to the cookstove where she pulled the pots off the heat and opened the oven door. She went out to the mulberry trees where Gordon was playing with Jack and picked up the dust covered child and headed for the barn, Jack trotting along behind.

From the barn door she called the horses up from the pasture, shooed the mares and colts out of the way and fastened Dan in the barn and gave him a good feed of corn. By one o'clock she had fed the family its own dinner, rushed Sarah and Otis through a wash-up and into a change of clean clothes and had them in the buggy, ready for a trip to Little Axe some fifteen or twenty miles away.

Standing with her hand shading her eyes as she looked up at Sarah, she was struck by the change in her appearance since she came in from the cotton patch wearing a dirty dress and a worn-out bonnet, her face streaked with sweat and red from the heat. Now she looked so clean and fresh in her cool summer dress and broad-brimmed hat that no one would ever suspect she had ever set foot on a farm.

The thought of this made her give Sarah a final piece of advice. "Remember, Sarah. Farmers don't like town people. So let him know right away that you were raised on a farm right down there at Briggs. He might even have known your papa, or more likely Grandpa Roberts. Or maybe Grandpa Lane. And one last thing. If you get a chance, you might show some interest in his wife. It could make a difference."

Sarah smiled and nodded and Otis lifted the lines off Dan's back and gave them a shake, starting the horse out the driveway at a trot. She waited until the buggy had turned south and passed behind the pair of blackjacks, and then she hurried back into the kitchen where Agnes and Edith were doing the dishes.

In a few minutes, having put Gordon down for his nap and left Edith to watch after him and finish churning and taking up the butter, she was on her way to the cotton patch with the rest of the family, her eyes squinting against the glare of the hot sun in spite of the long brim of her bonnet.

Passing along the end of the weedy rows to where they were to start chopping, she was reminded again of how Mr. Koontz, poor old man, had let his farm go to crabgrass and cockleburs before he died, and she knew she didn't have an easy evening of hoeing ahead of her.

Late that night she was sitting at the kitchen table with the light turned low, waiting for Sarah and Otis to get back. She had set two places at the table for them, and had their supper waiting in the warming closet. Everybody else in the house was asleep, and she had fallen half asleep herself when she was startled by a loud "Whoa now!" from the driveway.

Hurrying out with a lantern for Otis to put Dan away, she could hardly wait to find out what Sarah had to say. But she stood at the buggy long enough to ask the yawning boy how Dan had held up on the long trip and to remind him to give the droopy, worn out horse an extra good feed.

Once back in the kitchen, she watched Sarah washing the grime off her face and neck and talking about the trip at the same time. Sarah said the head of the school board was a farmer. And he did have a friendly wife, so friendly she invited them to supper, where the farmer talked only about crops and the weather.

As for wanting teachers, he had told her while she was still in the buggy that if she was a Roman Catholic not to bother getting out. Later he said he was looking for two crackerjacks who wanted to teach school and not keep stirring up trouble. Sarah was not sure what "stirring up trouble" meant, and neither was she, but she felt better when Sarah went on to say, "I told him I didn't know how much of a crackerjack I was, but I said my interest would just be in teaching the pupils."

At noon a few days later, Otis brought back from his daily trip to the mailbox, a letter for Miss Sarah A. Roberts. The one-sentence letter, written with a pen, said she could have the job if she still wanted it. A happy Sarah promised to write an answer that very night.

She thought the offer of a job teaching school at seventy-five dollars a month and board was too important to be left to the mail. The letter could get delayed or lost, and from what Sarah had said about the head of the school board, he didn't seem like the kind of man who would wait very long before hiring someone else, especially since there were probably lots of people looking for one of those two teaching jobs.

Sarah agreed, and within an hour she was on her way to Little Axe again. This time it was Arthur's turn to be in the buggy beside her, grinning as he complained to Otis and Harold how unhappy he was to be missing those long hot hours of chopping cotton.

With a lighter heart than she had had for months, she turned back to the house to get herself ready for the cotton patch. Now if she could only hear that Monroe was alive and well, she wouldn't ask for anything more.

Chapter 41

After she had waited and worried for almost two years to hear from Monroe, all the while imagining every possible bad thing that could have happened to him, she had a letter from Rissy one day telling her that Monroe was alive and well. He had written to Browny, saying he was working as a lumberjack in Oregon and making lots of money, and that Browny could make lots of money if he would only come on out.

First she wrote a letter to Rissy, thanking her, and inviting the family to come for Sunday dinner whenever they could. The same night she wrote Monroe a long letter, saying how relieved and happy they were to hear from him, and telling him—beginning with Sarah's becoming a schoolteacher—the news of happenings on the farm since he left, especially the trouble with Mr. Watkins over Old Hazel.

Having seen that no fence could stop that long-legged cow if something she wanted to eat was on the other side of it, she had Otis put a yoke on her. Yet when Old Hazel was about ready to calve, the yoke was taken off to make it easier for her to get up and down when she was actually having the calf.

All went well until the second day after the calf was born and Old Hazel was allowed to go back to the pasture with the rest of the cows. That evening the cows came in at the usual time but Old Hazel was not with them.

Later in the evening one of the Watkins boys came to the kitchen door. He said his papa found the cow in his corn patch, that he had her in his lot, and to bring five dollars to get her.

Waiting until the Watkins boy was out of earshot, Otis said Mr. Watkins wouldn't dare do that if his papa were still alive. She thought so, too, but she didn't say so to Otis. Her main concern was that she didn't see how Old Hazel could have done half that much damage. Even so, she sent Otis to tell Mr. Watkins she would pay the five dollars as soon as she could, and in the meantime to please send the cow home.

Back came Otis mad as hops. The word from Mr. Watkins was that she was to send the money or he wouldn't let the cow out of his lot. Afraid to leave Old Hazel there overnight for fear her bag would cake with all that milk in it, and besides, Old Hazel's hungry calf was up in its pen right then, bawling for its supper.

She had Otis put Dan to the buggy and the boys loaded the new calf in it where she could hold it against the dashboard while Otis drove down to the Watkins and up to their barn lot gate. Their big brindled dog barking round the buggy set the calf to bawling again and brought Old Hazel charging to her bawling calf.

The old cow threw herself half over the barbed wire gate, snapping the top wires like string, and had her head in the buggy licking her calf before Mr. Watkins came rushing out of the house and up to the buggy.

She had never seen Mr. Watkins close up, and his long dark face and wild eyes scared her as he hollered at her as if she were an animal herself. She tried to explain about the calf needing to suck, but Mr. Watkins waved his hand in her face.

"Git that animal off my property," he shouted. "Next time it'll cost you plenty."

After that, Old Hazel had to wear her yoke even when she had her next calf.

She didn't tell Monroe about her recent trouble with Agnes, which had started one night when she was being kept awake by a full moon flooding the screened-in sleeping porch. At that warm time of year, the canvas on the porch was rolled all the way up, making the light inside so light that as she lay in bed she could clearly see Edith in her bed and Harold beyond her at the far end of the porch in his bed.

As usual on such moonlight nights, the mockingbird at the top of the big elm above the well was singing as if in broad daylight and she was half listening to it and thinking about Monroe.

During a lull in the mockingbird's song, she was sure she heard the front screen door shut. Since she couldn't imagine who or what could be coming in or going out of the house at this time of night, she slipped her feet to the floor next to Gordon's trundle bed, padded barefooted through the half-dark dining room and front room, and found the screen door closed as it should have been.

Glancing out across the shadowy front porch to the yard, she saw two dark figures come together on the far side of the front gate. Without thinking she called, "Agnes?" and the two figures separated. One faded away towards Duncan's lane and the other came into the yard.

She had been scared at first, but now she was so surprised that she could hardly believe what she was seeing. She stepped out on the porch and waited, and sure enough it was Agnes coming along the walk to the porch step, where she stopped and stood looking up, her face half in the moonlight.

"Agnes, how long has this been going on?"

"I don't know," Agnes burst out as if the matter was nobody's business but hers.

"I'm ashamed of you."

"We didn't do anything," Agnes burst out again.

"Well, you come in and go to bed—and stay there—and we'll talk about it tomorrow."

The next day while warning Agnes about the trouble she could bring on herself by slipping out at night to see Ralph Duncan, or any other boy, she was tempted to give her own experience as proof of the point she wanted to make, but she couldn't bring herself to confess it.

Only after Agnes had broken down and cried, and promised never to go out at night again to see Ralph, did she realize that her confession would have given Agnes something to hold over Sarah's head, and she was glad she had kept her mouth shut about it.

Naturally she couldn't write Monroe all of this, so she only wrote that Agnes had bobbed her hair and it looked becoming on her, which was true.

She closed the letter with love from the whole family, but on purpose she didn't ask Monroe when he was coming home, leaving it to him to bring up the subject. And then at the last moment, even as she was about to lick the flap to close the envelope, she had a change of heart and took out the letter and added another sentence, telling Monroe that she missed him and hoped that he would write soon.

The next morning when she sent Otis off on Dan—now wearing Nellie's old saddle—to take the letter to the mailbox, she felt happy with herself and Monroe for the first time since he ran away. Maybe it was her fault that he had run off, maybe he might just be waiting for her to give him a sign that she was no longer mad at him and maybe now he would write to her saying everything was all right between them.

A couple of weeks passed and she was still waiting for Monroe's answer when one night a sudden storm sent her running around through the house hurriedly closing windows and doors. Lamp in hand, she came to Agnes' room and found that Agnes was not in it.

Even as she stood looking down in surprise at the empty bed, she heard the front door, which she had just closed, open and let in the noise of the heavy rain. She turned and saw Agnes slipping inside, dripping wet, her bobbed hair plastered down like a boy's. Agnes came towards her, blinked at the lamplight and stopped, her rain-drenched face suddenly going white and her mouth falling open.

At first she was too hurt to be mad at Agnes, until flashing across her mind came the tearful promise Agnes had made to her the other morning right here in this room, and then came the thought that tonight was probably not the first night since then that Agnes had broken that promise.

Only the scared white face with rain running down it like tears kept her from lashing out at Agnes. Instead she walked past her without saying a word and went back to the sleeping porch to lay awake most of the rest of the night asking herself what was to be done.

The next morning she didn't mention Agnes's broken promise, leaving it to her to bring up the subject if she wanted to. By noon the sun and the wind had dried the cotton patch, and after dinner they all went back to picking again.

When the crop was all picked that fall, the ten bales she had hoped for, and counted on, had shrunk to seven. Even worse, the price was so low she wished she could afford to do like the Duncans and bring the bales home and store them in the yard until spring in hopes that the price might be a little higher then.

But she had to have the money now, and when she had sold the last bale and paid the taxes and the mortgage, she could see that while the farm was giving them a good place to live and enough to eat, at the present price of cotton she was losing money every year. And at the rate her bank account was going down, she could also see that one day she was not going to have any money left to make up the shortage.

She could always make do with the clothes she had, including the old black straw hat she had been wearing summer and winter for years, but the children either grew out of their clothes or wore them out, and she wanted to start them to school with new things, if she could.

All of these thoughts—and Agnes—were on her mind one Saturday when Papa and Tommy came by to take her and some of the children to town to get them fitted out for the start of school on Monday. She left the twins and Harold at home chopping wood, but she knew the sizes of everything she had to get for them.

As the noisy car bounced along over the dusty, rutted road, she scarcely listened to Edith and Gordon talking and laughing at the passing sights Edith was pointing out to him. Instead, most of her thoughts were on Agnes, who was sitting on the far side of the back seat, looking straight ahead and saying nothing to anyone.

She guessed that Agnes was still unhappy with her because of the two dresses of Sarah's she had made over for her to wear to school. She had worked on the dresses every spare minute she had for days—mainly after supper—and she was pleased with the way they turned out. Yet Agnes tried one of them on and said right out that it wouldn't do, even while she and Edith were both saying it looked fine on her.

Yet the unhappy, down-at-the-mouth look Agnes kept on her face as she tried on the second dress told her she didn't believe what they said. Agnes fussed back and forth before the looking glass, swinging her head this way and that to get a better look, and making the same complaint about the second dress. The waist was too high, the skirt didn't hang even, the neck wasn't right, and so on.

Her final complaint was, "But, Mama, they look so made over! I'd feel funny bein' seen in them at school."

"Um, maybe so. But I would've been happy to have had even one school dress as pretty as either one of these."

"But, Mama! Looks didn't matter way back then."

Once upon a time she wouldn't have let Agnes get away with such a silly statement, but since she was having so much trouble with her these days, she didn't feel like having an argument. She had said goodnight to the girls and left Agnes frowning at herself in the looking glass.

When they got to Kickapoo, Tommy drove down to Jenkins Feed Store and parked in back where they used to tie up the wagon and team in the old days. Now it was all cars. She smiled at Tommy hurrying off with a happy look on his face, knowing he was on his way to the Odeon Theater, where he would pay ten cents to see a moving picture show—something she had never seen, although Tommy had tried to tell her what it was like.

From her shopping trips with Grace Billings, she had learned where to get the best bargains, and after she had set the time with Papa when she would be back, she led the way up to Main Street and turned along it to a department store that stood on the spot where the Opera House used to be.

Agnes carried Gordon, who could have walked holding her hand if it hadn't been for the Saturday crowd of other farmers and their families filling the sidewalks. Edith gawked along in front of them as if alone, reminding her of herself long ago, before there were paved sidewalks in Kickapoo, when she, too, wanted to see everything at once.

She had no trouble getting Edith what she needed, but Agnes balked at everything she and the saleswoman showed her—shoes, stockings, underclothes, everything. Finally Agnes said, "Mama, why don't you just give me the money for my clothes and I'll get them while you're buying the things for the boys. I can meet you all back at the car later."

She was so surprised by this idea, and so glad to be able to put an end to all of the cross words, that she agreed. While she was counting out the money she had expected to spend for Agnes's clothes, she repeated to her the things she was to buy, and then she added two more dollar bills to the amount, just to be on the safe side.

Agnes took the money and disappeared, leaving Edith holding on to Gordon. That was the last they saw of her until much later when she came rushing up to the car, which had been all loaded up and waiting for her for more than half an hour. Several times Papa had taken his watch out and checked it against the sun. Each time while squinting at it he would say, "You don't reckin the child got lost do you, Mattie?"

Although she wasn't sure Agnes hadn't, she always answered, "Oh, no. I expect she'll be along any minute now, Papa."

When Agnes did appear, out of breath and carrying a single long flat box wrapped in bright paper, Tommy cranked up the engine while Edith began to question her sister about where she had been and why she took so long.

Agnes only gave Edith hard looks for answers as she settled down beside her, holding the long box leaning against her knees.

That night after supper was the time to try on the new clothes, and remembering what a happy time it had been for her when she was young, she still got a lot of pleasure out of watching the children look and feel, and even smell, the new clothes as they put them on and went around showing them off to each other. It was almost more fun than opening presents on Christmas morning, and in a few minutes the dining room table and the floor around it were cluttered with string and wrapping paper and shoeboxes.

Edith and the three boys were soon showing off their new clothes, and even Gordon was running around wearing Harold's new cap with the earflaps fastened under his chin. As usual most of the clothes were a size or two too big—especially the boys' things. They were bought that way on purpose because their arms and legs and feet were still growing, and the boots and everything else had to last until next spring.

After a while Arthur called it to everybody's attention that Agnes wasn't wearing any of her new clothes. Agnes said she didn't feel like dressing up, but the boys kept after her and when the rest joined in, she went to her room and came back carrying, draped over her arm, a gaudy red and yellow dress which she held out for everyone to see.

To keep from saying how awful the dress looked, she felt the material, which was smooth as ice, while Edith called out, "Scrumptious! Really scrumptious, Agnes. But it looks kind of short for you."

The boys only gave the dress a glance before one of them said, "And what else?"

Agnes looked at the floor and said, "This is all I got."

"What?" the boys all shouted at once. Then there was a long silence. Everybody looked wide-eyed at Agnes and waited to hear what the joke was. Even she didn't know what to expect, but watching the strained look on Agnes's face, she felt that whatever was going on in Agnes's mind was not a joke.

Suddenly Agnes pulled the dress out of Edith's hands and ran back to her room. The boys started calling and whistling after her, but she shushed them and turned their attention again to looking at gloves and caps and coats and lace-up boots as if nothing had happened.

Only later did she go into Agnes's room where Agnes was sitting in a chair and staring out the window. The red and yellow dress lay splashed across the bed next to the long, tissue-lined box it had come in. No other clothes were in sight.

"That looks like such an expensive dress, Agnes. How could you get it and all your other things, too?"

Without turning her head, Agnes said in a low voice, "I said that's all I got."

She couldn't believe her ears. "Don't tell me you spent all that money on this one dress?"

At the barely perceptible nod of the bobbed hair, she said, "But, Agnes, don't you see? As fine as it may be, we can't afford it. You have to have new shoes. And it'll be cold enough one of these days for a coat. And you need something for your head, and underclothes. Oh, Agnes, I don't see how we can keep such a dress. Where would you wear it? It's too fine even for church."

She was also thinking it was too loud for church, but seeing that Agnes already seemed almost in tears, she didn't want to make her feel any worse.

"Well," she began again, "don't put it on for church tomorrow and—"

"I didn't buy it for church," Agnes cut in, her voice strangely low, her gaze still out the window.

She wanted to say, "If you didn't buy it for church, and it won't do for school, then what DID you buy it for?" but all she actually said was, "I think you better put it back in the box and we'll take it back to the store next Saturday. There are a lot of things you simply have to have."

When Agnes didn't answer, she left her and went back to the dining room. With Agnes still on her mind she started everybody gathering up the string and wrapping paper and shoeboxes.

The next morning when Agnes was late for breakfast, she sent Edith to wake her up. In a moment Edith came running back through the house shouting, "She's gone! Agnes is not in her room Mama!"

But she had caught her breath and was no longer listening.

Now she knew what Agnes meant when she said, "I didn't buy it for church."

Chapter 42

While she was putting supper on the table one evening a few days after Agnes disappeared, the kitchen door opened and Agnes stood in the door, Ralph behind her.

Having been told earlier in the week by Mr. Duncan that the two of them had run off in his car to get married, she was ashamed to think Agnes was taking after her, and her shame of that night under the big oak tree came back to her more heartfelt than ever before. If Agnes had only talked to her, she would have had Reverend Willis marry them in the front room with both families present—even if Agnes was pregnant, or thought she was.

As she turned from the stove with a hot platter of fried potatoes, Agnes, in another new dress, stepped inside saying, "Hello, Mama."

Instantly she remembered how fearful she had felt bringing Hamp home for the first time after her elopement. She set the platter down quickly on the table, gave Agnes a forgiving hug and welcomed the blushing Ralph with a handshake.

"You're just in time for supper," she said.

"We jist came to say hello, Mama. They're waitin' supper for us."

After a few minutes of everybody talking at once, she told the children to start their supper, and she walked out to the rosebushes with the newlyweds, where she said good-bye and told them to come back soon.

Instead of going back to the house right away, she stood there with a lump in her throat, watching the two go across the road and up the lane, hand in hand. Whether they knew it yet or not, they were no longer a boy and a girl leaning over the fence talking and laughing the time away. With a few words to the justice of the peace they had put an end to those easy days forever. Within a few weeks Ralph had rented a farm down at the south end of the county, and one day she waved goodbye to Agnes and him as they rode off in a wagon loaded with secondhand furniture and a coop full of laying hens and leading a Duncan cow tied on.

After Christmas a letter came from Monroe, a few lines wishing everybody a Merry Christmas. In spite of her immediate answer, she waited through the rest of the winter without another word from him, although she was kept cheered up somewhat by the weekly letters from Sarah, who from the first day had found teaching school just right for her.

As for Agnes, months passed with no hint of a baby. Every now and then Agnes and Ralph drove home in the wagon to the Duncans for a Saturday night stay, and they always either walked down to the house for a visit or stopped by late Sunday evening as they left for the long drive back to their farm.

When spring came she was busier than ever. In addition to the gardening and everything else she had to do outside, she found that the cockleburs and crabgrass in the cotton patch were getting so far ahead of the cotton she had to help the children with the chopping to keep the crop from being sapped out. That fall she helped with the picking, too. The next year went the same way and the next.

On Andy's visits to the farm, he kept telling her that she was not going to have to depend on cotton much longer for a living, that the oil boom in the county was just around the corner. Yet with the price of cotton so low she couldn't bear to think about it, and even worse, an acre was making less cotton each year, she paid little attention to Andy's predictions of a prosperous future for her.

Instead, to cut down on expenses every way she could think of, she had Papa sell the mares once Dink and Seymour were old enough to work, for she could no longer afford to feed two teams.

Another worry was Agnes, married long enough to have had two babies by now, but none in sight. Nor any likely, she thought, from the way the two of them were always carping at each other during their visits. All the more reason to pay a visit to them.

One day she and Sarah drove down to the farm in Sarah's secondhand car. She was surprised to find Agnes wearing a dirty dress and her hair a bush. And that wasn't all. It was easy to see the floors had not been swept, and from what she could see of the bedroom, the bed had not been made. Even worse, Agnes served them a hodgepodge dinner—not a single fresh vegetable from the garden, even though this was the best of the growing season.

In the face of all these signs of an unhappy marriage, she was surprised on the way home to hear Sarah say she was going to get married herself one of these days. She already had her husband picked out—the son of a part-Cherokee farmer who had come from Iowa to make the Run. He had proposed but she had not said yes, yet.

"His name's Crider," Sarah went on. "John Crider. Doesn't sound very Indian, does he? Well, wait till you see him."

She listened to Sarah in quiet wonder. She had never doubted that Agnes and Edith were pretty enough to catch a husband without any trouble, but for years she had been afraid Sarah's homely looks might make an old maid of this best of her daughters, the way Alice's had done for her family. Now she was so happy to have stumbled on such good news that she wanted to tell someone.

Sarah must have guessed what she was thinking, for she said, "Now, Mama, all this is our secret till further notice."

No further notice came from Sarah in her letters that fall, or when she came home for Christmas. Yet in Monroe's Christmas letter there was a hint of news of another kind that took her interest somewhat away from Sarah's love affair.

Monroe said he had been down sick—although he did not say what the matter was—and he about had his fill of lumberjacking. Hoping this meant he might be coming home before long, she answered right away, asking Monroe about his sickness, but she got no answer.

Yet as another freeze-and-thaw winter wore itself out, she had another worry on her mind. Each Sunday morning, one look at poor skinny Alice—when Alice was able to come to church at all—was enough to make her feel sad for the rest of the week. She never expected to see Alice at church if the weather was bad, but one beautiful Sunday in March as soon as Tommy picked them up, he said, "Alice is very sick."

She could hardly wait for Tommy to get her to church, where she could question Papa. "Doc Williams says it's TB," Papa said, shaking his head. "Emma's been after her for some time to come out and live with them. So I reckin she'll go now."

As soon as she was back home and finished with dinner, she had Harold put Dan to the buggy, and taking Gordon with them, they drove off to see Alice. After visiting a little with the rest of the family on the front porch, she went upstairs to her and Emma's old room where Alice was lying in bed looking livelier than when she had seen her at church the last time. Yet with her graying hair stringing down on either side of her thin face, Alice looked as old as Mama.

Alice answered her greeting by saying, "Well, Matt, I guess I feel better now I know for sure what's the matter with me."

And as she sat down on the edge of her bed, Alice smiled up at her and poked her in the arm with a finger. "Did you hear I'm goin' out to Em's? They say it high and dry out there in the Panhandle. Jist what Doctor Williams says I need to git me well. And guess what? No work!"

"No work?"

"Noooo work!"

The very idea was so unheard of that the two of them stared at each other a long moment before bursting out laughing. As soon as Alice stopped coughing and got her voice back, she said, "And I'll git to ride out there on a railroad train, too. Ain't that nice? I always wanted to ride on one and never thought I'd git to."

"Alice, remember how scared we were the night we first heard a train whistle?"

"Do I? I remember Em runnin' out of the tent screamin' and wakin' everybody up."

She did, and one old happening called to mind another one. Soon they were jogging each other's memory in a light-hearted way they had never done with each other before, asking questions, telling secrets and laughing like school girls, until she chanced to say, "Alice, remember when you and Bob came on Fred Dawson trying to kiss me out at the buggy that time?"

Nodding, Alice suddenly turned sober and tears stood in her eyes. "Wish now I'd married Marvin Cole."

Before she could think of a suitable answer, Alice clutched her arm to give her another "remember" and they were laughing again.

A few days later, standing with Alice and Mama and Papa and Tommy at the railroad station, she could hardly believe her happy talk with Alice had ever taken place. Today it seemed more like a dream than ever. Here they were, the same two people face to face, yet once again as serious as they had always been with each other. Maybe it was too much to expect that she and Alice would be talking and laughing when Alice was about to go away, maybe to be gone forever.

Anyway, Alice was not smiling today, and her face looked even sadder and thinner than usual, what with her new brown hat stuck so far down over her ears—like a flower pot turned upside down on her head—the only hair showing was the gray bun at the back of her neck.

Here in the middle of the noisy hustle and bustle of dozens of people, the five of them stood bunched up hardly talking at all, just waiting against the time for Alice to disappear inside the long green car with her gripsack, bought new, like her hat, for the trip.

The train whistle filled the air with its mournful sound and the potbellied conductor called, "All aboarrred," up and down the platform.

A sudden flurry of hugs, kisses, tears, and loud good-byes started all around them. The family had tears in their eyes, too, but none were shed as Alice started with Papa and gave him a touch of her hand and a soft good-bye, and so on to each of them, Mama last.

She watched Alice follow the other passengers up the iron steps into the railroad car, her black, Sunday shoes showing with each slow step. The potbellied conductor swung himself lightly up behind Alice, and at the top of the steps he turned and slammed the door shut.

She and Mama and Tommy backed away, but she kept her eyes on the train as it gave a noisy jerk and started sliding away like a long green snake. A red light on its tail went rushing by and she watched it grow smaller and smaller until down the tracks it winked out of sight around a curve. Only then did she wipe away the tears sliding down her cheeks.

Within two weeks she was reading Alice's letter home to Mama, a letter mostly about Emma and Glenn's farm. It was so big—nearly a thousand acres, including what they leased—that their nearest neighbor lived a mile away. But they could see the house and barn clear as anything because the land was flat as a pancake and had no trees. Some years Glenn made over ten thousand bushels of wheat. TEN THOUSAND BUSHELS!

When she got her own letter from Alice, the best news was that the dry climate seemed to be doing her some good. Or maybe it was her doing no work that made her feel better. Alice was not sure which it was. The only part of Alice's letter she didn't like was hearing that sometimes the wind blew day and night without letting up. Reading this she knew such a wind would be too much for her. She had begun noticing that even a little wind put enough dust in the air to start her coughing, whether she was working in the field or trying to sleep at night.

Later in the summer in one of Sarah's letters, she got the "further notice" about John Crider that Sarah had promised her, an announcement that they were coming for a visit Sunday evening. By the time Sunday evening came, she was all curious to see what Sarah's beau was going to be like. Usually she changed out of her church dress right after dinner on Sunday, but today she didn't. After cleaning up in the kitchen and boiling a pot of tea and letting it steep, she took off her apron, washed her face in cool water and looked to her hair.

The boys had gone off somewhere, and she was sitting on the front porch listening to Edith practice saying "To A Waterfowl" for school the next day, when a black coupe turned off the road and stopped under the shade of the elms a few feet from the front gate.

As Sarah and her beau came up the walk, she went down the steps to meet them. She noticed that Sarah was taller, but as they got closer it was the dark face under the brim of his hat that held her attention. For an instant a feeling she had never felt before surged through her and she wished Sarah was not marrying an Indian.

They stopped before her, and the smiling Sarah said, "Mama, this is John."

John took off his hat and beamed on her. "I'm pleased to meet you, Miz. Roberts." His black eyes—as black and shining as his hair—twinkled into hers as he took her hand and she liked him at once.

They sat in the rockers on the front porch and talked hot weather until Edith came with a pitcher of cool tea and glasses, and went back for a plate of molasses cookies made that morning before church. When Sarah introduced John to Edith and he stood up to shake hands with her, a sudden blush came to her cheeks. But tea and cookies and John's good nature soon had everybody at ease and the talk moved on to other topics.

Several times Sarah brought John for a visit, usually on Sunday evening for a couple of hours, although once they came on Saturday and spent the day. It happened to be a day when Agnes and Ralph were home for a visit, and she was pleased to have them meet each other.

The two men seemed to get along well enough together, but later when she and Agnes were alone, Agnes said, "Mama, you never told me Sarah is marryin' an Indian."

"I guess I didn't think it's worth mentioning."

But at supper that night the subject came up among the children. She learned that Arthur and Edith did not like it that Sarah was marrying an Indian. Harold got so mad hearing them picking John apart just because he was an Indian that he raised his voice till it cracked, saying, "What difference does being an Indian make to anybody? Seymour Sloat is my best friend. And he's a full-blooded Delaware. You all ought to be ashamed of yourselves."

After letting them argue for a while, she calmed everybody down, and then repeated what she had said to Agnes earlier in the day, adding, the only thing that matters is that John Crider is an honest man and he and Sarah love each other."

Yet here was something she had not expected, for the children had known all along about the Indian blood in the family, about Grandpa having some Cherokee in him, and all about Grandma Lane's mama walking the Cherokee Trail of Tears from the Great Smoky Mountains to The Indian Territory when she was little more than a baby. And as for herself, the children were always after her to tell them once more about the time at Oakridge School she slapped Bonnie Stevens in the mouth for calling her "Indian face."

Without saying anymore about it, she was not swayed by those who did not want Sarah to marry an Indian. When Sarah left her alone with John on the front porch one evening, she was not surprised when he asked her permission to marry Sarah.

She gave it, wishing him and Sarah, who had suddenly returned to the porch, much happiness.

Chapter 43

She was sitting in the shade of the big elm with Papa and Tommy, listening to Papa tell how he had suddenly found a good buyer for his school lease and had sold everything but one team of mules and the cows and chickens.

He sounded as pleased with the world as if he had made it himself, and she was happy for him. But when Papa went on to say he was going to buy the farm on the corner half a mile north of her, a treeless worn-out farm she had looked at with Andy, she felt her smile dry up.

Poor Mama. Ever since Papa had argued her into leaving a perfectly good farm in Arkansas, with a year-around creek running through it, to try for a free homestead in Oklahoma Territory, Mama had been working and waiting all these years with never a complaint that anyone ever heard of. And now instead of the free homestead on the new ground they had expected in this land of milk and honey, finally they had to settle for buying a farm about as used up as they were.

Papa's next piece of news was that he was going to stop raising cotton, and make a living from milk and eggs. With no cotton to chop and pick, Tommy could handle all the fieldwork and the new farm by himself, so Papa said, and went on to say that beginning in the fall he was taking a job as janitor up at Brinton School.

Giving half an ear to the mockingbird's song from the elm above her, she wished she could be as pleased to hear Papa's news as he seemed to be to tell it. Yet all the while she was asking herself how a man who had worked out-of-doors with crops and animals all his life could bear to give it up to sweep floors, keep water coolers full, and carry heavy buckets of coal to all those stoves. Hamp had been right when he said spring was no different from any other time of year if you got up every morning to the same job.

She did not need to ask Papa what Mama thought about all of this knowing he probably had not even told her what he was going to do until he had made up his mind to do it. When she had a chance to talk to Mama, she found she had been right, but the closest Mama came to complaining about the new farm or Papa's new job was to say, "Far's I'm concerned, Mattie, the only good thang in all this is that we'll be neighbors. Course, I won't mind bein' out of the cotton parch for good, nuther."

Then Mama want on to say, half-jokingly, that maybe Alice's letter might have had something to do with Papa giving up farming, saying the letter was all about Emma and Glenn's farm—over a thousand acres, and a plow that could break as many acres of land in one day as on all of Papa's School lease fields. And in good years they made ten thousand bushels of wheat.

She had some news of her own for Alice. On Andy's advice, she had leased the exploration right to the farm to an oil company. That brought in enough money to pay the mortgage and taxes for a while. Yet the two men running around over the farm for one day in a pick-up truck pulling a little trailer-stopping here and there to fiddle around with dials on the trailer for no reason her boys could see seemed to be the beginning and end of her oil boom.

"It's too soon to know." Andy said one day at the well curb. "Mattie, you'll just have to have patience."

"Patience, Andy? Seems to me farmers have more patience than anything else."

———————————

Long before the wedding date, Sarah moved back home from Little Axe and went off and found herself a new teaching job for the fall in Seminole, a town in the next county that was having the kind of oil boom Andy kept predicting for Kickapoo.

It was near Seminole where John was going to take Sarah to live. His papa had a cousin married to a Seminole Indian living over there, and even though her husband had struck it rich and built a big house in town, he wanted someone to keep the old farm going as a farm in spite of all the oil wells on it.

She let Sarah—living at the home until the wedding day arrived—take the children to the cotton patch each morning to fight the crabgrass and cockleburs for another day in the sun and heat, work which she herself had been finding more tiring this spring than ever before. And on Sundays, as much as she enjoyed visiting with poor Molly between Sunday school and the sermon, she let Sarah take the children to church and she stayed home.

She liked having a few hours to herself with plenty of time to make something special for Sunday dinner, and she liked the near silence of Sunday morning. It was the only day of the week that the country was anywhere near as quite as it used to be all the time, for quietness was becoming a thing of the past even way out here miles from town, and all because of the automobile. Year after year more and more cars went roaring by the house, each car dragging a rooster tail of dust behind it.

Yet she noticed that one thing had not changed over the years. In the old days, she could tell all the people she knew by their saddle horse or team before the people got close enough to be recognized. Now she could tell them by their cars.

That was why one noontime, hearing a car coming up the driveway, she needed only a quick glance out the kitchen window to know it was a stranger. She was surprised to see a strange car headed for the back of the house, because strangers usually parked out front and came to the front door.

Even so, she would have stuck her head out of the kitchen door to see who it was, but the children were due in from the field and she was too busy getting dinner ready to put on the table to leave the stove just then. She turned back to her work and while waiting for whoever it was to get out of the car and come to the door, she checked her pots and pans and started turning a skillet of okra, browning just the way she wanted it to.

Not hearing any noise at the kitchen door, she almost jumped out of her skin when close behind her a familiar voice said, "Well I'm back."

Even as she gasped, she knew it was Monroe. Turning quickly, she stopped where she was, too overcome to speak or move. The Monroe she had expected was not looking at her. Instead of the young face she had last seen, she was staring up at a lean, hard-face man.

"Didn't mean to scare you, Mama."

She reached out and their hands met. He was Monroe again and she was suddenly afraid of breaking out in tears if she told him how happy she was to see him. Studying him from his neatly combed hair to his shiny brown shoes, she said, "You don't look like you been sick at all."

"Sick? Oh, that was a long time ago. I'm fit as a fiddle."

"Your face is... thinner."

"So's yours. You're still workin' too hard, Mama."

To keep herself under control, she said, "Where'd you come from?" and turned back to the stove to pull the okra off the heat and put a lid on the skillet.

"Well, that's a long story. I was in California a week ago."

"Is it as pretty as they say?"

"Some parts of it."

"Here," she said, pulling out a chair from the kitchen table. "Sit down and let me look at you. The children will be in from the field any second. You won't know Gordon he's so big. Or maybe Edith either."

Monroe sat down and looked up at her. "So Agnes and Ralph run off and got hitched. That didn't surprise me. Any kids?"

"No."

"How they gittin' along?"

"All right, I guess. Times are hard for farmers these days"

"Times are always hard for farmers." Monroe said, his own voice suddenly hard. "Farmers are even worse suckers than workin' stiffs. Only a real sucker would still try to make it farmin' these days."

Instead of taking this personally, she thought of all the times she had heard that same tone. It used to come out of an innocent face, but now Monroe's look was as hard as his words. He had no reason to be unhappy that she could think of, him with a good mind, a big strong body, and fine looks.

Yet there he sat, the Monroe she had been longing for years to see, not back in the house two minutes and already the old sneer in his voice. She didn't know what to say and was relieved when she heard Sarah and the children at the well. At the same time she was ashamed of herself for feeling relieved.

Chapter 44

When she told Monroe the others had come, the hard look left his face and he jumped up and went out to see them. She followed him to the door, and as she stood watching him go along the walk between the rows of hollyhocks, she tried to put his bitter words out of her mind. Beyond him she could see Sarah and the children at the well, busy washing off the dirt and sweat from the cotton patch while Otis pumped.

None of them seemed to notice Monroe at first, and then everybody was calling his name and crowding around him, everybody but Gordon. Forced out of the way by his noisy big brothers, he looked on while the others were making over Monroe.

She saw Sarah take hold of Monroe's shoulder and turn him around to Gordon. She couldn't hear what was said, but she saw Monroe reach down and lift the freckled faced boy up in the air and put him down and shake his hand.

At dinner everybody was so excited and noisy it was more like Thanksgiving or Christmas than a working day. Apparently Monroe thought so too, for when he was telling them what all he had seen in California, somebody asked something about moving pictures, and learning that none of them had ever seen one, he said, "I tell you what. Soon's dinner's over let's all go to town and see a movin' picture show."

"Yeah!" Arthur called, and the whole table fell silent and looked at her.

Her first thought was that Monroe didn't seem to remember that chopping cotton was a "can see to can't see" job. Any farmer that let his help out of the field at noon to sit all evening at a moving picture show wouldn't last long as a farmer. She would have liked it better if Monroe had offered to borrow her hoe and go to the cotton patch with the children after dinner and help out with the chopping.

Seeing the children looking at her and all but holding their breath, she looked slowly around at them. They seemed to have suddenly forgotten that the cotton wasn't simply waiting for them out there in the sunshine. While it waited it was being sapped every minute by faster growing weeds and grass, and if a rain should keep them out of the field for another week the cotton crop would be finished before it ever got started.

She was put out with Monroe. He should have known better than get the children's hopes up for nothing.

Yet in spite of how anxious she was to get the cotton chopped while it could still be saved, the longer she hesitated about saying "no" to his offer the more she realized she probably shouldn't say it. After all, it WAS something special to have Monroe home again, and nobody could be happier to see him than she was, even though this was the second time she had been upset with him in the few minutes since he got here.

Against her better judgment she thanked him, and set off a scramble among the children when she told them they could go if they washed up again and put on clean clothes.

She and Sarah spent the evening chopping cotton, stopping early enough to make a molasses cake for Monroe's homecoming supper, where the whole talk was about the moving picture show, and the ice cream cones Monroe had bought for them before the show.

The next morning at breakfast the children were still talking about the cowboy capturing the outlaws all by himself, with Otis wishing he had a silver mounted saddle like the cowboy's.

After Sarah and the children had gone to the field, she washed the breakfast dishes while Monroe sat at the kitchen table catching up on what had been going on in the family and in the county all these years. When she told him what Andy had said about the coming oil boom, he didn't have much to say, but he took a great interest in news about the Ku Kluck.

"Sounds like he's one his self," he said, the hardness coming in his voice. "Mister Duncan's got the answer for them whistle punks." He made pistol of his hand and fired it a couple of times. "They start chousing me around I'll give'm the same kind of answer."

Since she couldn't think of any reason why Monroe should need to be worried about the Ku Klucks, she went on with her work. The talk turned to the family, and when he said he thought he would drive down to see Agnes and Ralph and probably spend the night, she was reminded that she hadn't told him yet about Sarah getting married. But she decided she would let Sarah have the pleasure of breaking that news to him herself.

Monroe came back the next evening while they were having supper. Sarah set a place for him and as he ate he told them the latest about Agnes and Ralph, bringing the news that they were thinking of giving up farming and moving to Kickapoo.

She noticed, however, that Monroe was not the free and easy talker he had been yesterday. He seemed to have something on his mind besides what he was saying, and even though he answered Sarah's questions he never looked at her.

When supper was over, she excused the twins and Harold so they could go play ball, and she let Sarah and Edith clear the table while she stayed talking with Monroe, who got around to saying that Agnes and Ralph didn't seem to be getting along with each other. She could have told him a lot about this herself, but she only nodded, not wanting to tell it while Edith and Gordon were within earshot.

"By the way," Monroe said, raising his voice and looking towards

348

the kitchen, "nobody around here yesterday told me Sarah's getting married." At this a smiling Sarah stuck her head out of the kitchen and said, "I never got a chance. But I'm glad you'll be here for the wedding."

"Agnes tried to make me believe you're marryin' an Indian, Sarah. But I didn't fall for it. I told her you was too smart for anything like that."

Expecting to hear some old joke about marriage, she was so taken aback by the mean words behind Monroe's laugh that all she could do was look at Sarah's fallen face while he went on in the same mocking tone, "Big chief of the Cherokees is he?"

Sarah couldn't have missed his sarcasm now, but she gave no hint that it bothered her. Stepping all the way into the dining room she said, "No, John's grandpa gave up his tribal rights long ago when he moved to Iowa. John's papa made the Run here like everybody else."

"Well, I was just sorry to hear a sister of mine is marryin' an Indian."

Her mind leaped to Bonnie Stevens calling her "Indian face" and she leaned forward to remind Monroe of his own Indian blood, but before she could say it, Sarah said it for her. "Aren't you forgetting you're part Indian yourself?"

Monroe's set smile dried up. "No, I ain't. But I don't claim it. And I'm damn sure I wouldn't stoop to marryin' a good for nothin' Indian myself."

"Monroe!" she said. "What's got into you?"

"Don't look at me, Mama. I suppose next thing I hear, you'll be lettin' Edith marry a nigger."

A red-faced Edith appeared in the doorway and Monroe turned his eyes on her. "You hankerin' to marry a buck nigger one of these days, Edith?"

Before she could stand up and put a stop to Monroe, Edith was already calmly saying, "No, thank you."

"What? No nigger?" Monroe seemed surprised. "Well now. Maybe we can find a nice Jew boy for you. I ain't never seen a Jew farmer—they're too smart for that. But with all that money in

Kickapoo, there's bound to be a few big-nosed kikes around cheatin' the yokels out of it."

She was on her feet now. "Monroe, that's enough. You ought to be ashamed to yourself."

"I'm not the one who ought to be ashamed," he said, glaring at her as he abruptly pushed himself up from the table. "I'm not the one marryin' an Indian. You all think about that for a while."

He brushed past Sarah and Edith without looking at them, his footsteps crossed the kitchen and shortly she heard his car going out the driveway.

"Well, Sarah," she said, "I never heard the like,"

"Don't worry about it, Mama. It's what a lot of people would say if they said what they thought. I hear the pupils talking at recess. But I don't mind, and neither does John. I'm sorry he dragged you in to it, Edith."

"Oh, that's all right. I hear talk like this all the time at school."

Later that night, while she was giving Gordon's feet their nightly examination to see if he had washed them clean enough to put them in bed with him, he said to her, "Mama, what's a Jew?"

"Why, a Jew is just a person like you and me."

"Have I ever seen one?"

She told him she doubted it and went on to explain that not many Jews lived in this part of the world. And then she told him about the only one she had ever seen in her life, the little man in the store in Kickapoo a long time ago who gave his Aunt Alice a hat for nothing.

When she got to bed herself she couldn't go to sleep for thinking about Monroe. She had hoped that being out in the world among other kinds of people he might have learned not to be so quick-tempered and unhappy, that maybe he would come home with some of Hamp's easy disposition. But being away seemed to have made him worse. After running Sarah down the way he did, how could he ever look her in the face? Well, she wouldn't allow him to do it again, and she'd tell him so when he came back—if he came back.

Monroe was gone for several days, and Sarah and the children were on their last day of cotton chopping when he came in one morning with a big package of beefsteak. He was his friendly self again, as if his tirade of the other night had never taken place, but after she thanked him for the meat she got right to the point.

"About the other night, Monroe. You're—"

"Mama, you know I only said what had to be said."

"Maybe that's the way you see it, but I won't have you filling these children's heads with hate."

"They're better off learnin' them things young. Then they won't be such chumps when they grow up."

"Learn to despise everybody but your own kind?"

"You think they don't already despise us?"

"No, I don't believe it."

"Oh, Mama, the world ain't a Sunday school class. It's dog eat dog."

Seeing that he had an answer for everything she said, she finally gave up trying to reason with him. She had made up her mind what she was going to say to him if she had to, and now even though she was trembling inside at the thought of it, she said, "Monroe, you can think whatever you want to about Indians, Negroes and Jews. But I won't have any more talk in this house like the other night.

"As for Sarah, you owe her an apology. She's going to marry John Crider right in there in that front room next month. As far as I'm concerned you're welcome to be there—if Sarah still wants you. But whether you are or not, when you're in this house you are to treat John Crider with the same respect as you do me. Is that clear?"

Instead of another mocking answer, Monroe looked out the window for a time before turning back to her and saying almost softly, "I guess I didn't think I was upsettin' you so much, Mama."

She took this to mean he would see to it that it didn't happen again. On the surface this patched up the quarrel and she was glad to turn the talk to something else. Yet she doubted that any of the family would soon forget what Monroe had said.

Whatever the children thought of what he said about Indians, Negroes, and Jews, they hung on to every word he said about what he called "bumming around the West" before he became a lumberjack—hopping freight trains, fighting with railroad dicks, working a day or a few days here and there at any job just to get enough money to put food in his mouth, and even stealing food when he had no job and no money.

When he talked about stealing, her mind jumped back to Hamp and him at the supper table the time Hamp opened the tool chest and found that Monroe had stolen things from stores in Kickapoo to get money to buy whiskey. Now she had the feeling that he might have done worse than steal food, and stirring in her was the old fear of his being put in jail.

Yet he made it all sound so exciting that she seemed to be the only one around the table who saw the hardship and the danger in that kind of life, or the trouble it might get him in with the law. When she worried out loud to Monroe about these things, he just laughed and thought of another story for the wide-eyed boys. Or if he didn't, one of them would ask him to tell again about the time he did such and such to so and so.

Monroe still came and went at odd times, sometimes staying home for two or three days, and sometimes going off for days on end. After she had taken him to see Mama and Papa and his Uncle Tommy in their new home, he never stopped by to see them again, although he passed a couple of hundred yards from their house every time he went to Kickapoo.

Whenever she reminded him that his grandpa was always asking about him, he laughed his hard little laugh and said, "Probably wants to show me how deep to plow. Well, my farmin' days are over." And it was true that he never lifted a hand to help around the farm. He never even took enough interest in it to ask about the crops or the livestock.

Yet he seemed friendlier with the Duncans than before he went away. He paid them a visit almost every time he came home, walking or driving up the hill to be gone for hours on end, and sometimes he stopped by their house before he came home. Harold said he bet Monroe liked Opal Duncan, but Edith said he was too old for her, and besides, she already had a beau at school.

More than once Monroe came home smelling of whiskey, and one night he came home drunk and woke everybody up talking to

Jack for ages at the back door before he finally went to his room, where he slept until noon the next day. When he came out red-eyed and yawning she told him privately that if he wanted to get drunk that was his business, but he was to do it away from home.

"I won't have you drinking around the children," she said. "Or bringing whiskey to the house."

Monroe didn't say aye, yes, or no to this, but didn't come home drunk anymore. Yet instead of finding something to do and getting on with his life, he seemed content to laze around at home or down with Agnes and Ralph or—as she learned during a Sunday visit from Rissy and Brown—with Browny in Kickapoo.

Now that Monroe was a grown man, she didn't think it her place to tell him what to do with his life, but one day when he was talking about the high cost of everything, she did say to him that she hoped he would find something to do before he spent all of his money. He said he hoped so, too, but if he was looking for a job he never found one, and his coming-and-going habits didn't change.

The day before her wedding, Sarah came back from Kickapoo with an ice cream freezer, saying she wanted to have ice cream with her wedding cake.

It was the first time the children had ever seen ice cream made, and from the way Gordon hung around her, watching and asking questions while she was mixing the batter, pouring it in the shiny ice cream can and carrying it out to the well curb to set in the freezer, she could see that he was much more interested in the ice cream than he was in the wedding.

Out at the well curb, she showed the twins and Harold how to chip the ice in small pieces and put them in the freezer around the can until it was covered, and then she explained that they were to crank the freezer until the handle wouldn't turn the can anymore.

After that all they had to do was pack chipped ice on top of the can up to the top of the freezer, wrap the freezer in one of their cotton sacks to keep in the cold, and the ice cream would stay frozen for at least an hour.

She repeated her instructions and hurried back to the house to see that Sarah and Edith had everything else ready there.

Later she called from the kitchen door for the boys to hurry in and get into their church clothes. After that, seeing Gordon still fussing around with the cotton sack, she called for him to come along on the run.

By the time everything was ready, Monroe still hadn't come and neither had Agnes and Ralph, although they had all been invited. But the front room was more than full without them, what with the other children and Mama and Papa and Tommy, Reverend Willis and his wife, and John's parents and a light-skinned brother, Frank, who could have passed for a white man anywhere.

She had found a place for everybody and the wedding was going along quietly when Gordon burst in at the kitchen door shouting, "Mama, come quick. The ice cream's all MELTING!"

She turned to see the surprised boy stop short at the dining room door, his startled look telling her that he had forgotten all about the wedding. She wasn't concerned for the ice cream—that would just be melting ice seeping through the cotton sack—but how could she have not noticed that Gordon was missing Sarah's wedding?

Reverend Willis stopped reading, looked around and joined everybody in a good laugh. Then he called out to the sheepish looking Gordon, "Jist give us five more minutes, young man, and we'll all give you a hand with your ice cream problem."

Chapter 45

The morning after the wedding, she was sitting at the kitchen table talking with Otis and noticing the dark hair falling over his forehead as he was eating breakfast by lamplight.

He was the only one of the children to get her hair. As she had done countless times over the years, she was thinking how strange it was that while his dark hair made him look less like Hamp than any of the other boys, Otis was the one most like Hamp, especially when it came to working.

This morning was a good example. If Otis had wanted to, he could have stayed in bed like the rest of the boys, sleeping until the sun and heat forced them out to another day of loafing around the farm. The crops had all been laid by, and it was a slack time until summer school started.

Last summer Otis hadn't been old enough to do more than drive the scrap rake, but he had grown so much by this summer that he was now able to do anything on the hay crew a man could do, and he was being paid a man's wages. Already he was talking about the horse he was going to buy as soon as he had enough money saved up.

When he finished his fried eggs and thick slices of light bread smothered in crabapple butter, and drank a second glass of sweet milk, she followed him out to the driveway where Dan was grazing on the strip of Bermuda grass alongside the apple orchard fence. She stood by the rose bushes while Otis picked up Dan's trailing reins, climbed in the saddle and pulled his straw hat down tight.

"Make Mister Gray a good hand," she called, and Otis nodded for an answer as he rode off.

Watching him go, she saw again for a moment the happy Sarah and John riding off in the black car with "JUST MARRIED" painted on the back, and the boys whooping and hollering the newlyweds out to the road. She had not been surprised when Monroe did not show up for the wedding, and not wanting to believe that Agnes would also deliberately stay away, she was waiting until she saw her to hear her reason for not coming.

Now hearing one of the mules up in the barn lot nicker after Dan, she let Sarah's wedding fade out of her mind and walked out to the barbed wire gate at the entrance to the driveway and closed it. Then she went up to the barn lot gate and let Dink and Seymour out where they could graze on the Bermuda grass along the driveway without her having to worry about them wandering out into the road.

The sun was not up yet, but a familiar orange haze along the eastern skyline told her it was going to bring another scorcher of a day when it did come up from behind Duncan's house. With this in mind, she went to the back porch and picked up two buckets and headed for the garden to do her picking for dinner before the day got too hot.

Early morning had been her favorite time of day since she was a little girl, and she liked it even better the older she got because it was the only time she still felt fresh and alive—if only for a short while. The sights and sounds always seemed new early in the morning, especially the sounds. It was late in the season, but she could hear so many birds that only a nearby crow repeatedly calling "come quick" to other crows kept her attention.

Passing near the chicken house, she came across a scattering of chickens spreading out from the door; half-asleep hens stretching up on their toes, fluttering their wings and seemingly talking with each other as they strolled off looking for something to pick up for breakfast.

A few roosters milled around trying to interest the hens in something besides breakfast, sidling up to them with short steps, one stiffened wing dragging on the ground as they circled a hesitant hen and chortled who knew what promises to her until she consented by crouching to the ground to await the mounting rooster.

The brief mating finished, the hen stood up, shook her feathers and quietly went back to hunting for breakfast, while the rooster stood his ground and announced his conquest with one or more raucous crowings as he looked around for another likely hen.

The sun was well up and she was on her way out of the garden with her two buckets heavy with vegetables when the daily airplane carrying the mail—so the boys said—roared over the barn lot almost as low as the top of the barn. By now she was so used to it that she barely glanced up. Yet that first morning months ago it had not only set the chickens squawking but sent her ducking over the washboard until she looked up to see what was making such an awful roar.

Back in the house, she set the buckets of vegetables on the back porch, washed her hands and face, and turned to getting breakfast for the other children. She was pleased that for the rest of the day, unlike Otis working in Mr. Gray's hayfield, she would be able to stay out of the sun for it seemed to her that the sun must be getting hotter each summer. At least it was getting harder for her to bear.

A couple of weeks after Sarah's wedding, Monroe came home again. He did not mention the wedding, but he said he had passed through Seminole—which he called a lively burg—and had stopped by to see Sarah and John.

Remembering the mean things Monroe had said to Sarah about marrying an Indian, and the fact that he hadn't come to her wedding, she was surprised Monroe had the gall to go see them, but she was heartened to think the trip might mean he was trying to find work in the oil fields.

"Sarah writes there are plenty of jobs down there," she said.

"Yeah," Monroe said, and out came his hard little laugh. "Oh, I'm sure of it. Well, my hands used to fit an axe handle, but I ain't trying no pick and shovel. I can tell you that."

"Maybe there are other jobs down there"

"Maybe."

This was the last word on the subject until Sarah came home for a weekend visit, leaving John behind to look after their farm. Sarah said Monroe had been as friendly as could be, but he was not down in Seminole looking for work. John had told Sarah that Monroe was peddling moonshine whiskey.

Hearing Sarah say this, she closed her eyes, too ashamed to say anything. Her first thought was that Hamp was no longer alive to lay down the law to him. Then she realized Monroe was too old for that. If caught selling whiskey he would have to answer to the real law.

Pulling herself together, she said, "Oh, Sarah, what's to become of Monroe I don't know. Anymore than I know how he got this way." After she and Sarah commiserated with each other for a time, she tried to put Monroe out of her mind and find out how things were going with Sarah.

From then on, lying awake at night thinking about Monroe, she wished more than ever that Hamp could be here to tell her what to do about him. Yet even without Hamp here she knew what he would say. If he found out Monroe was breaking the law, he would give him a chance to stop it, and if Monroe didn't, Hamp would wash his hands of him.

She could hear Hamp saying it—and her agreeing with him—but she knew herself well enough to know she could never say, "Monroe, you stop selling whiskey or stop coming home. Make up your mind."

Her hope was that eventually she might be able to talk Monroe into changing his ways, and in the meantime she could not bear the thought of turning her back on him and never seeing him or trying to help him again. The next time Monroe came home it was the following morning before she could make a chance to be alone with him and tell him what she had heard about him from Sarah.

"Monroe, why are you getting yourself mixed up in something that's against the law?" she began. "You know it'll only lead to trouble."

"I suppose John blabbed to Sarah."

"It's you I'm worried about. You're breaking the law. Keep this up and you're bound to wind up in jail. And maybe even the penitentiary."

"I'll cross that bridge when I git to it."

"Why don't you try to find an honest job? I'm sure Andy Billings would give you a chance, if you want me to ask him."

"No thanks. Like Papa used to say, I guess I ain't cut out for an insurance salesman."

"So you're going to keep this up till one day I read about them arresting you."

"We'll see."

When she finally stopped her plea, all Monroe did was give her a steady look and say, "Mama, a man's got to eat."

She was a little surprised that Sarah's news about Monroe selling whiskey—if it was news to Agnes—did not seem to bother her a bit. Agnes said that down where they lived lots of farmers made and sold whiskey on the side.

Agnes was more interested in talking about how happy she was that now she had finally talked Ralph into giving up farming and moving to Kickapoo, where his friend got a job for him in the railroad shops starting the first of the year.

As she listened to Agnes saying this, she thought of her own urging that had moved Hamp off the farm to Kickapoo. Not only was Hamp's death still on her conscience for that, but she was coming to think the move to town might also be one reason Monroe was turning out bad.

Whatever the reason, she continued to worry about Monroe, so much so that one evening in the fall, after the crops were all in and the children had started to school, when a stranger came to the front door her heart flew to her mouth. She was sure the well-dressed man was from the sheriff's office, even though he was not wearing a big white cowboy hat like the sheriff and his deputies—including

Browny—wore.

But the man had nothing to do with the law. He named the oil company he was with and said it was getting ready to do some exploration in the area and he was here to talk to her about oil royalties.

She was so surprised she had to take a deep breath to keep a straight face. Sitting with the polite, smiling man on the front porch, she listened to this explanation of what the company was prepared to offer her and told him if he would come back in a week she would try to have an answer for him.

Excited at the thought of having some money again, she wrote Andy that night, asking his advice, and went to sleep for once without thinking about Monroe. Instead of getting a letter from Andy, in a few days he drove up to the well curb. He was looking a little fatter and a little older than when she had last seen him, but he seemed happier than ever to see her.

The first thing he said was, "Well, Mattie! Didn't I tell you, you was goin' to be a millionaire one day?" He went on predicting a rosy future that was going to be hers before long. He ended by advising her not to sell any royalty just yet, saying once an oil company brought in a producing well in the area, companies would be fighting each other to drill on her land. And that, he said, was where what he called "the real money" was made.

As hard up as she was for money, she took Andy's advice, and within a week she was sitting on the front porch, listening again to the polite, smiling oilman explaining again what his company was prepared to pay her for the oil rights to her farm. Knowing all the while that she was not ready to sell any royalty at any price, she felt guilty about taking so much of the man's time. She felt even more guilty when she realized she was saying "no" to enough cash to pay off the mortgage.

Chapter 46

Having taken Andy's advice and decided not to sell any royalties just then, although the boll weevils had ruined so much of the cotton crop that she hated to turn down a chance for some ready cash, she felt a little better about not selling when she learned that the Duncans hadn't sold their royalty either.

In talking to Mama about the offer, she set Mama wondering why the oilman hadn't come to their place. Later Mama told her she had found out from Papa that the oil rights to their farm had already been sold before he bought it, something he hadn't bothered to say anything about to her.

She felt sorry for both of them. Papa had to quit his job as janitor because his legs got too weak for him to climb the stairs to the second floor of the schoolhouse with heavy buckets of coal. This meant that now Mama and Papa and Tommy had to depend on their cows and chickens for a living, and she made up her mind that when—and if—she ever did get any oil money she would see that they got some of it.

Yet because she didn't want her children thinking they might have a lot of money one day, she said nothing to anyone but Sarah about what Andy had called "the coming oil boom around here."

One day during Christmas vacation, Sarah came and took her and the children to Seminole to see where she and John lived. She could see that the farm had been a pretty place once upon a time. The rock house stood in a pecan grove, the barn and out buildings a hundred yards behind it in the same grove, the land sloping down to a creek on either side.

But now, in all directions from the house, rusty oil derricks stuck up out of patches of oily water, and streaks of red and yellow clay ran across the fields to the closest creek. John told her that in some fields half the land was ruined for farming by this slush dumped out of the wells.

At each derrick a great black arm was going up and down without stopping. "Pumping oil," Sarah said. The engines making these arms go up and down sounded like pounding drums that never stopped. In a while all this movement and noise made her want to close her eyes and stop up her ears, but she never let on to Sarah.

After dinner when they drove into Seminole to see Sarah's school, she found the town even more of a mess than the country. In addition to the noisy oil derricks scattered here and there, tents, shacks and new brick buildings stood helter-skelter along the streets.

People and mud were everywhere. The rutted main street was so clogged with muddy teams and muddy cars, and muddy trucks and trailers carrying long rusty pipes, that she was reminded of hogs in a mudhole, except that everything in this mudhole was trying to go somewhere else.

Not only was the town a dirty, noisy place, a smell of rotten eggs hung in the air. The children held their noses at the stink, but Sarah said it was only sulfur from the oil and that she no longer minded it.

The school, located on the far edge of town, was a long, low building of pale yellow bricks. Sarah's classroom was half as big as all of Oakridge School down at Briggs, with blackboards on three walls, windows across the fourth, and rows of desks in between— each desk with a comfortable chair attached. It was beyond anything she had ever seen.

She could see why Sarah would be happy teaching in such a place, and after having already looked at so much she didn't like that day, she was pleased that the cleanest, prettiest building she saw was a schoolhouse.

Yet as they drove out of town, it crossed her mind that of all the hundreds upon hundreds of people she had seen there in the homeland of the Seminole Indians, not one, except John, looked like an Indian. She wasn't surprised when Sarah said most of her pupils were white.

When they were passing back through Kickapoo, Sarah suggested that they stop by and see Agnes. She felt like saying she had seen enough towns for one day, but because she hadn't had a chance to visit Agnes and Ralph since they moved from the country, she agreed.

She didn't mind that their house was tiny—all the easier to keep clean—or that it was not clean, something she had more than half expected knowing Agnes as well as she did. What she hadn't expected was to smell sooty dust in the air and see a covering of it on every surface in the house. An even bigger surprise was to hear a continual noise of nearby railroad engines starting and stopping, whistles tooting and bells ringing.

The engines made such a stir that as soon as the boys had said hello to their sister they ran back out of the house and down the street to see all this excitement for themselves.

Agnes explained that the engines were moving freight cars from track to track—switching cars, she called it—and she seemed proud to say that this switching went on day and night. She not only didn't seem to mind the noise and the sooty dust, she said more than once that she liked living here better than being stuck way off out there in the country, although once she did admit, "Ralph, he don't like it here. But I keep telling him he'll get used to it."

They were welcomed home at dusk by a bark from Jack, who went running along in the headlights as he helped the car up the driveway to the well and the big elm tree.

It had been a long day but once she was in the kitchen and had the lamp lit, she was so happy to be back in a clean, quiet place that she forgot all about being tired. While the boys went off to do the milking and the other chores, she put on an apron, built a fire in the cookstove and set to work with Sarah to make a good supper.

Until that day she had never thought about what an oil boom might do to the farms around here, but in thinking about it before she fell asleep that night, she could see that while it might make a lot of money for some people, an oil boom didn't leave most people with a place worth living in.

Oklahoma was getting noisier and dirtier all the time, and she now realized as never before how lucky she was to be living out here in the country, where she almost never heard a sound outside the house from the time she went to bed until the roosters crowed the next morning, except for a few yapping coyotes now and then.

Spring came in with the usual hot winds from the south, green shoots of poke salad sticking up in the fence rows, white and pink blossoms filling the orchards and making the air smell sweet, the sight and sound of birds everywhere, but no signs of an oil boom.

Yet an oil boom was the furthest thing from her mind one Saturday morning as she paused while getting breakfast to glance out the north kitchen window. A movement on the road had caught her eye, and in a moment she saw it was Dan coming along past the apple orchard as fast as he could run.

It was so unlike Otis to be riding Dan this hard that she hurried out in the yard to see what the matter was. Otis had gone up to the blacksmith shop to pick up some cultivator sweeps Mr. Stout had sharpened, and maybe he was just anxious to get back and get started to work. Still, that was no reason for him to be using Dan that way, and she'd have to tell him so.

Once outside the house, she could hear the beating of Dan's hoofs on the road, and she noticed that Dink and Seymour grazing on the Bermuda grass had lifted their heads in Dan's direction and pricked up their ears. As she rounded the rosebushes, Dan came streaking into the driveway and without seeming to see it at all ran right through the barbed wire gate, turned a somersault, and threw Otis to the ground way out in front of him.

Calling Otis's name, she rushed towards the still body as Dan struggled up out of the tangle of barbed wire and stood with the saddle hanging under his belly, a bleeding slash across his chest and his right front leg dangling.

Otis lay face down without moving, and she dropped on her knees beside him, too scared to touch him. Yet to get his face out of the dirt, she reached out and slowly eased him over on his back. His face was a mass of blood, his eyes closed. He groaned and she was scared all over again, but relieved, too.

Stripping off her apron, she tried with shaking hands to gently wipe the blood from his mouth with a corner of it, but the blood kept oozing out from where his teeth had cut through his lower lip.

Harold came rushing up and she sent him running for a wash pan of water. Before he got back with it, Otis opened his eyes and tried to say something, but he didn't seem to be able to open his mouth. Suddenly he sat up and she grabbed his shoulder and told him to sit still.

And then Arthur was there, asking over and over again, "What happened, Mama?" while Edith and Gordon, without paying any attention to Otis, started crying and carrying on about Dan's broken leg.

"Arthur!" she said. "You've got to run down to Grandpa's fast as you can. Tell your Uncle Tommy to come in a hurry. We have to take your brother to a doctor. Run now!"

Wetting a fresh corner of her apron in Harold's wash pan of water, she started to clean the bleeding mouth. She felt the teeth give way under her fingers and Otis jerked his head back.

"Sorry," she said and winced at the thought of Otis losing that row of teeth. Then she scolded herself for not being thankful he was alive. Not five minutes had passed since she was scared he was dead.

Holding on to his shoulder with one hand and taking care not to touch his mouth, she bathed his face and neck with the cool water. At the same time she tried to take Edith's and Gordon's mind off Dan's broken leg by sending them out in the road to watch for Uncle Tommy coming in his car to take their brother to the doctor.

Mr. Duncan and Ray came up and leaned close to Otis for a look and a word or two of sympathy before they walked over to Dan, where Mr. Duncan held the bridle while Ray un-cinched the saddle and dragged it out of the way. She didn't hear what Mr. Duncan said, but Ray went running off across the road and in a few minutes came back carrying the biggest rifle she had ever seen.

Knowing that the crippled Dan had to be shot and dragged over in the woods for the dogs and wolves to fight over, she called to Edith and told her to take Gordon in the house and keep him there. Then she told Harold to take the mules up to the barn, harness them and bring them back hitched to a doubletree and dragging the log chain.

She waited until Harold had the mules well out of the way, and then without looking at Dan again she nodded to Mr. Duncan, who was standing a few feet in front of the horse, the big rifle tucked under his arm.

She shut her eyes and braced herself for the rifle shot, but the burst of noise was so loud she flinched anyway, and felt Otis flinch, too. Instantly every bird sound stopped, and all she could hear for the longest time after Dan fell was the sound of his hoofs scraping and scraping against the hard ground of the driveway.

When Papa and Tommy and Arthur came in the car, she got in the back seat and had them help Otis in next to her, and with Arthur holding him on the other side, they roared off to town to find Dr. Fortson, leaving Papa behind to show Harold how to get Dan dragged away.

On the way to Kickapoo, she remembered that she still didn't know why Otis had been running Dan so fast, but he was in no condition to be asked about that now. Squeezing his arm, she looked at his bloody face and was surprised when he nodded at her as if everything was all right.

From his own first look, Dr. Fortson didn't seem as concerned about Otis's condition, laughing while he told him that getting thrown was the hard way to get off a horse. After he had cleaned up the mouth and eased the caved-in teeth back in place with his big fingers, saying "uh-huh" to himself a dozen times, he examined Otis all over.

"Well, Miz Roberts," he said, turning to her. "I guess you got a pretty tough young man here. No broken bones I can find. But he's going to have to do his eating through a straw for a while. Till the teeth get solid again. Then he'll be fit as a fiddle. Though if I was you, Otis, I think I'd stay off horses for a spell."

Otis could only nod his bandaged face, and it wasn't until days later that the family got a first-hand account of the accident from him, and then, before telling what happened he said, "Mama, it was all my fault."

He had tied the sweeps on behind the saddle and they hung down below the edge of the skirt on either side. He said he had done this on other trips to the blacksmith shop without any trouble, and even this time Dan was jogging quietly along home until Watkins' dog jumped out of the bushes across the road from their house and landed with a big woof right in front of him.

Dan dodged sideways so suddenly he almost threw Otis out of the saddle—and here Otis said if he had known what was about to happen he would have tried to get off right then and there. Instead, he grabbed for the saddle horn and started pulling himself back up in the seat while the sweeps, their points and wing tips sharper than spurs, swung away from Dan's sides when he dodged and then came flying back right into his flanks.

Instantly Dan took off, running faster and faster as the sweeps gouged him in the flanks every step he took, and with the dog barking at his heels. Having lost the reins when he was nearly thrown off, Otis could only hold on to the saddle horn and wait for Dan to stop at the gate, never thinking he wouldn't stop.

While no one came right out and agreed with Otis that the accident was his fault, she did notice that Edith and Gordon always showed more sympathy for Dan than they did for their brother. For days they talked about poor Dan but never did she hear a word about poor Otis, and she didn't want to make matters worse by saying, "What about a little sympathy for your brother?"

Yet Otis didn't seem to mind. He stayed out of school until he could eat and talk easily again, and before that time came he insisted on starting the planting, and she let him do it even though it made her uneasy to see him working around animals and machinery before he was well.

One night at supper she had a moment of uneasiness of another kind about Otis and his accident when she heard Harold say that C.T. Watkins told him someone had shot and killed their dog. She looked over at Otis, afraid he might have done it, although she hadn't seen him taking out either the shotgun or the twenty-two.

Before she could ask, Otis said, "Mama, I had nothing to do with it. But I can guess who did."

"So can I," said Arthur.

Suspecting that they meant Mr. Duncan or Ray, she said, "Well, we'll just leave the matter there."

She didn't approve of killing a dog for something like this, but she knew if one of the Duncans did it he did it out of regard for Otis, and what could she say about it now that the dog was dead? It would only make matters worse if she went to Mr. Watkins and told him her boys had nothing to do with it.

When the crops were ready by that summer Otis went back to working in the hay, and before the summer was over he bought a cow and traded her—with a little cash to boot he told her—for the horse he had been dickering for with a farmer for almost two years; a buckskin with a long black mane, and a cream-colored tail that swept the ground. Even Monroe joked that Buck was a fine looking nag, and Otis was too proud of his horse to seem to mind this kidding from his big brother.

Monroe had been staying away from home more and more lately, and most of the time he came in late at night, slept till noon, got up to eat dinner with them and went off again. When he did come home during the day he often brought something for the family to eat, a mess of beefsteak, pork chops, beef liver or the like.

One Saturday night when he drove in he came directly out to

the sleeping porch and told her in an excited whisper that if anyone came to the house asking about him, she was to say he had been home all night.

Since the first rooster had already crowed for daybreak, she thought it unlikely that anyone would be coming around asking for anybody at this hour, so she saw no point in making a fuss and waking the children by telling Monroe she wasn't going to do it.

The next day after Sunday dinner, when Monroe was getting ready to leave, she walked out to the car with him to bring up the subject privately.

"Monroe, you have to know," she began and paused, not sure how he was going to take what she had to say. "I'll help you anyway I can when you're doing the right thing. But you have to know if the law comes here asking questions, I'm going to tell them the truth. I won't lie for you."

Already in the car, Monroe looked around as if not sure he had heard right. His face hardened and she could see that he was about to say something furious. She knew that look and was sorry she had brought it on, but she kept looking at him and waited for whatever he was going to say.

"But I reckin you'd lie for Sarah."

The mocking tone didn't surprise her, but she was surprised by his dragging in Sarah. It made her hesitate about answering, not because there was any truth in what he said, but it was a reminder to her that for as far back as she could remember he had always been jealous of Sarah, maybe ever since he was born. Yet knowing that Monroe was going to be even unhappier by what she was about to say, she softened it as much as possible by answering, "I don't think I would. But I doubt if Sarah would ever ask me to."

Monroe laughed his hard little laugh and said, "Sure, Mama." Without another word he started the car and drove away.

She watched him out of sight and turned and walked slowly along between the dead hollyhocks to the kitchen to help Edith clean up after dinner, asking herself along the way the same question she was asking more and more often these days. What was going to become of Monroe?

Chapter 47

That night she went to sleep saddened to think Monroe might be so mad at her for refusing to tell a lie for him that he would never come home again. Yet as she was starting to make supper the next evening, the kitchen door burst open and instead of the first of the children home from school—as she thought from the way the door opened—it was Monroe, needing a shave and looking upset.

Usually she either saw or heard his car as it came up the driveway, but not this time. As soon as she saw him she knew something was wrong, and the only reason that came to mind was that he was ashamed of himself for asking her yesterday to lie for him and had come back to tell her so, something she had actually dreamed about last night.

The first thing Monroe did was look behind the kitchen door where Hamp's old shotgun and twenty-two rifle were always leaning in the corner. He didn't say anything about the guns, just looked and turned to her, and even then instead of saying hello or starting to apologize for yesterday, he said, "Anybody come around here last night?"

"Yes," she said, and started telling him about Papa forgetting to give her Saturday's butter and egg money at church and coming by with it and Mama and staying to visit, but before she could get it all told she saw him frown and start shaking his head.

"No. No. Mama. I mean strangers."

She shook her own head and he looked relieved, but his voice was still anxious when he said, "Well, there may be some trouble around here tonight."

Without giving her time to ask what he meant, he turned back to the kitchen door, glanced at the guns again, and was out on the step. Yet as he was about to shut the door, he stuck his head back in and said, "I'll be back in a while."

She had no idea what was bothering him, but he was already hurrying off towards the driveway. Through the window she saw him stop suddenly and crouch behind the rose bushes while a car went by. As she watched him hurry on down the driveway and out of sight, she guessed he had left his car up at the Duncans, although for what reason she couldn't imagine.

She went back to making supper, but her thoughts stayed on Monroe's strange behavior, especially his eyeing the guns as if seeing them for the first time. If he was in trouble with the law for selling whiskey, he must know he couldn't settle it with a gun.

After puzzling about this for a time, she walked over and picked up the guns, one in each hand, and for no other reason than the feeling she had from the way he had looked at them, she carried the guns to his room and hid them under his bed, the last place she thought he would look if he wanted to take one.

They were just finishing supper when Monroe appeared in the dining room door, once more without her having heard any sound of his car driving in. She asked Edith to get him a plate, even though all that was left to eat were some mashed potatoes and a couple of pieces of cornbread.

But Monroe shook his head and without greeting anyone said, "Mama, would you come out here for a minute?"

When she came into the kitchen he was already at the kitchen door and motioning to her. She didn't know what to make of this, but she stepped out in the cold night and he followed her and shut the door.

"I don't want to get them all scared up in there," he said, standing close to her in the moonlight and speaking in a low anxious voice. "So don't say more'n you have to. Jist keep everybody inside and let me and the Duncans handle it."

"But, Monroe," she said, taking hold of his arm, "if the law is after you, give yourself up."

"I'm not talking about the law," he said, raising his voice, and then in a friendlier tone he said, "Where'd the boys move the guns to?"

"Whatever trouble you're in, guns will just make it worse." Hearing him curse under his breath she said, "I hid them."

"Oh, for Christ's sake," he burst out, pulling away and heading for the driveway.

She expected him to turn towards the Duncans as he had earlier. Instead, he cut across the driveway, climbed over the apple orchard fence and faded away in the moonlight towards the Watkins.

She stood looking after him even when she could no longer see him, for she was trying to make sense of why he was going towards the Watkins when he had just talked about the Duncans and him handling the trouble. Not sure what to say to the children, she went back inside and told them there would be no studying tonight, and cut short their happy comments by telling them to get ready for bed right away.

Never had she said anything to any of them about Monroe selling whiskey, but when she got the twins aside in the kitchen to tell them as much as she knew of the trouble he had hinted at, she found they had known all along what he was doing. They knew even more about what might be going to happen tonight than she did.

"Mama, it's not the law that's after him," Otis said. "If anybody comes messin' around here tonight it'll be the Ku Klucks." At the mention of the Ku Klucks she was more scared for Monroe than before, but relieved that he hadn't taken a gun with him.

"Yeah," Arthur said. "We heard today they closed down a dance out near Briggs Saturday night. Beat up one of the guys selling whiskey. But the other guy got away."

She could guess now who the other guy was, but she kept it to herself and hurried everyone off to bed. She left the lamp lit on the dining room table among the dirty dishes, and went out the back door to the shadow of the big elm, Jack following her from his place beside the doorstep.

She looked up towards the Duncans, dark under the trees, and then around to the Watkins' house with its speck of light beyond the apple orchard. Everything looked as quiet and peaceful as usual, so much so that she couldn't believe something horrible might be going to happen to Monroe right here in front of her eyes, and that she couldn't do anything about it. She felt like running up to the Duncans to find out what was going on.

Before she could make up her mind to do it, she heard a car start down at the Watkins, and then another and another and another. Soon she was sure she could hear them coming up the road, but she saw no headlights, no lights of any kind.

Rushing back through the house to get a closer look from the front porch, she found all the children but Gordon whispering together out there in the near dark. Now she could see a whole line of cars inching up the moonlit road like a lot of dark, growling shadows. The first car crawled past the two blackjack trees at the entrance to the driveway, and stopped in the moonlight directly in front of the house. All the other cars stopped and their engines went silent. Once more everything but her beating heart seemed quiet and peaceful in the moonlight.

From the dark of the Duncans' lane a shotgun blast shattered the quiet, and like a gust of hailstones on a sheet-iron roof. A splatter of shot hit the front car and someone yelled.

She started grabbing the children and pushing them ahead of her through the front door as another shotgun blast came from the Duncans' pasture, and then another blast from way down in the pasture near the Watkins.

Already the front car had come to life, and she saw its headlights flash on as the car lurched back and forth across the road and swung around towards the Watkins, suddenly lighting up a line of cars with white hooded figures crouching next to them.

Terrified for Monroe, she looked towards the Watkins and caught her breath. A red glow lighted up the sky down there. She couldn't believe he had set fire to their house, but he must have.

No more shots burst out, just the confusion of engines starting, gears clashing and headlights cutting through the night in all directions as cars backed and turned in the road and roared off towards the Watkins.

From the backyard one of the boys yelled that Watkins' barn was on fire, and now she could see flames swirling up in the red glow. Hearing faint shouts coming from down there, she imagined the men trying to save the scared animals, and for a moment—in spite of all the turmoil in her mind—she thought how different their actions were now from what they had planned to do tonight.

Soon the glow in the sky had the roosters crowing in the chicken house, and they kept it up after the fire died down and she had sent everybody to bed, including Gordon. He had come wandering half-asleep through the house wanting to know what all the racket was about and why they weren't all in bed the way they were supposed to be.

Sleep was out of the question for her, but she lay in bed listening to the roosters and thinking of Monroe. Now that the Ku Klucks had failed to get their hands on him tonight, she was more scared for him than ever, for after this setback they would not stop until they did get him.

The moon was down and she could barely make out his face as she let him pull her out of earshot of the boys sleeping on the porch and felt the frosty grass chill her bare feet.

"I never set his barn on fire," was the first thing Monroe said, and when she didn't say anything, he went on. "I went down there to throw a match in his haystack... to scare the bastards away from up here in case buckshot didn't do it. But the hay floor was full of Ku Klucks talkin' and laughin' about what they was gonna do to me. Soon as they went to their cars, I cut across to the haystack and saw smoke comin' out of the barn."

Maybe he was telling the truth and maybe he wasn't. He had told her so many lies she didn't know what to believe, and now she didn't say anything.

"I swear it, Mama."

He sounded as if she had doubted his word out loud. When she still didn't say anything, he said, "Well, I'm goin'."

"Promise me you'll try to change, Monroe."

"Goodbye, Mama," was all he said.

She held back her tears and watched him hurry around the corner of the sleeping porch to the front yard, heard the car start and saw it go down the road south without any headlights. Back in bed, even while crying because Monroe was gone, she couldn't help thinking of all the worry he had been ever since he came home from Oregon.

At breakfast she told the children their brother had come by to say good-bye and that he was going back out West. She only suspected that was where he was going, but she told them not to mention it or say anything about what they had seen and heard last night.

"Remember," she said, looking from face to face. "None of you had anything to do with what went on around here last night. So nobody at this table has anything to be ashamed of this morning. Let the others say what they want to about the Ku Klucks, the Duncans firing their shotguns, the barn burning, or whatever. Just keep your thoughts to yourself and everything will be all right."

About mid-morning she heard someone talking in the backyard and found Mr. Duncan petting Jack with one hand and carrying his shotgun under his other arm. As he greeted her, his smile was the same as always, and the twinkle in his blue eyes, too. He said he hoped he didn't scare her too much with the shooting, and went on to say that while Ralph and Ray were using buckshot, he had used birdshot on the front car knowing it wouldn't hurt anyone too bad at that distance.

This was the first she knew about Ralph firing one of the guns, but she let that news pass and thanked him for helping Monroe. She wanted to say she hoped this would be a lesson to Monroe about selling whiskey, but knowing that the Duncans' view of whiskey was different from hers, she turned the subject to Watkins' barn and said she was sorry he had lost a mule.

"He's got nobody to blame but hisself," Mr. Duncan said, shaking his head. "Maybe it'll learn him to mind his own business. I reckon Monroe got off all right did he?"

She nodded, suddenly too choked up to speak. Even though this time Monroe was going away a grown man with money and a car, she wouldn't rest easy until she was sure he was a long way away from this part of the country.

After a bite of dinner scrounged from what was left over from breakfast, she went out for a look around the place. It was a perfect fall day, clear and cool, and the stock were scattered around the barn lot drowsing in the sun.

She stopped south of the horse barn to look again at where the new well and windmill were going. Sarah had written that a neighbor had given John a windmill—if he would take it down—and since they already had a windmill, it was John's idea to bring this one up here to the farm, dig a well over there near that young post oak, and make it easier to water the stock than having to keep the water trough filled from the pump. Sarah said John had already signed up a well digger who owed him a favor.

She walked on to the top of the hill and was looking across the fields to the back of the farm when she saw a man come out of the little patch of woods back there just below where Mr. Koontz had built his first house, which had been blown away by a cyclone.

The man was too far away for her to tell who it was, but since he was coming towards her, she held on to a fence post and waited. He came down the slope, disappeared beneath the rise of the second field, and when he came in sight again he was close enough that his fast walk reminded her of Otis. Yet she knew this wasn't possible for it was still hours before school let out.

But it was Otis. When he got close to the gate down the fence line from her, she called to him and went along the fence to meet him. She was curious why he was out of school this time of day and why he hadn't walked home the usual way on the road, but when they met at the gate, she didn't say anything about either of the two whys.

"I quit school, Mama."

"Oh."

"I got in a fight... two fights. Both the Ferris boys got in it. And the Principal, he said because I started it he was going to keep me after school and give me a whipping. So I ran off and I'm not going back."

As much as she was dying to ask him why he couldn't have stayed out of trouble on a day when she already had enough trouble, she waited for him to go on.

"I'm going to Seminole and get me a job in the oil fields," he said as they walked along to the house, and without her asking a question he told her about knocking M.L. Ferris down at noon recess for calling Monroe a bootlegger, and when M.L.'s cousin took his side, he beat him up, too.

Mr. Henry took all three of them to his office where he reminded them what the punishment was for fighting. Otis admitted he hit M. L. first, but wouldn't tell the Principal why, and that was when he was singled out for the whipping.

"Why didn't you tell Mr. Henry why you hit the Ferris boy?" she asked.

Otis shrugged and looked away.

Try as she might, she couldn't change his mind about quitting school, and rather than have him go off empty-handed she found Hamp's old grip sack—stiff as a board now—and filled it bulging full with Otis' clothes. She had a few dollars of butter and egg money in her purse and she tried to get him to take some for the bus from Kickapoo to Seminole, but he said he still had money left over from his hay baling wages.

She waited in the driveway while Otis ran up to the barn lot to say goodbye to Buck, and when he came back they walked out past the spot where she had rushed only a few months before to his body lying on the ground, sure that he was dead.

Otis waved once from down the road and she waved and turned back to the house drying her eyes on her apron. Monroe had run away at eighteen, and now Otis was gone at fifteen.

At first the children would hardly believe that Otis had quit school and gone to Seminole, especially since he was a hero at school for having beaten up two bullies in one day. Yet before supper was over they were laughing and joking and outdoing each other telling what they had heard about the Ku Klucks last night. No one said anything about Monroe's close call with the Ku Klucks.

She let them talk and laugh without joining in, sad that Otis was gone, and scared now for the future of the farm. From experience she knew that Arthur was a lot like Monroe. He could do as much work as anyone when he wanted to, but he didn't always want to. Yet she had no choice but to depend on him. Knowing it would only make things worse if she let on that she was worried about the farming, she tried to be her usual self as she cleared the table and got the children started on their schoolwork.

During the next few days the sight of all those white-hooded Ku Klucks crouching by their cars in the sudden glare of the headlights stayed fresh in her mind, but the children soon stopped coming home from school with stories about that night.

When Saturday morning came, she had Arthur in the field breaking land at an early hour, while she went with Harold and Gordon to the woods where Harold used the axe and she and Gordon did the sawing. It came as a surprise to the boys that she knew how to handle her end of a crosscut saw, even though she hadn't had to do it since she was a girl.

By the time the day was over, she realized that sawing wood was not as easy as it used to be, but there was no point in telling the children that.

Chapter 48

On her way from church the first Sunday after the Ku Klucks had been scared away, she agreed with Papa that it was a shame Watkin's barn burned up and a mule with it, and was relieved when Papa gave no hint that he thought the fire anything but an accident. Even so, she put off telling him that Monroe had gone out West again, thinking this was news that could wait awhile.

As time passed, Arthur took to the extra farm work better than she expected, although getting him out of bed in the morning was a daily nuisance that sometimes forced her to threaten him with a dipper of cold water on his head. Once he was on his feet, Arthur went silently about doing whatever he had to do, and on Saturdays he put in a full day in the field plowing, except when Harold spelled him because Harold wanted to prove to the family he was big enough to plow with a twelve-inch moldboard plow.

Sarah's first letter after Otis arrived on her doorstep said he was living with them and looking for a job, and the next one said he was working for a pipeline company and making more than twice as much money as he had made baling hay. On the Saturday morning following Sarah's second letter, a light drizzle that would not have stopped Otis brought Arthur in from plowing, and when Papa and Tommy came by at noon, Arthur said he believed he would go to town with them.

That evening when Papa came back with her groceries and change, he told her that Arthur had left Jenkins' store with Tommy to go to the picture show, but Tommy said when they got there Arthur borrowed a dollar from him and went off by himself, saying he was going to Seminole.

She never let on to Papa how upset she was that Arthur would leave home when he could see how much she was depending on him to help keep the farm going. And to sneak off without saying goodbye was even worse. But what bothered her most of all was that he apparently thought his schooling was not doing him any good, or likely to. It scared her for what it might make the others start thinking.

At supper after the evening Arthur ran off to Seminole, as she sat across the kitchen table from Harold, with Gordon on her right and Edith on her left, she felt all their eyes on her. She could sense from the way she was having to do all the talking that they did not know what to make of first Otis and now Arthur suddenly leaving home.

She tried to lift their spirits by pointing out that with Otis already having a good job, Arthur was bound to get one soon. "For the rest of us," she said, looking around at each sober face, "we'll just have to all pitch in and do the best we can. Harold, I expect Uncle Tommy will help us out when we get in a pinch when spring comes. In the meantime you'll have to take Arthur's place with the plowing. Think you can?"

"Sure," Harold said. "I already been spellin' Arthur whenever he felt like a nap."

In the days that followed, in spite of trying to keep so busy she had little time to think, she could not get out of her mind how fast the family was breaking up. It was not as if she had not seen children in other families grow up and leave home, or that she had not done it herself. She had always known it would happen one day, but it was not until the shock of Arthur going off to town and not coming back that her eyes were opened wide to what probably lay ahead for her and the farm.

After struggling with the children to get the cotton all picked, and getting Tommy to haul it to the gin, she realized that to raise another such crop was out of the question now. Yet she could not help pay the taxes and the mortgage without a cash crop. And when Harold's time came to leave home, she would be hard put to raise a crop of any kind with just her and Gordon and Edith. Yet as she stared at the dark ceiling of the sleeping porch night after night, trying to think of a way out of her predicament, she knew there was nothing else she could do but keep on doing.

The coming of Christmas only made her feel sadder, in spite of the happy Christmas Eve celebration at church, and all the family except Monroe at home for Christmas dinner. Sarah brought Otis, and Arthur, whose sheepish look showed he was ashamed of the way he had left home.

But she offered him her hand and said, "Welcome home, Arthur."

"Hello, Mama," was all Arthur seemed to be able to say, and since he made no apology for sneaking off, she did not bring up the subject.

Instead, she said, "You're looking well," and went on to praise his new coat. Brightening a little, Arthur said, "I jist bought it pay day, Mama. I always wanted a sheepskin coat and I finally got me one."

Agnes and Ralph walked down from the Duncans' for Christmas dinner, the two of them friendly as usual with the family and her, but snapping at each other, making her worry about their marriage, especially since they had not had any children after all these years. Today so much was going on in the house, and she was so busy making dinner, she had no time or privacy for any real talk with Agnes. Yet it was easy to see that the prospect of moving to town had not erased the unhappy expression habitually on Agnes' face now.

As winter passed, she got used to taking care of a small family again, fewer mouths to feed, fewer clothes to wash and iron and mend, and fewer noisy spats to settle, all of which made her life easier. When the three came home from school they went quietly about their chores, ate supper, and without any fuss worked at their studies until she sent them off to bed at eight o'clock.

Every morning she was up at daylight or before, getting breakfast while the boys were out doing the chores, which were easier to do now that they kept fewer cows and hogs. By eight o'clock the children were on their way to school, leaving her with the whole day to herself in the silent house.

In the old days she had liked this winter season of the year best because it was the only time when she had a few hours in the day to call her own. Now being alone mainly meant she had more time to think about the missing children and what it was like in the old days before any of them had left home. Sometimes she even let her mind take her back to the misery of the time she lived believing she had drowned Tommy. To her surprise and disappointment at feeling no change in her life when she joined the church, she had ceased to worry about her soul—if she had one.

As she had hoped he would, Tommy came to help Harold with the spring plowing, and that was not all. Papa came too, seemingly pleased to use Dink and Seymour to do the planting for her. Later he helped Harold with the cultivating, saying he liked being a farmer again.

Once the small cotton crop was ready, she spent her days chopping it to a stand, determined to keep down the crabgrass and cockleburs if it killed her. On Saturdays the children chopped with her, and she was tempted to take them to the field on Sundays, but knowing this would bring on a fight with Papa, she did not dare try it.

One day as she stood at the end of a row of cotton, noticing how much chopping was still to be done when the children got out of school next week, her thoughts were interrupted by someone calling her name. She looked around and saw Andy Billings coming a few yards away.

His spick-and-span summery town clothes looked so completely out of place here in the heat and dirt of the cotton patch that it was almost comical. But she was too conscious of her own worn-out dress and shoes to smile. Her main thought was that she hoped Andy would not begin by telling her again she was going to be a millionaire one day, and he didn't.

After cussing the heat a little, he started talking about the special Fourth of July celebration he was helping put together in Kickapoo this year, saying it was going to be the greatest one the town had ever seen, a regular celebration during the day, and a pageant at night that traced the history of Oklahoma from the beginning right up to the present.

She hung her hoe on the fence and they walked to the house, with Andy still talking about the pageant. After drinks of fresh water from the well, she asked about Grace and they started swapping family news. When she mentioned that Monroe had gone back out West, Andy said he used to run into Monroe in town, and had offered him a job more than once, adding that Monroe always thanked him but turned his offers down.

"Stubborner than his papa used to be," Andy said, laughing. "But enough like him to make a great salesman... if he wanted to do it. Well, Mattie, I came out to see if you and the family would like to make a day of it with me and Grace at the celebration when it gits here."

Thinking of the children, she said, "Thanks, Andy, we'd be happy to."

Later, as Andy was leaving, he remarked that in case she had not already heard it, the oil boom that had taken over the south end of the county was going to move right up around Kickapoo soon.

She was used to his saying things like this, but desperate now as she was for money, she listened with a new interest. Andy finished by telling her again to hold on to the farm, made his usual prediction that she was going to be a millionaire one day, and drove off in his shiny black car.

She watched him go and couldn't help thinking about what she would do if they struck oil on the farm and she did have a lot of money. The only thing she was sure of was that she would like to go back to Bear Valley for a long, long visit with Aunt Sis, who had retired from teaching. But first she would pay off all the mortgage and give some money to Mama and Papa.

In a few weeks, news of drilling for oil in the neighborhood was in the newspaper, and farmers were talking about it at church. Yet as for Harold and Edith and Gordon, all they talked about these days, as they worked and sweated with her to finish the cotton chopping, was what they were going to see and do at the big Fourth of July celebration, even though it was still weeks away.

When it arrived, the daytime part of the celebration turned out to be pretty much like the one she had seen with Hamp and the children when they lived in town: marching bands, marching soldiers and marching civilians. It was more marching than she wanted to stand on the hot pavement and watch, with her old straw hat not keeping the hot sun out of her eyes. Then it was on to the park for more band music, speeches and much eating of barbecued beef.

At dusk she and the children, after Andy had taken them back to the farm to hurry through the chores and back to his house for supper, were sitting with Grace and him and hundreds upon hundreds of other people on bales of hay lined up in rows across a hillside north of Kickapoo, out where the prairie began.

At the bottom of the hill ran a fence and a row of the tallest posts she had ever seen. Beyond the fence was open, flat prairie, recently mowed. She guessed the hay from that prairie might be the fragrant, new bales they were sitting on now.

Having watched the practices for the pageant, Grace was saying, "Mattie, what's going to happen out there on that hayfield is just like a picture show."

"Well, Grace," she said with a laugh, "that doesn't tell me much. I've never seen a picture show." But the children had, and at sundown when lights flashed on from the tops of the tall posts and turned the prairie back into bright daylight, she felt the way they looked, excited for something magic about to happen out there.

The band, on a platform beyond the fence, had been playing all kinds of songs from "Old Black Joe" to "Red River Valley." Now it struck up "The Star Spangled Banner" and the noise quieted down as everybody stood up and faced the flag high on a pole at the bandstand.

Once the crowd was seated again, a single note from some kind of horn sounded for several seconds, and off to the right from out of the shadows a nearly naked Indian man came walking across the prairie into the light. A few yards behind the Indian, a swarthy man followed on a dark horse, the rider wearing a shiny helmet turned up at the ends like a paper hat, and a vest of shiny armor. A sword hung at the rider's side, and in his right hand he carried a shiny-pointed lance sticking straight up.

"Coronado," Grace said.

"Yes," she said, remembering Mrs. Whitaker saying in class that this Indian had later been killed by the Spaniards for leading them on a wild goose chase all over the plains, pretending to lead them to golden cities that never existed, while all the Indian wanted was to get out of slavery and home to his tribe.

Coronado kept his horse at a slow prance across the prairie, followed a few yards back by more helmeted riders on prancing horses. Once the Spanish horsemen disappeared, another long sound from the horn brought a little band of trappers out onto the lighted prairie, half a dozen riders in buckskins and slouch hats, rifles at the ready as they moved quietly along with their pack horses bunched in the middle.

Suddenly, screeching war whoops hushed the crowd, reminding her that probably there were people in the audience old enough to have heard real war whoops—and been terrified by them. From every direction, near naked Indians on paint horses raced towards the trappers, circling round and round the huddle of men and horses, shooting at the trappers, now off their horses and shooting back at the Indians.

From out of the darkness, bursts from a bugle shrilled above the clamor of war whoops and gunshots. A troop of cavalry thundered into the light, troopers firing as they came, and chased the Indians away. As the crowd cheered, she noticed that Harold and Gordon were cheering for the Indians.

Before the dust had time to settle, it was stirred up again by wagons, buggies and men on horseback, all lining up to start a run for homesteads. A U.S. Cavalry officer trotted his sleek bay horse along the line and back, wheeled the horse, drew his revolver, pointed it at the stars and, after a long pause, pulled the trigger. The sound of the shot was almost drowned out by the sudden roar from the surging line of yelling homesteaders and the watching crowd.

After the homesteaders disappeared, a lone cowboy loped his cow pony out under the lights and met an Indian girl riding a paint pony, her long braid of black hair bouncing on the back of her buckskin dress as she rode along. The two turned and rode to the bandstand and dismounted. There on the bandstand they were welcomed by Uncle Sam wearing a tall, flag-striped hat.

And then in a mock wedding ceremony, Uncle Sam married Miss Indian Territory to Mr. Oklahoma Territory. As the newlyweds rode off in a surrey carrying a banner reading STATE of OKLAHOMA, she shed a tear, reminded of Hamp and her riding up to their honeymoon log cabin.

Next, a massed team of thirty mules—according to Harold's count—came slowly across the prairie pulling an oil derrick lying flat on the running gears of a huge wagon and trailer. A man on a piebald horse held lines to the lead span of mules and urged the mass of straining animals along by cracking his blacksnake over their backs like pistol shots.

After all this, the noise and spectacle of fireworks kept everybody clapping and oohing and aahing to such a late hour that by the time Andy had driven them home, she was as tired as if she had done a day's work in the field.

As much as she enjoyed the pageant, she thought it had left out her most important picture of Oklahoma history—a man, woman, and children working and sweating in a sun-drenched cotton field.

The next Sunday on the way to church, Tommy stopped the car

along the south side of Ricketts' farm to show her where the first oil well was going to be drilled in this part of the county. Looking at the rusty derrick lying on the bright yellow oat stubble, she remembered the ruined fields around John and Sarah's house and thought of the sight, sound and rotten-egg smell of the oil boomtown of Seminole.

Chapter 49

As a dry summer slipped into a dry fall, two more oil derricks appeared within two miles of the one on Ricketts' farm, and soon all the talk going around the churchyard after church was about how rich the farmers were going to be if and when those drilling rigs struck oil. She heard this talk, but she tried to put it out of her mind, torn between worrying that it would never happen and worrying that it would ruin the fields for farming if it did.

Besides, it was cotton picking time again, and she was so worn-out picking every day except Sunday she had no time or energy left to think much about anything else. As fast as she and the children picked a bale of cotton, Tommy hauled it to the gin for them, and when the scanty crop was all picked and sold, as usual she asked him to take her to town to pay the taxes and the mortgage.

This year after she had settled up at the tax office and taken from her bank account the amount needed to complete the mortgage payment, she found she had less than twenty dollars left in the bank. What a relief it would be now if Brown would pay back even a little of the money he had borrowed from Hamp. But she had given up hope for any help from him. Hamp had been right long ago when he advised her not to try to hold her breath until Brown paid for the peanut thresher. The same now for the bank loan.

Leaving the nineteen dollars and fifteen cents in the bank, she made her way slowly across Main Street and down to Jenkins for a sack of flour and a few other things she had to have. From then on, every Sunday when she passed the oil derrick drilling in Ricketts' old oat field, she tried to take more notice of the growing streak of red mud cutting across the field towards the creek.

One Sunday dinner at Mama's, Mama was full of news—some of it old news—about the family, including Aunt Sis, who had just written she had planned a surprise visit to see them but had taken sick before she left home and didn't know now when she could risk the trip. Alice had written she was fit as a fiddle, tired of doing nothing, and was thinking of moving to New Mexico and getting a job. Emma and her family were getting along fine, but they needed rain if the wheat crop was to sprout this fall.

Papa broke in to remind everybody that the whole State had been bone dry for a year, and said maybe what was coming was the seven lean years the Bible talked about. After a pause, Mama asked about the boys and set her talking and thinking about Monroe, gone this time for nearly a year and still no word from him, nor from Otis and Arthur from whom she was used to hearing about only through Sarah's letters.

Maybe it was too much to expect that young men going out in the world could know how much those they left behind wanted to at least know they were alive and well. She would have to remember this more than ever now, since Otis and Arthur had left Seminole and gone to work in a new oil field hundreds of miles away in East Texas, and she no longer had any news of them, not even secondhand news.

At Christmas time Monroe surprised her with a few lines, telling her he was well and working in a copper mine in northern California. She answered at once with a letter filled with all the news she could think of, except the hand-to-mouth existence the family had come down to. Neither did she say anything to Sarah during her Christmas visit about having to live from week to week on the butter and egg money, because she already knew from Sarah's letters it was costing them more to live in Seminole than they had expected, and also more to get their house furnished and the farm going again in spite of—or because of—all those wells.

So she kept on counting her pennies, seeing that the children had plenty to eat but skimping on everything else, and watching the streak of red mud in Rickett's field slowly get longer and longer, or so she thought. She never noticed when it stopped growing, but one Saturday on his stop back from town with her groceries, Papa made her heart skip a beat when he said he heard the drilling at Rickett's well had shut down.

The news at church the next day was that drilling had also shut down at the other two wells. Some said it was just a trick of the oil companies so they could come around now and buy up a lot of royalty dirt cheap, and then go back and bring in the wells. But nobody came around offering to buy any royalty.

Before the month was out, Andy was at the back door with a long face to explain to her what had happened. He said it did not mean there was no oil around. He still bet there was a lot of it, but since each well had been drilled as deep as it was supposed to go and showed only a dry hole, the oil companies were not going to spend any more money drilling in this area when they had plenty of good prospects elsewhere. One day they would come back, drill deeper and probably bring in a gusher. In spite of his parting prediction, she noticed he never told her she was going to be a millionaire one day. Yet he did tell her to hold on to the farm, adding, "It ain't over yet, Mattie."

To keep even a hint of her disappointment from showing when the children came home from school, she decided to splurge and make a pan of gingerbread for them. After that she took a walk up through the barn lot to the top of the hill, still thinking about the end of her oil boom. At the barn door a bantie rooster gave a couple of sharp warnings to the rest of the barnyard to be on the lookout, and then went on scratching and pecking for something to eat. Stopping to look at the grunting old sow heavy with pigs, she laughed and felt better when the silly thought crossed her mind that not an animal in the barnyard seemed upset because an oil well was not going to be drilled on the farm and make her rich.

As the next six months turned out, it was too dry for more than half a cotton crop, and she could have saved herself and the children, and Papa and Tommy—everybody—a lot of hard work for almost nothing if she had not bought cotton seed and planted them and worked the fields and picked the crop and sold it, for she only made enough cotton to pay the taxes. With no money to pay the mortgage, all she could do was worry about it.

Yet as hard as times were for her this fall, from what she read in the paper they were worse for others around the country. She had been reading of troubles back East so bad she could hardly believe what she read. Something called The New York Stock Exchange had gone bust like her oil boom, and some men were committing suicide by jumping out of windows. When she read this her first thought was she hoped they did not leave a wife and children depending on them.

As weeks became months, and the months another dry year, she saw no sign that the oil bust was going to change for the better. Every week she was reminded of it when she rode with Papa and Tommy and the children to and from church past the rusting on derrick with its fading streak of red clay surrounded by more and more weeds.

One fall day after Sunday dinner, the boys went off hunting for pecans, and she was getting ready to take off her church dress when Edith came running in from the front porch with her book still in her hand to say a strange man had just driven up to the front gate in a big car.

She was about to tell Edith to go back and invite the man in, but she changed her mind, smoothed her dress down and went to the door herself in time to see a tall man dressed in a blue suit and brown shoes coming up the walk with an easy stride that seemed familiar.

Stepping out on the porch, she saw the man's sunbrown face

break into a grin and suddenly realized she was looking at Vernon Carpenter, older but handsomer now that his face had filled out. Where, she asked herself, was his long-ago present of the golden heart on the gold chain? She had not seen it or thought about it in years.

"Howdy, Mattie," Vernon said, hat in hand, his short sandy hair thinner but sticking up as she remembered it. All the time she was shaking hands with Vernon at the top of the steps, telling him she was glad to see him and inviting him to sit in one of the rockers, her mind was somewhere else.

She was thinking of the pie supper and the twenty-one dollars Vernon had paid for her apple pie, of Fred Dawson leaving the church in a huff because he had run out of money, of Vernon taking her home in his buggy and kissing her goodnight and coming around Christmas Day to propose marriage, of her thanking him but telling him she was going to be a schoolteacher and never get married. And then she met Hamp.

She felt her face getting warm and guessed she was blushing, although she did not know why. After all, she and Vernon were old friends, and in no time they were sitting in the rocking chairs and talking like old friends, going way back to the days of picking cotton side by side.

She learned that Vernon's mama and papa were both dead, his brother Virgil had the homeplace, and the rest of his brothers and sisters had married and moved away. Turning the talk to himself, Vernon told her he had been living for several years on the old banker Lacey's homestead southwest of town. She didn't know the farm he meant until he explained that Lacey had died a long time ago and a lawyer named Marlowe had bought the place and lived there for a few years till he drank himself to death.

When Vernon went on to say he had bought Marlowe's foreclosed farm from the bank—lock, stock and barrel, furniture and all— after Marlowe's widow had moved back East, she was reminded of teaching little Orin Marlowe in a breezy, upstairs corner room of the big yellow house on that beautiful farm. And then she saw herself driving Old Nellie away from that house one evening, starting up the road in the hot sunshine, stopping to offer a walking man a lift and having a young man turn and look up at her with a friendly smile she could still see at this very instant.

"Oklahoma's been good to me," Vernon was saying. "I think about it a lot these days, seein's so many farmers already wore out their land and moved on. I got me two hundred acres of bottomland good as any in the county, if I do say so myself. Every acre's paid for, too."

Her thoughts leaped to her own unpaid mortgage, while Vernon went on to say, "Course I've had to work for it. Now I got me a hired hand and his wife that lives on the place and heps out. But many's the day I still work from 'can see to cain't see,' as Papa used to say."

After they had a little laugh over his papa's old saying, she told Vernon how she knew the Marlowe house and asked him if he knew anything about the Marlowe children. When Vernon said all he knew was that one had been killed in the war, tears came to her eyes for little Orin.

For some minutes now, even though she was enjoying talking over old times with Vernon, she was getting more and more curious about why he had come to see her after all these years. Then without any change in his voice, Vernon said, "I guess you heard I lost my wife last year."

Before she could say she hadn't, he added, "I've come to ask you again to marry me, Mattie."

If she had known Vernon's wife had died, then the purpose of his visit might not have come as such a surprise, but the idea of marriage to anyone was so far from her mind that she must have looked as surprised as she felt. Before she could say she was sorry about his wife or anything, Vernon said, "I'm not lookin' for a cook, Mattie. You won't have to lift a finger if you don't want to."

That she could be Vernon's cook easier than she could be his wife was only one of the thoughts suddenly crowding her mind, and to keep from bursting into tears right in front of him, she grabbed her face in her hands and shook her head, half whispering sadly, "Oh, Vernon...."

When she was able to get herself under control, she lifted her head and faced him. "I'm sorry, Vernon," she said, and without telling him that she could never love him, she started in the kindest way she knew how to tell him that marriage was out of the question for her.

"Don't worry about your children," Vernon interrupted before she had a chance to mention them. "You know it's a big house and I'll treat them like I treated my own before they up and married and moved away. We never had but two. Then Loreen, she couldn't have no more."

Later, trying to recall everything she said, she realized she had been so anxious to spare Vernon's feelings she could not remember her exact words that finally started him nodding his head and seemed to make him understand that, for her, marriage really was out of the question.

He said he understood, and said it again with many more nods of his head. He got to his feet and they went down the steps and along the walk together. At the front gate they stood shaking hands and saying goodbye in a friendly way.

Vernon put his hat on and was turning to leave when, without any warning, he stopped and looked back at her. "I loved you the first time I seen you, Matt," he said, his eyes full of tears. "And I always will."

She was too full of tears herself to more than nod and stand without moving until Vernon drove away. Then she closed the gate and slowly went along the walk, silently grieving for Vernon, for little Orin, and for all the sorrow in the world.

Chapter 50

Many times after the Sunday evening Vernon came to ask her a second time to marry him, she thought about living in his big yellow house with all its fine furniture and never having to lift a finger. She thought about it most often on the hottest days when she was working in the field or the garden and so sweaty and dirty and tired she could hardly stand it.

She would catch herself trying to imagine what it would be like right then to be taking a long soak in that big white tub and then lolling about in the cool of those breezy upstairs rooms for as long as she wanted to.

But the picture that came to her most often—and saddened her every time—was of Vernon turning back at the front gate with tears in his eyes to tell her he had loved her ever since he first saw her, and he always would. She had no doubt it was the Mattie of long, long ago he still loved, and she had tried to convince him that she was no longer that girl. Yet his final words told her he didn't believe her—or his own eyes, either.

Love had also captured Otis. Unlike Arthur, who left the Texas oil fields about as broke as when he got there—so Otis said—and went hitchhiking off out West to find Monroe, Otis came home with money in his pocket and driving a new car. Within a few months he was married to a sweet, handsome girl named Leah, a girl as lovely as the sound of her name, and had started buying and selling livestock for a living.

For the second year in a row, sparse showers brought on scanty crops, and farmers were beginning to doubt if it ever was going to rain again. For a good while they had called it a long dry spell and talked about "when it rains." But now in the churchyard she heard Papa and the other men calling it a drought and saying, "if it ever rains again," and so on.

Many farmers—mostly renters and leasers—had already given up waiting for rain, sold out for what little they could get, and gone out West. Brown was one of those, selling his dairy for a song, as Rissy put it, and moving to Idaho where they had a married son.

Hearing of Brown's sale, she was curious to see if he would now pay off his debt to her—or some of it—before he left Oklahoma. But on his and Rissy's last visit he did not mention the debt, and she did not mention it to him.

The continuing drought brought bad news from Emma. The blowing sand out in the Panhandle had become more than Alice could bear, and she had moved to a little mountain town over in New Mexico to where Emma's neighbors had relatives. She had a job there, but Emma did not say doing what.

The worst news was that Glenn had lost so much money on his last two wheat crops he had to give up his leased land. The parched land now produced such a skimpy crop that it cost him more to raise a bushel of wheat than he could sell it for.

While she sympathized with Emma and Glenn's troubles, she could not forget that her own hard times were so bad she could no longer buy new shirts and overalls for Harold and Gordon to start to school in. She had to send them off in patched clothes, and Edith had to make do with the same dresses until she wore them out or outgrew them.

All the farmers around her were about as hard up she was, yet she did not hear any complaints, except about the weather. Most farmers seemed to be satisfied enough if they could keep body and soul together these awful days with no relief in sight.

She felt the same way, and in spite of the drought hanging on and on, her main worry was not the day-to-day living. Unlike the city people she saw in the newspaper standing in line for a bowl of soup or a loaf of bread, she and the children had enough to eat. And by scrimping and saving, by selling every egg and pound of butter they didn't need, by selling a few old hens or a calf or a hog when a really tight pinch came, they got along.

What kept her awake nights was worrying about ever again making a big enough cotton crop to pay the taxes and catch up on the mortgage. If she lost the farm she had no idea where she would go, what she would do, or how she would be able to keep the rest of the children in school.

Monroe had put an end to her dream of having every one of the children finish high school. And then as one by one Agnes, Otis and Arthur also quit, she had started worrying more and more that she had set a bad example for them by ending her own education the way she did. That was another reason she was trying so hard to make it possible for the rest of them to finish high school no matter what she had to do—except marry Vernon Carpenter.

Her hope now was that Harold would graduate from Brinton next spring, and she took it as a good sign that he was already talking about going to college, although she could not imagine a cotton crop big enough to pay the taxes and mortgage and still help pay his way there. It would take more than one good rain to make a crop that big, and as the summer went on she knew of no one who held out hope for any rain.

Her only good news that summer was that Agnes was going to have a baby around Christmas time. Instead of simply being pleased by the news as she normally would have been, she first thought— even as she was listening to Agnes telling her the news—that maybe the baby would put an end to the endless quarreling of Agnes and Ralph.

In November, more important to her than Mr. Roosevelt's winning the election was that once again she had not made enough on the cotton crop to pay the mortgage. Hearing more and more about banks foreclosing on farms, she was finally scared into writing Sarah about how little money she had left in the bank and how far behind she was on her mortgage payments.

"Mama, you should have told me this a long time ago," Sarah's answer began. "Now you stop worrying. I'll take next Friday off and come up to Kickapoo and see what can be done."

Far from stopping her worrying, she spent the week on pins and needles, hoping that Sarah might be able to help, but unhappy that she had to call on her for that help. Late Friday evening Sarah came driving in, all smiles at supper with the family and telling her privately as they washed and dried the dishes,

"Mama, you wouldn't believe it. The man was so pleased that any payments at all are going to be made... the word 'foreclosure' never came up. I found out that the banks already have more foreclosed farms on their hands than they know what to do with. So you're not to worry anymore about them wanting this one."

That good news, which she carried around on the tip of her mind for days, was the start of more good news than she had had in a long time. At Christmas, Sarah came with John, the car loaded with groceries and with presents for everyone. The day after Christmas Mr. Duncan knocked at the kitchen door to say Agnes had had a baby girl and named her Betty Louise after Ralph's mama. And a late Christmas letter from Monroe said Arthur had found him and they were working and living together.

But the weather that winter brought no good news. Not much rain fell, or snow either. When spring planting started, instead of the usual warm rains that sent the new plants shooting out of the ground, scorching winds from the south turned the already dry ground to dust and started blowing it out of the fields before the new plants were big enough to hold it in place. The wind filled the air with so much sand that some days a halo circled the sun at noon and turned it blood red long before it set.

As usual Papa and Tommy came to do the planting, otherwise

Harold would never have found time to get the seed in the ground. Red-eyed from the blowing sand in the air, Papa and Tommy came back and stirred up more dust as they rode the cultivators through the fields, rolling the dry dirt up close to the plants to keep them from blowing away.

She had her own problems with sand inside the house. Dust as fine as powder somehow sifted through every crack and crevice, in spite of closed doors and windows, and left a coating on everything no matter how many times a day she wiped it off with a damp rag.

Yet as the time for Harold's graduation from high school got closer, her excitement about this big coming event made it easier for her to pay less attention to the sand in the air, and the cough she was getting from it. Having missed Sarah's high school graduation years before in Kickapoo, she had made up her mind to go to Harold's, and she wrote to Sarah about it.

Sarah came on a Saturday to take Harold to Kickapoo and buy him his first suit of clothes. Once back at home, Harold dressed up in the light gray trousers and coat and paraded around the house for everyone to admire him.

She was reminded of the tight-fitting suit Hamp used to wear to Bill's office every day, and she found it hard to keep from smiling at Harold because there seemed to be so much more suit there than boy. Yet before he was back in his overalls and on his way with Gordon to do the chores, her smile disappeared at the sight of a new dress Sarah had bought for her, and a stylish pair of white shoes to go with it.

The dress was so pretty, and such a surprise to her, especially since she had not dared think about a new dress for years, that she had to turn away and hold the dress up to the sunlight while she blinked back her tears. The white material had a little pink design in it that reminded her of the shape of the sheep sorrel leaves she used to find around the farm on Bear Creek and chew when she was little.

As soon as she could speak, she said, "I'm sorry, Sarah. It's a very pretty dress, but you'll have to take it back. I have my church dress I can wear. Besides, after spending nearly fifteen dollars on that suit for Harold, you can't afford a dress like this, too."

And then Sarah did bring her to tears by saying, "Think of Harold, Mama. He'd be proud to see you in a new dress in front of his friends."

Several days later, feeling a little ill at ease in her stylish dress and white shoes, she was sitting in the sticky-hot gymnasium with Sarah and hundreds of others watching all the hustle and bustle around them as Brinton Consolidated High School was getting ready to start its tenth commencement exercise.

Ahead of her in the front row at the foot of the stage, she could see the back of Harold's blond head next to Seymour's black one as he sat in the row of Seniors, his new suit covered by a rented, black robe. Up on the stage, three men sat behind the speaker's stand. Of the three, the only one she recognized was Mr. Henry, the mild-looking Principal who had promised Otis a whipping that time.

Every now and then, to make sure she was not dreaming, she would stop fanning herself with her program, turn it over and run her eyes down the list of twenty-seven graduating seniors until she came to Harold Kent Roberts. With a lump rising in her throat she would silently read the name a couple of times and think of Hamp, wishing he could be seeing this.

The Commencement started with a prayer, and then everybody sang "America." After that, she sat for an hour or more listening to a mixture of speeches and songs—a girls' quartet, a boys' quartet, a glee club of boys and girls, and along the way a senior girl playing a piano solo. In spite of the variety and enthusiasm in the presentations, the heat inside the gymnasium was about to lull her into a nap when the Commencement Speaker, a homespun looking professor from the local university, brought her awake and kept her listening for every word after he began in a clear, quiet voice, "Consider the lilies of the field, how they grow; they toil not, neither do they spin: And yet I say unto you, that even Solomon in all his glory was not arrayed like one of these."

And on the speaker went, lifting her mind beyond the sticky-hot gymnasium, beyond her new dress and shoes—lovely as they were—beyond the hot sweaty evening of chopping cotton ahead of her, and placing it on the importance of this great occasion for Harold and the others, and for the community and the country, too.

While she was still marveling at how this ordinary looking man had seen to the heart of the occasion and made her see it, too, the seniors were being called up to the stage one by one to be awarded their diplomas. When Harold's name was read out she felt as if someone had pinched her. She leaned forward, all eyes, and watched his long legs go up the steps to the stage, the bell-bottom trousers of the new suit showing from the knees down.

Harold took the rolled-up diploma from Mr. Henry and shook hands with him, smiling Hamp's easy smile as he thanked him, and then crossed the rest of the stage in three strides and hurried down the steps and back to his seat. His time on the stage had taken only a few seconds, but after so many years of looking forward to such a day, she knew she would never forget these few seconds.

In the midst of her pride for Harold, she silently spoke the names of four other Roberts' children who had never gone up those steps, and was sad for them.

Two hours later, having eaten dinner and said good-bye to Sarah returning to Seminole, she and the children, all wearing patched work clothes and carrying on their shoulders hoes freshly sharpened by Harold, headed for the cotton patch, the new graduate stepping out in the lead.

Watching Harold striding along, she was too happy to mind the heat of the sun, or the thin haze of dust making her cough. She was already picturing the day when Edith, now walking beside her and taller than she was, would be going up those steps to get her diploma. And then one day, Gordon.

In the meantime, if it would only rain.

Chapter 51

One weekday morning a few weeks after Harold's graduation from high school, she went to church with Papa and Tommy to a special prayer meeting for rain, a kind of meeting going on at a lot of churches this summer. She took Edith and Gordon with her, but left Harold at home laying by the rows of stunted, sickly looking corn.

Under the arbor at church they joined the gathering, the usual wrinkled, dried-up old timers like the Butlers and Couches and Simpsons and Watsons and Wisdoms, farmers who had worn-out their farms scratching a living out of the soil ever since the start, and were now too old and worn-out themselves to pick up and head off somewhere else looking for new land.

Reverend Willis, looking as old and tired as any of the farmers, started the prayer meeting by leading them in singing "We gather together to ask the Lord's blessing." Then one after another as the spirit moved them, a farmer would kneel down and in his own way raise his voice to ask the Lord to forgive them for whatever sins they might have committed, to stop the drought if it was meant to be a punishment for their sins, and to make the rain come again.

Reverend Willis prayed last and longest, and afterwards he led them through the hymn reminding God He had been their "help in ages past," and beseeching Him to "be Thou our guide while life shall last."

When Tommy dropped her and the children off at home, she found Harold sitting with Seymour Sloat in the shade of the big elm at the well curb. Seymour was after Harold to hitchhike with him to the World's Fair in Chicago—whatever that was all about—and she was unhappy to see that Harold was already in a fidget to go.

After what she had just been hearing at church, the idea of anyone thinking about going off on such a lark in these hard times was so far from her own feeling that right there in front of Seymour she lit into Harold.

"What in the world are you thinking of? We can't afford to have you go traipsing off halfway across the country to see a FAIR! Probably no different from the State Fair. Which you've seen twice."

"But, Mama—"

"Besides, hard as things are with us right now, instead of thinking about running off somewhere to have fun, once you finish with that corn and kaffir corn you ought to be out rustling up some work in the alfalfa fields to help pay for your tuition, in case you try to go to college this fall."

As she talked, Harold twisted his long thin face into a painful expression while Seymour sat laughing at him, his perfect white teeth flashing in a face dark as a Negro's. "Too bad you're not enough Indian, Harold," Seymour joked. "You could go up to Haskell Institute with me this fall and have Uncle Sam pay your tuition. Room and board, too."

Paying no attention to Seymour, Harold said, "Mama, I can sell my cow for enough money to make the trip. So it won't cost you a penny! And Seymour's already got us a car ride far as St. Louis. I'll never get another chance like this in my whole lifetime, Mama!"

In spite of every argument she could think of against his going, in two days Harold had sold his cow to Otis, had shown Gordon how to finish laying-by the corn and kaffir corn, spent hours watching him practice doing it, and was gone at daylight the third morning after rushing through the big breakfast she made him sit down long enough to eat.

After ten days or so a postcard came from Chicago. "Having fun" was all Harold wrote, but on the other side of the postcard was a picture of a simpering woman, apparently stark naked except for the high heeled shoes she was standing in and a couple of fans covering some other parts of her.

When Gordon handed her the postcard, she did not think much of the picture on it and was surprised that such an indecent thing was allowed in the mail. Yet since it was addressed to Gordon, she gave it back to him and saw him grin as he passed it on to Edith, who said, "Look at that wavy hair! Wish I had wavy hair like that, Mama."

Still mad at Harold, but thinking nothing could be prettier than Edith's hair at this very moment, she reached out and pushed back a blonde strand from her smooth sun-browned cheek and said nothing.

The drought went on, a scorching sun beating down day after day, and blistering south winds stirring up the dust. The heat lasted through the night and left her as tired when she got up as when she went to bed, sometimes even more tired, for some nights dust hung in the air of the sleeping porch and she spent much of her time sitting up in bed coughing.

In the midst of this heat Sarah gave birth to a healthy, nine pound boy. Reading that they named him Robert Edward for Sarah's Uncle Bob, she was reminded of the young Sarah being so grief stricken by Bob's death from lightning that soon afterwards she joined the church.

Almost in the same mail came a letter from Alice, announcing she had just got married. "ALICE AMANDA LANE MARRIED? An old maid on the far side of fifty, married?" It was almost beyond belief. She sat looking in wonder at nothing for a long time before she could go on reading. The next thing that caught her attention was that the husband was a widower.

Having heard Alice say a thousand times she would never marry a man with children, she was relieved a little to read farther and learn that his children were all grown, married and gone from home.

Harold came back from Chicago half dead from lack of food and sleep but still as happy as when he left. That fall, after helping them start picking the sparse, heat-blasted cotton crop, he rode off with Sarah, who drove him away to a teacher's college in Ada, a little town beyond Seminole.

In his first letter home, Harold wrote he was working as night clerk in a hotel, a job that paid for his room and board and left him a little spending money. Later when he wrote it was easy to make good grades, she thought her hope was being realized at last, and she saw Harold already a college graduate, and maybe a schoolteacher like Sarah.

Yet when Harold came home for his Christmas vacation, he crushed her hope by announcing at supper he was not going back to college. "Mama, talk about working from can see to can't see. I been studying and working day and night. I guess I could stick it out some more if I liked what I was learning. But it's all dry as dust. So I'm going to stop for the time being and see some more of the country."

She wanted to say, "That's what comes of my letting you go off to Chicago." Instead, she said, "It may get more interesting as time goes by."

"Maybe. But, Mama, I want to have some fun now."

"More fan dancers?" Gordon teased.

"No, not that."

"I still have your Sally Rand postcard."

As if he did not hear Gordon, Harold said, "Everybody's going to California these days. I been thinking I'd go out where Monroe and Arthur are, and maybe they could get me a job in the copper mine."

Too upset to know what to say to Harold, she let the children go on with the talk and did not bring up the subject again. She had made plans to have all three families home for Christmas dinner, and she would find a time that day to see if Sarah could do something to keep Harold in college.

When Christmas Day came, she was happy to have the house full again, and she was especially happy to have her two grandchildren together for the first time, not to mention the one that Leah was expecting in February. Yet as the day went on she noticed that instead of bringing Agnes and Ralph together, little Betty Louise—walking and talking now—had given them something else to bicker over.

Through it all, fat little Robert Edward Crider lay quietly in Sarah's arms, but he kept his big eyes on his fretful, red-headed cousin Betty Louise whether she was up close or across the room.

As for Harold, in spite of Otis and the others telling him how lucky he was to have any kind of a job these days when so many millions were out of work and times getting worse instead of better, and in spite of Sarah telling him he should stay in college at least until he completed his first year, he smiled and shrugged and kept on eating.

Yet it was not until she overheard Sarah repeat her advice to Harold as she was leaving for home that he made her heart sink for good by saying, "It's too late now, Sis. I gave my job to another boy."

For all her disappointment at Harold's quitting college, she was glad to have him home, and when he said he would stay and put in the crop in the spring and go to California later, she secretly hoped something might happen in the meantime to keep him from going away at all.

She had not said anything about it to anyone yet, but she was not sure that Monroe and Arthur were still at the copper mine in California. A letter of hers had come back from there, and it was well after Christmas and no letter from Monroe yet—none from Arthur either, but since she had never had a letter from him she did not expect one.

Not only did Harold take over the outside chores, he pruned the orchards, fixed the fences and gates, cleaned out the horse barn and, when the weather was fit, he had Dink and Seymour in the field by sunup, breaking land for spring planting.

For weeks she listened to him day and night trying to talk her into letting him plant more kaffir corn this year instead of cotton, to his arguing that kaffir corn would stand the drought better, and that cotton was not making any money these days anyway.

The day she finally let herself be convinced it was the best thing to do, she felt as if a weight she had been carrying forever was lifted from her mind and body. No more fighting day after day with cockleburs and crab grass, her blistered hands trying to get them hoed out of the ground while chopping the cotton to a stand so that a cultivator could roll the dirt around the spindly stalks, making them grow big and produce lots of bolls of cotton. And then, no more bending over row after row of those full-grown stalks, picking the bolls one by one while dragging a heavy sack of cotton, her back a never-ending ache from the sweltering heat of September to the finger-freezing days of November, her fingers already scarred by countless stabs from the four pointed burrs on every boll of cotton.

She thought she would hang her cotton hoe permanently at the back door to remind herself she was not ever going to plant another seed of cotton as long as she lived, but she could not bring herself to do this. It did not matter that now, with Otis and Leah's new boy, she was a grandma three times, she was determined to keep her hoe busy, not let the farm go back to crabgrass and cockleburs the way it was when she bought it.

In May, the children brought home from the mailbox a letter they said was from Monroe, but she saw that while it was postmarked in California, the writing was not Monroe's. It turned out to be from Arthur, just a few sentences that said he had left the mine—for what reason he did not say—and was working on a horse ranch north of San Francisco. He did not mention Monroe.

To her long answer to his few sentences, Arthur wrote back that he did not know where Monroe was, he had not seen him since they left the mine. From this she supposed they must have had a falling out, something they used to do regularly when they were growing up together, although in those days the two of them were usually on the same side against Otis.

Arthur went on to say the valley he was now living in was the prettiest place he had ever seen, all ranches and grape vineyards, with such a perfect climate. It had never been too hot or too cold in the year he had been there, with no Oklahoma dust storms like the ones he had been reading about. He closed by saying since Harold knew how to handle horses it would be easy enough for him to find a job somewhere in the valley.

When reading this letter to the children at suppertime, she was tempted to leave out the part about it being easy for Harold to get a job in California, for she knew what was likely to happen as soon as he heard this. But her conscience would not let her fail to read all of the letter.

Within a week she was saying goodbye to Harold and watching him ride away with Otis in his red pickup truck to catch a bus to San Francisco, using money he had borrowed from Otis.

There was a time when she would have shed as many tears over Harold's going as she had when Monroe ran away. Yet after all the years of seeing the children go away, she had finally learned to try not to feel unhappy over something she could do nothing about. Anyway, maybe it was not right for her to be unhappy when they seemed so happy to be heading off on their adventures.

With no cotton to chop, she did not have to spend all her days in the field that spring. She thought it kind of a joke that she could still work in the field but she could no longer go to church. As often as not she had a coughing spell during the service—whether dust was in the air or not—and had to go outside. Finally she started letting Tommy and Papa take the children to church, and, like Mama, she stayed home.

One Sunday evening the worst dust storm they had ever suffered through raged down on them, blotting out the sun and keeping her and the children sweltering for hours in the closed-up house while swirling sand scratched at the doors and windows, and dust hung in the rooms like fog.

Yet a few days later the air was almost clear when Emma and her two girls drove in from the Panhandle in a sand-scarred car to say goodbye before their family all moved to California. At dinner at Mama's, Emma, grown stout over the years but spunky as ever, surprised everyone at the table, Papa most of all, by interrupting him when he started talking about how bad the last dust storm had been.

"Papa, this is far from the heart of the Dust Bowl. You have no idea what real dust storms are like. We got no farm left! Jist a house, a barn and some outbuildings. All the topsoil's gone. Blowed away. Clear down to hardpan. Half our cattle are already dead from dust pneumonia. Glenn and the boys are out there right this minute tryin' to sell the rest for what little they can git for 'em. More like givin' 'em away."

"I had no idea—" Papa began, but Emma had not finished.

"You ain't heard the worst yet. Last Sunday while we was in the house sittin' out the last one—the day dark as inside a cow— the livin' room ceilin' caved in. Dumped half a ton of sand on us that had been seepin' in the attic from all the other dust storms. That done it. We both said so. Soon's I git back to the Panhandle, we're headin' for California while we still got enough money left in the bank to make a new start."

"You done sold the farm?"

"Sold, Papa? Who'd buy it? We're leavin' it for anybody crazy enough to try to take it away from the jackrabbits. They're all that can last out there these days."

Everyone sat silent around the table until Papa cleared his throat and agreed he had never heard of anything so bad, but he said he expected the drought would soon be over. "The way I figger it, we still got two more lean years to go. I guess we can stand it, Mandy, if it don't git no worse."

Without looking at Papa, Mama moved her mouse-gray head slowly from side to side as she looked down at her worn hands and said, "Ain't nothin' else in this world we can do, Jim, 'cept lay down and die."

Chapter 52

Another lean year came and went, and she saw no signs that hard times were about to get better anytime soon. The drought and the dust storms went on as before, and more and more farmers sold out for what little they could get, or just pulled up stakes and headed for California or Oregon—or at least out West, she noticed, always out West.

California had been the right direction for Emma and Glenn, for thanks to Emma's sharp eyes it brought them a piece of good luck soon after they got there. Reading Emma's letter, she could just hear Emma saying to Glenn, as they were driving through country flat as a floor and passed a sign that said Bear Valley Ranch, "That sure ain't like Bear Valley in Arkansas."

And then Emma was yelling at Glenn to stop the car. She noticed the name of the owner was James A. Lane, Jr. "It might be my brother Jimmy! The one that run away cause Papa whipped him for ridin' Nellie too hard."

And it was Jimmy, although Emma's letter said she would never have known him in a million years if she had accidently bumped into him face to face. He was taller than Papa and fat as a hog at butchering time.

Emma went on to say she guessed Jimmy could afford to be fat, him sitting pretty on more land than she and Glenn went off and left back in Panhandle—all of it in fruit trees and all the irrigation water he wanted. And wasn't it great he could use a good farmer like Glenn on his farm?

When she showed Emma's letter to Mama and Papa, saying the long lost Jimmy was alive and prospering in California, she was not surprised that Papa started making noises about wanting to move out there himself. But not Mama, for what little her opinion was worth.

Their dispute reminded her of their arguments long, long ago over moving to Oklahoma Territory, and she had a feeling it would end with Papa and Mama and Tommy moving to California.

As the hot summer crawled by, she thought almost any place would be better to live in than Oklahoma. The sweltering heat lasted day and night, week after week, with no let up, and the dust in the air made it worse. It was so hot that one morning, tired of trying to keep the sand out of her long hair, she let Edith talk her into cutting it off, although not quite so short as Edith's. After a while she came to like her hair short, because it was so much easier to take care of, and cooler, too.

This was the first summer fruit trees started dying, and plants in the garden that did not burn up were wilted by noon in spite of daily watering. Out in the field, kaffir corn leaves hung limp, the heads half filled out with grains, and when the corn stalks tassled, the leaves had already turned yellow and started to wither and shrivel up to nothing.

To keep the corn crop from being a total loss, she had Gordon cut a feeding of the shriveled stalks every day for the stock. Since the pasture had already dried up, this corn fodder was about all the bony animals had to eat. As the summer wore on, she took Otis's advice, saved back her two best cows and a heifer, and let the government buy the rest and kill them —putting money in circulation, the government called it.

Otis and Gordon drove the sold cattle over to the dried up pond over in the woods for the two army officers to shoot with their rifles. Otis brought back as much meat as she could use before it spoiled, also some for Mama, the Duncans, and for himself.

She worried that the rest of the meat, amounting to no telling how many hundreds of pounds, had to be left over there in the woods for the wolves and dogs to fight over while millions of people around the country were going hungry every day. Yet she was thankful to get what money she could for cattle Otis said were even too poor to sell.

In spite of her worry over the drought and hard times that had been around so long it seemed like forever, she took satisfaction in the progress Edith and Gordon were making in school. In the spring she watched Edith graduate from high school, proud that she was first in her class, and surprised that the honor carried with it a partial scholarship to Sarah's university near Kickapoo.

Edith would be able to pay the rest of her expenses by working in the University's print shop. She was especially pleased when Edith talked about becoming a schoolteacher. Yet as summer drew to an end it seemed that Edith's main interest was in a shy, handsome young man she had met at her graduation, a friend of one of the boys in her class.

At first, Will, who lived on a farm along the river near Kickapoo, had started coming to the house to see Edith Sunday evenings, but before the summer was over, he was coming on Saturday nights to take her to a picture show in Kickapoo, driving off in the near dark and coming back who knew when.

The fall harvest was early and short. With no cotton to pick, and the shriveled-up corn already cut and fed during the summer, the only crops left to bring in were cane hay and kaffir corn. Otis came to help Gordon, and they had the crops all in the barn well before school started.

Late one evening, on a September day still hot as the dog days of August, she was coming out of the cellar carrying a colander of Irish potatoes for supper when she saw a man walking up the road by the apple orchard. Instead of going on in the house, she went to the well and set colander down on the well curb. She pumped herself a dipper of fresh water and drank it while keeping one eye on the man.

When he passed the Duncans' gateposts he looked up their lane, but he kept on walking and turned into her driveway. She took her eyes off him long enough to give her face a quick swipe with a corner of her apron and push back her short hair.

Then looking closely at the man, she noticed he was wearing a kind of uniform—a hat and shirt and trousers, all khaki. Just as she was thinking that the man walked like a man tired of walking, and maybe looking for a drink of fresh water to cool him off, she recognized the walk.

"Monroe!" she called and held onto the pump.

Still halfway down the driveway, Monroe lifted a hand instead of calling back, and kept on coming. When he got closer he said, "Wasn't sure it was you, Mama. You've bobbed your hair."

Shocked nearly to tears to see Monroe thin as a stick, his sweaty clothes hanging on him, she stepped down off the well curb and, keeping her eyes on his face with its several days' growth of whiskers, she said, "Glad you're home, Monroe. What a surprise."

Their eyes met, and their hands, she was shocked again to find his hands as hard and calloused as her own. Monroe doing manual labor? His eyes steady, but not happy. To have something to say, she said, "You look like you could use a drink of fresh water."

He could, more than one dipper, and they were soon sitting in the old willow chairs under the elm while she told him about each one of the family. All the time she was talking she was thinking Monroe looked more like a scarecrow than a man, although once he took his hat off, his close-cut hair reminded her more of the picture of some escaped convicts from McAllister she had seen last week in the paper.

Since Monroe seemed to have only the clothes on his back, after a while she said, "Let me scare you up a change of clothes and you can wash up out here before supper. Gordon should be along from school anytime."

She went in the house and dug out of the trunk a shirt and pair of trousers of Hamp's, and found Monroe a pair of Gordon's socks. Monroe took the clothes and washed up at the pump while she was in the kitchen finishing making supper, adding more potatoes and throwing together a fresh pan of cornbread.

Monroe came in the kitchen carrying his old clothes under his arm and looking for a match from the holder on top of the warming closet. He went back out and burned the clothes under the wash pot in the backyard. Given a chance, she would have cut the buttons off the clothes and saved them but she never said anything.

The next time she looked out, Monroe was walking up to the barnyard with Gordon, who was carrying a milk bucket. Noticing Gordon was as tall as Monroe, she remembered the last time Monroe came back from the West Gordon was little enough that Monroe could pick him up and hold him above his head.

At supper, she was so anxious to hear where Monroe had been all these years and what he had been doing—and what had happened between him and Arthur—that she forgot her manners. She started asking him questions almost as soon as he sat down with her and Gordon and went to eating as if he had not eaten all day, and maybe longer.

In answering her, Monroe seemed to pick and choose his words carefully. All he would say about Arthur was, "Well, Mama, after the way he done me, if I never see him again, brother or no brother, that'll be soon enough for me."

Once the meal was over, after Monroe, always a finicky eater, had astonished her by finishing the dish of beans, the platter of fried potatoes and all the cornbread, while washing everything down along the way with three glasses of sweet milk, she asked him where he had been since he left the copper mine and what he had been doing.

Monroe smiled at her in a way that made her think they were about to hear a long story like the ones he had told when he came home last time. Yet when he spoke it was in the same chilly voice he had used in talking about Arthur. "Oh, Mama," he said, "let's jist say I been here and there, doing this and that."

His answer told her she was not to ask any more questions, and she didn't. The next day she wrote a letter to Arthur and one to Harold. She got no answer from Arthur, but Harold wrote that Arthur told him he didn't know where Monroe had been and didn't want to know.

After she had given Monroe a couple of weeks to catch up on his eating and sleeping and visiting up at the Duncans—and shaving with Hamp's straight razor from his papa's trunk—she told him his grandpa had told her that he could get him a job working for a relief program of the President's. Monroe just laughed and said, "No, thanks. Uncle Sam can keep his handouts."

The next Saturday Monroe rode to town with Papa and Tommy. A week later he was back, driving a car and wearing new clothes, and once more he started his old life of coming in late at night—when he came in at all—and sleeping until noon.

She never asked him where he got the money for new clothes and a car, and he never said, although he did mention having seen his cousin Browny, and said Browny told him that Uncle Brown and Aunt Rissy were doing fine in Idaho. Knowing that Browny was now a deputy sheriff, she hoped he might be a good influence in helping Monroe find a job, settle down and make something of himself, even in these hard times.

Yet of all the people she knew, Otis was the only one who seemed to be able to prosper in spite of the drought and the hard times. He was on the road early and late, scouring the county and beyond in his red pickup truck—a new one every year—buying and selling and trading livestock. Once or twice a week he came roaring up the driveway to pass the time of day with her and see if she needed anything, or if anything needed to be done around the farm that Gordon could not handle.

If Monroe was at home, Otis did not stay long. She remembered Otis had once fought two boys for calling Monroe a bootlegger, but now he had little to say to his brother and never brought his name up to her. She never asked Otis what had come between him and Monroe, but she guessed one reason for it might be that Monroe was always teasing him about making his good living by cheating the farmers out of their livestock.

Otis would usually laugh and say, "Well, if I don't do it someone else will. So I figger it might as well be me." Yet sometimes when Monroe kept at him, Otis would answer without laughing, saying, "If you think it's such an easy way to make a livin', Monroe, you jist try it for awhile."

She had no idea how Monroe was making his money, but he always seemed to have some, and once when she was putting his washed socks and underwear away in his drawer she could hardly believe her eyes when she uncovered—without counting—a stack of greenbacks there.

As in the old days, Monroe often brought home something to eat. Usually it was a mess of beefsteak or the like, although once it was a side of bacon and once even a sack of flour.

She had no proof, but from something Monroe said to his grandpa out at the well one day, she guessed, since the Ku Klucks were no longer active around the county, Monroe might be selling moonshine whiskey again. Papa was saying that even though Prohibition had been voted down in most states around the country, he was proud the good Christian people of Oklahoma had voted to keep whiskey out of the State.

Quick as a flash, Monroe said, "Me, too, Grampa. If the good Christian people of Oklahoma ever vote like they drink, whiskey'll be legal here and bootleggers'll be out of business."

Papa had sucked his teeth at this and said nothing, but she thought even though it might be true it was still a mean thing for Monroe to say to his grandpa. Yet what worried her most about Monroe, as she thought about him during the day, or while sitting up in bed at night unable to sleep for coughing, was what was going to become of him.

Chapter 53

Still feeling numb from what Dr. Fortson had just told her, she sat silent beside Tommy as he drove out of Kickapoo, the hot, morning air rushing unnoticed through the open windows of the car. She was trying to put the doctor's advice out of her mind because she had no intention of following it. It would not be fair to Gordon, and he was the only one left to think about now that Edith would be gone to California in less than a month.

It was funny the way Edith had changed. She had been one of the children who complained about Sarah marrying a part Cherokee. Yet as soon as she finished her first year of college she was going to marry a part Pottawatomie Indian and go off to California looking for work.

Last week the paper said more people were out of work than ever before in the history of the country. The Great Depression they were calling it now. Even Andy, when he dropped by to say hello and take home his first load of "groceries" that spring, even he no longer talked about good times being just round the corner.

"I never saw business worse," he said. "It's no wonder there's so much crime. And I don't jist mean the likes of Pretty Boy Floyd or Bonnie and Clyde holdin' up banks. People are even robbin' fillin' stations and grocery stores these days. I tell you, Mattie, times are desperate."

Tommy picked up speed across the flat, bottomland, every field of cotton, corn and alfalfa already starving for rain, and the car went roaring up Carpenter's hill. Papa's news from last winter about seeing Vernon Carpenter in Kickapoo with a new wife on his arm had made her feel better than she could ever have told him. It wiped her conscience clean of Vernon's tearful good-bye for her second refusal to marry him.

Monroe's car was still there when they got home. She got out of Tommy's car at the well curb, putting her hand on Old Jack's head and rubbing it as she thanked Tommy and asked him if he wanted a drink of fresh water. Tommy shook his head and drove off.

She found Monroe at the kitchen table, finishing fried eggs and coffee, along with some blackberry jelly and leftover biscuits. In the months since he came back from California he had put on weight, his short hair had grown out and he looked like Hamp again, except for the hard set to his face.

Monroe smiled Hamp's smile up at her and said, "I was gittin' worried about you, Mama. Afraid you might've took off out West like everybody else these days. Lookin' for work and a better climate."

"No, I had to go to town," she said, struck by how close he had come to repeating what the doctor had prescribed for her.

"Where's the scholar today?" Monroe asked.

"Working that piece of kaffir corn on top of the hill," she said, not liking it that Monroe was making fun of Gordon when he used that word for him. Yet she was to blame for his using that nickname, something he had done ever since she told him one day how well Gordon was doing in school. Now she went on to say, "He ought to be in for dinner soon."

Taking off her hat as she left the kitchen, she shook out her hair. She picked up her apron from the head of the bed and went back to the kitchen to finish making the dinner she had started for Gordon before Tommy came to take her to the doctor.

When Gordon came in, brown and skinny, his cowlick flat from having just been slicked down at the pump, Monroe laughingly accused him of being off reading in the shade instead of working.

"Wish I could," Gordon said, laughing back at him. "It's too hot to read. But if you like, Monroe, you go finish that piece of kaffir corn this evening. I'll take a book up there in the shade and do my best to read."

"I would," Monroe said, making a serious face and holding out his hands, hands free of the calluses they had on them when he came home from the West, "But these won't fit them cultivator handles no more."

"Oh, Grandpa got us another cultivator since that one. Now you do it all with your feet. I can show you how in no time."

"I'd like to," Monroe said, smiling as he wiggled off the hook, "but now I think about it I got an important engagement that won't wait."

Later, as Monroe was driving away, Gordon said, "You know, Mama, he carries a gun under the front seat."

"A gun?"

"A pistol."

"Well, don't you touch it. It might be loaded."

"Oh, it's loaded all right. I already looked at it."

Until Gordon left to go back to the field, she kept the talk on his cultivating, and then she hurried to her bed. Last winter she had put a half bed in the corner of the dining room, thinking it would be warmer sleeping in the house and maybe cut down on her coughing. She still slept there, if you could call propped up with a pillow and coughing half the night sleeping.

Between a fever every evening, and coughing and hot sweats at night, she was tired most of the time. Yet until recently she had still been able to keep up with all her work inside the house and out. If anyone had told her the day would ever come when she couldn't put on her bonnet, pick up her hoe and go to the field and do a day's work in the hottest weather, she would not have believed it.

And then a couple of weeks back while she was hoeing in the

garden, a long coughing spell ended in a gush of blood. Suddenly so weak she thought she was going to faint, she dropped to her knees, still holding onto the hoe handle for support. But she had not fainted, and once she made it to the well and washed herself clean and got the sickly sweet taste of blood out of her mouth she felt better.

For more than a year she had been coughing up a little blood now and then, but until the mess in the garden she thought the bleeding was coming from the sand in the air keeping her throat raw. In Dr. Fortson's office she had learned it was something else.

"Now, Miz Roberts, if I said too much hard work, I'd be about as right as if I said TB. But for the record I've got to say it's tuberculosis. You'll have to get yourself out to a high dry climate... Arizona, New Mexico, Colorado. That'll do you more good than anything I can do for you. And rest. You got to get lots of rest."

She knew that for her lots of rest was easier to talk about than get. She would get as much as she could, but not in any of the places the doctor mentioned. Gordon had to have his chance to finish high school the same as the others. This meant keeping him up there at Brinton where he was doing so well. Sooner or later she would have to tell Sarah what the doctor had said, but she would worry about that when the time came.

Lately in a letter, Edith had hinted at having her wedding at the home of Will's favorite sister, but she had written her they would have the ceremony right in the front room where Sarah had been married. But now she was relieved that it could be held somewhere else, for if she felt on the wedding day the way she had been feeling since her trouble in the garden, she would not even be able to be there.

As it turned out, when Sarah came to take her and Gordon to the wedding, she did not feel like going, although she never told Sarah exactly why. Since Monroe had complained one day in Edith's presence about having another good-for-nothing Indian in the family, he was not invited, which he said suited him just fine.

Still feeling miserable the morning after the wedding, she was making breakfast when Edith and Will came to say a hurried good-bye, too anxious about the long road to California ahead of them to eat anything. Gordon seemed to be the only happy one in the kitchen, joking with the newlyweds to send him an orange to let him know they got there all right.

While waving and trying to smile, she called a final reminder to Edith to look up Emma. She found it hard to hold back the tears, for she had a feeling this was the last time she would ever see Edith.

It was soon another summer of heat and drought and dust storms. Whenever she saw a cloud darkening the sky in the west, she knew it was time to turn the pots and pans and dishes and glasses upside down, for sand would soon start swirling around the house like a snowstorm. With every door and window shut tight, she could keep most of the sand out, but fine dust seeping into every room made the air almost too close to breathe. Sleep was out of the question.

After one such sleepless night early in the fall, she had just said good-bye to Gordon going off to school and was starting to clear the breakfast dishes off the kitchen table, when a cough started another hemorrhage like the one in the garden, but with more blood this time. As she held onto the table, waiting to get enough strength to reach out to the washstand for the wash pan, all she thought of was being thankful that the blood could be washed off the oil cloth without staining it.

Lying in bed later, she decided the next time Sarah came she would tell her everything, and while she was at it, she would tell her she was giving her the farm. Also, as soon as she felt a little better, she was going to take another look at some of the old places out around Briggs.

She talked to Tommy about it one day and was waiting in the shade of the elm tree the Sunday evening he came for her. They drove towards Briggs without talking, the car pulling a rooster tail of dust past run-down farmhouses with run-down cars in the driveways and run-down farms out back, fence rows banked with drifted sand.

Gazing at the worn-out fields, some with rows of scraggly cotton ready to be picked, she could almost feel her back aching from years of bending over cotton stalks, picking the prickly bolls and dragging a heavy cotton sack. On every side, up every driveway and across every field, the country looked as tired and worn-out as she felt—sad and weary, as the old song said.

All that was left of Briggs was the old general store, which now had two gasoline pumps standing in front of it. At the corner on the road to the little log cabin of her honeymoon days, she asked Tommy to turn, and sat silent and stiff as the car jounced along the washboard road she and Hamp used to jolt over in a wagon behind a span of ear-flapping mules.

She saw the three blackjack trees first, and then the clump of lilacs twenty feet tall. The little log cabin was nowhere in sight, every trace of it gone as completely as if it had never stood there. As she sat in the car, a heaviness in her heart, looking and remembering, she was surprised after a while to find herself feeling relieved, and then even pleased. Nothing was left now to keep their honeymoon cabin from being just the way she remembered it.

She could not bear to go by the farm she had talked Hamp into selling and leaving, and when they came roundabout to Oakridge School, all that was left were the foundation stones half-hidden in the weeds. She wandered out among the weeds and stopped at the scattered stones of the schoolhouse steps. Here Bonnie Stevens had thrown her down after she had slapped Bonnie in the mouth for calling her "Indian face," which she took as an insult to Aunt Sis.

They turned at the corner where Fred Dawson—after walking with her from school—used to climb on his horse, Carrots, and lope off towards his own home, leaving her and Molly and Emma to stand in front of Molly's house to talk and talk. So far as she knew, Fred and poor Molly were still living their unhappy lives in there with the Wisdoms. As much as she would have liked to see Molly, she felt in no condition to face all of them.

When she came to where the big oak tree used to stand, she could not believe her eyes. Not only was it gone, so was the knoll it used to stand on, all cut away to widen the road. Watson's barbed wire fence she had used to help her climb the tree that evening was still there, but it was on the edge of a cut bank of red earth ten feet above the road. As for the ground itself, the leaf-covered place where in a few minutes she changed her life forever, that place no longer existed, except in her own mind.

At the church house a few minutes later, it was still in her mind as she listened to a bobwhite calling from Simpson's woods while she was zigzagging her way across the graveyard to keep from stepping on anyone's grave. After each call, a faint answer would come from a bobwhite in the pasture south of the graveyard.

At Hamp's grave she put a hand on the rough top of the rosy-marble headstone and stood looking down at the narrow mound of red dirt covering him. As always when she stood there close to Hamp she was flooded with so many feelings she had a hard time thinking, but she no longer broke down and cried.

On Hamp's grave lay a scattering of dead lilacs, already rusty red as the ground around them. Each spring when the lilacs next to the sleeping porch started to bloom, she would pick the first bouquet for Hamp, even though she knew he had never been much for flowers. Of late, Gordon had carried them to church and put them on the grave for her.

She bent down and gathered up some of the dead lilacs and stood sniffing and touching the rusty, crumbly flowers, remembering their blue gray color and their scent of springtime when she wrapped them in a piece of newspaper and gave it to Gordon, warning him not to crush the blossoms.

Live matter dying and turning back to earth to make more live matter, and so on and on forever. That was what it all came down to, for these lilacs and everything else in the world, for the bobwhite calling to its mate, for Hamp and her on fire under the big oak tree, for the once eager settlers in a new land, now moldering in their graves all around her. Whether they believed it or not, they had already had their heaven or hell.

When she was young, she never thought about such things. She was too full of dreams of the exciting life she was going to have teaching school when she was grown up. Those dreams ended in shame and tears back up the road there. The excitement that came afterwards was from something she had never dreamed about. Maybe that was what happened to all dreams after a long enough time—even when the dreams came true.

Holding the dead lilacs against her cheek, she stood looking down at Hamp's grave and thinking of hers next to it. Long ago, on the road from Arkansas to Oklahoma Territory, she had looked down at two graves in the moonlight and could not imagine being dead and down in the ground, and the world going on without her. Now it seemed as natural as plowing under dead stalks in the field, making the ground ready for the next planting.

She laid the dead lilacs on Hamp's grave and took a long time to tear her gaze away from the narrow red mound. Letting her hand linger on the rough headstone a final time, she felt hot tears brimming her eyelids and closed her eyes to squeeze them back. Slowly she turned and made her way past the other silent gravestones towards Tommy waiting in the car.

The bobwhite was still calling to its mate, but as she passed by the familiar gravestones again, her thoughts were on these settlers and their wives full of the fever of life, coming from all over the country, eager for a new start in a new land. And now in these graves on either side of her they lay at rest, their fever of life over, forever.

"And rest," Dr. Fortson had said. "You have to get lots of rest."

Chapter 54

Although it did not ease her evening fever, or her nightly sweats, it did give her peace of mind when she finally got it settled with Alice and Sarah that she would not accept Alice's repeated invitations to come live with her in New Mexico.

Sarah and John agreed to move in next summer and take over the farm, with Sarah teaching up at Brinton when an opening came along. The most important thing of all was that Gordon would be able to stay in Brinton until he graduated, no matter what happened to her.

When she told Monroe about her TB, and about the farm going to Sarah, his only concern seemed to be her health. Yet later, when she remarked one morning that Sarah and John would be coming to live here next summer, Monroe shoved himself away from the table, muttering, "Christ! What next?"

Grabbing his hat hanging behind the kitchen door, he slammed out of the house without another word. She did not see him again for days, although when he did come back he was friendly as could be, and never mentioned Sarah and her family moving in.

Usually she sat and talked family news with Monroe while he ate, always careful never to ask him where he had been since she last saw him, what he had been doing or where he was going. For his part, Monroe never said. When he had finished eating and was ready to leave he would pause at the kitchen door, hat in hand and say, "Well, Mama, take care of yourself."

Never knowing when she was going to see him again, she would watch from the kitchen window until he had driven out of sight past the rose bushes, always hoping as she turned away that one day he would come walking through the kitchen door and say, "Well, Mama, I got a job today."

With Monroe only at home now and then that winter, and with Gordon gone all day at school and out on the sleeping porch at night, it seemed to her that she was living in an all but empty house. Every evening as she lay on her half-bed in the shadowy corner of the dining room, she kept an eye on the shaft of sunshine slanting in from the back porch. Like a gauzy curtain filled with bright, floating specks of dust, it would slide across the floor until it had cut the room in half.

Once she saw the slant of sunshine start inching up the east wall, she got out of bed, whether she felt like it or not, took a bucket from the back porch and went to the chicken house to gather the eggs, her only outside work these days.

She was usually at work in the kitchen when Gordon came in from school. He would ask her how she was feeling and stand and talk a little about school before he looked in the warming closet for a bite to eat. While he was out doing the chores, she would finish making supper.

After they had eaten supper at the kitchen table, she would wash the dishes and then join Gordon at the dining room table. There she would read the day-old newspaper or his English or history book while he did his schoolwork, pleased that now and then he would ask her to listen and make suggestions when he practiced saying a poem or a speech he had to give in school. The subject they never talked about was her TB, although she and Mama talked about it every time they were together.

One evening when she was coming down to the house with her daily bucket of eggs, she saw Tommy driving up to the well, Papa sitting beside him, and Mama in the back seat. Curious about what could be bringing all of them out for a visit this late in the day, especially Mama, she hurried through the gate.

Papa and Tommy barely replied to her greeting, and it seemed to take Mama forever to climb down out of the back seat. Mama turned a tear-stained face to her and held out a crumpled letter.

She set her bucket of eggs on the ground, too scared to try to think what the trouble could be. As she reached out and took the letter, Mama said in a breaking voice, "Poor thang. Alice has took her own life."

According to the letter, all anyone knew about her death was that while he was gone on his regular run to Kansas City and back on the railroad, Alice shot herself with his pistol. She left no note, and neither he nor the police knew of any reason why Alice had taken her life, especially since she was soon to have their first baby.

When the husband sent Alice's coffin home by itself instead of coming with it, she thought that was for the best. Remembering Alice with Marvin, she realized Alice herself had already shown her deepest feeling about their marriage. Anything else would have been prying.

At the funeral, Reverend Willis did not preach that in the midst of life we are in death, as he had at Hamp's funeral, but the thought had been running through her mind ever since she re-read the crumpled letter.

She herself found it hard not to think about death as she lay in a sweat night after night, propped up in bed coughing and spitting blood into torn-up pieces of worn-out bed sheets, which she dropped into a paper sack beside the bed and burned in the stove the next day.

Yet by the time another winter began to wear itself out, she was coughing less and feeling so much better she thought she might be getting well. Even so, she never mentioned her health when she wrote to Aunt Sis, and Emma and Edith and Harold in California, giving all the other news she could think of. She would have written to Arthur, but Harold's last letter said Arthur had quit his job and gone off to Montana to work in the copper mines there.

One morning when spring was just around the corner, and the orchards all pink and white and smelling sweet and full of promise, she found a fine smoked ham on the kitchen table and knew Monroe had left it there when he came in during the night. She had lost her appetite for meat, but this morning she was feeling so good she took a sudden notion to have some of that ham cooked with a mess of poke salad.

As soon as Gordon left for school, she went straight to the woods along in back of the garden. With fingers long since shriveled to bony claws, she raked the dead leaves from around the first rotten stump she came to. She was pleased but not surprised when she uncovered a pale green shoot of pokeweed. She cut if off low down with her knife, dropped it in the bucket and raked around for more green shoots, some already sticking up through the dead leaves.

When she had gathered enough greens, she stopped to clean the knife on her apron and listen to a flicker hammering away in the distance on a post or a dead tree, a cardinal calling "pretty-pretty-pretty" up near the barn, and from somewhere a turtle dove's mournful song—sadder than death itself—hanging in her mind long after the sound had melted away.

She was going to surprise Monroe by having the ham and greens cooked when he got up at noon, but as she stopped at the well to wash the greens, Monroe came hurrying out of the house. She thanked him for the ham and offered to make him some breakfast, but he said he didn't have time. Thanking him again for the ham, she asked out of sudden curiosity, "Monroe, what do they get these days for such a fine ham as that one?"

Instantly, Monroe said, "Ask me no questions and I'll tell you no lies." Then coloring a little, as if sorry for his childish answer, he added, offhand like, "I forgot, Mama, exactly what I did pay for it."

She let Monroe drive away without saying anything else to him, ashamed that she had been so nosy about his gift. Yet his childish answer came back to her later in the morning when Otis dropped by—something he was doing more often now that he knew about her TB.

When she motioned to the ham, Otis laughed and said, "Mama, if I didn't know you better, I'd have the law on you for stealin' that ham."

Without stopping peeling potatoes, she said, "You might say I came by it honestly."

"Sarah bring it?"

"No, Monroe brought it in last night. Wasn't that thoughtful of him?"

Otis caught his breath, then slowly said, "Well, I'll be damned."

She raised her eyebrows and stared up at him without speaking.

"I'll... be... damned," Otis said again as he walked over and put a hand on the ham. "Last night two masked men robbed Charlie Kerr's Market again. The same two as before, he says. On the way out one took a ham." Shame and fear tingled her cheeks and she wished the floor would open and swallow her up. As if thinking out loud, Otis said, "So he wasn't jist sellin' whiskey." He stopped looking at the ham and turned around. "Well, Mama, now what?"

"Oh," she said, shaking her head, "I'll have to face him with it."

"He'll lie out of it to you."

"Leave it to me," she said quickly, afraid they might get in a knock-down-drag-out fight if Otis said anything to Monroe about the ham.

While she waited day and night for Monroe to come back, the ham stayed where it was in spite of Gordon asking and asking when he could have a slice of it. Sometimes she was so anxious to get the trouble cleared up she wished Monroe would drive in that very instant, yet the next car she heard coming up the driveway would start her heart pounding until she saw it was Tommy or Otis, or anyone but Monroe.

At other times, especially at night, the thought of facing Monroe—and saying what she had to say—made her so sick at heart she doubted if she would ever be able to go through with it. And each morning there on the counter of the safe, under a dishtowel to keep out the sand, laid the ham, a constant reminder of something awful waiting to happen.

She was still awake the night Monroe did come back, and she stayed awake for the rest of the night, going again and again through the awful meeting ahead of her, before he finally appeared in the kitchen the next day about noon. She was so nervous by then it was a relief to be out on the back porch finishing her churning.

When Monroe came back in from the outhouse, she had got her courage up and was waiting for him in the kitchen. As calmly as she could she asked him if he would like some breakfast. "A couple of eggs would be fine, Mama. And if you got any to spare, maybe a piece of that ham."

She had meant to let Monroe eat before she said anything about the ham, but when he said the word, out of her mouth came what had been on her mind all these days and nights. "It didn't come from Charlie Kerr's did it?"

"What?"

Trembling in spite of her back pushed so hard against the safe she rattled the dishes in it, she saw Monroe's startled look soften to the friendliest of smiles. "Whatever give you that idea, Mama?"

"Otis told me about the robbery. Then I read it in the paper."

"Well, I don't know anything about that. But," Monroe went on, an edge coming in his voice, "I can tell you one thang for sure. I paid good money for this ham. And I can prove it."

After a long silence, she made up her mind. "Monroe, I don't know what I ever did—or your papa either—to make you turn out like this...."

"You sayin' you don't believe me?"

Unable to go on, she stood without answering.

"Mama, I'm telling you the truth. And I can prove it."

Her eyes met his, and finally she said, "Either we go to the law right now with your story... or I never want to see you in this house again."

"Now, Mama, listen. This is silly." Monroe explained that he would go get the man he bought the ham from and bring him right back to her.

As she listened without believing a word he said, she got hold of herself. When he finished, she took a deep breath and said, "Monroe, you leave this house. And don't ever come back to these parts. For if you do... sure's I'm alive I'll have the law on you."

Unable to meet his hard stare, she slumped down in a chair at the table, her head in her hands. She heard him walk past her to his room, come back and leave the house. She stayed where she was, tears running out between her fingers, until she heard him drive away.

Then she staggered up and raked the ham into her apron. Still crying, she carried the heavy thing up to the hog pen with Old Jack sniffing along beside her. Without waiting for the grunting old sow and her new pigs to get up and come to the fence, she shoved the ham into their pen.

Coughing and half-blinded by tears, she stumbled back to the house and collapsed on her bed, her last memory a picture of Monroe walking into Charlie Kerr's place, that loaded pistol in his hand, the hard look on his face half covered by a mask.

Chapter 55

She woke to find Gordon shaking her shoulder and asking, "Mama, you all right?" As she struggled to turn over, she saw him stare down at her as if seeing a ghost, or worse. "Mama! What happened?"

Following his gaze, she saw the front of her dress covered with blood. She gasped as the fight with Monroe came back to her. "I guess I coughed up a little blood," she said, surprised that her voice came out in a whisper. Still in a whisper she asked for a drink of water, and Gordon rushed away to the kitchen.

The water soothed her throat, but she sipped it slowly, afraid it was about to make her start coughing. After emptying the glass she whispered, "Better get Grandma and Grandpa."

Without a word Gordon was gone, leaving her looking down at the blood on her dress and finally noticing her shoes. Ashamed for Mama to find her on the bed with her shoes on, she tried to sit up and take them off, but she didn't have the strength to do it. Closing her eyes, she lay back down to rest awhile and then try again.

A soft voice calling her name woke her, and Mama stood bending over her, Gordon holding the lamp, Papa and Tommy staring from the foot of the bed. She started to say something but Mama shushed her, told Gordon to set the lamp on the table, and asked all of them to leave the room.

Having Mama bathe her and put her in a clean nightgown made her feel like a baby again. Later as she lay propped up on pillows in the clean bed, Mama eased spoonfuls of barely warm broth down her burning throat. After that it was easy to go back to sleep again.

Whenever she woke during the night, hot and sweating, Mama was a dark shadow beside the bed, cooling her face and arms with a damp towel. The next morning as she was swallowing some oatmeal, Otis came rushing in saying, "Gordon ought to come for me last night, Mama."

His face was almost as white as his big hat, which in his haste he had not taken off. "This come from havin' it out with Monroe?" Afraid to try to speak, she looked up at Otis and nodded. "Damn him," Otis muttered, shaking his head. "Damn him." And while still looking at her, he said, "Grandma, what can I do?"

"Git Sarah," Grandma said.

The shaft of mid-evening sunshine was inching its daily curtain across her room when Sarah, red-eyed but trying to smile, appeared through it. "Oh, Mama," she said softly, and stood holding her hand while Grandma told her how Gordon had found her on the bloody bed and come running for help.

She added nothing to Mama's account, thinking later would be soon enough to tell Sarah the story about Monroe and the ham.

In a few minutes Dr. Fortson came in looking as hearty as ever. Yet when he said, "Evenin', Miz Roberts," his voice was so soft she hardly recognized it. She half expected he might say something about her not taking his advice to go out West, but he never even hinted at it.

After he felt her pulse, he slid a little metal gadget over her bony chest and her back. Then he looked down her throat with a little light. His final words were, "You stay put now, Miz Roberts, and don't talk more'n you have to."

She guessed he must have left her some kind of medicine, for a little while after sipping the strange tasting glass of water Sarah held for her, she felt herself dozing off. All this fuss, and the doctor never told her what the matter was, although she reckoned it was just another hemorrhage after her fight with Monroe.

All his robberies around here almost under her nose—and maybe pulling off more somewhere else right now—and to think she was so ashamed she let him go scot-free to keep from disgracing her and the family. If she had it to do over again she would go straight to the law. Yet maybe she wouldn't have the heart to do it, for whenever she told herself she would, she saw a teary-eyed little Monroe lifting his face from her lap and promising to do better.

The next morning she was pleased to see Agnes, and later the Duncans—Mrs. Duncan gaunt and inches taller than he was—the first time in all these years either of them had ever set foot in her house. She noticed this kindest of all neighbors had no twinkle in his eyes today and no chuckle in his voice. Also for the first time, he spoke her name, turning red as he said, "Good-bye, Mattie, we're hopin' you'll soon be mendin'."

That evening Reverend Willis was sitting by the bed when she opened her eyes from a doze, and she wasn't sure the hot room hadn't made him doze off, too. But when she stirred, the eyes opened in his wrinkled old face, and right away he asked her how she was feeling. Her answer all day had been, "Better." Tired and weaker would have been the truth, but again she said, "Better."

She saw him nod as if that was the answer he expected, and then he went on to talk about how hot the weather was for this time of year, and on to tell her they were praying for her at church. All the time he was talking, she was remembering looking up at his sweaty face hanging over hers that night at the revival meeting as she knelt at the altar to confess her sin of drowning Tommy, and her disappointment then, and later when he baptized her, that she felt no sign that she had been saved.

Yet she felt no need to talk about her soul now—if there was a God, He already knew her story—but she let Reverend Willis take her hands in his, bow his balding head over them and pray for her, ending with "... and Thy will be done. Amen."

Dozing and sleeping, waking up weaker and weaker, she lost track of time. She would be thinking of something, usually the old days in Bear Valley, and the next thing she knew it was daylight, or sometimes the lamp was lit and Sarah or Mama was telling her to swallow some soup or gruel, or more medicine.

The one thing she looked forward to each evening was the sun slanting its gauzy curtain across the middle of the room. Spellbound by the glittering specks of dust floating in this curtain, she would follow a single speck twisting and turning for a few seconds like a shiny live thing only to disappear without warning. Then her eyes would latch on to another speck, and soon another, until she was lost in the past. She would come to, not sure whether she had been dreaming or daydreaming.

One evening as she was playing her little game, a fleshy woman with graying hair and sad brown eyes in a sagging face burst through the gauzy curtain. She might not have recognized the woman right away but for her voice. Yet the instant she heard "Maat...tie!" in that well remembered Texas drawl, the troubled face became the Molly Wisdom of other days.

She tried to answer Molly in the same exciting tone, but it didn't come out that way, and she saw Molly's own excitement dry up at the sound of her half-whispered name.

And then Molly was on the bed beside her giving her a hug, crying and saying, "Oh, Mattie, I'm sorry. They didn't... I didn't know you were so sick." Molly straightened up and sniffed a couple of times while wiping the tears from her cheeks with the back of her hand. "Here I been grievin' about my own troubles. But I didn't come to tell you my troubles, Mattie."

She gave Molly's arm a squeeze to let her know she understood, and this brought on more tears from Molly as she talked about all the shame and misery Fred had put her and her parents through over the years, ending with the news that Fred had now left her for good and gone off out West with another woman.

As sick as she felt, she couldn't help sympathizing with her old friend and shedding tears over her troubles, so much so that when Molly finally left, she slumped down on the pillows exhausted. She never knew when the hemorrhaging started, but she woke up coughing and choking on blood, Sarah was holding her sitting up.

Feeling more dead than alive, she half heard Sarah saying again and again, "Hold on, Mama. Doctor Fortson's coming." It wasn't too long before Dr. Fortson was at the bed, poking around again with his metal gadget. But no light in her throat this time. Whatever kind of medicine he left with Sarah—after talking low to her for some time in the kitchen—it must have been stronger than usual, for she felt herself feeling sleepy almost as soon as she forced down the last swallow.

Yet in giving the empty glass back to Sarah and looking up at her, she was struck by the tired face and dark smudges under her eyes. A sudden urge to tell Sarah what a loving daughter she had been all these years roused her.

"I never could have done it without you, Sarah," she whispered, and went on until Sarah's tears and sobs stopped her.

More medicine in the morning, and all the time now she felt like she was in a never-ending doze instead of ever sleeping or coming wide awake. She knew she was lying in her bed, but the bed didn't seem to be touching her. At the foot of the bed Papa was on his knees in his church clothes, praying. The curtain of sunshine, all fuzzy now, was slanting halfway across the room. Far far away people seemed to be talking in whispers.

"Is dying like this?" she asked herself. Grandma Hale was telling her again how the white soldiers rode into the yard one morning at breakfast time and drove the family away like cattle, without letting her say goodbye to her favorite tree. In the mulberry tree down on Bear Creek she and Bob were eating mulberries and talking about growing up. "When Mattie grows up," Aunt Sis was telling everybody at the Sunday dinner table, "she is going to be a great schoolteacher. Just you all wait and see if she's not."

Someone was coming through the fuzzy curtain. Gordon's face was coming closer and closer. She must tell him she was sorry she hadn't lasted to see him graduate. She felt his lips touch her forehead.

"Be a good boy, Gordon."

"I WILL, Mama. I WILL!"

He was gone, and she was swooping down towards Aunt Sis's window to finally confess what happened that kept her from ever becoming a schoolteacher. But there stood Hamp, smiling at her from the dear sunshine beneath the big oak tree.

"Hamp!" she called and rushed into his arms.

The End

Family Trees

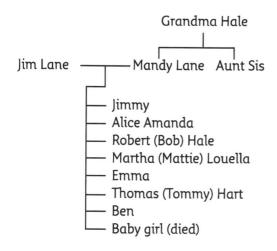

Grandma Hale

Jim Lane ——— Mandy Lane   Aunt Sis

— Jimmy
— Alice Amanda
— Robert (Bob) Hale
— Martha (Mattie) Louella
— Emma
— Thomas (Tommy) Hart
— Ben
— Baby girl (died)

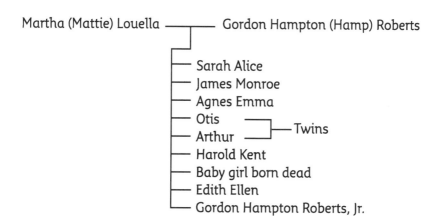

Martha (Mattie) Louella ——— Gordon Hampton (Hamp) Roberts

— Sarah Alice
— James Monroe
— Agnes Emma
— Otis
— Arthur   — Twins
— Harold Kent
— Baby girl born dead
— Edith Ellen
— Gordon Hampton Roberts, Jr.

About the Author

Roy Penny was born in Shawnee Oklahoma in 1918. His father and mother, as children, were part of the land rush of the 1890's when 180-acre farms were made available in Indian Territory, and settlers came in covered wagons to claim them. His father was killed in an accident in April, 1921, when Roy was 3 years old. The family had been planning to move to Colorado at the end of that month, but those plans were cancelled after the death of his father. He grew up with eight brothers and sisters, plowing fields with a team of mules, working in the vegetable garden, raising cattle, and riding his horse "Buck." As a youngster, he developed a life-long love of reading. His favorite first book was "The Mysterious Rider" by Zane Grey. He graduated from Bethel High School as the valedictorian of his class, and went on to attend Oklahoma Baptist University for two years.

He fought in the US Army during World War II. He was a Major, and commanded an anti-aircraft battery. His unit landed on the beaches during the American invasions of Leyte (October, 1944) and Okinawa (April, 1945). The war in the South Pacific put things in perspective for him, and whenever anything went wrong after that his comment was "It's not raining and no one is shooting at us." After the war he attended UCLA and received a bachelor's degree in English. He also worked for a time in New York.

In 1954, he met Isabelle Harris in Tripoli, Libya. Isabelle, who was from Wilkes-Barre, Pennsylvania, was in Libya to visit her uncle, a state department official. At that time, Roy Penny was working for a US government contractor in Tripoli building a Strategic Air Command air base. Isabelle had also grown up riding horses, and the name of her horse had also been "Buck." They were married in 1954. After their marriage, they spent 3 years travelling and living in Libya, Ethiopia, the Middle East and Europe This was a magical time for them.

They returned to the United States in 1957 to start a family. Roy Penny Jr. was born in 1958 and Chris Penny in 1962. Pursuing his life-long interest in literature, Roy became an English teacher, a career that he followed for 42 years. Most of that time was spent teaching at St. Georges, a private high school located in Newport, Rhode Island. Isabelle was also an English teacher and vice principal. The school where she worked was re-named "Pennfield School" after her upon her retirement. Roy was a trustee of the school. In 1975 he and Isabelle purchased a 38 acre farm in Middletown, Rhode Island, and he spent the next 18 years bringing the farm up to his standards after years of neglect, fencing it, and raising cattle. He and Isabelle sold their farm and moved to Colorado in 1993 to be closer to their children.

In addition to his legacy as a wonderful husband, father and friend, he is most proud of his book "Till We Meet Again," a story of life in Oklahoma during the period 1890 to 1937.

Made in the USA
Charleston, SC
11 March 2013